I0708945

FLICKER

THE ARDENTIS CHRONICLES

ALICE CORNELIUS

CRIMSON QUILL PUBLISHING

This is a work of fiction. Names, characters, organisations, places, events, and incidents are either products of the author's imagination or are used fictitiously. Otherwise, any resemblance to actual persons, living or dead, is purely coincidental.

Text Copyright © 2026 Alice Cornelius. All rights reserved.

No part of this book may be reproduced, or stored in a retrieval system, or transmitted in any form or by any means, electronic, mechanical, photocopying, recording, or otherwise, without express written permission of the publisher.

ISBN: 978-1-7640909-5-7

eBook ISBN: 978-1-7640909-6-4

Published in Australia by Crimson Quill Publishing. Copyright © 2026 by Alice Cornelius.

The right of Alice Cornelius to be identified as the Author of the work has been asserted in accordance with Copyright, Designs and Patents Act 1988. All rights reserved. No part of this publication may be reproduced, stored in a retrieval system, or transmitted in any form or by any means without the prior written permission of the publisher, nor be otherwise circulated in any form of binding or cover other that in which it is published and without a similar condition being imposed on the subsequent purchaser. No generative artificial intelligence (AI) was used in the writing of this book. It is prohibited to use this publication to train AI technologies to generate text under any circumstances. The author reserves all rights to licence uses of this work in AI training and development.

The story, all names, characters, and incidents portrayed in this production are fictitious. No identification with actual persons (living or deceased), places, buildings, and products is intended or should be inferred.

This book is forged in storms.
It carries violence, grief, bloodshed, and betrayal.
It carries the weight of the hunted, mothers lost too soon, and
power that others would kill to bury.
It speaks of cruelty, of being shunned, of never belonging.
But it also carries defiance. Love that grows in the ashes.
And the truth that even lightning cannot be caged.

ALSO BY ALICE CORNELIUS

HELLSPIRE ACADEMY

THE SOCIETY

I dedicate this book to my best friend, paired-partner, soul-mate, and husband, Glen.

Thank you for always being my biggest supporter, and still loving me when I'm stuck in my writing bubble for weeks at a time.

You mean the world to me.

TO DISTANT NORTHERN WATER
OBSIDIAN AERIE
VELINDRA
DUSKMIRE ACADEMY
VERATURA ACADEMY
SKYSPIRE
FARITIA
ANGORA
ASHENCLIFF
CRUDELIT
TO SOUTHERN SEAS

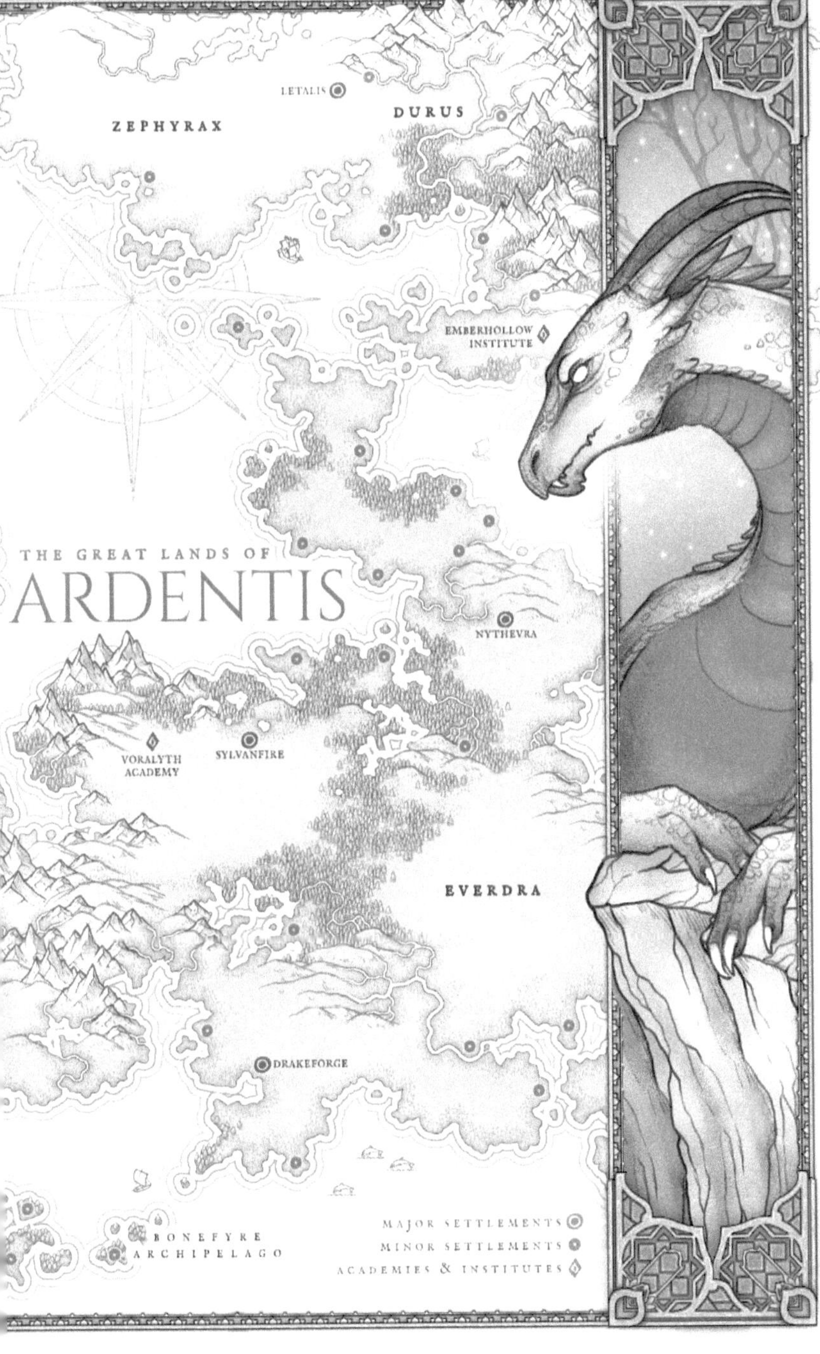

THE GREAT LANDS OF
ARDENTIS
ZEPHYRAX
LETALIS
DURUS
EMBERHOLLOW INSTITUTE
NYTHEVRA
VORALYTH ACADEMY
SYLVANFIRE
EVERDRA
DRAKEFORGE
BONEFYRE ARCHIPELAGO
MAJOR SETTLEMENTS
MINOR SETTLEMENTS
ACADEMIES & INSTITUTES

CHAPTER ONE

Today, the sea was angry.

The waves smashed against the rocky cliffs with thundering booms, the wind howled and roared as I battled to keep my skirts from flying up around my head. The bitter cold seeped into my bones as I made my way down the street. I ducked into the store, grabbed the packet of spinach and hurried to the counter.

"Wild out there, eh?" The older lady chuckled, scanning the packet before handing it back to me. "On your parents' account?" She smiled, and I nodded as I tucked my collar up higher.

"Yes, please, Ruth. Make sure you stay warm!" I wasted no time in tucking it into my jacket and heading back out. People bustled past, they pulled their hoods lower or held onto their hats. The town usually bunkered down in weather like this, as storms could last for days.

I very much looked forward to getting inside to the warmth.

Another boom sounded, and I rolled my shoulders with unease.

I hated when it stormed.

The grey stone and timber houses all blended together, identical except for the different coloured doors, the wild flowers in planters out the front. Even though they were built over three hundred years ago, people still wanted to make them unique. To make it theirs.

The gravel track was worn smooth, the occasional rock underfoot as I hurried home. We lived on the outskirts of town, one of the rare larger houses with a proper fence. It was built from slabs of rock and the odd fossil if you knew where to look. I loved it. It had character, a story, and the scratched and dented floorboards told of many people walking through its halls.

Apparently, a captain used to live there.

Our island used to be a fishing port, but over the years, more people started to move here and made a living from other things. Now, it boasted almost anything you could need. Books, food, clothes, a school, a small pub, a post office, you name it.

Our island's only source of power came from the two stormglasses, and when it stormed, they weren't very reliable. It charged them, yes, but usually caused them to overload. There was a high chance the power would be out when I got home. I didn't mind, to be honest. It was nice to live off the land, and if we had to go without power, we knew what to do to keep us going.

I opened the door to an intoxicating smell, risotto that mum was stirring in the kitchen. I kicked my boots off at the front door, smiling. I shucked off my jacket and hung it before making my way through to the living room. I was glad to be out of that weather. It was getting fierce out there. I placed the spinach down beside Mum in the deliciously warm kitchen.

"Thank you, sweetheart." Mum gave me a one-armed hug as she took the spinach from me, rinsing it before adding it to the pot. Her dark grey hair was tied back in a braid, but small bits had fallen out and framed her kind face. Her light blue eyes twinkled with life, always quick to smile. I was an odd mix of my parents, but I didn't share their colouring.

Back out in the living room, I plopped down on the couch beside dad who was playing a card game with Kai, who was cursing quietly as he lost another round. He was a sore loser, which was why I never played with him, because I always tended to win.

Kai frowned at his cards as the lights flickered, taking forever to choose the right one that would win him the game. His chocolate-coloured hair was pushed back off his face, like he'd been running his hands through it over and over. But Dad, sitting opposite him on the tattered couch, was smirking like he'd already won the game, which he probably had. He was just waiting to kick Kai's ass. The wrinkles around his mouth and eyes were a tell-tale sign that he liked to smile a lot and laugh. He had one of those laughs that you could hear from a block away.

It always made me smile.

His dark brown hair had begun to grey at the temples, a short beard looked more salt than pepper. But his dark brown eyes were cunning, always two steps ahead.

Kai made his move, looking triumphant for a full five seconds before Dad slapped down his card, trumping anything Kai had done.

"Oh, come on, I almost had you!" Kai growled, leaning back and taking a swig of his whiskey. Dad just chuckled and shuffled the deck with expert flicks of his fingers.

"Another round?" He winked, and Kai muttered quietly about cheating. But before he could reply, Mum called out from the kitchen.

"Dinner's ready!"

Dad groaned, struggling to stand - his joints seemed to stiffen with storms - as he slowly pulled himself upright. Thunder rumbled closer and closer, a distant flash setting me on edge.

"It's going to be a rough one tonight. Make sure your windows are latched and locked. We might lose power at some point, too," Dad said through a mouthful, spraying crumbs onto the table, earning a raised eyebrow from Mum. I nodded. Storms weren't unusual around here, but we seemed to be getting them more often lately.

All four of us played a round of cards, and Kai finally won, laughing in our faces as he danced around. He was such a damn show-off. Mum and Dad went to finish the dishes, talking quietly as I packed away the cards.

"Make sure you drink your tea before bed, sweetheart, otherwise it will be a sleepless night for you," Mum called from the kitchen. If I didn't have my chamomile tea, I would toss and turn with the storm raging outside, the lightning begging to be played with as another shiver passed through me.

No, thank you.

Mum put my tea on the coffee table with a sad smile, touching me on the shoulder on her way past, before sitting heavily onto the couch with a sigh. As soon as I'd finished, I hugged them goodnight, dodging a punch to the arm from Kai as I slipped into my room and shut the door. I could hear him calling goodnight through the door, calling me little punk - his annoying nickname for me.

The thunder rumbled closer with every boom, making my hair stand on end as it filled me with nervous energy.

I laid down on my bed, planning on reading to help drown out the storm, when I heard a sudden *CRACK, CRACK* noise from the living room, followed by a loud *THUMP, THUMP.*

Ice skittered along my veins as I sat back up, creeping towards my bedroom door.

Did the house get hit by lightning?

I eased open my door and came face to face with a tall, bearded man wearing all black, curved swords hanging on his hips and an evil smile. A bolt of lightning lit him up briefly before being plunged back into darkness. I screamed and went to slam the door in his face when he reached out a hand and grabbed me by the arm, pulling me towards him. I struggled, trying to peel off his iron grip. Panic quickly set in as he threw me into the wall, backhanding me. I cried out, the pain radiating like fire. Kai swung open his door and advanced on the man, smashing him right in the face with his fist. The man grunted and let me go as they fought. I used the chance to run out into the living room, a cry on my lips, and nearly tripped over something dark lying on the floor. I stumbled to a stop, my stomach dropping so fast I felt dizzy. I slapped a hand over my mouth to stop myself from making any noise.

No.

Mum and Dad lay there, bleeding as a giant puddle of blood spread out from underneath them.

Dead.

My lungs constricted as I tried to make sense of what I was seeing.

No, they can't be.

"Terribly sorry, sweetheart. But it had to be done." A gravely voice shattered my spiralling thoughts. I looked up at the man who held a shining pistol in his hand, standing by the open front door. He was huge. Startling yellow eyes met mine as my chest heaved, spots dancing at the edge of my vision. I could hear distant screams splitting the night, as if the rest of the island were being attacked.

Kai thundered up behind me, wrapping me in his arms. He took in the other three men in the room and shoved me behind him without hesitation.

"Run, Ria, run for your fucking life," He breathed and pushed me away, advancing on the man with the gun. Two men came towards me, and I ran, but not away. Dad had been training me since I was old enough to walk. He kept telling me it was better to be prepared for anything, just in case.

I just hoped he wasn't trying to escape the rogue dragons and their riders. Everyone knew there wasn't a place in the whole of Ardentis that you could go without them finding you.

But I knew that a ghost was haunting him. He constantly kept an eye on everyone who came to town. He'd trained Kai and me to be able to take someone down, to defend ourselves. But he never told us who would come after us, why he constantly looked over his shoulder.

A roar sounded from outside, and my blood turned to ice. That wasn't a sound I'd ever heard in my life. It was what I'd imagine a dragon to sound like. I banished the thought from my head as I leapt over the dead bodies of my parents and aimed my fist right for the man's chin, snapping his head up with a crack. Now wasn't the time to let fear in. I dodged and darted around them as quickly as the lightning that was flashing outside. Another man went down, a cry on his lips as I yanked the sword from his grip, and ran him through all the way to the hilt with a scream. I didn't think, I just acted - letting autopilot take over.

"*Enough!* You will stop this instant, or your brother dies too." The man by the door yelled, holding a bleeding Kai by the throat, a gun to his head. My chest heaved, throat burning as I glared daggers at him. The room was so dark that I could barely make out any other features. "You're a savage little silver fox, aren't you?" He grumbled, sounding impressed. He turned to one of his men. "Take the girl and cuff her. Put him with the others." Strong arms wrapped around me before I could take a step. I kicked and screamed as I was carried out of the room. Kai yelled after me, but it was no use.

Even through the sheeting rain and storm clouds, there was no mistaking the giant dragon before me.

I shook my head, dug my heels in, anything to try and get away from the beast spewing fire into my neighbour's houses.

"Get your fucking hands off me." I cried, but the rest of the words died on my lips as the beast turned my way. I got stuck in its golden gaze, and I couldn't breathe.

"We came here for *her?*" A feminine voice sounded to my right, and a tall woman stood before us with arms crossed. A black mask covered her face, but there was no mistaking her icy-blue eyes.

"Thornton, what the hell are you doing over here? Get back to the others." Regali snapped, his hand tightening on me.

"Everything *is* secure." Even the tone of her voice implied that she thought all of this was below her.

"If you want to continue flying with us, then get your ass back over there and stay there." He snapped, and she rolled her eyes before they landed on me, and narrowed.

"Maybe I don't want to fly with you anymore, especially if we have to come to remote holes like this for little girls." She snarled, looking down at me. I was too numb to feel more anger.

"Done. You can stay with *him* as his guard dog." Regali went to turn, but she took a step toward us.

"Don't you dare leave me there, with him." She snarled, but Regali only chuckled.

"Sweetheart, then you need to get better at doing as you're fucking told. Understand?"

"Fine." She hurled back before turning her back on us and storming away.

Regali cursed as he continued to drag me away.

I barely noticed the cuffs snapping around my wrists, the cold, heavy iron pulling me down. All I could see was the dragon, its bared teeth, its giant claws and barbed tail.

It growled, the feeling reverberating through the ground and up my bare feet as it lowered its head.

"Let's get out of this hellhole." The man who killed my parents snapped as he stepped up beside me, dragging me towards the beast. I thrashed and kicked, but it did me no good. "*Stop...fighting...me.*" He grunted as one of my heels kicked him in the shins.

The last thing I saw was the glowing eyes in the night, and the snarl vibrating through my whole body before a sharp pain exploded in my head.

I woke to wind whipping at my ears, the feeling of weightlessness. I swallowed as my memory came back to me, remembering that I was on the back of a *fucking dragon*.

My hands were still chained in front of me, the large man at my back. I was too scared to open my eyes, to look down at the ground rushing past us at an unnatural speed.

Who the hell are these men? And what do they want with me?

"They've been hunting your father for twenty years, girl."

Shit, how the hell does he know I'm awake?

"You can't hide anything from a dragon." He chuckled darkly, so I sat up straighter, opening my eyes. I had to slap a hand to my mouth as I looked around. The sun was shining to my right, the clouds below us, and land to be seen ahead. I began to shake, my mind not comprehending what was really happening.

"What do you want with me?" I croaked, my throat tight from the fear, sadness, and anger simmering in my veins.

"I'm just the messenger, the one to get my hands dirty." His arms tightened slightly as the dragon banked to the side, earning a squeak from me as I had thoughts of falling, and what would happen to me.

"But you, my dear, I've heard rumours of those born with silver hair and storm clouds in their eyes."

Oh, Gods. I tried to hide my flinch, but my pulse was *sprinting*.

"They say you have extraordinary powers." His voice was loud in my ear. Would he be able to hear my heart racing? It was almost too loud in my own head to hear what else he had to say.

I couldn't let him figure out what ran through my veins.

CHAPTER TWO

The rest of the flight passed in a blur.

I was too panicked to think about where I was headed, not to mention frozen stiff, barely dressed. All I could think about was whether the dragon was going to eat me. I had no idea how long we flew for, but this man must have needed me for something, because Kai and the others weren't there.

The landing was enough to jar each and every bone in my body. The man kept one arm around my waist as he hauled me off his monstrous dragon. My ass was numb, I couldn't feel my legs, and my wrists chafed with the cuffs around them. It was taking everything in me to hold myself together when all I wanted to do was break down and fall to pieces.

Not yet. When I was alone, I would let myself mourn for my parents, Kai, and my home.

No other dragons landed, it seemed to be just us. As soon as the man had his pack and was clear, the dragon crouched down and launched into the sky, its massive wings beating loudly in the silent morning air.

Yellow dragon. From what I'd studied at school, it was a Galadron - the meanest and most temperamental dragon in Everdra.

Like rider like dragon, it seemed.

"Come on, the Viscount is eagerly awaiting your arrival." The man's grip on my arm was hard enough to bruise. I kept my whimper behind my gritted teeth. I would not show this man any weakness.

We exited the grassy field and arrived at a door hidden in a hedge taller than my house. A guard stood by, watching our every move.

"Regali, your mission was successful then, I see." The guard smirked as he glared down at me. "She'll make a fine new pet." He looked me up and down, and I couldn't stop my shiver of revulsion.

"That she will." The man smiled, his pockmarked face harsh in the early morning light. The guard stepped back and unlocked the door, ushering us in and locking it behind us.

Opulent gardens filled my vision. Fountains, ornamental trees, rose gardens, and patios. Anything you could want, it was here.

I tried to take in everything to help form a plan to get away, but I knew that I wouldn't be allowed to come outside to appreciate the flowers. I didn't want to think about what they wanted with me.

We approached the most lavish manor I'd ever seen. Or was it a palace? Shining columns stood before me, large carved wooden doors, windows bigger than me overlooking the gardens. And this wasn't even the front door. Two more guards let us in, both commenting about this man's mission.

Obviously, *I* was the mission.

The thought didn't sit well with me.

I barely had time to look around inside when the man pulled me into a doorway on my right, where he shoved me into a chair before locking my cuffs to the damn thing.

"So, tell me, silver fox, what powers do you possess?" He leaned in closer and grabbed my chin, turning my head this way and that before he released me, only to trail a finger along the scar on my neck. I couldn't shove him away, so I smashed my head into his face as hard as I could. The satisfying crunch was loud in the small room. He yelled and fell back on his ass, clutching his bleeding nose. I expected anger or for him to strike me, but a barked laugh cracked through the tension. He stood, holding his nose as he reached into his pocket, mopping up the mess with a cloth.

"You're a fucking delight, fox, but I wouldn't expect anything less from the daughter of Albert Everhart." He chuckled again as he set his nose straight with a sickening crunch. His yellow gaze burned right through to my soul.

"You belong to us now, Nymeria, the Stormborne."

No. How does he know?

I needed to change the subject.

"What have you done with my brother?" I snapped as he walked to the back of the room, sat down and poured himself a glass of whiskey. He leaned back as he lazily looked me over, placing an arm over the back of his chair. His leathers looked well-worn, stained and dirty. I didn't focus too hard on the splotches that looked like blood.

"Your brother is currently on his way to Crudelitas, where he'll be put to use." He sipped his whiskey, keeping his eyes on me. "If you behave, then he'll be treated fairly and remain unharmed. But if you try anything, then there will be consequences." My stomach churned, threatening to spill its meagre contents. "The same rules go for him, if he missteps, then it'll be you who will suffer."

I swallowed, the words sending shivers over my skin. I was sure that he wouldn't hesitate to hurt my brother or me.

He grunted as he got to his feet, walked over to the window and looked out, crossing his large arms over his chest. "It seems that we have upset the sea. Perhaps it did not agree with our plans to sack your island and take all the inhabitants to sell as slaves." He mused. He said it so casually, like we were discussing the weather.

I felt *sick*.

He had taken everyone and sold them as slaves?

This man is a fucking monster.

I couldn't do much with my hands tied, but I *would* find a way to kill him.

"No matter, I'm sure the rest of my riot was successful." He muttered, scratching his chin absentmindedly, as if we were discussing what to wear for dinner. I was nearly burning alive with fury.

Thumping boots announced an arrival, interrupting my thoughts of revenge. A large belly, his grey button-down shirt stretching to its limits were the first thing I saw, then a red face shiny with sweat as his eyes swept from the rider to me.

"Regali. What...what have you brought me?" he wheezed, obviously not used to walking at all. "What happened to your nose?" he gasped, a look of surprise crossing his puffy face.

"A savage little beast head-butted me for getting too close. I should have known a wild animal would bite when cornered." His yellow gaze locked on mine, and I gave him my best grin. His eye twitched as he turned back to the wheezing man. "I probably deserved it, though. I did murder her parents."

Fuck. You.

"Oh, I see." The man cleared his throat, side-eyeing me. "Perhaps I should ask *who* you brought me?" I didn't like the way his dark, beady eyes examined me.

"This, my dear Walter, is the Viscount's new prize. I call her the Silver Fox." The man he called Regali smiled at me, and I wanted nothing more than to run him through with his own sword.

This Walter man grinned like it was his lucky day, rubbing his chubby, ring-clad fingers together.

"Excellent, excellent. I'll take her to the holding cell until his return. You've done well." Fat Walter shook Regali's hand, "He'll reward you handsomely."

"He better. That place was miserable." Regali strode past me, throwing one last look over his shoulder. "See you soon, silver fox." He winked. I raised my cuffed hands and flipped him off before he walked out, earning me a chuckle as he left me alone with fat Walter.

"Alright, no trouble from you, girl, and you won't have any trouble from me. Come along," he barked, but not before he showed me the longsword hanging from his belt. I sighed and heaved myself to my feet, the exhaustion falling over me like a weight. He clipped a long chain onto my cuffs and tugged me out, making anger boil in my veins. I wasn't some mongrel dog to be dragged around.

We wound our way through the giant building, the halls eerily quiet. I would have thought a palace of this size would have people running about at all times of day and night.

He nodded at the guards as he led me down into a stairwell that appeared on my left.

Great, underground.

The air felt stale down there, and I tried not to listen to the quiet wails down the halls that seemed to echo like ghosts. Walter tugged me along, down, down, until I swore that I could hear water dripping. The stale stench of mould and mildew was strong in my nose. Holding cell, my ass. More like a dungeon.

"You will start off down here until we can trust that you won't fight us, then we can move you to better lodgings once the Viscount returns in a few days' time."

—◦✦◦—

My stomach was too uneasy to eat when the guards dropped my pathetic excuse of a meal. Hard bread, a soft apple, and water that tasted like mud.

Did they attack our entire island?

Where's Kai?

Gods, I exhausted myself worrying about everyone as my mind raced. I'd cried so much it nearly made me vomit. The pain of the loss of my parents was almost too unbearable.

What do they want with me?

I spent four days in that disgusting hole. It was dark, wet, and freezing. My teeth constantly chattered, my hands shook as I curled into a ball to reserve any warmth. I think they forgot to feed me more than once a day.

But *finally*, a group of men came to the bars of my cell, jingling the keys as they sneered at me.

"Come on then, girl. You're not scary at all, are you? A pretty little timid thing." One crooned, smiling at me with three missing teeth as he swung the door open, then clipped a long chain on my cuffs again, giving it a hard yank, hard enough that I nearly fell to my knees. Anger replaced the bone-deep cold that had settled since arriving.

"Easy now, she broke Regali's nose." A deep, gravelly voice echoed around the stone walls, making fear slither along my spine.

Now, *that* was a voice I didn't want to mess with.

A mountain of a man appeared out of the shadows, so tall that I had to crane my neck to see his scarred face. He didn't have a single weapon on him, but I knew he didn't need any, judging by his build.

"Rex, what are you doing off your leash?" Another guard drawled, leaning against the wall like he had nothing better to do.

"I've been sent to retrieve my recruit and to make sure that she arrives in one piece. She belongs to the Viscount, after all." He crossed his arms as he met each and every one of their eyes, widening his stance.

"We wouldn't dare lay a hand on her, *slave*. I don't know why you would ever think that." The one who held my chain gave it another yank, making me stumble as he laughed. "But, by all means. Lead the way."

I ground my jaw as I was dragged out of the dank dungeons by a chain. But I could finally draw a full breath when we arrived on the first floor. I had no chance of remembering which way we'd turned. There were too many, and I was busy trying not to stumble and trip, with the asshole yanking on the chain every so often.

We walked past room after room of luxury and over-the-top flourishes, some of the golden candlesticks would be enough to feed a family for a whole year, and they had at least six in the first room.

Down into the belly of the palace, into rooms that looked the most practical that I'd seen. Training rooms, but not a weapon to be seen.

"You'll train in here with him." The guard thrust his chin in man-mountains direction. "The Viscount wants you to keep...trim." The guards chuckled, looking me over as I crossed my arms across my chest.

I was still in my pyjamas, no shoes, no bra.

"We'll be back later to fetch her, then we'll have to make sure she's presentable." The others filed out, but the one holding my chain yanked me towards him. I wanted to resist, but I was too busy keeping my tears at bay. "Remember, play nice." He unlocked my cuffs before he walked out of the room. I heaved a sigh of relief and rubbed my sore, raw wrists.

I turned to the giant man before me, hesitating. I had no idea who he was or how he was going to 'train' me.

"Look, I don't know what you did to get the Viscount's attention, but I'm sorry. I'm Rex, and as long as you're here, I'll be keeping you fit." His dark brown eyes assessed me, but not in the same way the guards did.

"What does he want with me?" I croaked, wishing I could curl in on myself.

"I don't know, but you must have something he wants. Come on." He turned and headed for a chest of drawers at the other side of the room. He pulled out a handful of clothes and walked back, lumping them in my arms. "Go change, then we'll get started." He pointed to a closed door to my right. I ducked in, glad to have something else to cover me. They were baggy but comfy, the shoes slightly too big, but I didn't feel so vulnerable anymore.

Rex was setting up machines I'd never even seen before, and I wouldn't be surprised if they were torture devices. I used to train with Dad, but this was going to be completely different.

I had to bite my lip to stop the sob building in my chest.

Mum. Dad. *Dead.*

I swallowed my sorrow, turning it into revenge instead.

"The men who took me, their leader was Regali."
Rex turned at my words, eyes narrowed slightly.

"Who are they? Are all dragon riders assholes?" I planted my feet, refusing to move until he gave me some answers. Rex slowly turned, scratching his chin as he thought.

"Yes, I think most riders are assholes. But Regali and his riot are in their own category. They're rogue, working for the Viscount who isn't a rider. He pays them very well to do his dirty work."

I let the words sink in. Rogue dragon riders.

"When do I meet this Viscount? Will he tell me why he killed my family and sacked my island? My brother was taken, and I have no idea where he is!" My hands were balled into fists at my sides, tears pricking my eyes as I tried so hard to control myself. But a tear slipped down my cheek, and I angrily wiped it away.

"I want some fucking answers!" I yelled, feeling so completely overwhelmed that I wanted to smash something, break it like how I felt inside. Completely broken.

"You will get your answers, but not until *he* decides so." He took a step toward me, and I shook my head in warning. "Use that anger, girl. Use it fuel you and keep you going. You're going to need it."

Hours later, the guards escorted me back down the halls to a lavish room with windows overlooking the ocean. But this place was still a prison, just a fancy one. I saw the cuffs attached to the walls, the bars on the windows.

"We'll have a servant come around and prepare you for the Viscount." The guards waited outside my door, letting in the older woman before locking the door behind them.

The woman didn't meet my eyes, kept her gaze down as she rummaged through her basket.

"Excuse me, milady." Her voice was barely above a whisper, but I could hear how it trembled, the fear.

"I am definitely not a lady. You can call me Ria." I took a small step, but her shoulders seemed to rise higher. "I'm not going to hurt you. I don't want to be here." I sat in the chair by the window, sighing. I felt bone tired, and they expected me to go and be nice to my kidnapper?

"Alright, Miss Ria. We need to get you washed and dressed, if that's alright?" She still hadn't met my eyes, but at least her shoulders weren't up near her chin.

"What's your name?" I asked as we made our way into the stupidly large bathroom. Honestly, it was bigger than my bedroom back home.

Shit. Don't think about that.

I gritted my teeth and attempted a smile, but the woman shook her head.

"We aren't allowed to give away our names, Miss Ria. Follow me." She shuffled in front and got to work helping me wash. It was mortifying. I could clean myself, thank you very much. But she would probably be punished if I refused her. So I shut my eyes, let her do her job, brush my hair and tie it up. She put stuff on my face, the cosmetics some of the girls like to wear. I'd never bothered, I didn't want to cover up who I was.

Once we'd finished in the bathroom, we made our way back out into the main room, where she pulled a dress out of the cupboard.

They already had clothes here, and I could almost guarantee they were my size.

I swallowed the boiling rage. How long had they planned this?

"I don't want to wear that." I shook my head, backing away. The woman paled as she held it up, her hands began to shake. I scrubbed both hands over my face as I tried to calm myself.

Breathe in. Breathe out.

I opened my eyes and sat heavily on the bed, holding onto the towel wrapped around me like a lifeline. The poor woman looked terrified.

"Fine. Let's get this over and done with." I shut my eyes and let her guide me, lifting my arms when she told me so she could slide the silky material over my head and tied it up at the back.

Of course, it had a corset built into it as she yanked on the strings.

Nothing like struggling to breathe while facing down your enemy in a pretty dress.

CHAPTER THREE

The woman knocked on the door once she deemed me presentable, to notify the guards. I didn't look in the mirror. I knew I wouldn't see *myself* looking back.

The guards whistled and cajoled as they took me in, the woman disappeared down the hall on silent feet. The guard clamped the cuffs back over my wrists, giving me a savage smile for good measure.

"You clean up alright, sweetheart," he tugged me behind him, and began our walk down the shining halls. Chattering and laughter could be heard, echoing through the palace as we made our way through. They all stopped and stared, their gaze like a brand on me as I kept my chin high.

They would not see any weakness in me.

The halls got fancier the further we walked. The floor shone, the windows sparkled, and priceless artifacts stood on plinths. Disgusting wealth, especially when some people were starved throughout the world.

My stomach knotted the closer I got, my skin began to prickle.

No, not now.

I gripped my hands together, making any attempt to keep them out of view. Since I couldn't shove them in my pockets or under my arms, I was going to have to concentrate.

Two guards stood by carved, wooden doors, they swung them open at our arrival, revealing bright sunlight beyond.

My pulse was sprinting, sweat beading my brow as I focused everything I had on keeping my hands from crackling. My body knew I was in danger and was trying to protect me, but this was so *not* the time.

"Ah, here she is." A man boomed from a pile of cushions, it was hard to see the person from the pillows. "Your silver hair and grey eyes are obvious tells that you are Arcborn." His gaze turned hungry as he sat up, and my stomach dropped. I'd only heard my mother mutter that name to my father one night after my fifth birthday, after I'd accidentally shocked a bully at school. I was something people would hunt down, used as a weapon, and this viscount knew what I was.

"I know what a powerhouse you are." His eyes darkened, and I swallowed my nerves as he waved to a guard pull him to his feet. He slowly approached me. "I've had my spies keep an eye on you, and they confirmed my suspicions." He was only a few feet away from me now, and my palms were sweaty with fear.

"Your powers will rival the brutes on those flying, overgrown lizards. I want you to grow and thrive to your full potential. I don't want to hurt you. I want you to become what you were born to be!" His eyes were wide as he approached me, practically quivering with excitement. "Together, we will show them that they aren't the only ones who can rule the sky!"

I blinked back my shock, wishing that I could back away from this man who had obviously let power go to his head. He reached out, grabbed me by the arms, and held tight, his fingers digging into my skin.

Nope. This asshole will not *touch me.*

I took a deep breath and drew on the electricity in the room as I sucked it into me, the lights above us flickering and buzzing. I flung it out in a burst of energy that travelled down my arms and into the viscount, and sent him flying. The windows, the lights, and even the dark evercast in the corner all exploded in a shower of glass. He flew backwards, crashing into a chest of drawers and clattering to the ground in a heap. Guards rushed me, aiming their guns at me, but the viscount only laughed as he pulled himself to his feet.

"And that, my girl, is exactly what I want. But you can cool off a little down in the cells for a bit, while I make up a more...suitable room for you."

Before I could draw on any more electricity or fight back, I was shackled around the wrists, ankles, waist, and throat with a heavy chain. They frog marched me down, down, down into the belly of this ridiculously large building. I was hopelessly lost as we went through different doors, corridors and stairs until we reached the dank, dark and smelly dungeons again.

I sighed internally.

The guards tossed me into a cell without any windows and a poor excuse for a bed. I puffed out an annoyed breath as I picked myself up off the filthy, cold stone floor. My chains were so heavy that they made it almost impossible to stand on my own.

I wished that I had something to cover the disgusting mattress with, the dark brown stains looked suspiciously like dried blood. The guards laughed at me as they walked away, their footsteps slowly fading and leaving me there alone in the dark. Only a distant light flickered down the hall near the door, which they bolted from the other side.

The Viscount obviously held a grudge against dragon riders, and the fact that he had some in his employ confused me more than anything.

I'd managed to get some sleep before a guard bashed on my cell with a baton, telling me dinner was served.

Slop.

I wouldn't call it dinner, let alone food. But I needed to keep my strength.

I held my nose while I slurped it down, grimacing at the foul taste.

Three days, they fed me this slop they called 'food'. Once a morning - I presumed, as the guards were fresh and clean, then once more of an evening when they were yawning, dirty, and irritable.

I would pace my cell, holding onto my chains so they didn't drag along the floor, trying to do what I could to move around. I couldn't stop the shivers passing over me. It was ridiculously cold down here, especially in a stupid silk dress. The worst part was that there was nothing I could do about it.

The chains were so heavy that I could barely lift them without toppling over.

Finally, the viscount appeared at my cell, a smile splitting his gruesome, pockmarked face.

"Alright, my dear. I've got a room just for you, and a fancy band that will wrap around your wrist and ankle. We don't want anymore...accidents." He smirked, stepped aside and let the guard unlock my cell door. He stepped in and cuffed my wrist and ankle with a small black band, blue veins glowing slightly.

It instantly made me feel nauseous and dizzy.

I stumbled back a step, attempting to blink away the fuzziness in my head.

"Yes, the bands will take a little while for you to adjust. You can rest for a few days before I want to see you train." The viscount walked away, the guard tugging on my wrists to force me to follow.

But as soon as I was in my own room, I would find a way to escape and find Kai.

I was allowed to rest for two days before the guards came to escort me to my 'training' with Rex.

The whole time I was violently sick, too dizzy to stand without falling. Whatever was in these bands was toxic, and anything that touched them didn't even scratch or leave a mark.

The viscount had a chair brought in to watch my session, but it was useless as I couldn't stay on my feet for very long.

"Perhaps only one band is needed, seeing as she hasn't gotten used to it yet." The viscount waved to a guard who removed a shiny black square of glass wrapped in cord and came my way. I tried to see what it was and how it unlocked, but he blocked my view as he knelt at my feet.

The relief was instant, and I couldn't smother my sigh. He shoved both the band and the black glass into his pocket before I could get a good look. But if I wanted to remove the one on my wrist, I needed a piece of that glass.

Removing the band made a big difference, but I still felt sick. My body knew that it was *wrong*.

Rex ran through a few stretches and had me running the perimeter of the room, the viscount watching all the while. Rex seemed happy enough with my fighting skills, but we both knew they needed more work. It had been a while since I'd trained.

The viscount declared he would follow my progress and went to leave, but he paused at the threshold, turning back to lock eyes with me.

"I have a plan to hone your powers, and I'll have Walter keep me updated. I can't wait to see who you become, Voltrite." The door shut behind him with a click that echoed in the room, Rex standing beside me with clenched fists.

"I have a bad feeling about this." He muttered before walking away.

Every day I trained with Rex, becoming stronger, faster. It wasn't long until I moved onto weapons. The viscount liked things to be more personal, and anyone could shoot a gun. But a dagger, that had to be close, you had to mean it.

I didn't want to think about why he was training me. But I'd caught Rex looking at me with sad eyes more than once. If I were to stay here and spend my days with Rex, I should at least get to know him.

"How long have you been here for? I heard the guard on the first day call you...slave." I was attempting to do twenty chin-ups, but my arms shook at only fourteen.

"I've been here for the past thirty years. I used to live in Crudelitas as a merchant, and the Viscount appeared one day and offered me something I couldn't refuse. I took him at his word, but he wasn't entirely truthful." He frowned as he watched me struggle, arms folded across his large chest.

"He only wanted me for my strength and to fight for his entertainment." He turned, putting things away, head down. "What about you? Who taught you to fight?" he peeked at me over his shoulder, raising his eyebrows when I hadn't moved. I grunted as I lifted again.

"I'm twenty," I huffed, wanting this torture session to be over already. "And my father taught me." Once I'd finished, I dropped to the ground, my shaking hands on my knees while I caught my breath.

"Well then, spring chicken, show me what you got," he turned, lowered into a crouch, beckoning me with his finger. I sucked on my teeth before I sprang at him. I knew I was fast, but this man had the muscle to back him. I aimed a punch at his left shoulder, but he moved at the last minute, coat-hanging me and knocking my ass to the ground, winding me.

"Pathetic. Try again," he laughed in my face, making me feel weak as I pulled myself to my feet.

"I don't know how to fight men the size of mountains," I wheezed, trying to get enough breath into my lungs.

"Do you think anyone cares? They will tear you *limb from limb*. Now, attack me," he barked, making me see red. I flew at him with everything I had. I didn't manage to get a good hit on him, but he wasn't able to get one on me either.

"What the hell do you mean they'll tear me apart?" I snapped, straightening up with my fists in front of my face, chest heaving. He paled, swallowing before meeting my gaze.

"The Viscount wants you to do what I used to. Fight for his entertainment before he deems you worthy to be by his side." He cocked his head to the side. "That's why I've been training you. I want to give you the best fighting chance. Again." He charged, barely giving me any time to block him.

My anger boiled in my veins and clouded my vision.

"You're letting your anger take over. *Control it*. Use that to fuel your hits and kicks. Otherwise, you won't last ten minutes out there." He stood and glared down at me, watching me struggle to hold myself together.

We did that for hours until I couldn't even stand or lift my arms. I just wanted to fall into a heap and stay there. But Rex wasn't going to allow that. So he changed tactics, grilling me instead about the best way to take someone down while I pulled myself together.

Food was delivered shortly after, and I swore I'd never tasted anything so good. As soon as I'd finished, I was forced back on my feet until the sky turned dark out the tiny window.

And that was to be my everyday.

My room was escape-proof. I'd examined every corner, every window, even the furniture, which was bolted to the floor. So there was no point in even trying. I'd have to try to escape elsewhere.

For three months, I trained and built up my skills. Then they would send me out to fight for their entertainment. I tried not to think about it, because when I did, it made me sick to my stomach.

Normally, we weren't allowed weapons in the arena, but the viscount wanted Rex to teach me anyway, claiming that I would be foolish not knowing how to use them, just in case. You could never promise that someone wouldn't smuggle one into a fight.

Rex was the one who was to determine whether I was ready or not for the pits, and every time Walter came to inquire, he would tell them, *not yet*. I didn't know if he still thought I wasn't good enough, or if he was doing it out of kindness. He was a gruff man of few words, but we worked together in companionable silence.

I told him about Kai, and if he were able to get any word out to someone who could give me any information. I needed to know if he was alive.

I felt incredibly useless in here, training while Kai was out there doing Gods knows what.

I just hoped Kai didn't do anything stupid enough to get himself killed.

The weeks flew by, quickly turning into months, when Walter came to watch our training session, keeping his dark, beady eyes glued to me the whole time. And he announced he thought I was good enough to fight.

I didn't sleep at all that night.

CHAPTER FOUR

My first fight was against a scrawny man who growled at me like a feral animal, teeth bared.

I rolled my shoulders and looked around at the viscount, who gave me an encouraging nod. Rex had instructed me to drag it out and make him bleed as much as I could - the viscount would enjoy that.

Wonderful.

I swallowed down my nerves as he ran at me, no doubt to try and knock me over and strangle me. That's what Rex said most of the untrained ones try first. If I let them do that, I was a goner.

I dodged his tackle and kicked him in the ass, making the small crowd laugh. I tried not to fidget with my silver fox mask, which the viscount demanded I wear to hide my identity. I was only going to be known as the Silver Fox. The man growled and turned back to me, crouching low. I jumped over him like a game of leapfrog, using his back to propel me. The crowd roared with laughter once again as the man stumbled. I chanced a quick look at Rex, and he raised his eyebrows at me, crossing his arms.

Right. He wanted me to start making him bleed.

I have a bad feeling it's going to be to the death.

I gritted my teeth and ran at him instead, punching him in the side of the head, right on his ear as he howled. I latched my fingers onto said ear and, using my sharp fingernails to cut into his neck, made blood run down his throat. I dragged it out as long as possible, dislocating his shoulder, breaking a few fingers and possibly his ankle before I couldn't take it any longer. I broke his neck with a twist of his head, the sickening crunch loud enough for even the crowd to hear.

They were ecstatic as they clapped and cheered, calling my name.

"Well done, well done. What a fabulous match." The Viscount was standing, clapping his large, ring-clad fingers. "I hope to see more of that." He winked my way, but it was a struggle to keep the sneer off my face. I gritted my teeth and bowed my head slightly.

I didn't remember much after that. I think I was in too much shock as they led me out of the arena and back to my rooms.

I vomited into the toilet for the rest of the day, but Rex told me that the Viscount was proud and to keep up the good work. Rewarding me with nicer clothes, an evercast in my room, and better food.

For the next one thousand and ninety-five days, I fought in the pits, putting on a gruesome show, and training with Rex, who'd become a sort of father figure to me. He would never admit that he cared, but I could sometimes see it written on his face, in the tone of his voice, especially when he was patching me up after a violent battle.

The worst part? They whipped me when I didn't put on a good enough show.

And they made Rex do it.

I nearly died five times. One of the other slaves they pitted me against had gotten me onto my back, their hands on my throat as they choked me. That's the only time I had used my *'gifts'* as my mother used to call it.

I would electrocute them from the inside out. The band around my wrist cut off pretty much all of my powers, but I was able to draw on the smallest amount. Enough to get them off me, anyway. I swore the Viscount loved those days the most. He wanted me to use my powers. Wanted to see what I was capable of.

One particular battle had the crowd going completely insane. I was fighting against a man who hadn't lost a fight in the past two years. He smirked as he looked me over.

"Oh, sugar. How cruel of them to make me kill you. I would much rather do way more interesting things with you." He winked at me as I cracked my knuckles, my top lip curling in disgust. Rex had warned me against him, that he was cruel and frighteningly strong. I had to wear him out and not let him get his hands on me.

Easier said than done.

The fight seemed to drag on for over an hour, both of us panting and exhausted as our bodies ached from the many hits and kicks. He growled at me, something silver glittering in the palm of his hand as he approached me.

He had a knife.

The fucker.

Weapons were meant to be banned.

I dodged his swipe, rolling to the side as he grunted, exhaustion catching up to him. He reached down and threw a handful of dirt in my eyes, making them sting and water, temporarily blinding me as I tried to blink it away. I was disoriented as he approached too quickly, swiping at my stomach. I managed to jump back, but not quickly enough as the blade skirted across my ribs. I barked out in pain, my hand going to my stomach, coming away red.

"Sorry, sweetheart, but I'm going to win this." I could hear the crowd yelling and stomping, but Rex's voice was unmistakable as I heard him yell about this man's weapon. Their solution was to throw in a small knife at the edge of the arena, so I could have one too.

I ran like my life depended on it. Which it did.

He was hot on my heels, but I was faster.

I scooped the knife and darted away as he swiped at my head. I managed to roll away under his arm and slash his thigh, making him cry out in pain and anger.

Now the fight was about to get really bloody.

Lately, I'd been training with throwing blades with Rex, and it turned out that I was pretty good, but if I did throw it, I would lose my only weapon. I had to make a decision quickly. My eyes still stung from the dirt he threw earlier.

He snarled and ran right at me. I took a deep breath and squared my shoulders, rolling my neck. I lifted my arm, holding my small knife by the blade, and flicked it with all my strength. It spun through the air as if in slow motion, over, and over, and over.

The brute of a man stumbled to a sudden stop, his eyes widening as he rocked back on his heels. My knife stuck right out of the middle of his forehead, all the way to the hilt. He toppled over backwards with an almighty thump, dust floating in the breeze.

The crowd was deafening as they cheered. I felt like I wanted to fall into a heap and cry tears of relief.

I was rewarded with a bunch of flowers and an oily smile from the Viscount. He leaned over and spoke to Walter, who turned my way and nodded.

Something settled in my stomach, uneasy shivered over my skin.

Did he think I'd proven myself?

Rex walked me to my room, silent as I breathed a breath of relief.

"You fought well today. Good throw," he said gruffly, refusing to look at me as I stared at him in shock.

Did he just compliment me?

"You're not going soft on me, are you, Rex?" I joked, seeing his mouth twitch like he was trying not to smile.

"I fear that he'll take you out of the arena any day now," he mentioned in a monotonous voice, like he was trying not to let any emotion slip. I continued to stare at him as we walked. "He'll want you to hone your powers next." My stomach sank like a stone. As much as I hated being locked up here, forced to fight and kill people, I'd come to enjoy my training with Rex. He was the only sort of family

I had left. Seeing as no one would give me any information about Kai. Rex had his friends looking, but they all came back with nothing.

He'd simply vanished with the rogue dragon riders.

"What does he really want with me?" I whispered, stopping him with my hand on his arm. He ground his teeth, his jaw twitching before looking down at me.

"I don't know, but you're twenty-three now. I've heard rumours he's looking for someone to take down his enemies." His dark brown eyes softened as his gaze met mine. "I'm sorry, Ria. I'll do what I can to try and help, but the viscount has eyes and ears all over Ardentis."

"Then I'll escape. I'll kill my way out if I have to. I'll refuse to do his dirty work."

"What of your brother? Won't he pay the price for your disobedience?" he said quietly behind me, regret lacing his tone.

That stopped me in my tracks.

Fuck.

"Then it looks like I'm going to have to do what the viscount wants," I whispered, continuing to my room, where a guard opened the door for me, then locking it behind me with a final clunk.

I didn't allow myself to break down. I needed to come up with a plan. There was no way that I was going to let that murdering prick get his way.

⋯⊰✦⊱⋯

I gasped awake, blinking against the crushing blackness of my room as another boom shook the building. I knew a storm was coming. I could feel it approaching all day, my skin tingling. I heard the guards whispering about the odd marks on my neck and face that weren't there yesterday when they delivered my breakfast.

My lightning scars only appeared when a storm was nearby.

Another wave of electricity passed through me, making me shudder and grind my teeth.

Fuck sake, I'm not going to get any sleep now.

I rolled my neck, the tension building as another boom sounded. The band on my wrist blocked me from using my most of my powers. I'd had a constant headache the whole time I'd been wearing it.

It must be one hell of a storm if it's shaking the building.

Wait.

That's not just thunder.

Another shudder, closer this time. The ground shuddered, and dust rained down. I could feel something almost pushing against my mind, like it was trying to get in. Panic gripped me, and I used the electricity in the air to create a bubble of sorts around my mind, just like my mother taught me. It was the only thing I could do with the damn band on me.

Keys jingled in my door, and I bolted out of bed, grabbing the closest thing I could use as a weapon - one of those ridiculous golden candlesticks. Even in the darkness, I knew who it was immediately.

"Ria, you need to get out." Rex puffed, like he'd run all the way here. He handed me a blade as I shook my head.

"What are you talking about?" I put the blade down and ran about my room, looking for clothes before shoving boots on.

"They've come for you. The real riders."

My head snapped up, the breath catching in my throat.

"What the hell do you mean by the *real riders?*" I laced up my boots, sticking the blade down inside.

"No time to explain, this is your only chance to get away. Go." He reached into his pocket and grabbed a small square piece of black glass. He waved it over the band on my wrist, and the thing clicked open. I sighed in relief, my headache finally gone. Rex shoved the thing in his pocket.

I shivered at the electricity surging through me, crackling over my fingers. Rex nodded once before he grabbed my wrist and tugged me along behind him, out the door and down the hall. Guards lay on the ground in a heap every few corners. I wasn't sure if they breathed, but right now, I didn't care. Rex had obviously taken them down, making use of the darkness.

Another boom shook the building, the power was completely out in the whole palace by the look of things.

Not surprisingly, large storms often took out the skyline relays and stormglass. They'll be fully charged by morning, but right now, they were volatile and almost overloaded.

We didn't pass a soul, and for that, I was thankful.

Rex towed me down to the garden doors and out into the pouring rain. That's when I could feel it. The presence of a dragon. I swallowed, shaking my head and pulling back against him.

"I won't go with them. Dragon riders killed my parents!" I shouted to be heard over the pouring rain, attempting to dig my heels in. Rex turned back, his eyes wide, pleading with me.

Before he could open his mouth, a man appeared out of nowhere right in front of me.

To my credit, I didn't shriek like I wanted to, but I raised my blade as he smirked.

By the Gods. He's gorgeous.

"We gotta move, now." He murmured, taking a step toward me.

"Who are you?" I snapped, taking a step back as a shuddering boom sounded.

"Right now, I'm your only hope of getting out of this place. We need to move." He took a step towards me, and I took another back.

"I'm not going with you." I turned pleading eyes to Rex. He should know better than anyone that I never wanted to see another dragon rider.

"You need to go with him, Ria. He's not like the ones who killed your family. He's one of the good guys." Rex stepped up and grabbed both of my arms, squeezing them. "Please, this is your only chance."

"How the hell do you know that?" I gritted my teeth.

I will not cry. I will not cry.

"Look, you can interrogate me the whole way back, but we're running out of time. I've been sent here to get you out, so that's what I'm going to do." The man growled, looking impatient as he looked around the rain-soaked yard.

"Sent by who?" I raised a brow as I turned to him, and he rolled his eyes. Clearly impatient.

"A behemoth who will eat me if I don't rescue you." He took another step.

"Say that again?" I frowned. What the hell is he talking about? Clearly frustrated, he rubbed his face.

"Look, can I grab your arm and tow you out of here, or not?"

"Oh, well, when you put it like that, sure," I grumbled. But I didn't miss the word *rescue*. He reacted fast and wrapped a large hand around my arm.

"Stay safe, Ria. I'll keep an ear out for your brother and send word if I hear anything." Rex surprised me by pulling me in for a hug. He held for a moment, two, before letting me go. He mashed his lips together as he nodded encouragingly at me. "Go, Silver Fox."

"Rex." I croaked, feeling tears prick my eyes. "What about you?"

"I'll be fine. Go." He pushed me gently toward the handsome rider, turned, and ran.

But before we could move, six guards rounded the corner, and we froze.

"Shit," The rider muttered. I could feel more electricity buzzing in my veins thanks to the storm, and something else I could feel that wasn't there before. I was filled with a sudden urge to blast the men up and around. My hands moved on their own as I watched in horror as the guards were picked up by an invisible force and thrown around the gardens.

Their screams were muffled by the rain and wind. When they landed, their joints were sticking out in grotesque angles.

They'd been thrown around like rag-dolls.

I'd done that.

My rescuer looked down at me with raised brows. "Well, that's one way to do it." He muttered, making me bark a laugh before my eyes rolled up into the back of my head.

I groaned as I woke, something cold pelting my face, stinging like needles.

Is that rain?

I opened my eyes and almost cried out. Strong arms were wrapped around my waist, and I was sitting on something that was moving...but not on the ground...

No.

"Easy," the deep voice mumbled into my ear, making me shiver as his warmth slowly leeched into my back.

Breathe. Don't freak out.

The rain continued to pelt my skin as we flew through the dark, the distant rumble of thunder thankfully in the opposite direction, as it got quieter. My heart began to trip over itself as I started to realise that this was *real*.

This was actually happening.

Chapter Five

"We've got another four hours until we can land. Are you alright?" he murmured, and I could feel the reverberations through my back. The smell of his wet leathers set my pulse racing. It brought me back to the last time I was on the back of a dragon.

No, I'm not alright. I wanted to shout, but it would do me no good to panic. I took a calming breath and blew it out slowly.

"I don't know, to be honest. I have no idea who you are, and where we are going, for starters." The wind tried to steal away my words, but the man rumbled a laugh.

"My name is Brodie McTavish. I'm from Sylvanfire, and this is my dragon, Drathruin."

I couldn't even tell what colour dragon it was, but I guess it didn't matter. It could still eat me if it felt so inclined.

"I was sent here to save you from that slimy, fat bastard by a very cantankerous, black behemoth called Vexirion," he grumbled, huffing out a long breath.

He doesn't mean…?

"A dragon…sent you to get me?" I tried to turn to make sure I heard him correctly. He just tightened his arms.

"Yes, he's a Tenebrae, a void dragon, and a breed that we haven't seen in these lands for a very long time. He landed two days ago and demanded that we get you out. He had a vision of you long ago. He's going to bond with you."

My heart *stopped*. I tried to absorb what he just said, but it made absolutely no sense.

"So, what you're saying is that a giant, rare dragon turns up out of nowhere and demands that you specifically come and bust me out of the creep viscount's house of horrors?"

"Yeah, that pretty much sums it up. And that he will raze my house and those I love if I don't."

"He sounds charming." My breath caught at his words. Rex did promise me that he was one of the good guys. But it didn't mean that I was going to trust him.

"Oh, you've got no idea." He chuckled darkly as his breath tickled my ear.

"Why the hell would he pick me?" My breaths were choppy and my hands sweaty as I gripped them together. "I'm no one, haven't been for the past three years." I swallowed my sorrow.

Mum. Dad. Kai - wherever the hell he was - not even Rex could find out anything for me with his many contacts.

"Look, I don't know why he wants you, but he said if you were to stay there, bad shit would happen. And that he's been destined to bond with you since you were born." Brodie sounded almost bored, like he didn't care for such drama. I shuddered and pulled the jacket tighter around me.

"Who *are* you?" I asked again, because this dragon wouldn't just ask anyone to do its bidding, surely? I could feel him sigh against my back as his chest expanded with a deep breath.

"It doesn't really matter who I am. I'm just the messenger. Once you bond with Vexirion, you'll probably go to Emberhollow Institute and never see me again."

He couldn't just be a nobody. The biggest dragon in Ardentis wouldn't have picked just anyone. So I changed tactics.

"Why didn't he come and get me himself then?"

"Because a dragon can't exactly sneak in and out unseen. He's rather noticeable," he quipped sarcastically, and I rolled my eyes.

"No shit. I mean, why isn't he here to meet me?"

"Because that's how he wanted it to happen. I don't know what he's thinking. You don't question dragons if you value your own life," he grumbled, shifting his weight behind me.

I shut my mouth and let my thoughts run wild.

Emberhollow Institute? Where on Ardentis was that? I thought that the closest dragon academy was Voralyth? I could feel a tugging at my shield again, and I started to wonder if it might be the dragon trying to link with me. But what the hell would I know? Dragons didn't come to the Bonefyre Archipelago, there hadn't been a sighting for over three hundred years. Until three years ago.

But Father used to tell Kai and I stories of when he was younger, and could see their gigantic silhouettes soaring in the sky above them. He never got close to one, but he'd heard that once you were bonded to a dragon, they were loyal to you for life, and not to mention the magic you would get from them.

It seemed more like a fairytale than real life. And here I was, on the back of another one, and off to meet another who wanted to bond because of a dream he had.

I'd read that the different breeds of dragons gave you different powers. Like the green dragons were fire, the blue dragons water, the yellow dragons air, and the red dragons earth.

But the other three breeds? The black, purple and brown were shrouded in secrets.

The sky began to lighten on my right.

We must be flying north, then.

The silence was starting to get awkward, and my ass went numb hours ago. I tried not to fidget, but it was getting more and more uncomfortable.

"We're nearly there," he grumbled, shuffling away from me as I wriggled. I could see a city ahead, something that looked like a castle in the distance.

And we were heading right for it.

The burning orange sun peeked over the horizon as we flew around the back of the castle, landing in a large, open field. My heart was in my throat as Drathruin landed, jarring me from head to toe. I tried to stifle a yawn, but lost the battle. I felt *exhausted*.

"How...how do I get off a dragon?" I yawned, and Brodie's arms dropped away from me as soon as we touched down. I missed his warmth, and I didn't want to admit it to myself, but I thought I'd felt something like safety in his arms.

"You'll want to slide down her foreleg, bend your knees when you hit the ground. I'm guessing your ass is numb, so you shouldn't feel a thing," he chuckled, the vibration sending shivers through me. I took a deep breath and assessed the challenge before me. I wanted to get down before there were more eyes on me. I moved before I could think more of it, forced my stiff legs to work, my numb ass skating over Drathruin's scales as I hit the ground with a grunt. My legs gave way beneath me, and I fell into a heap. I scuttled away from the beast as quickly as I could. A man came rushing over to help me, my cheeks burning with embarrassment.

"Are you alright?" His voice was eerily similar to Brodie's, but I froze as I looked at him.

I blinked. And blinked again.

Shit. They're identical.

"Yes...I'm alright. Just a bit tired," I croaked as I continued to stare. He pulled me up. I was still unsteady, but I was able to stand on my own.

"I'm Elias, but you can call me Eli. You've already met Brodie by the looks." He smiled, and it lit up his face. He was gorgeous, just like his twin brother. A woman dressed in similar clothing ran to us, looking me over. Eli's eyes warmed as he looked at her, and she gave him a cheeky wink before he wrapped an arm around her shoulder, kissing the top of her head. I heard a quiet grunt behind me, meaning that Brodie had dismounted. Lia stuck out her hand, her grip firm.

"I'm Vidalia, but you can call me Lia."

I didn't trust these people. I didn't want to give them my name.

As soon as I could, I'd get away and begin my search for Kai.

I opened my mouth to give them a fake name when a *boom* shook the ground. The hair on the back of my neck stood on end, and I broke out in goosebumps. That force pressing at my shields doubled, and I turned slowly. The biggest, meanest-looking dragon I'd ever seen had just landed behind us, and its piercing gold eyes were pinned on me. On instinct, I dropped my shields, and a cold, low voice slithered in.

Nymeria Everhart, finally, you let me in. He growled, making me shiver as he took a thundering step. *I am Vexirion, born of the great Tenebrae and Pravius line, or as they call me, the Void dragon of shadows and space. You will be my rider until our forms return to the stars.* I stood rooted to the ground, trying to take all of him in. He took another few steps towards me, lowering his head until it was level with me. *I dreamed of you over a hundred years ago. I have been waiting for you, but you were pulled away from your chosen path, and I had to intervene.* He growled again, still advancing on me. I was frozen, terror gripping me so tightly that all I could do was stare. *I was waiting for you to come to me, but I had to take matters into my own hands. I don't like chasing girls like some hormonal teenage boy.*

My hackles rose, like being kidnapped was *my* fault.

"Now, hold on just a minute," I growled out loud, folding my arms across my chest. I heard a gasp behind me, but I ploughed on. "Do you think my parents getting murdered in my own home, me getting kidnapped and forced to fight for three fucking years, was *my* fault?" My voice had turned shrill as I started to yell. "Don't you come saying that it was such an effort to threaten others to do your dirty work, all for what? Some dream you had over a hundred years ago?" I felt someone step up beside me, but Vexirion glared at them, baring his teeth until they backed away again.

Good. I wanted to see if they had broken you, but you still have a fire burning in your soul, Voltrite. His voice almost sounded smug, like he was happy that I'd started to yell at him. I sucked in a lungful of air, ready for round two, when he butted in again. *There is a stone in my chest. Come and collect it, then step back twenty paces.* The command in his voice brooked no arguments, and I almost didn't want to do it because he had baited me to anger. I couldn't deny the feeling in my soul, my very bones, though, that this was what I was born to do. I just never imagined that it would lead me to a dragon. I slowly made my way towards him, and he sat up straighter, exposing his chest to me. My heart was thundering in my throat as I approached him, the warmth coming off him was surprising. As I reached his chest, I saw something glimmering between his black, shimmering scales. With a shaking hand, I reached for it, and it was embedded deeper than I thought.

Remove it and hold it in your right hand. Vexirion rumbled into my mind. I finally wrapped my fingers around the hard stone. It was the size of a duck egg and glistened like an opal in the early morning light.

It was beautiful.

I stepped back twenty paces and stared at the dragon that somehow wanted to bond with me.

Close your eyes and hold your breath, little storm. His voice was loud in my head as my pulse sprinted. I heard someone curse behind me and loud footsteps as they quickly backed away. I sucked in a long breath and closed my eyes, having no idea what was about to happen.

The stone in your hand will protect you. Do not drop it. Do not open your eyes and do not breathe in.

"What do you mean?" I asked, he only grumbled, so I sucked in a breath before I was engulfed in blistering black dragon flames.

CHAPTER SIX

It felt like I was being wrapped in a cocoon, or a warm blanket. I could feel heat all around me, but it didn't burn. A tingling started in my fingers, moving up my hand, wrist and arm with a sting that felt like someone was poking me with a thousand needles. My lungs began to burn with the need to breathe, but I held on, and on. Just as I was sure that I would collapse, his voice was clearer in my head.

You are safe to open your eyes, little storm. I sucked in a beautiful lungful of air and blinked open heavy eyes. I quickly looked down at myself, assessing for damage, but found none.

A little warning would have been nice. I snipped, trying to catch my breath.

It wasn't anything you couldn't handle. Stop being dramatic. He drawled, lifting his head higher as he looked behind me. *Tell them that we will remain here to train before the year starts at Voralyth. We have much to do. Now go wash, sleep, and eat. In that order.* He huffed out a loud breath, but I cut in before he took off and left me here.

Wait. How am I to trust these people? I crossed my arms across my chest, standing my ground.

They are not like the ones who took you. Those riders are a disgrace and use their power for money. These riders are honourable.

I still don't trust them.

Vexirion didn't deign with a response before flexing his giant wings, crouching, and launching into the sky.

Okay then. See you around, I guess.

"Your arm," Lia gasped behind me. I turned to see her hazel eyes wide open as she stared at me. I looked down at my right arm and froze. The stone I was holding was no longer there, but it had seemed that the dragon flame had somehow dissolved it, and into my skin. Black and silver flames started at my middle finger and curled around my wrist, snaking their way up my arm and into my sleeve.

"It's beautiful. I'd only heard of the way Void dragons leave their brand, but to see it in action was a little terrifying," Eli breathed as he came to Lia's side, huffing out a laugh. "How do you feel?"

Brodie slowly made his way over, eyeing me like I was about to combust or something.

"I feel the same, I think. I'm too exhausted to feel much else. Vexirion told me that I was to remain here to train until Voralyth starts for the year, and to wash, sleep, and eat. In that exact order." I rolled my eyes, and he grumbled, his voice slightly quieter.

I heard that. And you can call me Vex.

Are you always going to be inside my head? Even when you're not close?

Yes. Get used to it, and learn to block me out.

"You're to stay here? He doesn't want to take you back to Emberhollow?" Brodie folded his arms across his chest like the idea displeased him. Eli, on the other hand, looked delighted.

"That's great! Imagine the faces in the boots section when they learn a Void dragon is here. They'll shit their pants." He laughed, and Lia just rolled her eyes, shaking her head.

"Honestly, you're always looking for ways to shove something in their faces." She frowned at him, but Brodie and Eli only chuckled. She met my confused expression, her lips twitching. "The infantry at Voralyth is called the Boots section, and the riders are the Jaw section."

"Ah, right. Thanks," I nodded, still a little confused.

"Yeah, but they always do the same to us," Eli argued, but Brodie cut him off from saying more.

"So, since it seems like you're to stay here, we'd better know who you are." I turned to look at him. His light green eyes were framed with the longest, darkest lashes, and his black hair was almost long enough to get into his eyes, the waves looking as soft as silk. He towered over Lia and me. The two brothers were equal in height, but Eli had startling blue eyes, otherwise, they looked exactly the same. It was going to be hard to tell them apart if you couldn't see them straight on.

I hesitated. I wasn't ready to tell them anything yet. What if they weren't honourable at all?

"You can call me Ria." I blinked as I took a wobbly step back, my head suddenly feeling a little too heavy for my neck. "And I think I need a lie down," I whispered as the ground rushed up to meet me.

Brodie moved, swift as a snake, and caught me before I hit the damp earth. I was too exhausted to complain as he carried me inside. I shut my eyes as nausea rose as swiftly as the tide. I swallowed it down, breathing deep as Lia and Eli chatted quietly ahead of us. The rocking sensation lulled me to sleep as Brodie carried me in his strong arms.

A dark room greeted me as I cracked open my heavy eyes. The curtains were drawn, and the mattress underneath me was soft, the sheets pulled tight.

Finally, a comfortable bed.

`I would be rather surprised if the king of Everdra had lumpy beds.` Vex grumbled, making me suddenly *very* awake.

Why am I in the castle?

`Where else do you think the princes would have taken you? I thought you were smart, little storm.`

I beg your pardon? Princes?

`Yes. Prince Elias and Brodie McTavish.` He drawled like I was stupid, like I should have known that the man who saved me was a fucking prince of Everdra.

By the stars.

I swung my legs over the side of the bed, rubbing the sleep from my eyes. I pulled the curtain aside and glanced out my window. I was greeted with a view of a stunning garden, hedges all in a neat row, flower beds and weeping willows decorating the land. The garden was almost as big as my village back on the Bonefyre Archipelago. I swallowed, my throat dry and raw.

Right.

What the hell am I meant to do now?

I opened my bedroom door, half surprised to find it unlocked as I swung it open. The hallway was quiet and empty, the dim lights glowing softly above me. I looked around, having no idea where to even begin. The place looked huge from the air. I was sure to get lost as soon as I left my room. But I didn't plan on staying here. I needed to get out and find Kai, hopefully with the help of my new dragon.

This has to be some sort of sick joke, or at least a dream.

`Then you're going to be in for a nasty surprise, little Storm.`

"Excuse me, miss?"

I jumped as a guard approached me. I went to my hip on reflex, but of course, I had nothing on me. "I didn't mean to startle you, but I was told that when you woke, I'm to help you find your way to the dining room." He looked sincere as he stopped a few feet away and gave me a tentative smile. His dark blue eyes and brown curly hair made him look boyish, even though he was probably Kai's age.

"My name's Levi." He held out his hand for me to shake. I hesitantly shook his hand in return as he smiled at me. "Come on, then. This way." He walked ahead, making me blink in surprise. I took a steadying breath and decided to follow. I *was* hungry, and I couldn't remember the last time I'd had something filling.

The hallways all looked the same, and I was hopelessly lost already. Lush carpets lined the floor, which softened our steps, and paintings of landscapes and the royal family were scattered around every so often.

I realised with mortification that I didn't have a bra on. And it wasn't that warm in the halls. My nipples would be on show for everyone to see as I'd left my jacket back in my room.

Fucking great.

I crossed my arms over my chest, attempting to hide them as we rounded a corner, and Levi opened a wide set of wooden doors. Thankfully, no one else was in here as we made our way down the long table. Honestly, this thing could have sat at least twenty people.

"You can sit anywhere from here down, and I'll get one of the maids to come and get you something to eat. I'll wait outside until you're finished." He smiled at me again and wandered off, closing the doors quietly behind him. Before I could pull out a seat, a maid came trotting over.

"You must be Miss Ria! Please take a seat. What can I get for you today?" She looked at me kindly, her round face and pink cheeks, her brown eyes warm as they crinkled at the sides. I swallowed the sudden emotion clogging my throat. I hadn't been spoken to so kindly for a very long time, especially by another woman.

"Thank you," I croaked, having to clear my throat. "I..." my words disappeared like someone had stolen them from my very throat. I didn't know what I wanted. I hadn't been able to make any decisions for myself in years.

I tried again, but I snapped my mouth shut as the words wouldn't come. I felt my cheeks burn as tears pricked the backs of my eyes.

"It's alright, sweetheart." She spoke softly, touching me on the arm as I gritted my teeth. "How about I bring out a couple of things, and you eat what you like, okay? Take a seat and get comfy. I won't be long." She shuffled away, and I sat heavily, practically falling into the chair.

I took a sip of the apple juice before me, savouring the tart taste as I swallowed. I couldn't remember the last time

I'd had fresh juice. I was on strict rations at the viscount's palace.

I shut my eyes and leaned back into the chair, letting the emotions roll through me - sadness, gratitude, homesickness - before taking a deep breath.

"I hope I'm not interrupting," A deep voice jarred me from my thoughts. I snapped my eyes open, and my gaze landed on Brodie, who was standing opposite me, his hands gripping the back of a chair. His hair was still damp, the dark waves falling over his forehead as his sharp eyes locked onto me.

Prince.

This man before me is gods-damned prince.

"I should be asking you that question, *prince*. Seeing as this is your castle." I clenched my jaw to stop what else I wanted to say. I reached for my juice instead, only for something to do because I couldn't reach for a knife. I didn't miss the steel in his gaze, the way his knuckles turned white as he gripped the back of the chair.

"That was quick," he breathed, and I swore that I saw hurt flash in his light eyes. "I was wondering how long it would take you to treat me differently once you found out."

"I don't care that you're a prince," I snapped, leaning forward in my seat. "It's the fact that you didn't tell me. You said you were a nobody."

"And I am. My brother is the favourite, the one destined for the throne. I'm the back-up. The *spare*," he grumbled, pulling the seat out and sitting with a sigh.

"Oh, as if. I don't believe that for a second," I mumbled, taking another drink of my juice. He opened his mouth to retort when the kind maid shuffled out with a tray full of food. She placed it all down in front of me and gave me a wink before turning a sharp gaze on Brodie.

"I hope you're being nice to our guest, Cookie?" The maid crossed her arms across her ample chest as Brodie looked annoyed, opening his mouth only to be cut off again. "Make sure you and your devilish brother behave." She threw him a stern look before walking away. "I'll be sure to bring out your usual." She called out over her shoulder, and the kitchen doors swung shut behind her.

"By the stars, I haven't even had breakfast, and I'm already in trouble." He grabbed the closest glass of water and drained it before running a hand through his damp hair.

"So, 'Cookie' huh?" I fought against the grin that pulled at my lips, but gave up trying. He sighed and raised a brow at me.

"Yeah, I used to steal them all the time when I was little, so she calls me cookie, and Eli is muffin." He pretended like it annoyed him, but I saw the fondness for the older maid on his handsome face.

"They're adorable nicknames."

Fancy the princes of Everdra have the cutest nicknames I've ever heard.

"She only calls me that when she wants to embarrass me," he grumbled, and I laughed. He looked up, and something flashed in his eyes. He cleared his throat and looked away as my laughter died.

It had been years since I'd laughed properly. It felt strange, almost like I'd forgotten how to do it.

I looked down at the plates she'd set before me, and my stomach grumbled loudly. I should have been embarrassed, but I was past the point of caring. I was bloody starving.

I dug in, having a little bit of everything. Eggs, porridge, toast, muesli, yoghurt, and fruit. Brodie's own breakfast was delivered, and I didn't miss the maid ruffling his hair before wandering away, or the slight pink staining his cheeks. The plates were still half full, but I couldn't fit anything else in. My stomach wasn't used to such good food. If I'd eaten anymore, I'd have made myself sick.

I was surprised at the comfortable silence as we ate our breakfast. I was delighted when the coffee was brought out, and I drained it in about three mouthfuls. When the doors opened again, Eli and Lia wandered in, hand in hand.

"Oh, good morning, Ria. I hope you're feeling a little better?" Lia asked as she sat down beside me, Eli sitting next to his brother, who ruffled his hair, just like the maid had. Eli's hair was shorter, the sides shaved and a bit longer on top, his waves a mess. I suddenly felt insecure again as I took in Lia's lovely clothes. I hadn't even looked in the mirror when I left my room this morning. I probably looked like a hot mess with my bed hair.

"I'm feeling much better, thank you," I murmured, loosely folding my arms over my chest to hide my bra-less boobs. "I was just talking to Cookie here about his adorable nickname, and yours is Muffin?" I had to bite the insides of my cheeks to stop myself from smiling as Eli choked on his coffee, and Lia roared with laughter.

"Oh my gods. How have I never heard that before?" Lia cackled, leaning back in her chair as I joined her. It was too much, I couldn't stop laughing as I wiped tears from my eyes, stomach hurting as we both laughed. I'd forgotten how good it felt.

The twins looked slightly put out as we finally wound down.

"Had your laugh, have you? Feel better?" Brodie narrowed his eyes at me, and I hiccupped.

"Man, Ria is serious trouble. You should have left her where you found her," Eli grumbled and drained his coffee, but I didn't miss Lia kicking him under the table. "I'm joking!" he hissed at her, rubbing his shin with a wince. "I'm sorry for what they did to you." Eli's voice dropped, causing me to look up. "I promise you we're nothing like those brutes." He looked sincere, but something in me couldn't trust him. Trust them.

The maids darted out and collected my plates, setting some down in front of Eli and Lia with a smile. I thanked them and blinked sleepily, feeling warm, comfortable, and full for the first time in ages.

"And don't you dare tell anyone else our nicknames," Eli grumbled, attempting to lighten the conversation, looking so eerily like Brodie as he pointed his finger at me.

"Don't you want the people to know the princes of Everdra have cute pet names? I think it will make you more relatable."

"That was quick," Eli griped, sharing a look with his brother, echoing what Brodie had said only minutes ago.

"Was it Moranna that told you we're princes?" He leaned on the table, eyes narrowed on me.

"Who's Moranna?" I shrugged, looking at the twins.

"The maid that so kindly told you her pet names for us," Brodie said, digging into his scrambled eggs with a side of bacon.

"Oh, no, it was Vex."

CHAPTER SEVEN

*D*on't *go throwing me in the deep end, thank you very much.* Vex rumbled into my head, making me jump. I'd forgotten he was there. Which earned me a growl in response.

"Alright, Ria. Let's find you some clothes and give you a tour." Lia smiled at me, and I attempted a smile in return.

I made sure to keep my arms over my chest as we made our way out of the dining room, the boys grumbled to each other as the doors shut behind us.

"So, that's where we normally have our meals, that sort of thing. I'll take you to get some clothes." Lia turned and grimaced at me. "Sorry, I would have left some things in your room if I knew you'd be up so early." She obviously noticed my discomfort.

"That's alright."

An awkward silence bloomed between us.

"Did the viscount really get you to fight for his entertainment?" she breathed, peeking a look at me from the corner of her eyes. I didn't want to think about it, but I guess there was no going back now.

I had no idea how she found out, either. It wasn't like I was going to tell them.

"Yes. I was there for three years." I tried to swallow past the lump growing in my throat. Once I got some clothes, I would start hunting Kai down. I didn't want to go to some school.

"They made me wear a mask so people wouldn't know my true identity. They called me the Silver Fox."

I heard Lia gasp beside me. She'd obviously heard of me before.

"That was you? Oh my Gods, Ria," She stopped and placed a comforting hand on my arm. "I'm so sorry for what they made you do. I can't even begin to imagine what it was like for you." I saw her wipe a tear from her eye, truly meaning her words. I didn't want to admit it to myself, but it even made me feel uncomfortable.

"Thank you. I'd made a friend there, Rex. He was the one who trained me - he was like a father figure to me." My words trailed off, my throat too tight.

We arrived at a door at the end of the hall, where Lia knocked softly. A soft *'enter'* called from inside, and she swung open the door.

The room was like a rainbow had exploded inside it. There were multiple coloured fabrics strewn around it, pins, cushions, hats, you name it.

"Jane, would you have anything for my friend Ria, please? I'm afraid she wasn't able to bring anything with her." The plump older lady swivelled on her chair and looked me up and down, brown eyes wide. "We just need something basic so we can go into town and find her some more clothes." Lia was about the same height as me.

"Yes. I think I have something here suitable for Miss Everhart." Her voice was low but firm. I flinched.

How does she know my name?

The old woman smirked like she could read my mind.

"It's your hair and eyes, my dear. I have only met one other of you before, and she was an Everhart. Plus, news travels quickly, especially when someone bonds to the biggest dragon we've seen here in about three hundred years." Jane raised a brow at me before turning away to dig through a pile of clothes. "I've got something here that will fit. I was going to give it to you, Vidalia, but I think the colouring will suit Nymeria better." She turned around with a gorgeous olive green dress draped over her arm.

"How do you know my full name?" I breathed, taking a step back towards the door, unease slithering through me.

"I have ears and eyes everywhere, girl. And someone doesn't forget someone with your...colouring." She stood to her full height, eyes locked on me. "I mean you no harm. You can trust me, and those who help you here."

She turned her back, flinging clothes everywhere while I stood rooted to the spot.

She knew of someone like me? Another Everhart?

I never met any of my grandparents. As far as I knew, my parents were only children.

"Here, I think this will be good enough until you visit the shops. I'll make you something for the ball in a few weeks. I'm already nearly done with yours, Vidalia, but no peeking!" She shoved us out the door, Lia stifling a giggle as Jane slammed it behind us.

"Are you alright? You look a little pale." Lia stopped by the door, but I couldn't meet her gaze.

"Yeah, I'll be fine. Just not used to people knowing who I am." I cleared my throat and attempted a smile.

"Come on, I'll grab you some underwear and get you feeling a little more comfortable." She offered me a shy smile, and I returned it. The expression felt a little strained as I wasn't used to so much smiling or laughing as I had done in the past hour. Something akin to guilt slithered under my skin, which dampened my mood instantly.

Lia gave me some of her spare toiletries and told me to knock on her door across the hall once I'd finished. It was going to take me at least an hour to tame the hair on my legs. I heaved a loud sigh and got to work.

Swirling grey eyes stared back at me in the mirror as I brushed out my long, silver hair. I'd never liked my eyes, but my parents told me they were beautiful. That they told a story.

I looked away as my mother stared back. What I wouldn't give to see them one more time. To speak to them, to have them hold me and tell me everything was going to be alright.

It does not do well to dwell on the past. You need to focus on the now. Vex grumbled, making me shiver as I swallowed my sorrow.

I know you're right, but I just want someone who loves me to tell me things are going to work out.

I'm not going to say that, because I can't foresee the future. It is what you make it, little storm. Now, get dressed, find something suitable to wear, and come and see me. We need to soar the skies, and you need to learn how to fly. I've seen your memories, and you can already fight. That is good, you'll need it.

His words didn't fill me with confidence, but at least he'd complimented me.

That was a good start.

The dress fitted me perfectly, and I ran my fingers down the smooth material. Lia had given me some sandals to wear with it and a pretty blue claw-clip to tie my hair back with. I hazarded another look in the mirror, and it almost brought me to tears.

I was a woman now. Not the girl who was taken in the night. That girl was dead and gone. The woman staring back at me was a killer. Scars littered her mind and body like jewellery. I felt stripped to my bare bones, my soul lying tattered as it struggled to hold on to who I was.

It all begins and ends in your mind. What you give power to has power over you, if you allow it. You aren't that same person anymore. Move on. Evolve.

Vex was right. I had to shed that skin and be who I wanted to be, right now. And I wanted to be strong and take charge of my future.

I turned away from the mirror and knocked on Lia's door. The smile she gave me was radiant as she looked me over.

"By the stars, Ria. You look beautiful."

"Thank you. I haven't worn a dress in...a very long time." I ignored how it hurt, choosing instead to focus on the now. I had bonded to the biggest dragon in Ardentis, and I would rather die than go back into a cell ever again.

A little dramatic, but I won't allow that to happen.

I mentally huffed a laugh as Lia led me down the hall.

"I need to know what the hell you were doing two nights ago. And a Void dragon in the area? How long did you think it would take me to find out a Tenebrae was here?" A stern voice cut through the silence. It was a voice that made me straighten my spine, lift my chin a little as we rounded the corner.

The man turned our way and smiled at Lia, giving her a subtle nod before his eyes landed on me. Brodie and Eli were shoulder-to-shoulder with their hands behind their backs, jaws ticking.

"And this must be the new rider you dashed off into the night to steal from..." He cleared his throat, the words dying as his eyes scanned the hall, before he turned to

Brodie, raising his brows. He nodded, not even looking my way.

"Let's continue this conversation elsewhere. Follow me." He gestured his hand down the hall, where the twins began to walk. We followed in awkward silence.

Shit. That's their father. The king. The king!

Do I bow? What do I do?

`Keep your chin up and spine straight. Do not cower before this man. I don't. It's the queen you need to worry about.`

That's because you're a dragon and you do what you want. And what do you mean, I need to worry about the queen?

"Don't worry, he's really nice. He's been nothing but kind to me." Lia whispered in my ear, and I nodded, my stomach settling a little.

Eli held open a large wooden door with a smile, winking at Lia as we crowded into the comfy room. The large bay windows overlooked the sparkling ocean, the sun glinting off the water like diamonds. I could have sat there and stared at it all day. The king moved behind his large desk by the windows and sat with a sigh. The others followed as soon as he did.

He turned his full attention to me. He was a very handsome man, just like his sons, but his blue eyes looked tired as they landed on me. "I'm Euan McTavish - welcome to my home."

"Thank you, your majesty. You have a lovely home. I've heard wonderful things about Sylvanfire." I managed to keep my voice even, though my hands threatened to shake.

"So, please, tell me about yourself, and how you ended up at Viscount Mordane's?" He leaned back in his chair and fixed his light blue eyes on me. I swallowed my nerves, all attention on me.

"My name is Nymeria Everhart, and I'm from the Bonefyre Archipelago." I resisted the urge to close my eyes and picture the island I'd called home, but I did what Vex told me to do instead. Move on.

A darkness fell over the room as I spoke, and the king's eyes dulled a little. I gritted my teeth as I thought about the cruel way my parents had died.

I *would* get my revenge on the rogue rider and the viscount one day.

`And you will.` The deep voice rumbled into my mind. It made me feel better knowing Vex was on my side.

I cleared my throat when I spoke about Kai, hating the stinging in my eyes as I swallowed the tears.

"I want to begin by saying how very sorry I am, Nymeria." The king leaned forward, elbows resting on his desk. "The news about Viscount Mordane is concerning.

Leave him with me. In the meantime, I will see what I can find out about your brother. You are welcome here." He leaned back again, his all-seeing gaze travelling over each of us. "You will train with my sons before attending Voralyth, to give you the best fighting chance. The academy is tough but necessary."

"Oh, I was hoping that I could go on my way to search for him myself." It took everything in me not to shrink from all the eyes on me. "I've already done my schooling." I cleared my throat, but the king smiled kindly at me.

"All new dragon riders are legally required to attend an academy or institute of the dragon's choosing. We're making sure that you know how to handle the powers you'll manifest, how to ride in a riot and work together. It's necessary when you graduate and enter the real world. Many riders are sent around the Ardentis, or wherever their king or queen chooses."

My hopes and dreams were crushed in those few words.

"As for your brother, I'll have some of my men search for him. Welcome to Sylvanfire. May you fly strong and land safe."

CHAPTER EIGHT

Sylvanfire was the most beautiful city I had ever seen.

Tall buildings kissed the sky, and people smiled and waved at each other as they passed in the streets. Flowers were growing in pots out the front of buildings, trees lining the streets. Bright. Happy. Cheerful.

Lia had been given the go-ahead from the king to put my things on his account and to get whatever I needed. Eli had come with us, hand-in-hand with his girlfriend, as they walked ahead. He was constantly touching her, tucking her beautiful blonde hair behind her ear, or kissing her because he could.

The king had asked for a list of names of people I knew from my island. He said he would do what he could to see if they lived and if he could find them. I had thanked him with tears slipping down my cheeks.

Shop after shop we visited, the owners promising to deliver the items to me at the castle. I had never owned so much before. Where the hell was I going to put it all? Sure, the room they had given me was enormous, stupidly big. But what was I going to do when I went to Voralyth?

"We need to get you fitted with some leathers, so you can ride Vexirion and begin your training. It gets very cold up there." Lia flipped through some books on the shelves, tucking some under her arms for herself. I couldn't remember the last time I'd read a book, so I made sure I grabbed several on Lia's recommendation.

Eli didn't care for books unless they told you how to dismember someone, apparently, but got something for his brother. I don't know why, but it made me smile. It was something Kai would do.

"When can I start?" I asked, trailing my fingers along the spines, breathing in the calming smell of paper, leather, and binding glue.

"As soon as we get you sorted with clothes. I'm sure that he wants to see you as soon as we get back." Lia smiled my way, and I nodded back.

"Yeah, he told me to hurry along and stop shopping an hour ago." I sighed, ignoring the huff of annoyance I felt through our bond. It was only ten in the morning, and he was already bossing me around.

And I will continue to do so until you return.

What's the hurry? Got somewhere to be?

He ignored me. I rolled my eyes as I kept wandering.

We grabbed some treats from the bakery and made our way back to the castle. We decided to walk, enjoying the sun on our faces, the morning already warm. A shadow passed over us, soaring away into the distance. I looked up. *Dragons.* It sent a shiver down my spine as I watched them fly. It was going to take me a while to get used to that. And even longer to get used to the fact that I had my own.

But my heart raced with fear at the same time.

I'd been having nightmares about that night ever since it happened, and Regali and his damned dragon starred in it every time.

Banishing my dark thoughts, I found myself eager to get my flying leathers on and go out into the field where my dragon was impatiently waiting for me. To my surprise, Brodie was out there with his dragon, Drathruin. I realised with a start that his eyes were the same colour as his dragon.

I looked over to Vex and simply admired him and how magnificent he was. This still didn't feel real.

"Alright, the best way to mount is to run up their foreleg, using the scales to grip onto, and climb. There is a smooth bit of scales just behind their neck, near the wing joints, which is where you can sit. We call it the saddle. There should be a curved scale just in front of the saddle for you to grip onto, called the pommel." He finally looked at me, and I shivered. His gaze was darting over me as I stood before him in my leathers, feeling a little self-conscious. "You'll want to hold on by squeezing your thighs, but usually your dragon helps you out until you're strong enough to hold on yourself." His voice was gruff and emotionless, like he'd done this a hundred times. He had stubble growing on his chin, making him look like anything but a prince. I just nodded as I tried to remember everything he told me. I was usually a quick learner, so I wasn't feeling too overwhelmed for once.

"Alright, let's see what you got." He turned and ran up his dragon's leg, making it look easier than it was. Once he was settled, he nodded for me to do the same.

Right. I can do that.

`Hurry up, little storm, we don't have all day.`

Are you always this impatient?

`Yes.`

I blew out a sigh and made a run for it. I leapt, grabbing hold of a scale and hauling myself up his ridiculously large leg. I slipped, not able to get a good enough hold, and I slid down and landed on my ass with a grunt.

Great.

Again. Vex barked, glaring down at me.

I stood, brushed myself off, backed up a few steps and tried again. And again. And again.

I. Can't. Do. It.

I felt the embarrassment burning my cheeks as I sucked in lungfuls of air.

I could feel his sigh from here as he angled his leg out for me, and I could have sworn that he raised a scaled brow at me.

`I won't do this again. You'll get up on your own next time.`

Another long breath before I ran again, this time making it up his legs and onto his back. I scrambled my way across his scales, making sure to stay away from the sharp and deadly-looking spikes that trailed down his spine. I found the saddle and gratefully sat, catching my breath. Vex swivelled his head around to look at me over his shoulder, golden eyes raking over me before turning away.

`Hold on, little storm. Let's fly.`

He crouched down, flaring his gigantic wings out with a whoosh before we suddenly became airborne. Up, up, and up we flew, Vex's wings flapping with loud beats as the ground quickly dropped away. My hands and legs were gripping so tightly that they started to ache.

You don't need to hold on so tight just yet. I've got my magic around you. If you're silly enough to fall, I'll catch you.

I relaxed just a little, feeling his magic wrapping around my legs like a band. Brodie and Drathruin soared behind us as we banked, and my world tilted. I swallowed my scream as Vex turned dangerously fast, the air rushing past us. When he finally evened out, I flipped down my goggles, the difference immediate as my eyes stopped watering.

Vex made sure that he showed me every move as I struggled to stay conscious. It was thrilling, yes, but also terrifying. We eventually landed an hour or so later, and my whole body ached.

We will meet every day to train for two hours, and when you're not with me, you'll be training with them.

No rest for the wicked, huh?

Vex blew a gust of hot air into my face, making me stumble back a step as he extended his wings and took off into the sky. I watched him go, shaking my head. Still shocked that he bonded with *me*.

"That was good. Let's head in and get some lunch before we start on weights." Brodie appeared beside me, making me jump. I hadn't even heard him land. I nodded and followed the prince. I shook my head again as I thought about everything that had happened in the last few days.

A prince rescued me from the palace of pain, and now I was flying on the back of a dragon. It seemed too good to be true.

For the past week, I'd had both princes training me, and I preferred Eli. He was quick to smile, tell a joke, and was super friendly. But Brodie was stern, serious, and I didn't think I'd seen him smile properly once.

Which was fine with me.

Even though I was a dragon rider now, it didn't mean I had to trust them.

Every breakfast, I'd arrive to find Brodie already there. He'd nod in greeting and avoid my gaze. I couldn't help but look up every so often, wondering if I should try to talk to him. But my distrust stopped me. It wasn't like he was trying to have a conversation with me either.

In the halls, he'd continue on his way, as if he were busy on an errand. But if I saw Eli, he'd stop and talk.

They might be twins, but they were chalk and cheese with me.

I'd talked myself into peeking into my mirror again, finally looking at the extent of my brand from Vexirion. I'd gotten used to the black and silver flames on my hand and arm, but it wound up around my shoulder before turning into a gigantic dragon that covered my whole back. A claw was half around my throat, as if it was gripping onto me, the wings were outstretched across my shoulders and upper arms, and its body trailed down, its long tail curling around my left thigh. Honestly, he'd covered half of my body with his brand.

But I had to admit: it was *beautiful*.

The bigger the brand, the more magic I can transfer to you. And being a Tenebrae means I'm more powerful than the other four common breeds here. So buckle up, little storm, and prove to me you can handle it.

The more I looked at the brand, the more beautiful I found it. And I didn't fail to notice that it covered a lot of my scars from the whippings I used to get on my back, the knife scar on my thigh, and the small scar on my throat.

Thank you. It truly is beautiful.

`I don't see you training.` But his voice lacked his usual bite.

I smiled.

Brodie's eyes normally looked elsewhere when I entered the room, but occasionally I saw him looking at my brand with drawn brows. I don't know what it was about that man, but I was drawn to him in ways I couldn't explain. I had to force myself to look away. Perhaps it was just because he rescued me from the viscounts, and I was appreciative of him.

He sure didn't want anything to do with me.

Chapter Nine

Voralyth was still another two months away, so I'd been training full-time with Lia, Eli, and Brodie. Now it was time to see how I fared in the sparring ring.

I bounced on my toes as I stretched my arms, getting ready to fight Lia on the mat. I felt strong, my legs were now able to grip onto Vex without him holding me, unless he turned quickly, then I slid right off. The first time, a scream burst from my throat, terror gripping me as the ground approached me at a sickening speed. Vex caught me in his claws before flinging me into the air, and I landed on his back with a grunt.

I still had bruises, and continued to add to them with my constant falls. But I *was* getting better.

"Ready, Ria?" Lia grinned at me from the other side of the mat. She and I had become good friends these past weeks. I'd never had a proper friend who was a girl before.

"Yep, bring it on." I winked as she laughed. Levi, Eli, and Brodie were all standing around to watch. Whoever won this round would fight the winner of the next round.

We circled each other, crouched down, ready for the attack. We lunged at the same time, a tangle of limbs and curses. She got me good on the ribs, but I'd managed to get her chin with my elbow. Here, on the mat, we weren't friends. This was serious business.

She managed to sweep my legs out from under me, my breath hissing out as I gasped for air. She landed on me, going for my throat when I wrapped my legs around her and flipped us until I was sitting on her, my arm against her throat. She tapped out when her lips began to turn blue.

I'd won.

Levi clapped as Eli helped his girlfriend up, who grinned at me.

"Well done, Ria. You're quick. I can see why they called you the Silver Fox." Lia huffed as laugh as I gave her a tight smile as the name raked over my locked-away memories. I hated it. "Alright, to make it fair, two of you need to fight before the winner takes on Ria."

"I'll fight." Levi stepped onto the mat, rotating his shoulders and stretching his arms. "Which one of you wants to take me on? Been a while." He smirked and narrowed his eyes as they played rock-paper-scissors to decide who would fight him.

Brodie lost.

Eli chuckled and slapped him on the back as Brodie made his way to the mat. They crouched low and began to circle each other.

"What's the deal with riders and the infantry?" I whispered to Lia, who was rotating her shoulder with a wince.

"It's a strained relationship between the Jaw Section and the Boots Section." I raised my brows in confusion. "They have us train as one to try to make us all get along and work better together. In theory, it works, but I don't think they'll ever get us to all like each other." We stopped and watched for a moment, the sight of them stirred unpleasant memories. "But these three have always been friendly enough with each other, but it's strained." Their fists were flying, grunting as they landed. "They were all the best in their year, and they grew up together, fighting for their parent's attention and approval." I watched in awe as they moved about like deadly dancers, their forms perfect, their hits precise. Rex would have loved to have trained them. I cleared my tight throat and pushed him from my mind. Truth be told, I missed him terribly.

"But why? What's the problem? That we get magic and they don't?"

"Yeah, pretty much. The government are a body that says they stand for the non-magical folk, so they have a voice." Lia wrinkled her nose when Levi's fist cracked into the side of Brodie's jaw. I gritted my teeth, but Brodie was lightning quick as he swiped his legs out from under Levi, sending him crashing to the ground. There was a flurry of curses, Brodie managing to get his forearm against Levi's throat until he had to tap out.

Damn. They can fight.

`And so can you. They didn't call you the Silver Fox for nothing. Use your speed to your advantage.`

Brodie's eyes meet mine, and my skin tingled. I didn't know what it was, but it seemed my body was overriding any rational thought as I forced myself to blink, plastering a bored look on my face.

"Looks like Brodie and Nymeria are going to battle it out." Eli grinned widely, and I narrowed my eyes at him. I swore he had been throwing the two of us together at every opportunity. But little did he know that Brodie didn't want to be anywhere near me, and I didn't want to be with him either. Good-looking or not, I wasn't going to trust a rider.

We were given a ten-minute break to catch our breath before the next round began.

"So, Nymeria. Where did you come before here?" Levi leaned against the table as I sipped at my water bottle, the cold settling into my stomach with a churn.

I'd been asked to keep my history to myself. Viscount Mordane was meant to be an ally to the royal family, and he couldn't find out that his prisoner had been taken by them. I filtered through my memories and tried to remember exactly what I was meant to say.

"I'm from Nythevra." I gave him a tight smile as his gaze locked on mine, head tilted to the side as he assessed me.

"What's it like there? I've heard it's beautiful." He sipped from his drink, but his eyes never left mine. Brodie loudly cleared his throat from across the room.

"It is. The city is surrounded by thick forests, and we tend to keep to ourselves out there." I took another mouthful of water, hoping they'd call the match any second.

"And what did you parent's think when you just wandered off on a hunch?"

"My parents died four years ago. I was fending for myself, so..." I trailed off with a shrug. My scalp tingled as

I turned my head and caught Brodie staring at us. I cleared my throat and stepped away from Levi, my eyes still stuck on the prince.

"Ready, Everhart?" he grumbled, his voice giving me shivers. I don't think he had ever said my first name. Perhaps it was too personal. But the thing that annoyed me most was that I didn't tell him my full name.

"Are you?" I winked, desperately wanting to call him Cookie, but I knew he would kick my ass if I did. He gave me a wicked grin that popped a dimple in his left cheek.

Oh, Gods.

He's got dimples?

I almost swoon.

`For goodness sake, girl, get a grip on your hormones!` Vex growled down the bond, snapping me out of it. Brodie must have known the power of his dimples, because he smirked before winking at me.

The bastard wasn't playing fair.

I shook out my hands as I stepped onto the mat. Lia called out *'good luck'* behind me.

I crouched low and began to circle, trying to remember everything my father and Rex had shown me about how to take down an opponent larger than me.

He rushed at me like a bull, and I quickly danced out of his way, my fist finding his ribs as he grunted. *Yes.* I got the first hit. But it didn't last long. He was quick for someone so large. Within moments, he was assaulting me with punches that I could only deflect with my arms, always on the defensive.

Move! Hit the boy!

I would if I could! I shouted down the bond. It was easy for him to give me orders when he wasn't fighting. *Stay out of my head.* I growled and ducked another swipe. I rolled and managed to knock one of Brodie's legs out, crashing him to one knee. I used the chance to boot him in the back and sent him tumbling. But he rolled and moved so quickly that I didn't see it until it was too late. He wiped both of my legs out from under me, then he straddled me, breathing heavily. He threw me another disgustingly charming grin as he went for my throat.

Nuh uh.

I wrapped my legs around his waist and twisted, causing him to lose his balance. I wasn't able to roll him as I did with Lia, but it was enough for me to wriggle free and land on his back. I heard Lia cheering me on, and Eli laughing. I wrapped my arms around his throat, my legs still around his waist as he tried to pull me off. But I was stuck like a limpet. He sucked in a long breath before pushing it out with force. Then he reached up and *pulled*. He flung me off him like I weighed nothing, and I landed on the mat with a grunt, the air knocked out of my lungs in a whoosh. I heard Lia and Eli gasp behind me as I tried to clear the stars from my vision. He came for me again, but I kicked him in the stomach before I rolled away. I got to my feet, and we stood there glaring at each other, our chests heaving.

"I think it's a draw," Eli chuckled, coming over to throw an arm over his brother's shoulder. I stood up straight as I still struggled to breathe normally.

"Agreed. I haven't seen anyone else fight as dirty as you, McTavish," Levi laughed and came to stand beside me. "You're full of surprises, Nymeria." I accepted my water bottle with thanks and drank long, forcing my gaze from Brodie's heavy one.

"Fine. Draw it is," he said before walking away.

`Next time you will win. The boy isn't used to losing, so make sure you practice.`

Don't worry, I will.

⸻❖⸻

I felt like I was falling.

Which was odd, because all I was doing was walking from my room into another. But the room was the gym. And the gym wasn't attached to my bedroom.

A cold gust of wind made me shiver.

I gasped awake as I landed heavily on something warm. My eyes flew open, and I looked at the ceiling of the gym. I was very familiar with the gym ceiling from the many times I'd been knocked on my ass in training.

What the hell?

"Storm?" A familiar, low voice sounded surprised, coming from right above me. I craned my neck and realised that Brodie was holding me in his arms. My eyes widened as I stared at him, and he stared right back.

"Ria?" Eli called, "where the hell did you just come from?" His voice came closer until he was beside me, his cerulean eyes full of surprise, like his brothers.

"Am I in the gym?" I asked quietly, brow furrowing as I tried to figure out how the hell I ended up here.

"Yeah. You just fell from the roof," Brodie muttered, blinked, then set me down, stepping away quickly. He cleared his throat as he ran a hand over his face. "You literally fell from the ceiling, out of nowhere."

"Yeah. I thought you went to bed hours ago?" Eli asked, cocking his head to the side as he scratched his chin. I gasped and looked down. Yep. I was wearing just a singlet and pink underwear.

I *was* in bed, asleep, last time I checked.

I could feel my blush rise from my chest, up my throat and stain my cheeks. I must have been glowing red as a tomato.

By the stars. This is mortifying.

"What the hell just happened?" I breathed, trying to cover my nipples that are no doubt showing through my thin singlet. It was rather chilly down here, but both twins had their shirts off, sweaty and breathing heavy like they were working out.

"I don't have the faintest idea. But I wonder if it has something to do with Vexirion's powers beginning to channel into you. We don't know how the powers of a Void dragon work," Eli wondered, looking into space. Thank the gods. But I was too afraid to look at Brodie. I didn't want him to see how embarrassed I was.

He called me *Storm*, not Everhart.

Did he just give me a nickname?

"I think you just teleported," he whispered, and my eyes shot to his. His light, sage green eyes were pinned on me, and I couldn't look away.

Eli quickly shoved a shirt on, eyes constantly darting to the door.

"There's no other explanation. You were asleep? weren't you?" Brodie grabbed his shirt from his bag, but he looked at me like I was a puzzle.

I nodded my head, chewing on my bottom lip as I could see the thoughts swirling behind his eyes.

"Vex must be starting to channel, and it's manifesting into teleportation."

I felt like someone had ripped the ground out from under me. I stumbled back, and he stepped towards me, his hand wrapping around my bare arm to steady me. "We need to get you back to your room before someone comes in."

"Get her outta here, Bro, you know that O'Connell would take her if he found this out." Eli nervously chewed his fingernails, and I had no idea why.

"You good?" Brodie let go, and I nodded weakly, still feeling a little lightheaded. He ran a hand through his tousled hair. "I'll meet you back here in half an hour." He called to Eli as he came my way. He took my arm again and led me out of the gym.

"Don't freak out, but I'm going to turn you invisible so others don't see you," he whispered into my ear, and I turned to him. He wasn't joking. His eyes were serious as they met mine.

"I beg your pardon?"

"Just keep your mouth shut and follow my lead."

108

Chapter Ten

He wasn't joking.

The bastard had turned me completely invisible. I stifled my cry when I looked down and only saw a faint outline of my body. He hushed me as he towed me out of the gym and into the cold halls. It was freezing out there, and I couldn't stop the shiver that passed through me.

We hurried along at a quick pace that had me almost tripping over my own feet.

When we heard steps coming our way, he slowed his pace to more of a dawdle. It was a man in uniform, and I felt Brodie's hand stiffen around my arm before he pushed me behind him.

"Take hold of my arm," he hissed, and I wasted no time in grabbing him. I tried to control my breathing as the man's eyes narrowed on Brodie.

"A bit late for you to be wandering around, Prince McTavish?" he drawled, coming to a stop in the hall. Brodie inched towards the wall, careful not to squish me.

"I could say the same for you, Captain O'Connell," Brodie said in a bored tone, not wanting to stop, but the man stepped in front of him, forcing us to a halt.

"What are you really up to? I saw you leave and return at dawn a few weeks ago, with another person on the back of your dragon." His voice was full of suspicion as he leaned in.

My heart began to hammer in my chest, but I made sure to steady my breathing so as not give myself away. Brodie stepped back, and I was pushed against the icy wall, Brodie's warm back flush against my front.

"What are you talking about, O'Connell? I was here the whole time," Brodie sounded calm, but his posture said otherwise. "More importantly, why are you watching the comings and goings of dragons and their riders?"

O'Connell narrowed his eyes at the prince before smirking, stepping away to clear the hall.

"You should watch how you speak to me, prince." The captain growled, "It was just an observation." I could hear the mocking in his voice as he shrugged nonchalantly.

Brodie shoved past the Captain and stormed away up the hall. I made sure to step lightly as I watched O'Connell narrow his eyes at Brodie's back before storming away.

"What the hell was that all about?" I whispered, but Brodie just took my hand and pulled me along faster.

We finally reached the hall where my room was before he plunged himself invisible and tugged me along. I couldn't see him at all. We quickly darted through my door, and I heard the faint click of the lock before letting me go. We both come back into view.

A thought hit me so hard I blurted it out before he could say anything.

"That's how you snuck into the palace grounds, isn't it?" I breathed. His jaw ticked, but he nodded his head, his posture stiff. "Does anyone else know of your powers?" My heart was racing. Holy hell. His eyes met mine, and the green was now dark, like they changed with his mood.

"No. Especially O'Connell. Only a select few know, and I would like to keep it that way," he whispered. I swallowed, nodding.

He can turn invisible. This is huge.

"And I would ask you to do the same with yours. Especially since we have no idea how your powers work, and you haven't even taken the plunge yet." He was standing there, stiff as a statue, his face unreadable.

"So, what now? How do I even start to try to learn how to use it?" I took a step towards him. "And what's the plunge?"

"The plunge is when your dragon opens the floodgates of their magic into you, and you need to dive into yourself to gather that magic. Let it fill you before you return to the surface. But if you take too much, you get trapped inside yourself, and you'll wither away into an empty husk. And being a Tenebrae dragon, he will have a lot of magic coming through that bond."

My mind emptied at the thought of doing such a thing.

"And when am I supposed to take this plunge? How do I know if it's too much?" My stomach twisted as I started to feel lightheaded.

`I will guide you. We will do it together. Fear not, little storm`

Where were you earlier? Was it your powers that made me teleport?

`None of your concern, and yes. But I did not know what powers it would manifest into. It depends on our bond.`

You will need to train so you don't
do it in your sleep again.

And how do I train something like that?
We'll figure it out.

Super helpful. Thanks.

Brodie took a step towards me as I blinked away the panic threatening to overwhelm me.

"You'll feel a shiver run through you, your body will tingle, and you'll know, Vex will know. You can feel the magic flowing through your veins. We just have to make sure you're nearby so the doctors can help if you get into trouble."

"What kind of trouble?" I whispered as he came to a stop right in front of me. I craned my neck to look him in the eyes. I only came up to his collarbone.

I should step back. Shouldn't let him get so close.

"Something I don't think you'll need to worry about, Storm. You're stronger than you look." With that, he turned and walked away, shutting my door quietly behind him.

I stumbled back until I reached my bed and fell into a heap.

Teleportation.

The plunge.

Magic.

It all felt a little too much, and there was no way I was going to be able to fall asleep again. I took a hot shower and sat with my head in my hands until I no longer felt the water pelting down on my back.

⸻❖⸻

"Are you alright, Ria?" Lia asked from beside me as I continued to stare at the food on my plate. I felt too sick to eat.

"I didn't get a good sleep last night," I mumbled, downing the rest of my coffee. The twins shared a look before checking over their shoulders. Lia stiffened beside me and shot Eli a look. He shrugged innocently, but Lia's gaze then snapped to Brodie, who narrowed his eyes at Eli.

It was like they were having a silent argument that I couldn't hear.

"I think she's getting close to taking the plunge," Brodie bit out, unable to say my name like a normal person. Lia turned to me with wide eyes.

"Oh, that's super exciting! I can't wait to see what kind of powers you'll manifest. We have no idea what you'll get, as a Tenebrae has never bonded here before."

So they haven't told her yet, then. I tried to ignore the brooding prince sitting opposite me, but I needed to know when I could start my training.

It seemed odd that I would have to hide my powers. Wasn't that the norm for dragon riders?

But their words about the government tickled the back of my mind. I think they were suspicious of those with great powers, and I'd heard of powerful riders going missing and never seen again.

"When can I start my other training?" I asked no one in particular, but I saw Eli quickly glance at his brother.

Eli leaned back in his seat, his hands behind his head as he checked over his shoulder again.

"Today. And we'll need to figure out a plan for when you're sleeping. So it doesn't happen again." Eli ignored the heated glare from Brodie as he ploughed on. "I haven't heard of anyone else with that sort of power before, so we'll need to visit our father."

"Are you already manifesting your power?" Lia asked quietly, catching on that this might be a conversation no one else should hear.

"I think so. I apparently teleported last night. I was asleep and fell through the gym roof."

She gasped and slapped a hand over her mouth. The twins nodded, looking tired as they leaned back in their chairs. Perhaps I wasn't the only one to have a sleepless night.

"Brodie caught her before she hit the ground," Eli said around a yawn, pouring himself another coffee. I felt my cheeks turn pink as I remembered how he held me in his arms, no shirt on, and me barely dressed.

I need to stop that. I don't trust him.

"By the stars, Ria. That's a very strong power." She whispered just as the dining-room door swung open and in waltzed Levi. The twins slumped further into their seats and rolled their eyes.

"Ah, good morning, Nymeria," he said with a spring in his step, sitting down next to me.

"Morning, Levi." I reached for the jug of coffee and poured myself another mug. I was going to need a lot of coffee today.

He smiled at me, and I gave him a small one back. I could see Eli pulling a face and mimicking him across the table. I had to bite the inside of my cheeks to stop myself from laughing.

Breakfast continued in awkward silence, but every so often, I saw one of the twins' shoulders shake, like they were holding in laughter.

"Alright, time we get out there. A pleasure as always, Levi." Brodie muttered before walking out. Lia, Eli and I followed.

"Hey, Nymeria," Levi called, and I stopped, my hand rested on the door to the hall as I turned. "If you ever want someone else to train you, let me know. I might not ride a dragon, but I sure know my way around the gym and fighting ring. It's good to have someone else with a different perspective, perhaps." He gave me a cheeky grin.

"Thanks, Levi. And you can call me Ria." I walked out to a dark look from Brodie as he raised a brow at me. I ignored him and stalked past, mentally high-fiving myself for annoying him for a change. Lia headed off to visit Jane, something about her dress alterations for the ball, and promised to catch up with us later.

Eli and Brodie led the way to their father's office to discuss the delicate nature of my new powers.

It made me feel a little nauseous, but Lia assured me I was in good hands. If anyone knew how to keep a secret, then it was the McTavish twins.

Their father called for us to enter, and we sat before his desk, papers strewn around as he smiled our way. You could see where the twins got their looks, but I was still to hear of their mother, the queen.

"What can I do for you three today?" He leaned back in his seat and looked us over. The brothers shared a look, and Brodie sighed.

"We think that Miss Everhart can teleport."

Does he simply refuse to say my first name?

The king sat forward and rested his arms on his desk, eyes locked on me.

"Tell me."

"I was dreaming of walking from one room into another when I felt a gust of cold air. I woke when Brodie caught me." I fought my blush as the king's eyes widened.

Gods. Get a grip.

"I see. And it was just the two of you there?" He turned to his sons, who both nodded.

"Yes. I managed to sneak her back to her room without anyone seeing."

"Good. Good."

"Miss Everhart," the King began.

"Please, call me Ria," I interrupted, hating the formality. The King smiled, the corners of his eyes wrinkling.

"Ria, do you remember anything else from last night?"

"Nothing else, Your Majesty." I heard Eli cough over a laugh. I managed to keep my cool, indifferent mask on, even though I wanted to throw something at him.

"Thank you." The king leaned back again and scratched his chin, a move that Eli did all the time. "It looks like we need to do some digging through the records to see if there is anything on teleportation. But, in the meantime, I want you to keep this to yourselves. We all know how hungry the government is when it comes to the powers riders possess." He looked up at the ceiling, deep in thought. "Oh, and try to figure out how to harness this gift as soon as you can. Go and visit George before he leaves for Voralyth." He stood and looked out of the window, the sea a swirling mess of white caps and spray as the wind picked up.

"Yes, sir," the brothers said in unison as they stood. I took that as our leave and quickly followed. They set a hurried pace down the hall, and I sped to keep up.

Eli knocked on the door and swung it open. A frazzled-looking older man glanced up from his messy desk and beamed at the twins.

"Ah! If it isn't my favourite princes!" He hurried over and gripped their hands in a firm handshake. His large yellow eyes swung my way, and I felt pinned to the spot. They reminded me of Lion's eyes, tawny gold, wild and bold. "Who do we have here? No, don't tell me. You're the one bonded to the terrifying Tenebrae, aren't you?" I nodded, and he beamed, taking both of my hands in his. "Amazing! Oh, I can feel the magic beginning to stir in you already. You will take the plunge in a matter of days, my dear." He chuckled, making me feel a little ill as he let go. "Sit, sit, tell me what's going on."

"Well, we need your help with Nymeria here. We think she's developing a rather powerful gift." Eli spoke softly, but the professor was nodding, his eyes lighting up.

"I knew it. Let me try and guess what it is." The twins huffed and smirked at each other as the professor cocked his head to the side. "May I?" He reached out his hand. I shrugged and put my hand in his again. He closed his eyes, and I felt a tingling in my fingertips.

"Oh, by the gods above and below," he gasped, eyes flying open. "You're a teleporter, and Arcborne."

CHAPTER ELEVEN

Both twins swivelled their heads in my direction, and I shrank under their heavy gaze.

"What the hell is an Arcborn?" Brodie breathed. Eli simply looked confused.

"This young lady is a powerhouse. Not only will she be able to teleport, and possibly more after she takes the plunge, but she is what they call Arcborn, a Voltrite." The professor looked at me with sparkling eyes.

"Is that how you threw those guards around like rag dolls?" Brodie turned to me, and I nodded.

"I was able to draw on the electricity in the storm and use it to my advantage, controlling their biolectirics. But I've barely used it, especially like that, so it was too much for me after years of being shackled." I spoke into my lap, twisting my hands together.

"So, what does this mean?" Brodie asked the professor. I looked up into his kind face as he gave me a sad smile.

"It means she'll be hunted for her powers, not only being a Voltrite, but also being bonded to a Tenebrae too. No doubt why the Viscount took her."

"Is there anything we can do to help her stop teleporting in her sleep?" Eli asked, his face paler now.

"I'm afraid not. Not until she makes the plunge. There is nothing much to do, unless you know what kind of bands were used when you were in Drakeforge, at the Viscount's manor?"

"We will *not* be shackling her. She still bears the scars from what those monsters have done to her," Brodie snapped, and I raised my brows. I hadn't seen him lose his temper before. The professor smiled kindly at him.

"I'm not suggesting we use them, my boy, simply to find out what materials they used." He turned back to me, his yellow eyes seemingly endless. "To help nullify your powers, child, so we can put it in your room, or clothing. Otherwise, she simply cannot fall asleep until she makes the plunge." He looked back at the twins, who shared a concerned look, shoulders slumping. "I'll see what I can find out and get back to you before tonight." The professor stood and rifled through his drawers and papers, muttering under his breath.

"Excuse me, professor?" I spoke up, all three men turning my way. "The bands were black, with blue glowing veins in them, if that helps. It made me feel nauseous, dizzy and foggy."

Horrible, nasty thing it was.

The professor stood up straight, tapping his chin before scribbling something down on some paper.

"Thank you, Nymeria. That really helps." He sat and bent his head down as he continued writing. Brodie and Eli stood and thanked the professor.

We split up, heading in different directions as I slowly made my way to my room. We'd catch up for lunch later, but my appetite was gone.

I'll be making the plunge in a matter of days. People are going to continue to hunt me down. My panic was threatening to choke me as I tried to calm my breathing.

`And I will scorch the ground where they stand if they try to take you. You will train, and you will master these powers, and they will tremble with fear when they mention our names.`

Is it weak of me to admit that I'm scared?

No. You'd be a fool if it didn't frighten you.

I forced myself to sit down and take a moment, and simply breathe. I hung my head in my hands, running over everything that had happened in the past few weeks.

Would I really have to wait to graduate from this academy before I could go out and search for Kai? I needed to know what happened to him. I wouldn't be able to sleep, not without constantly worrying.

The last thing I wanted to do was sit around and twiddle my thumbs when I could be finding him instead.

I grabbed one of the books that I picked out the other day and lay down on the bed to read. Might as well escape my own life for a bit.

I swung the dining-room door open to reveal Lia and the others already waiting inside. I sat and stared at my plate, my mind a swirling mess as the others chatted around me. I hadn't been able to focus on my book, so I ended up sitting at the window just staring out.

"Ria, you should eat something," Lia said softly. I took a deep breath and gave her a small smile.

"I'm really not hungry."

"Did the meeting go that badly?" Her forest-hazel eyes looked me over. She tucked her long blonde hair behind her ear, twisting some strands between her fingers.

"King McTavish was very kind, no problems there." I tried to smile, but her brows pinched in worry.

"We went to visit Professor Korin after," Brodie said from across the table, and Lia's eyes widened in understanding. "He says she'll make the plunge any time now."

"Oh, you don't need to worry about that. No one has had any trouble in, like, sixty years." She patted my arm comfortingly, but it didn't ease the swirling of unease and nerves. I looked up and saw the twins shovelling in food, one shrugging slightly, one smirking. Lia returned to her lunch, but I didn't miss her kicking Eli under the table, making him yelp.

"Alright. Are you guys having some secret conversation, or is it some weird twin thing?" Their eyes snapped to mine, and I leaned back in my seat, crossing my arms. They shared a guilty look, and Brodie smirked.

"It's your secret, man. You tell her." He grinned, and Eli pulled a face at him.

"Alright, alright. Seeing as we're all sharing secrets. I'm telepathic." He shrugged like it was no big deal. But it was. "I can set up an open link between whoever I want. I have a permanent one with Lia and with Brodie. Sometimes I create a three-way connection on missions."

"That's seriously cool. I can imagine that would come in handy." They all nodded. I turned to Lia, who was suddenly very quiet. "What about you, Lia?" I smile and she offered me a shy grin.

"Okay, but I'm still perfecting it." She cleared her throat and looked around. "I can clone myself. And make multiple copies. And they can all act separately." She blushed like it was something to be embarrassed about.

My mouth dropped open.

By the stars.

"But I'm still figuring it out. I create beings out of the earth, like soldiers made from dirt. I'm still working on getting them to move on their own."

"That's fucking cool, Lia," I beamed at her, impressed by her powers. The books I read at school only claimed that riders possessed basic magical skills, and the occasional rider who could do something a little fancier. I guessed that they were probably at least ten years out of date.

"We told Lia about your other matter, too. Thinking she might be able to find out some information for you on the down-low while at Voralyth. They have more information about different powers in the library there." Eli said around a mouthful of spaghetti. I nodded, understanding that between the three of them, they shared everything.

I wish I had something like that.

`You have me, but don't think I'm going to get all soft and mushy on you. I don't do hugs.`

I snorted a laugh out loud, unable to stop myself as everyone's eyes met mine with confusion.

"Sorry, Vex actually has a sense of humour," I chuckled, shaking my head and picking at some fruit, my nauseous feeling finally starting to lessen.

"We've decided that the three of us will take turns keeping you company each night, to stop you from falling asleep, until we can figure out what we can do." Brodie sighed. He didn't look too happy about it.

Eli was trying to stop himself from smirking at his brother.

"And lucky you, I'm up first," Brodie grumbled, and I felt a bubble of laughter rise, but I clamped it down before it could escape.

"And we need to get you a whisperglass, because not all of us are telepathic," Lia chirped, sending a pulse on her own shard of smoothed and polished glass with speed. I'd only just gotten my whisperglass before my life went to hell four years ago. Not everyone had one, people in the poorer districts considered them a luxury item.

A soft ring sounded, and Brodie answered his, nodding as he listened to someone talk quickly.

"Okay, we'll be right over." He hung up and met my gaze. "Professor Korin has found something he thinks might work to keep you from vanishing into the night."

We knocked on the professor's door, who ushered us inside quickly with a harried look.

"I think I found something, but it's not going to be easy to get. And it's stupidly expensive." He ran a hand through his messy white hair, which it seemed like he'd been doing since we left a few hours ago.

"Well, what is it?" Brodie asked impatiently, shrugging his massive shoulders before crossing his arms over his large chest.

"It's called Gravemelt Dust. It's pulverised remnants of a meteorite said to have fallen during the first eclipse war." We all raised our brows, eyes wide as we tried to accept what he was telling us. "It dampens magic by weighing down the soul's pull on the veil between planes."

No. Tell him there needs to be another way. Vex growled, making me flinch at the anger in his voice.

"Vex doesn't like the sound of that," I replied quietly, and the professor shrugged.

"The only other option is Runestone Salt. It's highly toxic if used for too long, but it's effective for teleporters."

Absolutely not.

"Sorry. Vex doesn't like that either." I sighed.

"Then I'm afraid I've got nothing else." Korin ran his hands through his hair again, leaving them on the back of his neck. "Seems like you'll be staying awake until you make the plunge, which is dangerous enough as it is, without being sleep deprived," he grumbled, grunting as he got to his feet, and began pacing back and forth before his desk. The carpet there was worn, so it must have been something he did often.

Ask him about Veyrium. Vex demanded, his voice sending involuntary shivers over me. Even the word felt wrong in my head.

"Vexirion said to ask you about…Veyrium," I said quietly, and all eyes turned to me. It tasted foul on my tongue to even say it.

"How does your dragon know about Veyrium?" The professor asked, voice barely loud enough for us to hear. "No matter, no matter. It is nearly impossible to find, and that's only if you make it out alive." The room fell so silent that you could hear a pin drop. My heart was loud in my ears as I felt that we were treading in dangerous territory. "It's said to be a shadow-forged mineral found only in the rift-cracked mine, somewhere in Ardentis. It's apparently known to disrupt arcane threads of movement and displacement." A shiver passed over me, goosebumps prickling my arms.

"And where would we even begin to look for something like that?" Brodie asked, tone harsh as he glared at the professor with unease.

"That I cannot tell you. It seems only dark beings know where to find it, and perhaps dragons." The professor turned back to me. "Your Void dragon might know, as he's tied to space and shadows."

I know where to go. But it will be perilous. But hell of a lot safer than using Gravemelt dust and Runestone salt. And I can guarantee that's what they used in those bands.

"Vex said he knows where to go. And is this...mineral the safest option for me to stop teleporting in my sleep? Isn't it safer to just keep me awake for a few days? Or to use the other options?" I twisted my hands together, my nerves wanting to get the better of me.

"No," the professor and Vex barked in unison. I winced at how loud it echoed in my head. "The...Veyrium," the

Professor gasped out, as if it pained him to say it. "Is extremely powerful and rare. It's also instrumental to our technology and healers. Even a little bit would go such a long way. I'm guessing that it's what they used in your shackles. It's known for its black appearance and blue veins." He paced a few more times before stopping in front of me. "I feel that this is essential."

I feel that we need to do this alone.

`You can't get in there and out by yourself, as I cannot be with you.`

I don't want to drag these people into something that sounds extremely dangerous. They've done enough for me.

`It's not your decision.`

"Then I'll go alone and fetch it. I don't want to drag anyone else into my troubles." I went to leave, but Brodie blocked my way, green eyes dark as they pinned me to the spot.

"Not a chance, Storm. We're coming with you." I opened my mouth to protest, but he shook his head. "No arguments. Gear up, we leave in half an hour." He went to turn but I blocked his path, shaking my head.

"No. There is no chance that I'm risking both of the princes for something so trivial as helping me stay in my own bed. If you won't let me go alone, I won't go at all." I folded my arms across my chest, which Brodie copied.

"You heard the Professor, I'll make the plunge in a matter of days anyway."

Brodie leaned in a little closer, and I felt frozen, trapped in his gaze. "We can't risk you falling out of ceilings anywhere in the castle. There are people here who would pay a lot of money for information like that. So, no, we're coming." He spun on his heels and walked away, leaving me standing there with my mouth open in shock.

"You won't be able to change his mind. Once he makes a decision, that's it. But he's right, we're coming too. You got proper gear, yeah?" Eli was beside me, gripping onto Lia's hand tightly as they made their way out of the Professor's room.

"Yeah, it arrived the other day. So what, we're just going to fly off into gods know where on what sounds like a pretty perilous journey? Just because I apparently shouldn't be teleporting in my sleep? This feels a little extreme." I shook my head, my nails digging into my palms.

"No. It makes perfect sense. I've dreamed about this." Professor Korin's eyes looked glazed as he stumbled our way. "I couldn't see your face in my dream, just a silver aura. This is meant to happen. You must go there right now." He pushed us out the door and slammed it behind us.

"Well, that settles it. Meet out in the field in half an hour. Ready for your first deadly mission, Everhart?"

CHAPTER
TWELVE

I began strapping my new weapons to myself like fine jewellery.

Guns and technology will be useless. You'll want fine steel and blades.

Anything else you want to share about this rift-cracked mine?

Once we are closer.

Alright then.

I had on my flight leathers, sheathed with as many weapons as I could find. It was a wonder that I didn't rattle as I walked. I'd tied my silver hair back into two braids, securing the ends on the top of my head. It almost looked like a crown. A small pack with supplies that Moranna dropped off only minutes ago. She said that Brodie had requested some food and water to be handed to each of them. I thanked the older woman kindly and did one last check. My gaze caught on my reflection in the mirror, and I paused.

I looked like a rider.

And I looked badass.

Lia walked me to the flight field, adjusting the straps on her pack.

"Any idea where we're heading?" she asked quietly, the yard surprisingly busy at that time of afternoon.

"Nope. Vex said he will give us some more information when we're closer." I grumbled, but we were stopped in our tracks by Levi Brown.

"Where are you two headed off, looking like you're ready for battle?" He blocked our way, looking casual, but his gaze was sharp.

"Nunya. Ever heard of it?" Lia quipped, leading us to step around him, but he stuck an arm out, halting me.

"Ria, I wanted to see if you were busy tomorrow night?" His blue eyes raked over every weapon on my body. "Why do you two have so many weapons? Is everything alright?"

"Everything's fine, Levi. We're off on a training exercise, and we don't know when we'll be back. But we need to leave, so if you'll excuse us." I'd never heard Lia be rude before, but she shoved his arm out of the way and towed me behind her with a firm grip on my wrist. I threw him an apologetic shrug over my shoulder and followed the fierce woman before me. Levi had been nothing but kind and pleasant to me. But I knew there was history between the three of them. Or perhaps it was as easy as riders vs infantry.

Alright, team, are we ready to head out? Sorry, can't control the volume!

"Argh!" I jumped, not used to having another person's voice in my head. Lia looked at me with a small laugh. I'd started to get used to Vex's low voice in the few weeks I'd been here, but this was something else.

"Yeah, you'll get used to it." Lia looked over them with fondness. I shook my head as we reached our dragons. Vex towered over the others as he looked at them like they were his subjects.

Yes. Any idea which direction we need to go in, Storm? Brodie's voice was almost identical to Eli's, his was just a little deeper, and to have it in my head gave me the shivers, as it seemed to caress every part of me.

This could be very dangerous. And very distracting.

Then you need to pay attention. We are to head east, towards Nythevra, in `the mountains`. Vex sounded bored, but his molten gold eyes locked onto mine as I approached him. I made a running jump before settling into the saddle. I'd finally managed to make it in one go, without him having to lower his leg.

I felt very proud of myself.

East, towards the mountains between here and Nythevra. I repeated to the group.

Alright, let's get this over with then. Brodie seemed to fall into the role of leader naturally. I really don't know why he thought he was the spare.

The others mounted their dragons - their colours were stunning in the glow of the setting sun. Brodie's dragon, Drathruin, shimmered a sage green, Eli's dragon, Morvanyx, was as blue as the ocean, and lastly, Lia's dragon, Cyndrithra, glowed as red as the sunset. They were *beautiful*.

Kai would love to see this. The thought brought tears to my eyes. I hastily wiped them before lowering my flying goggles.

`We will find him. Do not give up hope.`

We will, I just hope it's sooner rather than later.

Launching into the air, I didn't miss the eyes of Levi glued to us, waiting at the doorway with arms crossed.

We flew in silence for hours, Vex leading the party as the darkness settled in around us. The temperature plummeted as soon as the last rays slipped from view, and I was glad to have the extra layers.

`The cavern is rumoured to host shadow-wraiths from another realm, and they are the ones who protect the Veyrium. They are said to invade your mind to trick and turn you against each other. We will need to be on alert, and whatever you do, don't let them win.`

How the hell do we fight off something like that?

`Flame is a good deterrent, and a strong mind.`

I haven't learned to summon flames yet. I tried to swallow the panic that had begun to creep up my throat, but it stuck like a rock.

`Then you stay close to P1.`

What? Who's P1?

`The grumpy one who brought you out of the palace.`

Brodie? And does that stand for Prince One, and Eli is Prince Two?

`Yes.`

Then don't you call them by their names?
`They haven't earned that privilege yet, little storm. We're getting closer, prepare.`

As I let the others know, I heard a sharp wail from my left and saw Drathruin throw her head back, eyes rolling as Brodie swore. Morvanyx and Cyndrithra behaved the same way. They made a sharp turn, back the way we came.

`The darkness of the cavern hurts them. We will land, and you will have to go the rest of the way on foot.`

The dragons landed heavily, the ground shuddering with the impact, the trees swaying.

Well, this is a lovely night for a stroll. Which way, Ria?

I could practically feel Brodie roll his eyes from here at Eli's casualness.

Vex said we need to go north-east until we feel the pull. There are Shadow-Wraiths that will try to invade us. They don't like fire, and keep your shields up.

Awesome. A walk in the park, then.

Our feet hit the grass, and as soon as we were out of reach, the dragons were airborne again. But Vex remained at my back like a hulking statue.

They will retreat further back, where it doesn't cause them pain. But I will stay here. He growled, and a shiver passed over me.

This place felt *wrong*.

Lia and Eli, you two lead. Storm will be in the middle, and I'll bring up the rear. Keep a ball of flame in your hands, and whatever you do, don't drop your shields. Can you do either of those yet, Storm?

I can shield.

Good. Let's head out then.

Even though night had fallen, I could still see his sharp features. A bright ball of green flames flared to life in his left hand, a red one for Lia, and a blue one for Eli.

Will my flame be black when I learn?

Yes, or silver. Tell the others to be as quiet as they can. Even the trees have ears here. Vex paused, his voice low. *I do not know what else lies deep in the cavern, but the Veyrium will be a shard and only take what you need. One piece will be more than enough.*

I repeated to the others as I rolled my shoulders. It felt like something was crawling over my skin.

Thanks for giving me more ideas for my nightmares, Ria. Eli grumbled, sounding like his twin for once.

We continued in silence, only the crunch of gravel and leaves under our feet as we made our way through the thick, dark forest.

It was eerie here. No birds or other animals. Just tall, twisted trees, vines and thorny bushes that caught on my clothing and tore any exposed skin. I stumbled over tree roots and rocks more than I wanted to admit. I was the only one without a ball of fire to help guide me, and my sleepless night seemed to catch up to me.

We were gradually making our way down into a valley of sorts. I started to feel nauseous and sweaty. I tried to blink away the blurriness, but my head was spinning. Just like when I had the band on.

`It's the darkness trying to pull you in. You're more connected to the void because of your bond with me. It will affect you more than the others. Keep your wits about you, stay close to P1 behind you.`

How will staying close to him keep them away from me?
`He has fire and a strength about him that frightens them. He is not`

`so easily broken`. Vex grumbled, his voice getting fainter and fainter the further we descended into the forest. Even though I'd only been bonded to him for a short while, I had grown to like having him with me. It was comforting to know that I wasn't alone.

I...I can feel something ahead. Lia's voice was quiet in my head, like she was whispering.

I can too. It feels like someone is plucking at my clothes. What else should we expect in here, Ria? Eli's voice was equally quiet as we slowed our pace. We'd been walking for hours, but I still couldn't chase the chill that had settled into my bones.

Vex doesn't know. Only that it's a shard, and to take one piece.

Looks like we've reached the entrance. Is that...is that a skeleton? Brodie grabbed my arm to halt me, pulling me back behind him like the pile of bones was about to come to life and attack me.

The skeleton had a sword in its chest, still embedded in the stone behind it.

Awesome.

With a last glance at the poor soul, we took a steadying breath and plunged into the pitch-black entrance of the rift-cavern.

A quiet sort of buzzing noise started building in my head, making my ears ring. Pressure behind my eyes made my head ache as we slowly made our way down the slippery stone entrance. Eli grabbed Lia's hand, and I was surprised when Brodie reached for mine. I turned over my shoulder to take in the prince who came to stand beside me, gaze sharp as he raked over my face. He gave me a nod, and we continued following the others. My hand was so small in his, but his grip was comforting, safe.

Doesn't mean I trust him. I had to remind myself.

The hairs rose on the back of my neck, and I knew we were no longer alone.

A swirling black vortex sucked at the balls of flames, shrieking when it got too close as it circled us. We stopped and put our backs together, the others holding out their hands with the flames, encouraging them to grow bigger. My chest was heaving, the buzzing in my ears almost becoming too much.

Stay strong. Keep your shields up, keep moving. Brodie's voice was loud and commanding. It was obvious he was a born leader. But my breaths were shallow, my head spinning as I tried to concentrate on keeping my shields up.

It felt like it got worse the further down we went.

We shuffled along until the shadow moved on, but I could still feel it watching us as we continued. The tunnel came to a sudden opening, and inside, the cavern was *enormous*. The whole castle could have fit inside. We were on a rocky ledge, and between us and a jagged column of black, shimmering stone was a rickety bridge. The stone seemed to swirl with smoke and shadows, almost alive as it stuck out of the ground at an angle. It must have fallen from the open rift and impaled itself into the black soil. I staggered a step forward, as if pulled by an invisible string.

Storm. Brodie growled, yanking me back.

It's...it's pulling me. I gasped. I even sounded breathless in my own head.

Your nose is bleeding. He reached out and touched me gently, wiping the trickle of blood from my face. A movement caught my eye, and I heard Lia shriek inside my head.

Elias!

He had his head thrown back, arms stretched wide as black, swirling shadows twisted their way into his mouth, eyes, and nose.

Oh gods.

He opened his eyes, and they were wholly black. A twisted smile curved his lips as they locked onto me.

"Oh, it's been such a long time since I've tasted something so powerful." He licked his lips, his head turned to the side like a predator. "Let me taste your blood, Voltrite." He growled and pounced at me.

CHAPTER THIRTEEN

B rodie shoved me away as his twin brother came at me with a blade in his hand.

Lia was rooted to the spot, her eyes wide with terror as she watched.

Now. I have to try and get it now.

Go! Brodie yelled into my head, making me flinch as they went sword to sword. But Brodie's was lit with green fire, and Eli shrank back when it got too close as if it burned.

I bolted, the rickety bridge swaying in front of me like it was rocked by a phantom wind. I took one quick, deep breath. I could feel tendrils of darkness grabbing at my heels, trying to pull me in as I pumped my legs, harder, faster. The wooden slats groaned with each step, the rope harsh under my hands. A board snapped, and I fell. A scream tore from my throat as I gripped onto the splintered board before me.

"Nymeria!" A loud voice bellowed behind me, followed by a pained grunt. *Brodie.* "Get up!" He yelled again, his voice echoing around the vast cavern.

"Go, Ria. You can do it!" Lia shouted, panicked as the sound of swords clashing drowned her out. She let out a yelp behind me, but I refused to look. It would only distract me. I slowly hauled myself up, inch by inch. Splinters found their way into my fingers and under my nails as I gripped onto the rope and wooden boards with everything I had.

Finally, I was up. I continued to make my way, the darkness still pulling at me, weighing me down.

I could feel the pressure building in my head the closer I got, and I felt another warm trickle down my lips and chin. I was so close now, but something latched onto my ankles, trying to pull me back. I slashed at them with my blades, and they shrieked and retreated, only to be replaced by more.

So close. I could almost touch it.

YOU CANNOT ESCAPE US, DARK STORM. YOU BELONG TO US, WITH US.

GIVE IN, AND WE PROMISE IT WILL BE PEACEFUL.
WE WILL LET YOUR FRIENDS LIVE. THEY DON'T HAVE TO DIE HERE TODAY.

The voice was everywhere inside me. I could feel it reverberating through my bones. I heard another pained cry from behind me - it sounded like Brodie.

No. I went to turn, but something inside me pushed me forward. *Just a bit further.* It seemed to whisper. *You are strong enough.*

I sucked in a ragged breath and reached my hand out to touch the swirling stone. It hummed, the vibrations almost electric as my fingers hovered before it.

I slapped my hand to the stone and screamed.

Blistering pain. *Everywhere.*

The shadows shoved down my throat, in my eyes, ears, and nose. They were *hungry.* I felt like I was falling, but into myself.

`Nymeria Everhart!` A loud voice bellowed, and I halted. `The darkness has triggered the plunge, and you must focus!`

Vexirion. He sounded panicked, but his voice was faint.

I could feel more than the shadows inside me. I felt a raw power that was begging to be taken.

We will dive together, but we must be careful. The shadows will swallow your essence if we let them. It wants to take you into the void.

I don't know if I can. I'm scared.

Good. So you should be! Now dive with me. Our connection is too weak for me to hold for much longer.

Down, down, down, I sank like a stone through my consciousness. I thought I could hear a voice yelling my name, but I let it float away as I focused on the growing storm within me. It was a dark vortex that screamed my name, and I held out my arms, welcoming it into me. The force with which it hit me was enough to light me up, so blindingly bright that everywhere inside of me was white, and I was numb.

I could hear and feel the shadows retreating, shrieking in pain as the force of magic inside of me exploded.

Rise! NOW! Vex bellowed, and I bent my knees and jumped.

I shot up through all the layers, the pain, the sorrow, the scars. I saw glimpses of when I was a child with Kai, my loved ones' dead bodies, the fighting arena, and leaving Rex. Everything that has left a mark on me showed its face, and my heart wanted to break.

It all begins and ends in your mind. What you give power to has power over you, if you allow it. Vex repeated, and his words gave me strength.

I hadn't realised I'd stopped, hovering somewhere inside myself where all I could see and feel was my parents. Their love wrapped around me like a cocoon, making me feel warm and loved. Vex repeated his words, and I knew that I must move on. That was what my parents would want.

I forced myself away from the glowing faces of my family and rose.

I burst to the surface and gasped. I was lying on the cold stone, a shard of the Veyrium clutched in my hand. I could hear grunts of pain behind me, where Eli was laughing, and Lia was sobbing, a sword pointed at her boyfriend's chest. Electricity was flickering over my skin. I could see its silver sparks at my fingertips, and I knew that I had made the plunge. I now had pure, raw magic running through my veins.

I stood on shaky legs. I imagined myself taking one long step towards my friends, and suddenly, I had teleported myself to them. Lia cried out in surprise as I landed between Eli and Brodie, who was looking barely conscious. I reached out and grabbed Eli by the arm and sent my electricity into him. He screamed and thrashed under my touch, but the shadows began to pour out of him. He convulsed as they left his body, before collapsing to the cold ground in a heap. Lia cried out as she threw the sword down and rushed to him, touching his face, trying to wake him. I turned to Brodie, who looked at me with tears in his eyes. I didn't know what emotions were running through him, but I held out my hand. He took it and gripped me like I was his anchor. I turned and reached for Lia's other hand, as she wrapped her fingers with Eli's.

I closed my eyes and took a deep breath before making another jump.

It was like blinking. Easy as breathing.

We landed in a heap out in the dark forest. The dragons growled as they approached us. They shook their heads, Morvanyx huffing as he shoved Eli with his snout. They were snorting like they couldn't stand the stench of the shadows. Brodie and Lia were on the ground, hovering over Eli with glowing hands while I stood back and tried to catch my breath.

`Well done, little storm`

Is there anything I can do? What have I done?

`You saved the boy by banishing the darkness within him.`

But why isn't he waking up?

The darkness was too much. He needs rest, his heart is weak.

There has to be something? I shoved the shard of Veyrium into my pocket. It felt wrong, evil, and it burned where it touched my bare skin.

You can send a jolt of electricity into his heart. That ought to wake him.

Truly?

I would never lie to you.

Lia was sobbing as she crouched over Eli's chest, and Brodie was still trying to resuscitate him. I knelt beside them and placed my hands over his.

"I've got nothing left. The flames and constant shielding drained me." Lia's hands were shaking where they rested on Eli's chest, they were no longer glowing. Brodie's hands were flickering. They'd used up their magic.

"Let me try," I whispered, and Brodie turned tear-laden eyes to me. He mashed his lips together and gave me a faint nod. His hands slipped away, and I closed my eyes and focused on the bioelectric energy inside of him. I could feel a faint pulse, and I brought my powers to the surface. I felt the hair on the back of my neck stand on end as my skin crackled. I took a deep breath and sent a small jolt to his heart. His back arched off the ground, landing heavily. But his heartbeat was a little louder.

Again. The same voltage.

I did it one more time, and Eli gasped awake, crying out as his back arched again and hit the cold ground. He coughed, and Lia cried out with joy. I stood on shaky legs and leaned heavily against a large tree. Brodie brought Eli to a sitting position and wrapped him in a crushing hug.

"Don't you ever do that ever again, you hear me?" He growled, and it was enough to bring tears to my eyes.

"Thank you, Ria. I don't know how I can ever thank you enough." Lia smiled through the tears coursing down her cheeks before she turned and kissed Eli.

We need to leave. The shadows are coming back. And the princes are too weak to hold them off again. P2 needs to get back to a healer.

The others acted quickly after I relayed Vex's message.

"Then let's head out." Brodie pulled Eli to his feet and wrapped an arm around his shoulders. Morvanyx was gracious enough to let Brodie on his back to settle Eli into his saddle. Once we were all mounted, the dragons wasted no time in launching into the sky.

Eli was too weak to maintain the telepathic connection, so we flew back in silence.

I took the time to come to terms with what happened.

I'd made the plunge into my power, and now, my electricity seemed to have come alive as well. I could feel it under my skin, and the ease of teleporting seemed like I'd been doing it my whole life.

That is just the beginning, little storm. You have much to learn about the power you will possess. You must train and have control over it, otherwise it will have control over you.

As soon as we made it back, I gave the Veyrium shard to Professor Korin, who, with tongs and gloves, popped it into a glass vial. His eyes were as wide as saucers, and they darted to me every few seconds.

"You've taken the plunge." It wasn't a question, but a statement.

"Yes."

"I can see a slight shimmer under your skin, but only in certain places. It's in the shape of lightning." His head was tipped to the side as his eyes followed the curve of my throat.

"It must be shining through my scars. I can feel it closer to the surface now." I murmured as he nodded. "And I can teleport at will." His eyes lit up.

"Can you show me?" He breathed.

I stepped away until my back was against the door. I shut my eyes and took that mental step. I opened them to find myself behind his desk. He gasped in pleasure as he spun.

"Brilliant. Simply amazing." He took a deep breath and blew it out noisily before smiling at me. "Once we're back at the academy, I want to work with you. I look forward to seeing what else you're capable of, Nymeria."

I felt lighter now that I didn't have that evil shard in my pocket.

That first night, I slept like the dead. I woke to someone shaking me.

"Gods damnit, Storm. Wake the hell up." I peeled my gritty eyes open to see an angry prince hovering over me. He let go as soon as he saw my eyes open, and stepped back, running a hand through his messy black hair.

"Wha-what's the matter?" I got out through a yawn. I rubbed my eyes and sat up, my body protesting.

"You've been asleep for over twenty-four hours." He said, frowning as he crossed his large, tattooed arms.

"And is that a bad thing? I took the plunge, apparently, that kinda thing takes it out of a person," I grumbled. Why the hell was he so angry?

"You took the plunge?" he demanded, his voice low and lethal. He stepped forward, and I resisted the urge to roll my eyes.

"Yes. I was forced into it as soon as I touched the ve...rift mineral." I still couldn't say the word out loud. It burned my tongue almost as much as it burned my skin.

"Why the hell didn't you tell us?" He almost sounded hurt, which confused me even more.

"There were more important things going on, in case you forgot. And I'm fine. Professor Korin knows, and he's not worried."

"Bloody hell, Storm. Being forced into the plunge isn't a good thing." He sat on the edge of my bed, and I had to blink to make sure it was actually happening. He stared at the opposite wall, not meeting my eyes.

"What happened in there? I heard you scream, and then you were lifeless on the ground." His words were barely more than a whisper.

"As soon as I touched it, the shadows invaded me. As soon as I took my power into myself, the white light was too bright for them, and it chased them away."

He turned to look at me, his sage green eyes bright as they looked over my face, trailing down my throat. He reached out a hand as if to touch me, before blinking and tucking his hand under his leg.

"I saw the flash. It lit up the whole cavern, into terrifying clarity. Shadows were closing in, tugging at me, trying to get past my shields as I tried to stop my own brother from killing me." He cleared his throat before looking at his hands twisting in his lap. "Thank you for saving him," he whispered before turning back to me, his eyes lined in silver. I reached over and placed my hand on his, giving it a squeeze. The muscle in his jaw ticked, but he turned my hand and gripped it back.

CHAPTER FOURTEEN

Our training resumed as soon as we were back on our feet.

Korin often asked to come along, as he wanted to see my powers in action. We made sure to use the private training room, just for the royal family. Turned out that George Korin was the king's brother. Illegitimate, of course, but that explained why he was here, and why the twins were so fond of him.

Lia, in her own right, was one hell of a fighter. She moved like it was a dance, quick as a snake, but looked sweet and innocent at the same time. She was a joy to watch.

Eli, on the other hand, turned into a menace. He would cajole and bait you into annoyance, making you doubt yourself. But I couldn't help really liking them. I felt like they were my friends.

Brodie still kept to himself, and something in me was wary of him.

How come it was he who had to come to my rescue? And how did Rex know who he was?

I had so many questions, but I knew I'd never get answers from him.

"Ria!" Eli bounded my way, throwing a ball at the same time. I caught it at the last minute, blinking back my surprise. "Quick reflexes." He winked, but not before I threw it back at him. "How are you feeling after our little adventure the other night?" He wiped his forehead with the back of his hand, eyes travelling over my face.

Sometimes he was more of a kind big brother. It made my throat tight.

"Fine. My body is slowly getting used to my powers, but I wake in a sweat a lot. Probably from my nightmares, though." I attempted a laugh, but it came out strained.

"What do you dream about?" He cocked his head to the side as he studied me.

I hesitated. I didn't want to get into details. It was bad enough that they hounded my sleep.

"The night I was taken. The arena, that sorta stuff." I looked down at my feet, scuffing my boot on the floor.

"I'm sorry you still have to relive it. I couldn't begin to imagine what you've been through." He looked away for a bit, scratching his chin. "Come on, let's go climb some walls." He took off at a sprint to the indoor rock climbing wall, beckoning me over his shoulder.

I rolled my eyes but couldn't stop the smile. Damn him and his good moods.

We trained until we were sweaty messes, puffing as we lay there on the floor. Korin had long gone, claiming he needed to brew some tinctures. We headed off for the night, the halls quiet as we split up.

And much to my dismay, the ball was tomorrow night.

Lia insisted I go, telling me that Jane had a dress all ready. I just had to visit her to get the last measurements so she could finish. I was tempted to 'forget' to go see Jane, so I had an excuse not to attend the ball. Plus, I hadn't had anyone ask me.

I wasn't going to hold my breath. That would be silly. But there was still a small part of me that wished, hoped that someone would ask me. Lia told me that Eli would be more than happy to have two women on his arms.

The longer I stayed here, the more I liked Eli and Lia. But Brodie was something else. I just couldn't put my finger on it.

I dragged my feet to see Jane, at Lia's persistent nagging.

Jane eagerly told me to enter as soon as my knuckles touched her door. I looked up, suspecting to see a peephole or something. But nothing.

"Ah, good to see you again, Ms Everhart. I've been expecting you." The plump older lady gave me a knowing smile, her brown eyes all-seeing. "Strip down to your underwear, over there." She pointed to a small circular platform in the middle of the room.

Once I was stripped, I stood and waited for Jane, not looking in the mirrors that surrounded me.

I knew how many scars I had.

"I immediately knew what colour would suit you, my dear." She ambled over and told me to lift my arms up. She slipped the soft material over my head, moving my arms where she wanted them, like I was a giant doll.

"Hmm. Yes. This will be good." She walked around me a few times before nodding. "Don't move, I'm going to pin." As she got to work, adjusting here and there, her comment from the first time we met surfaced.

"Excuse me, Jane?" I was quiet, not wanting our conversation to be overheard.

"Yes, dear?" She murmured with pins in her mouth, busy trying not to prick me.

"The first time we met, you mentioned that you knew someone like me. Another Everhart?"

She stopped as if she was frozen. She slowly lifted her head and looked me right in the eye. The rich brown seemed to dim slightly.

"Yes," she breathed, paling. "A long time ago." She took a deep breath and continued to pin the outfit. "She was magnetic. Everyone loved her, but she had powers no one knew of. Couldn't know of." She gave me a knowing look, and I shuddered.

She knew I was a Voltrite.

"But someone did find out, and they showered her with gifts, enticing her to come back to his homeland with him. Told her that she could save the world with her powers." She breathed deep for a moment, just staring at the pins in her hands. "She only wanted to be loved. Her parents were scared of her and abandoned her as a child. She grew up suppressing her powers, and I think it started to take over. This man-" She seethed, hands clenching tight. "He used and abused her. And then she followed him to Durus, never to be heard from again."

My heart began to race. Was she related to me somehow? I never knew my grandparents...

"But you'll be just fine. You're in good hands, and a dragon to help keep you in your own mind." She patted my hand, shocking me out of my tumbling thoughts. "What do you think?" She stood back and pointed to the mirrors. I sucked in a deep breath and faced myself.

The dress was cobalt blue, a halter neck that plunged between my breasts. It hugged my figure, a split up the leg, dangerously high to show off Vex's brand curling around my thigh. I spun and gasped. The back scooped just above my ass, showing off the whole brand.

It was the most beautiful thing I'd ever seen.

"Jane. It's-"

"Yeah. It's something special." She winked at me, and I blushed. "Strip it off. I'll finish stitching it up and get it delivered to your room." She waddled away, and I gently tried to take it off without pricking myself. She was completely hidden by the time I was dressed. I called out a farewell anyway and let myself out.

The morning of the ball, Lia was knocking at my door just after dawn. Grumbling and moaning, I opened it to see her beaming.

"Let's go and get our nails done!" She went to grab my hand and yank me out, but I was still wearing my singlet and undies.

"Let me get dressed, woman," I grumbled, but her light mood was contagious. She shut the door behind her and flopped down onto my bed while I dug around my wardrobe for something comfortable to throw on.

I ran a brush through my hair, splashed some cold water on my face and messily threw my hair up.

We were out the door and into town before I'd gotten a chance to suggest breakfast. But she knew me too well. We stopped for pancakes and coffee before heading to the salon.

The ladies working there cheerfully fussed over us, Lia clearly having already made a name for herself. We were the first ones of the day, and they wouldn't be stopping until just before the ball. They were the best in town, according to Lia.

"So, you've got your dress all sorted?" Lia lay back, a facemask on, someone filing her fingers and toenails.

"Yeah. It's stunning." I smiled, everything in me trying not to laugh, or yank my feet away from the woman doing my toenails..

"I hope you're ready for a magical night." Lia sighed. "Full of dancing, drinking, fine food and amazing acrobats flitting around on ribbons."

"Sounds like a big night." I'd officially given up hope of being asked.

We finished up, and my nails were actually really pretty, matching my dress. I'd never had them done before.

Next on the agenda was hair and makeup. It seemed silly getting them done hours before the ball, but Lia assured me we didn't want to do it too late and feel rushed.

Just like the nails, I'd never been pampered so much in my life. The makeup artist was lovely, commenting on how beautiful my hair was and that she couldn't wait to make my eyes pop.

She spun me around to face the mirror, and I had to do a double-take. The woman looking back at me wasn't the same as before. Her grey eyes glistened, lined in silver and cobalt blue. Lashes so long they touched my eyelids, almost tickling my cheeks when I blinked. My hair tumbled around my shoulders in soft, feminine waves.

I was speechless.

"Oh, Ria." Lia gasped, coming to stand behind me. She had tears in her eyes. "You're absolutely stunning."

"Wow, look at you." I smiled. Her stunning hazel eyes popped with blue and green. Her lovely blonde hair fell in waves like mine, one side pinned up with a silver comb behind her ear.

"Come on, let's get something for lunch before heading back to the castle." She linked her arm with mine and towed me toward a restaurant down by the river.

We received many looks, some of them lingering a little too long. Lia ignored them, pretending they weren't even there. She must be used to it. All I could feel were their eyes, boring into me like knives.

It reminded me of the arena.

"Are you alright? You're very quiet." Lia swirled her lemonade with her straw, the tiny bubbles fizzing and popping.

"I don't like everyone looking. It makes me uneasy," I murmured, fighting the urge to look over my shoulder.

"Oh, I'm sorry, Ria. I didn't realise." She leaned over and placed her hand on mine, giving it a small squeeze. "We'll finish up and head off, okay? Oh!" she gasped. "I nearly forgot about our masks."

I frowned. We'd already done facemasks...

"It's a masked ball." Lia explained, "We need to pick them up before we leave. I got yours to match your dress, of course." She grinned, and I felt a little better. At least I'd have a mask on, so people might not recognise me. But on the other hand, it would remind me of playing the Silver Fox.

Damn it, everything is reminding me of the viscount.

`Then let these new memories replace those bad ones. Don't dwell on the past. You cannot change it.`

Are you always so wise?

`Yes.`

We headed to one last shop, not wanting to linger. The walls were covered in fine masks, ranging in so many styles. Animals, colours, feathers, sequins.

I let Lia handle it as I wandered. I tried ignoring the memory of fat Walter pushing the mask into my hands, trying to replace it with the magic of the ball, but the feeling settled in me.

A large box was sitting on my bed when we returned. I ignored it for the time being, placing the bag with the mask on top. I still didn't know if I wanted to go.

I stood in front of the mirror, trying to see past the makeup, the nice hair and the fake smile.

Perhaps it wouldn't hurt to be someone else for one night.

I opened the box, and a matching pair of heels sat on top. My heart sank. I hated wearing heels. I'd only ever worn them once when I went to a wedding on the island, and I hated the way they made me feel unstable.

But I didn't have a choice. I had nothing else to wear with the dress.

Sighing, I pulled it all out, the silky material of the dress slithered over my arm, cool to the touch.

It truly was very pretty.

I didn't think twice as I stripped off and shimmied into the dress. A g-string was the only thing I could wear with it. Not my first choice of underwear. I knew it would annoy me all night.

I strapped on the heels, a delicate strap around my ankle.

I wobbled as I took a step, but the effect in the mirror took my breath away.

It wasn't me that looked back.

I didn't know this woman. She looked confident, sexy, and someone who deserved to be here.

`Stop that. I don't want to hear those thoughts. You deserve to be here more than many others I know. So snap out of it, put your chin up, and shoulders straight.`

Yes, boss.

He was right. I had to stop thinking like that.

I slipped on the mask and allowed myself to admire how lovely I looked.

A knock on the door nearly had me tumbling over in surprise. I straightened my shoulders, concentrating as I wobbled over, expecting to see Lia in her gorgeous blood-red dress.

But it was Brodie who stood there, frozen.

His eyes were so wide as they travelled over me, his mouth parted in shock. My heart stumbled before it remembered how to work. He looked so freaking good in his suit, and his tie was cobalt blue, just like my dress.

"Storm," he gasped, eyes stuck on the slit in my dress for a moment before meeting my eyes. He cleared his throat, swallowed, then ran his tongue over his teeth.

I'd never seen the Prince of Everdra at a loss for words before.

It felt fucking amazing that it was because of me.

"Would you like to come to the ball with me?" he breathed, and I couldn't stop the smile from blooming. I nodded as he reached out his arm for me to take.

CHAPTER
FIFTEEN

We walked in silence down the hall, but Brodie held me steady.

Tension crackled between us, but I refused to turn and look. His mask covered half of his face, but I could still see his beautiful sage-green eyes. They glittered when they looked at me, and it made me feel things I hadn't felt in a long time. Things I shouldn't feel for this man.

I could hear the music before we reached the double wooden doors. Levi stood tall, a mask covering his face as he winked at us. They pulled open the door, and loud sounds of laughter and chatter assaulted us.

Our steps slowed as we reached the top of the curved stairs.

Damn it. I didn't know we would be making an entrance.

Sweat threatened to bead my brow, my mask suddenly feeling hot.

"Easy. I've got you." Brodie's breath brushed my ear, his arm tightening around mine as we took our first step. I swallowed my nerves, instead focusing on the man beside me.

We took slow, steady steps. A few faces looked up, but I couldn't miss the gigantic grin on Lia and Eli's faces as they waited for us at the bottom. I couldn't stop my own smile as we reached them. I felt light and giddy.

"Oh, Ria!" Lia cried as she wrapped her arms around my shoulders, squeezing me tight. I hugged her back just as fiercely. "You look amazing."

"So do you. That dress is too hot for something like this." I giggled, and she laughed as she pulled away, cheeks flushed under her mask. Eli winked at his brother, slapping him on the shoulder. I glanced at Brodie, but quickly looked away at the heat in his eyes. Why the hell was I feeling so nervous?

Brodie offered his arm again as we made our way through the crowd. I scooped a flute of champagne from a waiter on his way past. The tart bubbles popped on my tongue. I tried to ignore the lingering looks: the men on me, and the women on Brodie. I didn't fail to notice their glare at me after they checked him out.

I just gave them a savage grin in return.

The room didn't take long to fill, a never-ending trail of people flowing down the curved stairs. Euan sat on the small dais, smiling, a cup in hand.

It's a shame that the queen wasn't here. But perhaps that was for the best.

"Would you like to dance?" The words sent a shock through me. I turned slowly to Brodie, who stood so close that I could feel the heat of him beside me.

"I'm not very good, I'm afraid." I breathed, anxiety worming its way in as I thought of everyone watching us. Lia and Eli were already on the floor, spinning, looking like a dream as her red dress flew out around her.

"That's okay. We'll take it slow." He reached out his hand, and I hesitated a few seconds before I took it. "Just follow my lead. I'll step to your right, then we'll go left." He'd never spoken to me so softly before. His eyes had never lingered on me so much, either. I felt pinned beneath his gaze, like a butterfly on a board.

I took a small step to the side, just as he did. We swayed together, slowly turning in a circle. The rest of the room dropped away as we danced.

"That's it," he murmured, and I looked up. His eyes were locked on mine, and my chest tightened at what I saw. "I wish we didn't have to wear these masks. I'd like to see you properly."

My heart stumbled, my feet following. I swallowed my curse as I stepped on his toe.

"Oh, sorry!" I gasped, but he simply chuckled, shaking his head.

"I would be worried if you didn't step on my toes, Storm." He continued to slowly spin us around.

I never wanted the song to end.

"Nice suit," I said to him. A smile kicked up, and I saw a dimple pop. It hit me right in the gut every damn time.

"Thanks, Jane threatened to flay me alive if I didn't wear it," he chuckled, and I was incredibly aware of how the sound reverberated through his hand on my hip.

"I know the feeling. Between her and Lia, I was a little scared." We picked up our pace, and my feet began to move on their own.

"I'm glad I came in the end." His eyes raked over my mask, not daring to go any lower where my breasts were on show. Not like half the men in this room.

"Me too." I had no idea what was going on between us. I told myself that I didn't trust him, but I didn't know where his head was, either.

Was he interested? The heat in his eyes told me yes, but most of the time, he was so cold with me.

"Sorry to interrupt, but could I borrow Miss Everhart for a dance?" Brodie's hands tightened on me. Captain O'Connell stood beside us, his hand out, waiting to take mine, if Brodie allowed. I swallowed. I didn't want him to let me go.

Brodie gritted his teeth once, twice, before giving him a slight nod and dropping his hands from me. I tried not to show my disappointment, at how cold I felt without his touch. He gave me one last look before turning and disappearing into the crowd.

"Miss Everhart." The Captain swept in, his hands quickly replacing Brodie's.

All I wanted was to shake him off, but I slapped a smile on my face and stood up straight. I didn't know why I felt so nervous.

"You look lovely," he breathed as we began to slowly move. Unease slithered over me, but I refrained from rolling my neck.

"Thank you." I smiled, but it felt forced. We moved a few moments in silence, but my heart never stopped skipping over itself.

"How are you finding Sylvanfire?" He spun me around once, eyes glued to me as he waited for my answer.

"It's wonderful. The most beautiful city I've ever seen."

"I've heard that Nythevra rivals us, some say their city is much lovelier." His hands were tightly gripping me, and I felt trapped. Swallowing my nerves, I plastered a smile on my face.

"True. But in a different way. Nythevra has more trees and greenery, whereas Sylvanfire is filled with colour and music." We spun a few more times, his eyes searched mine as we danced, and I was glad for the song to come to an end.

"I hope to see more of you, Miss Everhart, and that dragon of yours." The Captain dropped his hands and stepped back, slightly nodding to me before walking away. I had to shake my hands out before I left the dance floor, heading to the drinks table.

"That looked...interesting." Lia was suddenly at my side, appearing out of nowhere.

"Where the heck did you just come from?" I gasped, stumbling back a step.

"I was watching you two from over there. The twins are out talking on the balcony. I didn't want to interrupt them." She took a sip of her drink, but I didn't miss her peeking at me out of the corner of her eye.

"He said he wanted to see more of Vex and me." I picked up another flute of champagne and downed half of it before meeting Lia's eyes.

"That doesn't bode well, Ria. He's the Captain of the military, and involved with their 'secret service'." Lia's face had paled slightly, her fingers gently wrapping around my free hand. "Stay away from him and his son Mitch at Voralyth."

I nodded, trying to calm my breathing. But something cold had settled in me, the way his eyes raked over me. Lia cleared her throat and smiled at me, her shoulders loosening.

"You know, he wasn't going to come at all. But being a prince, Euan made him." We made our way to the food tables, picking at pastries and chocolate. "And Eli told him he had to come. But I had no idea that Jane gave him a tie that matched your dress." She smiled, taking me in. "You truly look beyond beautiful." She touched my arm before perusing the table.

I wondered if the Captain noticed his tie too, but I pushed him from my mind. I wanted to find Brodie again and see if we could at least have another dance together. I grabbed him a drink, and I wandered out until I found the princes, leaning against the railing, looking slightly put out with each other.

"Ah, Ria. You look lovely, by the way. Have you seen Lia?" Eli walked towards me, but Brodie stayed where he was.

"Yeah, she's grabbing something to eat."

"Perfect. I'll see you later." He winked as he passed me, a cheeky glint in his eyes. I swore he was always up to no good. I slowly approached Brodie, who was leaning on his arms, looking out over the dark garden, lit by tiny lanterns.

"Hey." I slid next to him, passing him a drink.

He turned slowly, taking a deep breath.

"Thanks." His smile was sad, and his eyes were void of their spark. I desperately wanted to know what caused it, but I knew he'd never tell me.

"It's beautiful out here." I looked out over the gardens, the neatly trimmed hedges and pretty flowering trees.

"Very," he breathed. My breath hitched as I turned to see that his eyes were on me, suddenly feeling nervous. "Storm," he started, but closed his eyes a moment, as if he was fighting with himself. He took a step, his shoes almost touching mine. My heart was in my throat.

Did I want this?

My heart said yes, but my head said no.

"I'm sorry how cold I've been," he started, his knuckles white as they gripped his glass. He swallowed and put it down on the edge of the balcony. He took my hands in his, and it was as if he shocked my nervous system. "I just-"

The door behind us crashed open with a bang. The glass shattered as it slammed against the wall.

Brodie instantly shoved me behind him. A drunk man stumbled forward, coming right for us.

"Oh, did I dooo that?" he slurred, tripping over his own feet. Brodie gritted his teeth and grabbed the man by the arm.

"I think you need to leave," he snapped, turning over his shoulder to look at me, eyes filled with emotions I couldn't understand. "I'm sorry, Storm," he said and towed the man away.

I was left standing there in the cold. I wrapped my arms around myself as tears pricked the back of my eyes. I had no idea why I was so upset, but I knew that I wasn't staying at the ball any longer. I swallowed the lump in my throat and made my way inside. I stuck close to the walls, hurrying to get out of there without anyone spotting me.

I knew if Lia, or even Eli, asked if I was okay, I'd burst into tears. Which was utterly ridiculous.

I gritted my teeth so hard it gave me a headache as I fled through the halls. I kicked off my heels so I could run.

I wanted to get as far away from the ball as I could.

Chapter Sixteen

Lia didn't ask about why I left the ball so early. And I wasn't going to tell her. Eli seemed a little cool with Brodie in training, and the latter couldn't even look at me.

No one mentioned my dance with the Captain, but I knew it made them nervous.

Voralyth was starting the next week, and it filled me with more nerves than the perilous journey into the rift-cavern. It meant that I would have to be around more people, make friends, and pretty much go back to school. *Ugh*. I didn't like school enough as it was. Was it going to be somewhere that was filled with huge egos and pompous idiots?

More than likely.

Lia told me that I could hang with her and her wing, but she was in her third year, and a Furora.

Vexirion was a Tenebrae, and they didn't have that house at Voralyth, or Duskmire, the other academy over in Faritia. But Vex was adamant that he didn't want to take me to Emberhollow over on Durus. He said that place wasn't where I'm supposed to be. So here I was, about to attend an academy where a Tenebrae dragon hadn't been sighted for over three hundred years.

I spent every waking moment either training, flying, or practising teleporting. And when we were sure there was no one around, they had me using my Voltrite powers. At first, it was small sparks at my fingertips, then encasing my body with a fine layer that would shock anyone who touched me. Lia was looking forward to going back to the academy to see her friends, her wing, but would miss Eli. The princes had managed to keep me away from the captain as much as possible, as they obviously didn't like the way he was so interested in me.

But they couldn't hide me away forever.

I'd started running each morning and evening again, as it helped clear my head and eased the tension building in my shoulders. Having all of this power inside of me was exhausting. If I didn't let enough of it out, it started to give me a headache and made me irritable, sparks lighting at my fingertips.

⸺◦◦⸺

We're sitting around a fire-pit in the castle gardens. It'd been dug into the ground, comfy outdoor loungers and chairs surrounded the blazing pit in the middle. We'd been given snacks and drinks, Moranna insisting on bringing us out a treat for dinner, as it was mine and Lia's last night at the castle for a while.

I couldn't stop my gaze from landing on Brodie as he relaxed back with a drink, a cap turned backwards and laughing at something Eli said. He looked like a normal guy. Not a prince, not a brooding dragon rider, just...normal. But he was *anything* but normal, and I hated the way my body reacted when he was near.

I forced my eyes away and took another swig of my wine. I leaned back against the cushions and stared into the sky, taking in the glittering stars as they twinkled in the dark. I would never have dreamed that my life would come to this. Living in a castle, riding dragons, and going to an academy for god's sake. I was sure that Hellas, the god of fear and confusion, had been taunting me for the past four years, but perhaps now he'd left me. And for that, I was thankful. He could go and harass someone else for a change.

"Ria," Lia called, landing on the cushions beside me. "Are you alright?" Tonight, she had pinned her hair back in complicated-looking twists, but the effect was stunning. Her forest-hazel eyes were bright as the fire danced in their reflection.

"Yeah, I'm just thinking how crazy this all is." I waved my arm around to encompass everything there. "I've been living in a *castle*, for goodness sake. And I'm bonded to a *dragon*. If you asked fifteen-year-old me where I was going to be in eight years, I definitely wouldn't have thought this." Lia chuckled beside me, lying back with me.

"Yeah, I get it. I never would have thought that I'd be madly in love with a prince of Everdra. But here we are." I could hear the smile in her voice, and it made me thankful to have someone like her in my life. Even though we'd only known each other for a short while, it was starting to feel like I'd known her much longer.

"What's going to happen tomorrow when we land at Voralyth?" I turned to her, but she remained staring at the glittering stars above us.

"I'm not too sure. A Tenebrae has never trained at Voralyth, as far as I'm aware. So it will probably take them some time to figure out what to do. It's not like they can put you in your own wing. They'll have to put you into another house."

I looked away and steadied my breathing. I shouldn't spend time worrying about things that might or might not happen. I just needed to accept and evolve.

A bark of laughter drew our attention, and we both looked over at the twins, who were now cackling, heads bent towards each other as they cried with laughter. A smile bloomed on Lia's face, and I started to feel warm on the inside, too.

Friends. These people were my friends.

"I know Brodie can be a little standoffish and gruff, but it takes him a while to let his guard down." I felt Lia's eyes on me, but I couldn't meet them. "He's been through...things that will change someone. But it's his story to tell." She continued to stare, so I turned and met her gaze.

"Then why do I get the feeling that he wants nothing to do with me?"

"Because he's afraid of what he feels for you."

I turned away again and took in a deep breath, blowing it out noisily.

"He has a funny way of showing it."

It was going to take us a good few hours to fly to Voralyth from Sylvanfire. I had a stupidly big bag already loaded on Vex, and another pack on my back.

I could see the sun beginning to peek over the horizon, its golden pink rays promising a beautiful day. Eli had Lia wrapped in his arms as Brodie dumped her last pack at her feet. I turned away from them, arms wrapped around myself as I tried to gather my thoughts. I saw Brodie look my way and take one step towards me.

"Ria!" I turned to see Levi coming my way. I glanced back at Brodie, only to see him walking away. I tried to ignore the flare of hurt in my chest as he left, not even bothering to say goodbye.

"I wanted to see you before you left." Levi stopped at my side and smiled down at me. I forced my lips into something that resembled a smile, even though my stomach felt twisted and churning.

"Thanks. You didn't have to come out this early. You could have just sent me a pulse." I raised my brows, and he shrugged, giving me a cheeky grin.

"Yeah, but I wouldn't have been able to see you. You look good in rider's gear." I looked up into his dark blue eyes and heard Eli scoff behind us. Lia shushed him. "I'll miss seeing you around the halls. Take care of yourself." He winked before turning and heading back into the castle, leaving me standing there with a mixture of conflicting emotions - hurt at Brodie walking away, the odd warmth from Levi's words.

Perhaps riders and infantry could be friends after all.

"Fly strong, and land safe, Ria." Eli came to my side, Lia tucked under his arm. "And I'm glad he's not going to be following you there." He glared at Levi's retreating with narrowed eyes. "But stay away from Mitchell O'Connell." He raised his eyebrows at me until I nodded in agreement. I'd already been told by three different people to stay away from the captain's son.

"Thanks, and try not to get into too much mischief while we're gone," I replied, stopping myself from telling him to butt-out and mind his own business. "Tell your brother that I said goodbye, seeing as he left already." I failed at keeping the sting out of my words, clearing my throat and plastering a false smile on my stiff face. Eli gave me a sad look and opened his mouth like he wanted to say something.

Time to go.

"Alright, Vex says it's time to leave. Thank you for everything you guys have done for me, really. I don't know how I'll ever repay you." I looked up into his handsome face, so similar to the man who I couldn't seem to get out of my head. He smirked, shrugging like it was nothing.

"Any time, Ria. And I should be reminding you not to get into too much trouble." He lightly punched me on the arm as they turned back to Cyndrithra, where Lia ran up her dragon's foreleg. I turned and did the same, the heavy pack threatening to topple me backwards if I didn't concentrate.

I gave Eli a wave as Vex extended his wings, crouched, and launched into the sky.

Chapter Seventeen

The ground below us passed in a blur as the sun rose behind us, warming my back.

I could see the academy growing into existence before me. It was just as I imagined it, just perhaps not as big. It rivalled the size of the McTavish castle, but had more of a barracks kind of feel. Something more brutal, harsher as it came into view. Vex aimed for a large field out the south side of the academy, where there seemed to be a party waiting for our arrival. Lia said that the king notified them that Vex and I would be arriving. I didn't know how warm a welcome it was going to be. I could see the other four usual coloured dragons shimmering at the edges of the trees.

Busy bodies who have nothing else better to do, apparently. Vex grumbled with annoyance as we landed. My body ached, my butt numb again. I winced as I moved off the saddle and slid down his leg. I stifled my groan as I stood up straight, heaving my heavy bags over my shoulders. No one moved, not until I was slightly further away from Vex. He remained at my back, his head lowered as he watched them with interest.

I'm not leaving until I'm satisfied that they mean you no harm.

They're teachers and professors, Vex. I'm sure they wouldn't even think of that.

I'm still not moving. He growled, and a few of the younger students stepped back.

"Welcome, Nymeria Everhart, and Vexirion to Voralyth Academy." A woman stepped forward and bowed towards us, eyes down. She straightened, and two younger men stepped forward and offered to take my bags. I declined, not trusting anyone with my things just yet. "I'm Principal Anita Shields, and I'm also one of the Professors here."

"Thank you. I never thought I'd be attending this prestigious academy." I smiled as Vex huffed down the bond. I ignored him.

Lia came up to my side, nodding in greeting at the Principal.

"Ah, cadet Fairchild, welcome back. Now, let's head inside, and we can try to sort out where to put you." Many eyes continued to dart behind me and away again as they took in Vex, who was still glowering at them.

I'm fine, Vex. You can leave now.

`Fine. Any whiff of trouble and I'm tearing the place apart stone by stone.`

So dramatic.

I followed the crowd and looked around in awe. Dark stone, chipped and stained, lined the circular courtyard before us. On the ground was a mosaic of seven dragons flying around a globe, surrounded by stars, clouds, and planets. Their colours were displayed in beautiful, perfect detail. Something written in a different language circled them all. I stopped and took it in.

`It says Wind at your back, fire in your heart. When dragons rise, empires fall. It's written in the language of Volatus Comitium.`

What language is that?

`Dragon.`

I tore my eyes away from the artwork and hurried after the others, my shoulders already aching from my heavy packs. Half of the group broke away, until it was just me,

Principal Shields and two other Professors. We climbed a set of stairs until we were ushered into a dark office. Shields whipped open the curtains, bathing us in the golden rays of the morning sun.

"Alright, take a seat, everyone. We might be here a while. The others shouldn't be too far away." Just as she finished, two more professors knocked and entered the room, followed by four older students who had also been out on the field. Once everyone had settled into a chair, they turned their focus on me. I swallowed under their gazes. It took everything in me to keep my chin up and not shrink under their attention.

"Okay, so, we've found ourselves in a situation that I never thought would happen here. We have Miss Everhart here who needs to be sorted into a house. Wingmaster's, if you want Nymeria and Vexirion in your house, we will hear your pitch." She settled into her seat behind her large desk, placing her entwined hands on her desk. "Wingmaster Ficus, you're up first."

A young man with a shaved head and ice-blue eyes stood. His leathers were pristine, he had a small blue water droplet badge on the left side of his chest, as well as a badge with a pair of wings. Six silver darts sat on his shoulder.

"I know that cadet Everhart and her Tenebrae dragon, Vexirion, will be best suited to join the Ruleum house, as we are known for our gracefulness, cunning and intuitive natures. Some of our dragons are dark enough that they could pass as a Tenebrae in the dark."

I didn't fail to hear a few scoffs around me, including the grumpy dragon eavesdropping in my head.

No. I won't go with them.

"Thank you, Wingmaster Ficus. Skirvington, you're up next."

"Thank you, Principal Shields." A young man with long curly brown hair and beautiful moss green eyes stood in front of the room.

He has such lovely eyes.

"I would love to have cadet Everhart and Vexirion join us in Sinvidia. Some say we are fierce and impulsive, but I know we are loyal, and we look after those in our wing. We would be honoured to have you both." He kept his eyes on mine the whole time, talking only to me, not the room.

"Thank you, Wingmaster Skirvington, Moss, you're up."

A tough-looking woman stood and met everyone's eyes without fear. Her black hair was braided tightly against her skull, and her sunflower yellow eyes were a bright contrast to her dark hair and equally dark skin.

"Galadron's are wild, swift, and unpredictable. We don't know what Tenebrae dragons are like, but they look like they mean business, and so do we. It doesn't matter what colour scales they have, beneath them, they are all the same. I believe riders are the same way." She nodded my way and sat down.

"Thank you, Wingmaster Moss, and lastly, Wingmaster Ranger."

A woman who looked eerily like Lia stood and approached, giving the room a soft smile.

"Thank you, Principal. It is up to her dragon, Vexirion, as much as it is cadet Everhart to choose which house fits best. There are always going to be times when we all clash, but in Furora, we are steady, protective, and patient. I know that my wing will welcome you both, and we would be honoured if you were to join us."

Vex, what do you think? I'm thinking Sinvidia or Furora.

`Yes, I agree.`

"Cadet Everhart, we will let you sleep on the decision, but we will need to know for attendance tomorrow morning, when the rest of the first years arrive. For tonight, you can reside with cadet Fairchild." I turned and smiled at Lia, who grinned back. Wingmaster Ranger winked at Lia as she passed her and sat back in her seat.

"Thank you, Principal Shields. I look forward to having a look around the academy."

"Then please spend the day, Vidalia, making sure she visits all the important places. You're all dismissed." The room stood, and they filed out. I sighed as I heaved my bags back over my shoulders, but Wingmaster Skirvington stopped at my side.

"Can I help you with those?" His dark eyes sparkled, and I couldn't help but smile up at him. He looked trustworthy enough.

"Sure, that would be great. Thanks." He hefted the heavy one up and gestured for Lia to lead the way. She led us through the academy into her room in the Furora commons. It was warm and comforting in the main area they shared: loungers, lots of tables and plants littered the space. There were many strange looks from the people as we passed by.

Once my bags hit the floor, Wingmaster Skirvington turned to me, holding out his hand to shake.

"Call me Mick. It's nice to meet you, Nymeria. Your dragon is outstanding. I never thought I would be lucky enough to see a void dragon so close up."

"Earning yourself some brownie points there, Micky." Lia raised her brows and shook her head, gaining a laugh from the Sinvidia Wingmaster.

"Just being nice to our new cadet. I would do the same for anyone else."

"Yeah, I know, just teasing. You'd better clear out before people start gossiping." Lia smiled as she leaned against her bed. Mick nodded once before heading out.

"He seems nice, and so does Wingmaster Ranger." I sat on the small chair in the corner as Lia flopped down on her bed, yawning.

"Yeah, he's great. And Daniella - Wingmaster Ranger - is my cousin, in case you're wondering." She chuckled. "So, who are you thinking? I don't want to pressure you if you haven't decided yet."

"I'm not too sure, to be honest. I'm tossing up between Furora and Sinvidia."

"Both good choices. We'll grab something to eat, and I'll show you around."

We grabbed some egg and bacon pies on the go while Lia showed me around my new home for the next six years. The academy was mostly old but with a modern flair. It had chandeliers hanging by chains, but instead of candles, light globes flickered like actual flames. Rough stone walls surrounded us, some chipped and cracked. Rich, vibrant rugs lay on the floors, which muffled our steps as we climbed up staircases that hugged the walls. There was no way that I was going to remember all of the places we visited, or how to find them again. But Lia assured me that, once I picked a house, they would look after me. As a house and wing, we became family. And to me, that sounded perfect.

The hard part was: I had to pick one. Red or Green. Furora or Sinvidia. I needed to work out what was best for me, and for Vex.

`I think you know where you're going to pick, and I am fine with that choice.`

Thank you. Looks like we found our new family.

`I wouldn't go that far. You're my family now, that's it.`

What about your parents?

`They perished long ago. Do not forget, I am already three hundred years old. My parents were considered old when they had me.`

I'm sorry, Vex.

`Don't be. They weren't the maternal type, and this place is better off without them.`

⸺◈⸺

The circle court yard with the mosaic was where we were to gather each morning, every cadet, for attendance. We had history, weaponry, fitness training, mage class, and flying lessons. In the Jaw section, they had the junior cadets until we reached the fourth year, where you could become a Wingbearer - where you've just earned your wings, so to speak - and begin your leadership duties. They can carry the weight of the title and help look after their wing and sections. Then, in fifth year, was the Wingwarden: more responsibility by overseeing junior cadets and assisting instructors and their Wingmaster's. Then in the final year, Wingmaster's were top-tier leadership. They lead full squadrons and even influence strategy with the professors.

I would almost guarantee that Brodie and Eli were Wingmaster's in their final year.

`They were. And the most powerful the whole time they were here, even as first-year cadets.`

How do you know all of this?

`What else am I supposed to do while you're inside training? Drathruin was more than happy to fill me in on the people who are in your life now.`

I doubt I'll be seeing much of the princes from now on, anyway. Especially Brodie.

Don't hold your breath, little storm. I wouldn't want you to pass out.

Great.

I heaved a sigh as I followed Lia up the stairs to Principal Shield's office, where I was going to tell her of my decision. I just hoped it was the right one.

Overthinking is the biggest waste of energy. Trust yourself.

CHAPTER EIGHTEEN

Attendance the next morning was loud, overwhelming and enough to make me want to turn invisible just like a certain prince that lived in my head.

Principal Shields of the Jaw Section and Principal Peterson of the Boots section called for silence as they read through the roll, sorting cadets into their houses. And Principal Shields had left me to last, it seemed.

Awesome.

"I have an unusual announcement this morning. We are lucky enough to have a new cadet here, with a Tenebrae dragon." I could almost feel the ripple of shock as it spread through the courtyard. Whispers were hissed, eyes darting every which way. There was a clear divide between the riders and the infantry, and it wasn't just the uniform. They stood together in their neat little groups. Some of them wouldn't even acknowledge the rider beside them, and vice versa.

"Silence," Shields barked, gaining full attention again. "And seeing as we don't have a Tenebrae house here at Voralyth, they were allowed to select which house they would like to join. So it brings me great pleasure to announce that Nymeria Everhart has chosen house Sinvidia, jaw section."

The cheers that echoed around were deafening. A few others grumbled and cursed, but I felt my cheeks heat as fellow Sinvidia cadets slapped me on the back in congratulations as I made my way over to their group. I looked over to Lia, and she just smiled widely at me, giving me a small nod. I was worried that she would be upset that I didn't choose Furora, but I couldn't explain the pull towards Sinvidia.

Once the crowd had settled down, we were introduced to our chain of command. If we had an issue, we went to the Wingbearer, who was Jodelle Trivett. Tanned skin, her eyes a dark jade, and she had dark brown hair that floated around her head like a fluffy cloud. Wingwarden Sean McDonald had the lightest green eyes I'd ever seen, they were almost yellow, and his black hair was shaved close to his head. And I had already met Wingmaster Mick Skirvington. Within our Sinvidia house, we had the Boots Section, and they had a Swordbearer, Swordwarden, and Swordmaster they had to report to.

They didn't pay us much attention as they sorted themselves into two neat lines and strode into the academy.

"Hey, I'm Theon," a bulky guy with a beard introduced himself. He gave me a shy smile and a wave.

"Hey, nice to meet you. I'm Ria."

"Welcome to Sinvidia." His voice sounded like rocks rumbling against each other. "So you're the one with the Void dragon." He had the darkest green eyes, almost black, and with his brown hair and beard, they made him look like a bear.

"Yep." I didn't know what else to reply, so I followed our wing into the academy for our first lesson.

History.

Wingmaster Skirvington and Swordmaster Jacobs were placing us at intervals. One Jaw, one Boots, one Jaw, one Boots, and so on. I was placed down the end between two Boots who looked like they would rather be anywhere else. Principal Shields entered the room, and it fell silent. I'd noticed that our whole house was there, every year of

Sinvidia. It seemed they had us all studying together, rather than per year.

"In this class, I am your professor, and nothing more. Please welcome Professor Yates." A man entered who had the harshest face I had ever seen. His uniform was similar to what the Boots wore. A slate grey shirt and pants, with burnt red accents. His black boots shined like they had just been polished. His grizzled expression passed over us like he already found us lacking. His sharp, grey eyes lacked all warmth as they landed on me, lingering a little too long.

I heard Vex growl in my head, but I held my ground and didn't break contact. Even when my hands began to sweat. I was done being treated like shit by those who thought they were better than me. A muscle in his jaw ticked, but he narrowed his eyes and only looked away when Professor Shields tapped his shoulder.

That man needs to keep his eyes to himself. I could barely understand Vex's growled words.

"In this class, we'll speak of history that changed the world as we know it." Professor Yates prowled the front of the classroom like a predator, a sneer on his face. "It has always been the might of the foot soldiers, the infantry, keeping our proud country safe. And this academy was solely built for them until the dragons came." Even from his tone of voice, I could tell he didn't like us, or our dragons. I could see a few riders from the corner of my eye stiffen their shoulders.

`Make sure you stay away from him. I've been told he's as bitter as they come.`

I get the feeling he doesn't like us very much.
`You assume correctly.`

Professor Shields stepped up to the front of the room and tried to give us a friendly smile.

"Yes. The Principal at the time was welcoming and open to the idea of allowing us to train together. And it has been that way for over three hundred years. We share history class, gym, and weaponry. And we will work as one unit. You are house Sinvidia. These people in this room are your new family." I heard a scoff from beside me.

"In the coming days, the first years in Jaw Section will meet their dragons, and once both have accepted the bond, there is one more thing you need to do."

Oh, am I the only one who's already bonded?
`Yes. We had more important things to do than sit around and wait.`

"I'm not sure how many of you know our customs, but as soon as your dragons decide you're ready, you take the plunge, and then they will start channelling their magic into you." Muttering broke out around the room, and the Boots seemed to roll their eyes even more.

"But Professor Korin will tell you more about it in mage class."

"What happens if the dragon doesn't accept the bond?" One Boot cadet asked, a smirk playing on her lips.

"Then the dragon will scorch the ground where you stand, turning you to nothing but ash in seconds."

Fuck. That's brutal! But the dragon is the one who chooses, not the other way around.

`Just be thankful that I knew you were worth it. Not everyone gets that chance.`

I knew some of the history from when I was at school, but still I took notes and tried to concentrate. I felt a shiver pass through me as dread settled into my stomach.

No. Please, not on my first day. I begged the gods, to anyone who would listen.

An electrical storm was on its way.

⟶⟢✦⟣⟵

I was glad to get out of History and to see Professor Korin again. I hadn't had to deal with a storm since I took the plunge, and it frightened me what might happen. I could feel my skin tingling, and electricity zapping through me as I made my way along the halls. I hoped that the professor might have something to help me. I'd let my hair down to hide the left side of my face and neck, where my lightning scars tended to glow when it stormed. It was going to be challenging if it stormed here often.

"I hate how they separate us in history. The boring gravel grinders don't care less about our dragon history. And the dickhead beside me was muttering the whole time, and I missed some of what the professor said," a first-year woman grumbled, and I held in my chuckle. I think her name was Izzy.

Professor Korin was wiping down his board when we entered, but turned and smiled my way. I felt like I could breathe a little easier. He knew everything, and I trusted him.

"Cadet Everhart, good to see you. And a wise choice, choosing Sinvidia." His eyes crinkled at the edges when he smiled.

"And you, Professor, thank you. I went with my gut." I looked down at my hands for a moment as I twisted them together. "I was hoping for a word when you're free." I met his gaze, I could see him searching my face, understanding dancing in his eyes.

"Regarding the storm that's swiftly approaching?" he whispered as he watched me roll my shoulders as the tension began to build. I nodded with a grimace.

"Absolutely, sit at the back." He nodded to the back row and turned around to his board. I hurried that way as the room filled with every first-year cadet. I felt bad, but I couldn't focus on a word he said. The storm was blowing in so quickly that it would be here in a matter of hours. I felt jittery, on edge as my knee bounced, my pen tapping on the notebook before me.

I caught Theon looking at me a few times, a few others glancing my way, but they didn't say anything. At least Korin was talking about taking the plunge and what to expect. So I didn't feel too bad that I wasn't listening.

The bell rang, signalling the end of class, and I made sure I was last to leave.

"A quick word, cadet Everhart."

"Sure, Professor."

"She'll catch up with you in the cafeteria," he said to Theon, who was lingering by the door. He nodded my way and shut the door behind him.

"Thank you, professor." I rolled my shoulders again, feeling on edge.

"Here, let me have a look and see if I can make something up for you." He rummaged through his cabinets and drawers. He brought out something that looked like bark and had a pungent smell, making me wrinkle my nose. "Ashmellow bark, it's good for many things, but brewed for long enough, it helps dull the senses and blocks those pesky electrical currents from misfiring." He winked at me before glancing out the window. "I'll make a start now, and I'll come and find you after your next class. Then you can sip it until it passes."

"Thank you, professor. I really appreciate your help."

"Can't have you electrocuting kids on their first day, now can we?" he laughed, and I felt a little better. I hurried off to the cafeteria. The room was loud and a little stuffy with so many bodies crammed into it.

"There seems to be more riders this year than usual, according to Professor Shields," A second year said around a mouthful of salad.

"No one in my family has been a rider. I'm the first one. Ever." Izzy grinned, tucking a wild curl behind her ear.

"Me too," Theon grumbled, cutting his steak like he wanted to kill it all over again. "I didn't know what was happening until a dragon spoke to me, telling me to hurry up and get my ass to Voralyth." We laughed, his cheeks blushed a light pink.

"I don't think anyone from Classina has ever been a rider before. And now there are two of us? Crazy." Izzy downed her water in one go before turning to me, wiping her mouth with the back of her hand.

"When did you know you were a rider? And where did you come from? Oh, and how the hell have you already bonded to a Tenebrae dragon?" She fired the questions at me.

"I'm from Nythevra, and I had this feeling, these dreams that told me I needed to get to Sylvanfire. So I left everything I knew behind me and found Vexirion waiting for me at the castle. We bonded and only a few weeks, later I took the plunge."

The table stared at me with open mouths. It was almost comical.

"So you just up and left. What about your parents?" Theon leaned on the table, his chin propped up on his fist.

"They died four years ago. It's just me now." I looked away, back down at my half-eaten burger. I didn't feel very hungry anymore.

"Oh, I'm sorry." His voice softened, and I turned back to him, giving him a small smile.

"Thanks, but I've got some friends, and I have Vex now. Even though he told me he doesn't do hugs." Theon barked out a laugh, spraying us with his juice as he choked. It made me laugh in return, and I was glad to lighten the situation.

"Sor...sorry," he wheezed, thumping his chest with his large fist, which made us laugh more.

If this was how it was always going to be, then I might be alright.

Chapter Nineteen

"You alright there, Ria? You're looking a little pale." Theon said as we made our way to training.

"I think it's just been a long day," I muttered, any other excuse slipping from my mind. Before I could think of anything, I got shoved from behind, my scattered mind overreacting and making the lights above us explode in a shower of glass. I heard screams and shouts as people ducked, and light after light after light down the hall shattered in little *pops*.

Oops.

"Are you okay?" A voice asked, pulling my attention away from the glass littering the ground like tiny glittering diamonds. I turned to my left, where a man with chocolate coloured hair was looking at me worriedly. "You've got a cut on your cheek." He reached up, as if to touch it, but thought better of it. I wiped my cheek, and it came away bloody. "It's only small."

My gaze returned to his wheat-gold eyes as they assessed me.

"I'm fine, thanks. I've had worse." I forced myself to laugh, but on the inside, I was shaking.

The hall was starting to calm down, people brushing the tiny shards of glass off their clothing, cursing as it got stuck in their fingers.

"What the hell just happened?" He looked around, bent over and shook his floppy, chocolate brown hair. He stood back up, and his eyes latched onto me again. "I'm Ryler, by the way, a Wingbearer for Galadron."

"Nice to meet you. I'm Nymeria, first year in Sinvidia."

"Oh, you're the one with the Void dragon," he breathed, eyes wide. "I'm a little jealous that you chose them." He winked, and I huffed a laugh through my nose. "Well, I'd better get on my way and see if anyone else needs my help. Lovely to meet you, Nymeria." He threw me another cheeky wink before sauntering down the chaotic hall.

"Well, ain't he a sight for sore eyes." Izzy rested her arm on my shoulder as she watched Ryler walk away.

"I think he knows it, though." I shrugged as she watched him walk away.

"Who cares? Classina didn't have many options when it came to young, single men. So I'll happily take what I can get." Izzy flicked her curly hair over her shoulder, jogging to catch up with another first-year.

I don't know if someone shoved me on purpose or if it was an accident, but Professor Korin couldn't get here quickly enough.

I was thankful that I'd kept up my training with P1 and P2 - the damn nickname sticking, but it made me laugh when I thought of it. The training class sure wasn't mucking around.

Professor Potteira didn't take any prisoners. She had us climbing walls, swinging ropes, sparring, and skipping, all without having a break. There were a lot of first years who couldn't climb a rope, who couldn't throw a punch. That's where the others, like me, had to help them, especially those in our house. That was our responsibility: to get every cadet over the line in two months. As that was roughly how long a bond between a dragon and their rider was the weakest, and the dragon could reject the bond without harming the rider, if they want to, that is. The other option was sending that cadet home in a small box, with whatever they managed to sweep up off the ground.

Professor Korin was waiting for me out in the hall, nodding to students on their way past. He handed me some books, but I could feel a small bottle in the bag as well. The training class had done a good job of keeping me distracted, but the sound of the thunder now made me flinch.

"Take one sip now and then another every hour after that. I apologise about the taste, but there's nothing I can do about that." I nodded, thanking him quietly as others caught up. "Good luck, Ria." The professor walked away as another boom shook the academy. The hair on my neck stood on end, and I rolled my shoulders. My fingertips tingled, so I shoved them into my pockets, hoping they weren't sparking.

"I think I'm going to head to bed early tonight. I'm wiped out." I threw a yawn in there for good measure, rubbing my eyes.

"Yeah, I don't blame you. But I'm starving, so I'll catch you tomorrow." Theon headed off towards the cafeteria to grab something to eat, as I headed back to the Sinvidia common room, thanks to the little paper map they handed out earlier. I was halfway to the common room when I saw

Lia jogging towards me. Her eyes darted over my face, but seemed relieved.

"How was your first day?" She linked her arm with mine but quickly yelped, backing away.

"Sorry!" I mumbled, stepping away from her.

"Yeah, I thought you might not be having much fun. Do you need anything?" She rubbed her arm where I'd zapped her.

"Professor Korin gave me some Ashmellow bark, but I still feel a little on edge." I began walking again, and she fell in step beside me.

"I heard all the lights in the hallway to training blew." She mentioned quietly, and I nodded, embarrassed.

"Yeah, someone shoved me, and I'm so scattered that I couldn't help it."

"You're alright though?" She stopped me with a hand on my arm, and I made sure I kept my electricity to myself. Another boom rattled the panes of glass, shaking the chandeliers.

"Yeah, I'll be fine. I'm heading to bed, hopefully to sleep it off."

"Alright, but make sure you tell me if you need anything."

The kind gesture brought tears to my eyes. I had to mash my lips together, so I didn't start to cry. She gave my arm a comforting squeeze.

We parted ways, and I slipped into my new room. I'd received my key at this morning's attendance, and they told me I'd be sharing with a woman from the Boots section.

They were really trying to force us to get along.

My bags had been brought in from Lia's room and dumped on the bed. I sighed, flinching when another boom rattled the building. How was I going to keep my powers to myself? I couldn't fake an illness like I used to back home.

When I had my parents to help look after me. And Kai.

Stop that. I can't afford to think about them now, I'd never stop crying.

I mentally shook myself and began putting my things away, taking a sip of the potion Korin brewed for me.

I didn't sleep well, but at least I got some in the early hours once the storm had passed. My roommate was quiet, as I didn't hear her come in. But she was tucked in when I woke before dawn. I rolled out of bed and crept my way to the bathroom, needing a shower before I could face the day. I made sure the door was shut before turning on the light, the fluorescence's harsh on my sore eyes. I noticed that my scars still glowed slightly, and I blew out a breath. Great, normally they would disappear when the storm did, but it looked like things were changing.

Damn it.

`There are worse things to worry about, little storm.`

I guess you're right. But my secret won't stay hidden for very long.

`Then we will cross that bridge when we come to it. Don't borrow tomorrow's worries.`

Alright, alright, oh wise one.

I felt his annoyance down the bond, and I chuckled as I finished drying my hair and snuck out again. My roommate was yawning and stretching her arms when I re-entered.

"Morning, I'm Ria." I held out my hand for her to shake, but she gave me the best stink eye I'd ever seen. She looked me up and down again before scoffing and throwing off her blanket.

"Wow, that's rude," I muttered, but she ignored me and locked herself in the bathroom. "Awesome, my roommate is a bitch."

I grabbed my pack and headed down into the cafeteria to get some much-needed coffee. I made sure my hair was down around my face, my hood on. We hadn't been issued a proper uniform yet, but we got those today.

I grabbed a big mug of coffee on my way to the Sinvidia table and sat with a sigh, inhaling the aroma.

"Rough night?" Theon was cradling his mug with both hands, bags under his eyes.

"Yeah, you could say that. Also, my roommate is a complete bitch."

"Ugh, same! Mine didn't even speak to me." A woman called Sue butted in from across the table, she looked perplexed as she shook her head.

"I don't know why they think forcing us to spend time together is a good idea." Theon rumbled into his mug.

The smell of food was the first clue that we'd better get our asses to the front of the line. I needed to eat. My stomach grumbled so loudly it was drawing odd looks from the others at our table. I made a mental note to get some snacks to hide in my room for when the storms hit again.

"Good morning, Nymeria." I looked over my shoulder to see Ryler smiling my way. I replied with a small wave and returned to my bacon and eggs.

"Damn, looks like you've made a friend in the handsome Wingbearer." Izzy grinned into her coffee, but I shook my head.

"I'm not interested, so you can have him." I dug into my breakfast, eager to change the subject.

Weeks started to fly by, and before I knew it, I'd been there a month.

As much as I tried to stay under the radar, it seemed everyone else had other plans. Most students jumped out of my way, apologised, or offered their seat up for me, or to go first in the line at the cafeteria.

It was getting incredibly annoying.

`They know you will be the most powerful rider in the academy, and don't want to make an enemy of you.`

Well, they don't have to run away from me. I really don't care.

`Yeah, well, you'd better get used to it.`

I just wanted to do my work and get on with my day, but it seemed the cadets of Voralyth had other ideas.

I was pushing through one of the hellish leg presses when a handsome, blond-haired man strutted through the gym's double doors. I heard a few girls sigh in appreciation. I raised my brows but kept pushing. Five reps to go until I was free to leave their torture session.

I looked up, and his brown eyes landed on me, and I didn't bother looking pleasant. I wasn't in the mood to be nice or friendly.

He leaned against the frame of the machine I was using. "I'm Mitch, nice to meet you."

I almost froze as his name washed over me.

Mitchell O'Connell. The Captain's son.

He winked and extended a hand just as I finished my reps. I sat forward to shake his hand.

"Nymeria." I gave him a tight smile before standing and stretching. My legs were killing me. Mitch cocked his head to the side, his eyes trailing over the brand on my throat.

"Nice brand. I haven't seen one like that before."

"Because her dragon is the black beast you've no doubt seen flying around lately," Theon murmured as he set the weights down, running a hand through his wavy black hair.

Mitch's eyes widened as they rested on me again.

"No way. You've got the Void dragon?" He sounded shocked as he blatantly looked me up and down. He opened his mouth to say more when a ripple of conversation moved through the room like wildfire. Another cadet from Furora ran over and whispered something into Izzy's ear with a giggle and a blush. Izzy beamed and thanked her before turning to me with a grin.

"Apparently, two new guards have been called in to help with our training, seeing as there are so many of us first years this year. And they are drop-dead *gorgeous*." Her pale green eyes seemed to sparkle, her black curls bouncing in her ponytail as she moved. I don't know why, but I had a bad feeling about this.

"Want to spar, Ria?" Another first year came over, but I think her reason was to get closer to Mitch.

"Yeah, sure," I said as we headed over to the mats, but she turned to Mitch and batted her eyelashes.

"Do you think you could help me? I'm not sure if I'm doing it correctly." She pouts, popping one knee out. I rolled my eyes so hard I was worried they'd get stuck back there. A smile tugged at his lips. He dipped his head in acceptance as he made his way over.

"Why don't you make a start, and I'll watch, then go from there?" He stopped at the edge of our mat, arms loosely crossed over his chest. I tried hard to ignore him, but the twins' warning played constantly in the back of my mind.

It was clear that this first-year had no idea what she was doing. She flinched each time I came near her, her punches barely touched me, and she seemed to be just dancing around.

Mitch scrubbed his face. I could see he was trying hard to smother his laugh.

"Nymeria, why don't you spar with someone else while I try to instruct cadet..."

"Narelle." She beamed as he came closer. I was more than happy with that idea.

I walked to the next mat, pinched a first-year called Bree, and started again. At least she had some idea of how to fight.

I heard Mitch mutter something under his breath, pricking my interest when a low voice interrupted us.

"Why are you holding back, cadet Everhart?"

Oh no, are you freaking serious?

I dropped my arms and turned to look at one of our new guards, who was glaring at me, one eyebrow raised as he crossed his large, tattooed arms across his wide chest.

I ignored the fluttering in my chest, my body's ridiculous reaction upon seeing him.

"Why would you think that, McTavish?" I asked innocently, trying to keep my breathing under control as I felt Bree's gaze lock on me, then back to Brodie.

"Because I know you're better than that," he growled.

Damn him to the fiery pits of hell.

CHAPTER TWENTY

"I'll ask you again, cadet. Why are you holding back? You're not doing yourself or the other cadets any favours." He widened his legs in a stance I knew all too well, and continued to stare, waiting for my response.

"Because I don't want anymore attention than what I already get," I grumbled, crossing my arms. His gaze flicked to Bree beside me.

"Cadet, pair up with someone else. I'm going to make sure that cadet Everhart here actually trains properly."

Great. What did I do to deserve this?

`Stop complaining and get on with it.`

Easy for you to say. He's not glowering at you like he's a disappointed parent.

He wouldn't dare look at me that way.

I reined in my annoyance and turned my attention back to Brodie.

"I bet the other McTavish wasn't too thrilled to hear he was returning." I moved away from the others and shook out my hands, knowing Brodie was about to throw down.

"He was happy at first, until he realised that we're not allowed relations with cadets," Brodie smirked, and I tried to hide my grin, pretending like I didn't care.

Poor Lia.

"Now, come at me like you mean it." He crouched down and crooked a finger, showing me one of his dimples for good measure.

Damn it, he's not playing fair.

I tried to ignore the stares I could feel on us as I launched myself at him. Kings guard or not, I had a lot of built-up frustration, and he seemed like the best outlet right now. We danced around, landing a few hits here and there, until he got through my defences and into a headlock.

"Why are you holding back?" he asked again, his lips at my ear, sending shivers through me as I struggled to get my breathing under control.

"Because I'm sick of being treated differently. I just want to be left alone," I breathed, thinking fast on how to get him off me. I lifted both legs, causing him to lose balance as he re-adjusted. I used that opportunity to twist his arm away and behind his back, making him hiss in pain.

"You can't hide from who you are, Storm," he growled, breaking my grip, facing me again. "You're going to be the most powerful rider at the academy for the next six years. Get used to it."

"Then why do they either run away scared, or hang around like they want something from me? I don't care about hierarchy. I just want to train like everybody else."

"You will never be like everybody else, Storm. So you'd better start getting used to it. Trust me, I speak from experience." He launched at me again, tackling me around the middle. I landed on my back, the air whooshing out of me. "You need to do what's best for you, fuck everybody else."

I stared into his lovely green eyes, only inches from mine. He truly was beautiful, and I tried not to think about how his body felt above mine. I swallowed and offered him a small nod.

"Then you won't mind what I do next, then." I attempted to knee him in the balls. His eyes widened and rolled out of the way at the last minute. It was my turn to straddle him, my arm at his throat as I pushed down.

"You play dirty," he wheezed, but I saw his lips twitch, as if he was fighting a smile.

"Ah, it's good to see you've still got it, cadet Everhart." Another familiar voice sounded to my right. I spotted Eli grinning at us, his cerulean eyes sparkling with mischief as he saw me straddling his twin brother. I scrambled off Brodie and offered him my hand. He took it, a faint blush on his cheeks that made me feel things I shouldn't.

"Cadet Everhart, it seems that Prince McTavish was correct. You have been holding back." Professor Potteira *tsked*, shaking her head. "Next lesson, I hope to see your full involvement." She walked away. I turned hard eyes to Brodie. He just crossed his arms and glowered back.

"Good to see you, Ria," Eli whispered before moving away, the class over for the day. I was still stuck there having a staring competition with his brother. I didn't want to be the first one to look away. He leaned in, his face so close, his breath brushing my face.

"I'll be keeping a close eye on you, cadet Everhart. Can't have you slacking off, now can we?" He threw me a lopsided grin, his dimples punching me right in the chest as he winked and sauntered off. I watched him walk away, a storm of emotions going off inside of me.

Elias and Brodie McTavish were our new guards - here to help in any class that needed an extra hand.

And, apparently, that was every class I was in.

Fan-freaking-tastic.

"Oh. My. Gods." Bree was at my side, also watching Brodie as he slipped through the training doors. "You two have so much chemistry it's a wonder you didn't catch fire and burn the place down."

I rolled my eyes and shook the thoughts from my head.

"Don't be ridiculous. He just helped me train before I came here. Bossy prince…" I grumbled, walking to my locker and slinging my pack over my shoulder.

"Sure thing, Ria. And also, I don't want to spar with you anymore. You're going to destroy me with moves like that." She looked at me seriously, and I barked a laugh. "I mean it. You're lethal."

The halls began to quieten as classes finished for the day.

"I've just had good teachers, that's all." I shrugged, trying not to think about Brodie's body above me, or me straddling him.

Damn it. I didn't need those images in my head.

I lined up for dinner, trying to ignore all the new looks my way from training class, the muttering getting louder and louder.

Damn that bloody prince to the darkest pits of hell.

"Hey, Nymeria."

I almost sighed at the male voice on my left. But it was only Ryler grinning at me as he leaned against the counter.

"Hey, Ryler." I smiled, moving along with the line.

"Do you have any plans this weekend?" He gave me a lazy smirk, standing close.

"I think I'm just going to stay in, perhaps try some new flight maneuvers I learned." I smiled at the lunch lady and asked for a helping of salad. My stomach didn't feel like much else.

"Cadet Everhart has some catching up to do, so I'm afraid her weekend is booked out."

You've got to be fucking kidding me.

I looked over my shoulder to a glaring prince whose gaze was locked on Ryler with such intensity it made me flinch. Thank goodness he'd never looked at me like that.

"No worries. Perhaps next weekend." Ryler winked, grabbed his food and moved along. I ignored Brodie and stalked away towards my table, where Bree and Narelle were grinning, and Theon's brows were drawn.

"Hey, Nymeria," another guy called as I passed his table, "nice switchbacks yesterday."

I didn't reply, just gave him a polite smile and continued on my way.

"Is this what it's like every day?" Brodie said beside me, having easily caught up.

"Yep," I sighed, sitting down and shutting my eyes. I heard a chair scrape on the stone floor as Brodie pulled out the seat beside me.

"I see."

That was all he said.

I opened my eyes and turned his way, but he was looking down at his burger with interest. I sucked on my teeth, biting back the words I wanted to throw at him. I couldn't tell him how I really felt. Not in public, anyway.

Seething, I turned back to my salad and picked at it. My hunger disappeared completely.

I caught Lia's eye the next morning at attendance. She gave me a sympathetic smile, and I gave her one back. It must have sucked having your boyfriend there but not being allowed to touch each other. I didn't fail to notice our two new guards standing at the front with the other professors. I refused to meet his gaze, but I caught Eli's, and he winked, mischief written all over his face.

I managed to avoid them for the day, but I didn't like my chances for the weekend as, apparently, I had some 'catching up to do'.

My roommate was still ignoring me, and I was sick of it. So, I went out of my way to be extra friendly to her, especially when she was with her Boots friends. I could see her sneer at me, looking at me with disgust when I would smile and call out her name. I'd had to ask around for it, as she refused to speak to me. If she was going to be a bitch, then so was I.

Saturday morning rolled around, and I breathed a sigh of relief. My peace only lasted about three minutes until there was a loud banging on my door. Ava - my roommate - let out an annoyed sigh and rolled over. The bashing continued. I swung my legs out of bed, the floorboards cold on my bare feet. I swung open the door and put on my best annoyed face.

"Good morning, cadet..." but his voice tapered off, losing its bite. I looked up into the face of Brodie McTavish as his eyes looked over my bare legs. I still only slept in a singlet and underwear.

It was nice to make him speechless for once. So I bent one knee and cocked my head to the side.

"To what do I owe this honour, prince?" I replied sarcastically, and he narrowed his eyes as he met my gaze.

"Get dressed. We're heading outside for training. Cadet Fairchild will be along shortly." He spun on his heel and walked away, not looking back. I poked my tongue out at his retreating back and slammed the door, not caring that Ava was still in bed.

Screw her. Screw him, too.

I grumbled to myself as I showered and dressed. Ava had snuck out while I was showering, to avoid me speaking to her, I guess. I poked my tongue out at her bed on my way past.

Lia was waiting at the common room door with a wide grin on her face. It settled my nerves slightly, but I knew she would look forward to spending more time with the twins than I would.

"They managed to get us a weekend pass for training purposes." She used her fingers in the air for quotation marks. I smiled at her enthusiasm as she handed me a fresh egg and bacon roll with a hash brown shoved in the middle.

"Oh, Lia. You know you're my favourite, right?" I clutched the sandwich to my chest as I shut the door behind me, quickly inhaling it on our way through the academy. Not many cadets were out and about this early on a weekend, but those who were watched us with interest.

You'd better hurry, P1 is getting impatient. Vex grumbled.

Oh, poor little prince. I'd hate for him to get upset. I quipped as we walked through the courtyard. The cold wind whipped at my hair. Luckily, I had braided it back in two neat rows.

I could see our dragons in the distance, Vex towering over the others easily as they snorted in the chilly morning air.

Gods, he was huge.

I ignored Brodie and walked straight to Eli, who was grinning widely.

"Morning, Ria. Ready to hit the sky?" He quickly looked around before slinging an arm over Lia's shoulders.

She sighed and shoved him away, shaking her head. But a small smile played at her lips.

"Oh, you have no idea." I didn't wait for anyone else to speak before making my way up Vex's foreleg, settling into the saddle. Vex crouched down and launched into the sky. I was forced backwards at the steep incline, but managed to hold on as he climbed higher and higher.

Before we knew it, we were soaring above the academy and flying towards the mountains, the sunrise golden and filled with promise of adventure.

Chapter Twenty-One

The sky glowed in oranges and golds, the trees standing tall like dark statues. To my surprise, we turned away from Voralyth and circled around the back of the mountains. We landed in a large field, the morning mist hanging thickly around the dragon's clawed feet.

Have fun. Vex raised his head, flaring his wings ready for take off.

What? Are you not staying? I spun around, glaring at my dragon, who I swore was smirking.

Nope. Don't set the forest on fire. With a huff of hot air at my face, he soared into the golden sky, Drathruin leading the riot of dragons into the surrounding mountains.

Brodie and Eli unpacked various things from their packs, speaking quietly, heads bent together. Lia came to my side, stretching her arms above her head as Korin landed, looking too sprightly for this time of morning.

Now that I knew Korin and the princes were related, I could see the obvious signs.

In the mannerisms, the way they spoke, and the same sense of humour. I was glad the princes had another family member to love them. Unlike their mother.

"What of the queen? I haven't seen or heard of her," I asked Lia quietly. It seemed strange that the whole time I spent at the castle, not a word was spoken. Lia's face fell a little, making sure we were far back enough for the princes to not hear.

"The queen only lives at the castle for a few weeks every year. She prefers to spend her time at their holiday home in Pyrelith." She didn't take her eyes off them as Korin hugged them. "It was an arranged marriage. Queen Ivelle isn't a rider. They only wed to unite the people."

"Oh. That must be hard on the twins." I watched them smile and laugh, looking relaxed.

"Yes, ever since they were little boys, she's been distant. Now that she's done her duty, it seems she prefers to be with her people. And where there are no dragons." Lia's smile was full of love as she watched them.

"Oh, that's horrible."

"It is. But they've grown up strong and kind, and they will be wonderful rulers. Euan has done a great job."

I let the conversation drop as we walked toward them. Korin was pouring something that looked like coffee into mugs, and I could have kissed him.

"Here..."

I jumped, not hearing Brodie approach. I took the mug with a quiet thanks, inhaling the delicious smell before taking a sip.

"What made you choose Sinvidia?" His voice was low, quiet, and he was standing closer than I thought he ever would. I risked my stupid emotions and peeked a look up at him.

His gaze locked on mine, making my heart thump heavily in my chest as our eyes clashed.

"It was between Sinvidia and Furora." I hated how breathless I sounded, even to my own ears.

"Both good choices," he murmured, keeping his eyes on mine.

"I guess I went with my gut, and Wingmaster Skirvington gave a good pitch, too." My heart skipped a beat - He hadn't spoken to me much since the ball.

I need to get a freaking grip on myself.

"He's a good man, very honourable." He took a sip of his coffee, but continued to stare.

I felt too hot in my skin.

"He seems like it." *What else do I say?* My mind scrambled to keep him there, talking, but I came up blank. His eyes finally left mine, and I almost sagged to the ground. He turned and walked away, leaving me standing there like a stunned animal as he made his way back to the others.

What the hell just happened?

"Alright, the reason I've got you all up here is so Nymeria can train and hone her powers without watching eyes." Korin paced back and forth in front of us, and I deflated a little.

I was hoping it would be something more exciting than that.

"Have you been able to practice your teleporting?" Korin asked, and I felt a little embarrassed.

"No, I haven't had the opportunity to, unless you call teleporting from the bathroom door into the shower practice?"

"That's alright. Have you teleported while holding something before?"

"No." I frowned, and it dawned on me why the twins had packs.

"I want you to teleport, holding this rock across the clearing." He handed me a heavy rock about the size of my head. I ignored the stares of the others as I focused on the rock.

I made the mental step, but heard a loud thump back from where I was standing. I looked down at my empty hands.

Damn it.

"That's fine, keep trying."

Brodie and Eli trained together at the edge of the clearing, the sounds of their swords clashing echoing. Lia sat on a fallen tree, encouraging me on.

I teleported back to the ball, picked it up and tried again, and again, and again. Until I was at the point of sweating.

"How about we have a break for lunch?" Eli suggested, looking exhausted just from watching me. "I know I could do with some food."

I hadn't realised that I'd been at it for hours.

I dropped the rock and made my way beside Lia, gratefully sitting down. A headache had started at the base of my skull.

"I think we need to start with something smaller and work our way up." Korin tapped his chin, eyes in the sky before meeting my gaze. "I've never trained with a teleporter before, so this is all new for me, too." He looked at me a little sheepishly.

"Then we'll figure this out together." I smiled, glad to have someone like him helping me, and not just because he was the prince's uncle. Because *he* wanted to.

Eli handed out the sandwiches, then some fruit to finish with, before I got back to it.

Korin's whispergalss pulsed in his pocket, and he sighed when he read it. "I need to head back to the academy, but I trust you to keep it up." He nodded to the twins before calling his dragon Immskarr. The yellow dragon caught the sun like a beacon, almost too bright to look at. As soon as they'd cleared the field, it was back to it.

"Alright, let's keep going. Eli, you and Lia spar, I'll work with Storm." Brodie stood before me, clearly waiting for me to get up and back to work. I gritted my teeth as I got to my feet.

"Let's start with this." He handed me a book before he took a step back.

I closed my eyes, concentrated on taking it with me, and only stepped small.

Success.

I smothered my smile as I handed it back, waiting for the bigger item. So and so forth, the items got bigger until I was back to the rock.

At this point, I was sweating in my leathers.

The sun had started to go down past the trees, and my arms and legs were quivering from the strain. Eli and Lia had mentioned it at least an hour ago that we should head back. But Brodie always said - not yet.

But Lia announced she was leaving, and Eli was going with her.

I went to follow the others when Brodie stepped in front of me.

I stopped with a huff, staring at his enormous chest.

"I'm only pushing you so hard, so you have the best fighting chance, Storm." His voice was low and quiet. I gritted my teeth and craned my head to look him in the eyes.

"Because Korin asked you to?" I crossed my arms, refusing to back away.

"Because I want to." He admitted, taking a step closer. He was so close we were almost touching.

Too close. Too dangerous.

"They know you're out here. And they won't stop until they have you, and I *won't* allow it." I searched his eyes for a hint of what he was feeling, but he gave nothing away.

"I'm tired, I have a killer headache, and I can barely feel my arms and legs. Don't you think pushing me this hard only makes it easier for someone to get me when I'm like this? I can barely walk without falling over." I went to walk around him, but he blocked me again.

"Then why the hell didn't you say anything?" He snapped before sighing in frustration.

"Because would you listen or think I'm just whining?" I threw my arms down, fighting against my finger wanting to point at his chest. "If it's alright with you, I'm leaving for the day." I didn't give him a chance to speak as I walked off, glad that Vex was almost here.

Would you like me to singe P1?

As much as I want to say yes, it would only cause drama I don't want.

Not even a little bit?

You're incorrigible.

I shuffled my way into the cafeteria, weary and a little grumpy. Eli and Lia had decided to eat together elsewhere, and that was fine with me. I was too tired to speak, let alone pretend to be pleasant.

"You look dead on your feet." A voice chuckled in front of me in the line. I looked up, and Mitch stood before me, an easy grin on his face.

"I *feel* dead," I muttered, not really caring what I grabbed. I was starving.

"I heard you had special training today?" Mitch's voice dropped slightly as someone walked past, and I narrowed my eyes.

How the hell does he know about that?

The boy is a guard, he would know of all comings and goings. Use your brain, little storm.

"Yeah, you could say that," I grumbled, wanting to sit and be left alone.

"I hope they weren't too hard on you. The twins are known for being hard asses." Mitch kept pace with me as I walked to my table. But his tone wasn't friendly anymore.

That's right. Apparently, they didn't get along.

"You could say that again." I groaned as I lowered myself into my seat, closing my eyes for a moment.

"Do you mind if I sit with you?"

"Knock yourself out."

His question took me off guard, but I was too tired to come up with an excuse. I opened my eyes and began picking at my food, looking forward to my bed.

His chair scraped back before I felt him sit beside me. We didn't speak for the next few minutes, just content in eating, which was fine with me.

"What's it like being bonded to the most powerful dragon in the continent?"

No one had asked me that question before. I was surprised enough that I turned and met his gaze. His brown eyes were actually lovely.

"It's...different. I don't know how to explain it, but it challenges me every day." I racked my brain to think of a better way to explain it. "I feel in my bones that this is what I was meant to do, but I'm also worried that I won't be good enough. Won't be strong enough to handle it."

I don't know where the words came from, but they spilled from me before I could stop myself. I felt my cheeks heat at my admission. Why the hell was I spilling my thoughts to this complete stranger?

"I don't agree. I think you're handling it just like you should be. I've watched you train, you're incredibly talented." Mitch turned back to his food, "I know the princes can be amazing and alluring, but just don't fall for it, okay?"

That got my attention.

I turned his way, his eyes meeting mine again.

"They might seem perfect, but they've got ghosts, just like the rest of us."

CHAPTER
TWENTY-TWO

The next morning started the same way. But Eli was at my door, and handed me a coffee as soon as I greeted him.

"Ugh, you're a life-saver," I murmured as I took the cup. I turned back to face Ava, who had the blanket over her head. "By Ava! I hope you have a great day!" I shouted, and the only reaction I got was her giving me the middle finger.

"I'm not even going to ask." Eli chuckled, falling into step beside me. "Sorry about yesterday, if I'd have known he pushed you so far, I would have said something." It sounded like regret laced his tone. But I couldn't meet his gaze, I instead focused on the hall ahead of us. "I'll be training you today. He's staying here." He trailed away, and I breathed in a deep breath, relieved more than I should be.

We didn't speak the rest of the way. I happily sipped my coffee, making sure I finished it before climbing on the back of Vex.

I was surprised he didn't say anything as we headed for the same place as yesterday. But Eli was right, no grumpy prince.

We set up, Lia hugging me as soon as we'd landed. Today might actually be a good day.

But I was annoyed at myself that I couldn't teleport while holding the rock. The book was fine, my dagger was easy, but it seemed that something much larger, that I couldn't put in my pocket or wear, was what I struggled with. Eli let me go with my gut and to have a break when I needed one.

He didn't stand there and watch me, instead he trained with Lia, but also kept an eye on me at the same time.

I'd been at it for about an hour when I shut my eyes, concentrating on the ball in my hands. Trying a different tactic. I willed it as if it were a part of me, that it needed to come too, as I began to sweat. My arms felt heavy, but I kept my focus on the ball and myself together.

I made the jump, my mind pushing against the weight in my arms, wanting me to drop it, but I held on with a growl. As soon as my feet touched the ground, I looked down, a smile blooming across my face.

I'd done it.

Even if my limbs felt like they were filled with lead, and my head was thumping. I'd done it.

I collapsed onto the ground, staring up at the sky, the clouds lazily making their way past as I caught my breath.

"Well done, Ria!" Eli and Lia clapped, coming over to me and helping me back to my feet. Lia led me to the fallen tree and handed me a muslie bar.

"I think that's enough for today. Let's head back so you can have some of your weekend." Eli packed up their things, waving my way as Morvanyx landed with a thud.

"You should be proud of yourself, Ria." Lia hugged me briefly before making her way into the clearing, Cyndrithra landing as soon as it was clear.

I wouldn't mind walking some of the way back. I need to clear my head.

`I'll pick you up and drop you at the bottom of the mountain.`

I was happily wandering through the trees, enjoying the filtered sun on my face, when Vex thundered into my head.

`Something's wrong. Get back to the academy! I'm turning around.`

The ground began to vibrate, and birds squawked as they took flight.

Something was coming.

Before I could even raise my blade, at least a dozen soldiers ran straight for me out of the trees' shadows. I took a deep breath and made the mental jump. Only...I'd never jumped that far before...

I fell short, only managing a few hundred meters behind them. It was better than nothing, so I did it again, and again. A headache pounded, and it felt like my skull was about to split in two.

Faster!

Something shot past me, embedding into a tree. The thing started to hiss, and foul white smoke began spewing into the air. I choked as the bitter smell reached my nose. I ran, my magic felt slippery as I tried to reach for it.

Fuck.

I coughed as my head started to swim.

I couldn't reach Vex. My link to him was like smoke, there, but I couldn't get hold of it. I heard a screech from above, and the bellowing of a dragon shook the trees.

Oh...he's pissed.

I cried out as a burning pain bloomed in my leg, making me stumble. I looked down and saw a dart embedded in the back of my thigh. My vision swam as I staggered to a stop, falling to my knees, and suddenly I was surrounded.

Shit, they've...drugged...me.

I swung my dagger at any of those that tried to get close, but it was no use. They grabbed onto my arms and dragged me through the trees, towards what the military called a stormchariot. A monstrous thing with four wheels, enough seats to hold at least eight people, and it went too fast for something so compact. I'd seen them arriving at the viscount's palace all too often.

Two soldiers opened the back, ready to throw me in.

No, n-no, no. This c-can't be h-happening.

Vex roared above me, the trees swaying from the gust of his wings.

Through my twisting and warping vision, I thought I could see some of the soldiers falling.

I heard a grunt from behind me - the one holding me - his arms around me turned stiff before falling away. I collapsed to the ground, my body no longer wanting to work. I swore I could see soldiers made of dirt approach, swinging their swords at the others who swarmed out of the second stormchariot. That was all before I saw Brodie launch himself at the soldier in charge. He'd appeared out of nowhere and separated his head from his neck in one smooth slice.

Strong arms hauled me up from the ground, my head lolling to the side. A large, warm chest beat erratically under my ear as they held me.

"Storm..." His voice sounded calm, but his heart rate gave him away. "I've got you."

I blinked, trying to focus enough to see who was holding me, but it didn't matter, I knew it was Brodie. "They've fucking shot you?" His voice rose, and I felt a sharp sting in my leg as he pulled the dart out. I heard raised voices all around, but I couldn't for the life of me understand what they were saying. My eyes drifted shut, everything feeling so heavy.

"Open your goddamned eyes, Storm!" Brodie barked, and I forced them open, trying to get myself to meet his gaze. "Your eyes...what have they done to you?" His voice was low, dangerous as he brought his face closer to mine. "Fuck, they've drugged you."

I felt like we were swaying as shapes blurred past me.

I heard more yelling and orders being barked. I heard a dragon roaring into the sky, shadows passing over me.

"We're taking you back to the academy, so keep your eyes on me, dammit." I tried hard to keep them open, but I felt so tired. My mind was a fuzzy mess, begging me to rest. Before I knew it, I felt wind whipping at my hair, loud wings beating, making my head hurt.

"V...vex," I whispered, feeling his loss like a wound.

"He's right here, flying us back as we speak." Brodie's voice rumbled from behind me. He was holding me in the saddle, just like he did the night he rescued me from the viscount's palace.

Within what seemed like minutes, I was being carried again. Raised voices echoed around me, and I was placed on a bed. People began shining lights in my eyes, prodding and poking me. I groaned, wishing they would leave me alone.

"She's been poisoned by Runestone Salt. I'm guessing they loaded their dart gun with it, hoping it was enough to nullify her magic." An unfamiliar voice spoke, his hands were gentle as he pried my eyes open. "Shit. It's at a toxic level. We'll have to try to siphon it from her system before it does any more damage."

"What do you mean, more damage? Will she be alright?"

"She should make a full recovery."

"Should, or will?" Brodie's voice was so full of anger that I would have flinched if it were aimed at me.

"I'm doing all I can, Prince McTavish. Why don't you go and clean up? I'll let you know when she wakes."

I couldn't hear his reply as a loud beeping filled my head, making me groan. There was a sharp pinch in my arm that faded quickly as my eyes finally closed, and sweet, painless blackness swept in.

⁂

"How did they get so close to the academy? Aren't there guards posted at the towers?" A stern voice woke me from my sleep. He sounded slightly familiar, but I couldn't place it as I rolled over. A mumbled reply I couldn't catch.

I felt *so* tired. Why the hell was I awake?

`Glad to see you're finally in the land of the living.`

Glad to have you back in my head.

`Don't ever do something like that again!`

I didn't do it on purpose!

"Nymeria." The voice sounded again, and I groaned as they stopped by my bed. The last thing I wanted was my dragon to be yelling at me and someone asking questions.

"Let me sleep," I grumbled, refusing to open my eyes. The voice chuckled, but the sound of a chair being dragged over the floor was loud in the quiet room.

"I need to ask you what happened." He sounded closer now, and I knew that they weren't going to leave until I answered their questions. I cracked open my eyes to find Mitch sitting beside me, looking a little worried.

"Hey," he smiled, looking me over. "Sorry to wake you, but I need you to tell me what happened out there. The princes aren't saying anything."

I groaned as I shut my eyes briefly, scrubbing my face with both hands, but it tugged on the tubes on my arms.

"*Fiinnne.*" I dragged the word out as I attempted to sit up, but my arms shook.

"Here, let me help." Mitch grabbed me under the arms and hauled me up, plumping my pillow before letting me lie back.

"Thanks." I breathed. I felt so exhausted, and the last thing I wanted was to talk about it. But I knew he wouldn't leave until I did. "I wanted to walk through the trees to clear my head. I'd been training pretty hard." I turned my head to face Mitch. He nodded in understanding. "Vex shouted in my head that something was wrong, and to get back, but it was no use. Soldiers swarmed out of the trees and came right for me."

Mitch's eyes got darker and darker the more I spoke. I swallowed, my mouth suddenly feeling dry. He held out a glass of water and patiently waited for me to continue.

"They shot gas into the air and embedded a dart into my leg, drugging me. They attempted to put me in one of their stormchariot's, but the others came for me before they could." I lay back on my pillow, exhaustion nipping at my mind, blurring the room around me.

"Thank you, Nymeria. You can rest now." Mitch stood and walked away, but I swore that his voice had darkened.

I wasted no time in shutting my eyes, letting my body get the rest it desperately needed.

"You look like shit."

I chuckled, then winced. "Don't make me laugh. It hurts."

I peeled my eyes open and glared at the grumpy prince. He was leaning against the wall, arms crossed over his chest. He looked tired.

"How are you feeling?" He asked, eyes raking over me, at the tubes stuck in my arms.

"How I look. Like shit." I replied dryly, glad that my vision had stopped swimming.

"How the hell did they catch you?" He pushed off from the wall, standing at the side of my bed with a dark look.

If he has a problem, then he can come and see me. Vex growled.

"They ambushed me. I'm guessing you can figure out the rest." I coughed, my chest burning. He cursed under his breath, running a hand through his wavy hair.

Gods, my throat is dry.

I attempted to reach for the glass beside my bed, but Brodie handed it to me, his eyes never leaving mine.

"Those fucking assholes," he sighed, shutting his eyes and pinching the bridge of his nose. "If anyone asks, tell them it's none of their damn business."

I could only nod my head, feeling suddenly dizzy. Something warm trickled down over my lips, and Brodie's face darkened. He ripped a tissue from the box on the bedside table and handed it to me.

"The doctor said you'll get nosebleeds while your body heals. And to use no magic if you can help it for at least two weeks."

"Two weeks?" I gasped, hunching over as my stomach cramped.

"Storm?" Concern laced his tone as I struggled to get my breathing in order.

"Just...just a cramp or something." I breathed, putting the tissue back to my nose as I felt it begin to bleed again. "When can I get out of here and see Vex?" I muttered, shutting my eyes again as my stomach roiled.

"When you won't pass out from the altitude. So hopefully another day or two."

I groaned, annoyed that I'd be stuck there, missing out on training. I opened my tired eyes and rubbed them, hoping to clear the grit that felt lodged in them.

You are already far more advanced than the others in your year. A few days' rest won't kill you.

"I need to sort some things out. Don't go wandering. Stay in bed and rest." Brodie fixed a hard glare at me before leaving my room.

I rolled over and shut my eyes, glad that no more people were in here annoying me with their questions.

CHAPTER TWENTY-THREE

Lia and Eli had both visited, and they brought me books, snacks, and drinks.

They were the only people keeping me from going crazy.

By lunchtime the next day, I was sick of lying in bed, reading. I needed to get out and stretch my legs. Brodie hadn't been back to visit, so I thought that I could get out for some fresh air.

I avoided the mirror, knowing I would see a mess of tangled silver hair and dark circles under dull grey eyes. I shoved my shoes on, tied my hair back, and hurried out the door.

I was halfway to the dining room when Mitch stalked around the corner.

Shit. Too late for me to hide.

"Should you be up and about? You look dreadfully pale." He moved to my side and put a hand on my arm.

"I feel fine. And I needed to get out and stretch my legs." I tried to smile reassuringly at him, but he only frowned at me.

"Then at least let me walk with you." He stepped closer to me, his hand still on my arm.

"If she said she's fine, then she is, O'Connell."

Brodie stepped up beside me, no doubt doing what he does best, glowering and looking grumpy. I went to sigh, but I felt a warm trickle over my top lip. Cursing, I reached for the tissue that I'd shoved into my pocket.

"Ria, you really shouldn't be up and about." Mitch stepped a little closer.

"It's just a blood nose, Mitch. I'll be fine." I tried to smile with the tissue to my nose, but his worried expression didn't change. He turned cold eyes to the prince beside me.

"I thought you were training with her up the mountain, McTavish?" His tone dripped with distaste.

"I am." Brodie snapped. "How about you do your fucking job and keep assholes like that out of the forests."

Mitch let go and stepped into Brodie's face, both men staring each other down.

"Why don't you go back to your daddy, he's always got something important for you to do. Your talents are wasted here." Mitch growled, his hands balled into fists at his side.

Brodie's chest expanded, and his eyes turned black as he went to open his mouth.

I'd had enough of this shit.

"I'm going to have some lunch," I walked away, refusing to look back. "Mitch, McTavish." I dismissed them. I didn't care if I sounded annoyed, I *was* annoyed at their constant pissing contests.

"Take care of yourself, Nymeria," Mitch called and I smirked.

"You too, Mitch," I replied as I rounded the corner.

"I see she uses my first name, and not yours. Interesting." I could hear the smile in Mitch's voice, and I would almost bet he looked a little smug.

"Fuck off, O'Connell." Brodie barked, his boot steps getting louder behind me. He caught up to me in the hall. I ignored him, keeping my chin high as I tried to think of anything else. I didn't want to speak to either of them.

"Storm," he began, but I didn't stop. "Can you stop for a second?" He grabbed onto my arm to halt me

I ripped my arm away. "Look, you need to stay away from-"

"Mitch. I know." I folded my arms over my chest, waiting for another excuse.

"Then why the hell is he talking to you in the hall?" He barked, but backed off when I raised my eyebrows.

"One, don't you speak to me like that. And two, give me a good reason not to?" I glared at him, my anger rising swift as a wave. "He asked me about the attack because it's his job. That's it." I folded my arms across my chest, trying to calm myself.

"You two were sitting next to each other at dinner the other night!" He snapped, and all I could do was shake my head.

"You're unreal, you know that?" I bit out between gritted teeth. If I stayed there much longer, I would do something I regretted, like zap him or punch him.

My skin prickled as I forced my legs to move. He didn't follow, and for that I was thankful.

By the stars, that man is an asshole.

`You don't see it, do you?` Vex chuckled, clearly enjoying my frustration.

And you do? What is it?

If you don't know, then I'm not telling you.

Ugh, you're so frustrating, both of you.

The whole week was worse than I imagined. I couldn't use my magic, because every time I did, I would get stomach cramps and a nosebleed. Pretty sure Brodie's face had set into a permanent scowl by now.

Theon had asked a hundred questions about where I was, why wasn't I in class, and what was wrong as I looked pale. Honestly, he was becoming more like Kai every day.

Which just made me miss him even more.

Anyone who touched me got zapped, and I'd lost count of how many light bulbs I'd blown. By the second week, I was an irritated mess.

The next Friday night, I couldn't take it anymore. I stormed outside, deep into the forest and screamed into the sky. Birds squawked and took flight, but I felt a little lighter. I created a wide electric shield around me and summoned flames to my hand. I'd had to pretend I couldn't do it all last week, so I didn't set my body off into crash and burn mode. But I needed to release it, release *anything*.

Gorgeous black flames danced to life in my palm, the tips a shimmering silver. I heaved a sigh of relief, my mind feeling much better already. My breathing became easier, and my chest loosened.

Having a little magical meltdown, are we?

Yes. And it feels good.

Excellent, get it out of your system and teleport to the flight field.

Yes boss.

I did as I was told and made the mental jump. I made sure to keep to the tree line, keeping me hidden just in case. It looked like the princes were leaving. Lia looked devastated, pretending not to cry. I quickly walked their way, all heads snapping in my direction.

"Ah, there you are," Eli called, tucking Lia into a quick hug. "Just wanted to say goodbye. I'm sure we'll be back once father no longer needs us."

Oh.

"Sure," I was glad that Brodie was leaving. I hadn't spoken to him since the day in the halls. I didn't bother looking towards P1, who was checking his pack for something. "Fly strong, land safe."

Eli's eyes shuttered slightly, flicking between his brother and me.

"I'm sorry about everything." He whispered as he pulled me into a hug. I hated how my throat tightened, the tears pricking my eyes.

"Don't be afraid to reach out. Keep in touch." He stepped back and hugged Lia one last time.

"Thanks, have a safe trip." I forced a smile to my stiff face, but it threatened to wobble.

What is wrong with me?

Brodie came our way, gave Lia a one-armed hug, but hesitated when he looked at me. My heart raced as our eyes locked.

"Make sure you practise your teleporting," he sucked in a long breath, and I knew he was about to tell me to stay away from Mitch. I crossed my arms as I waited for it. "Keep out of trouble." He turned and left, running up Drathruin's leg. Eli waved before doing the same.

Annoyance simmered under my skin. What was it about that man that brought all my emotions out of me?

We stood there on the field, watching them fly off into the sunset until it started to get too cold. An uneasy feeling settled into my stomach, something oily and unnatural.

Things were improving now that I could wield again, but then came the discussion of whether we should tell the other professors that I could teleport. Professor Korin decided that everyone would know that I would manifest something powerful and that it would be expected. But we'd keep my Voltrite powers secret. I wasn't sure if Brodie would agree with that or not, but he wasn't my keeper.

I was sitting with Lia in a bay window in the academy's social room. It was a large room with pool tables, table tennis, bean bags, a lovely open wood fire and bookcases. All sorts of things we could do in our free time. I hadn't explored the whole room, but I was content here in the window. I'd had five '*Hey, Nymeria's*' tonight, and it was enough to drive me to go and hide in the library.

Lia had been a bit down since Eli had left, but I knew they talked on their whisp's every night. At least her room had reception. My room seemed to be a dead zone, the reception kicking in down the hall.

But at least we had it. I'd heard that Duskmire Academy, the other dragon-riding academy in Faritia, had nothing. It was only riders there, and too much magic in the air cut them off completely.

Poor souls.

Mitch walked into the room, and I slid down into my seat a little lower. Don't get me wrong, Mitch seemed like a nice guy but I didn't need another reason for P1 to yell at me.

"I heard you and Brodie had a heated...discussion the other day?" Lia's lips looked pinched as I met her gaze. I didn't want to talk about it, but she'd obviously heard about it from someone. "He told Eli and wanted to give you some space."

"I would have thought that a thirty-year-old man would have been better at keeping his emotions in check," I muttered under my breath. "Do you think Korin would let me train by myself, or do I have to have someone with me?"

I knew Lia would pick up on my annoyance and happily changed the subject with me.

"Why don't you ask him tomorrow? I'm sure he'll be fine with it." She ran her hands through her hair, a nervous gesture I was starting to think. "I know things are a little..." She didn't get a chance to finish as Mitch walked our way. Lia sighed quietly and crossed her arms. Mitch nodded to her in greeting before turning back to me.

"Nymeria, how are you feeling?" he kept his voice down, and for that I was thankful. I felt Theon's gaze from across the room. He raised a brow in question. He was like my big brother, keeping an eye out for me. I knew he and Kai would have gotten along. I gave him a small smile and turned back to Mitch.

"I'm fine now, thank you." He'd pulled a seat next to mine, leaning his arms on his knees.

"I just want you to know that it won't happen again, and I'm sorry it happened at all." His brown eyes were sincere as they locked onto me. "What's more concerning is that they had stormchariots. They're for the military only." His brows pulled together, worry bracketing his mouth. He sat back up, stretching his arms over his head. "I'll leave you to enjoy your night." He stood and left the room, some eyes tracking him. But it was all riders in there, the boots and jaws didn't mix unless they had to.

They had another room similar to ours down the hall.

But his words stuck in my head. Did that mean that the military had something to do with the attack? Were they working with the viscount?

I didn't want to stay there any longer, I wasn't in the mood to pretend to be polite. I waved to Lia on my way out, barely paying any attention to who I passed in the hall.

I wish Kai were here. I wanted to talk to him, tell him my worries and fears. I wanted him to tell me that everything was going to be alright. Eli told me that they still had no luck in tracking him down, but they wouldn't give up.

Some days, I just wanted to fly out of here and find him myself.

"Ria?" Korin broke my train of thought as he came my way. "Everything alright?" He stopped at my side, eyebrows pinched as I mashed my lips together, at everything that happened in the past few months caught up to me. A sob burst through as tears fell down my cheeks. Korin sighed as he pulled me in for a hug.

"Come on, let's get you somewhere more comfortable." I sniffled as he led the way to his office. He made quick work of lighting the fire and told me to sit. I dropped my head into my hands as I cried, and cried. A warm mug of tea was pushed into my hands when I lifted my head. "Here, this might help you level out a little." I blew on the tea before taking a sip. I gasped, tears welling again as I shut my eyes.

"My dear, whatever is the matter?" Korin sat in a chair beside me, patiently waiting for me to gather myself.

"I'm sorry." I hiccuped, wiping my eyes.

"Never apologise for your tears." Even his kind words and soft tone were almost enough to set me off again.

"My mother used to make me this tea when it was storming," I said thickly, taking another sip. It tasted like home. But home wasn't there anymore. Neither were my parents.

I would have thought that over three years, the pain would start to lessen. Some days, like today, felt as fresh and raw as they did that first day.

"Ah, I see," Korin murmured before getting to his feet. He rummaged in his desk for a moment before returning. "Here, a little chocolate always helps me feel better." He broke off a row of dark chocolate and handed it to me. I thanked him as I took it, taking a bite. It was heaven on my tongue. It had been ages since I'd had any. "Now, tell me what's going on?" He sat back in his chair, sipping his tea.

"I think everything has finally caught up to me. I hadn't allowed myself to fully process it, I think."

Korin leaned back and let me think, not pushing for answers. Simply listening. "I miss my brother terribly. I have people telling me what to do, then getting pissed off for things out of my control."

I didn't mean to let that one slip. My anger over Brodie's attitude still made me upset.

"You've been through so much, and you're only twenty-three."

"Twenty-four." I interrupted. Today was my birthday, and I deliberately didn't want anyone to know. I didn't want any more attention.

Korin's eyes softened as he leaned towards me. "You didn't want a fuss, did you?"

"No. I've caused enough trouble the past few years. I'm the reason my parents are dead." I stared into the fire, it was something I couldn't get out of my head.

Korin was silent for a moment before I heard his chair scrape on the floor. He took my tea from me, placed it on his desk and took both of my hands in his.

"Now, you listen to me, Nymeria Everhart," he kneeled before me, his silhouette fuzzy as the fire behind him blazed.

My eyes shot to his, and the intensity in his tawny-gold eyes trapped me. "It's not your fault, never was, and never will be." I'd opened my mouth to object, but he shushed me. "The one you should blame is the viscount. He was the one who signed their death warrant the day he sent the rogue riders."

I gritted my teeth, "but they wouldn't have been there at all if it wasn't for me."

"You can't change the past, Nymeria." I looked away, but he gripped my hands. "I will help you get your revenge and help you find Kai. I promise."

I could only nod my head. All words had left me as gratitude filled me.

"Now, off to bed. I think you could do with the rest. But finish your tea first."

I did as I was told, thanking the kindly professor on my way out.

Chapter
Twenty-Four

Professor Korin decided that today was the day to show off my teleportation.

My stomach felt like a writhing pit of snakes.

Our class were sparring, and I was about to go head-to-head with a giant of a man from Ruleum. It was all first years in the gym, rather than just our houses as we'd had recently.

"You got him easy, Ria. He's big, but you're fast." Theon was cracking his knuckles beside me, watching the others move with narrowed eyes. "You can wear him out if you have to. But you're light on your feet."

We were watching the current match of a rough Furora and Galadron go head-to-head. It was supposed to be a fight to the first blood, but these two seemed to be taking this to the death. Professor Korin and Potteira were watching with drawn brows, about ready to step in before someone broke something. I didn't want to watch.

I'd seen enough violence and death to last me a lifetime.

"Alright, that's enough! Both of you off," Potteira barked, stepping onto the mat and pulling the two men away from each other. "Everhart and Simpson, you're up."

I took a deep breath and stepped onto the mat. Korin caught my eye and winked.

"You got this," Theon murmured from beside me. "Pinch under his upper arm. He squeals like a pig." He kept his voice low. I felt a smile tug at my lips.

"Thanks," I rolled my neck and stretched my legs as Jason Simpson lumbered onto the mat. He was at least a head taller than me, with thick arms and legs, and was covered in hair like a bear. Even his dark blue eyes seemed to be almost black. I felt a sliver of nerves skate over my skin as his gaze locked on mine.

"Okay, no weapons." Korin nodded my way as we crouched, circling each other. "Begin."

Simpson ran at me, his steps so heavy on the ground that I could feel the vibrations. He swung for my head, but I ducked and rolled, kicking him in the ass. A few people laughed.

I knew that I couldn't dart around him for too long. So I switched it up and started my offence. Quick jabs and kicks that made him stumble, but he still looked unaffected as he smirked at me.

Damn it.

"She can't take him. How embarrassing," A girl from Galadron drawled, laughing. I made sure I paid her no attention.

Stop dancing around and show them how powerful you are.

Alright, alright.

I took a deep breath and let him run at me. I stood up straight and gave him a wide smile. He was so close that I could almost feel his fist on my jaw. That was when I made the step. I landed right behind him, my foot kicking him in the ass again as he stumbled and fell flat on his face. The room was quiet, but I couldn't stop the smile from blooming on my face.

"What the hell just happened?"

"Did you see that?"

"How did she get behind him so quickly?"

Muttering broke out in the room, and I heard Theon whistle behind me.

Simpson got up with a grunt and came at me again, only for me to do the same, but this time I ended up beside him and smashed my fist into his ribs. I continued to do this over and over, until he was a sweaty, bloody mess. He tried to use his powers against me, the water shaped into a shield, a spear, but they were classified as weapons and one more warning, he'd be disqualified. He attempted to swirl a bubble of water around my head, but I'd simply teleport away.

"Stop. Fucking. *Moving,*" he wheezed. My breath was burning in my lungs, and my stomach threatened to cramp, but I'd nearly gotten him. I just hoped I didn't get a bloody nose.

"Come get me, then." I winked, and he growled at me. This time, I went to him and landed right in his face. My fist whipped out and crashed into his stomach so hard that he was lifted off the ground and flew backwards. The floor shook as he landed, knocking the little wind out of his lungs. I was on him in an instant, my arm at this throat as he struggled to breathe.

"Cadet Everhart wins." Professor Korin clapped, but the room was silent a moment before my house erupted into cheers.

"She can teleport."

"Teleportation."

"No fucking way."

I turned to the girl from Galadron with a disgusted look on her face. I walked up to her and gave her a small smile. Her friends stepped back slightly.

"Good enough for you, Kortney?" I asked sweetly. She had always been a bitch, for reasons I would never know.

"Fuck off, loner." She turned off her whisperglass and stalked away.

"You can teleport?" Theon was stunned, eyes wide as she shook his head. "That's some serious shit."

"I didn't know I could do it until the fight began, I just...felt it." I shrugged, feeling a little bad for lying. I looked over to Professor Korin, who gave me a small smile, but his whisperglass trilled, he grimaced as he looked at the caller.

I gladly took the bottle of water Theon handed me, downing half in one go. It settled my stomach enough to ease the pain I had. Korin looked like he was having a difficult conversation, putting away his whisp away with a wince. He walked toward me, but my whisperglass rang from my bag. Korin hurried over and excused us from my friends.

"If I were you, I wouldn't answer your whisp." He looked apologetic as he ran a hand through his hair. "It seems that someone filmed your fight and live-streamed it to RoarBoard and Emberloop. So naturally, the whole of Ardentis now knows you can teleport."

Oh, shit.

I would almost bet that it was Brodie calling to yell at me for showing them my powers. And it seemed like Professor Korin also took an ear-beating.

"But that was a fantastic fight. Well done." He patted me on the shoulder and walked out as class finished.

I checked my whisperglass that night and winced. I had four missed calls and seven pulses.

Shit. Brodie is pissed.

I headed outside, where I could get reception and called him. He answered on the first ring.

'What the hell were you guys thinking?'

I closed my eyes and leaned against a tree.

"Professor Korin thought it was best that I tell them, as everyone is expecting me to have some great power. We tried to come up with something else I could use instead, but it either involved my Voltrite powers, which we don't want anyone knowing. So we had to."

'It's all over the fucking aetherweb!'

"How was I meant to know someone would film me? What's done is done, get over it." I snapped. I could hear him take a deep breath and blow it out again. I rolled my eyes at how dramatic he was being. "Look, if I had known she would film me, I wouldn't have done it. But let's focus on the things we can control."

'*Well, that certainly isn't you, is it?*'

"Fuck off, McTavish."

I hung up, seething that he thought this was *my* fault.

Fucking grumpy asshole.

I shot some electricity into the air, making sure I keep it contained to my shield. It sparked blue, silver, and purple as it cracked and hissed around me. I let it out until I felt calmer.

I crashed into bed, not bothering with being quiet. I didn't care what she thought.

It was somewhat freeing to know that everyone was aware of my powers now. I don't have to practice in secret, and some of the other riders respect me now, instead of fearing me. Still, I was struggling to make friends. Sure, I had Lia and Theon. But I still felt like the odd one out.

Vex insisted on being first in flying formation and wouldn't let other dragons get close or take charge. I began to feel the others resenting me for it. Lia tried to spend as much time with me as she could, but I wasn't her only friend here, let alone those in her house.

I entered the cafeteria, the noise buzzing for a Friday night. I saw Ava standing with her friends over by the windows, and I used the opportunity to annoy her.

"Ava!" I called. She had her back to me, but I knew she'd heard me by the slight rising of her shoulders. "Ava, have a good night with your friends!" I called again, and all her friends turned my way with narrowed eyes, their noses scrunched up like they smelled something foul. She finally turned around and gave me the best stink eye I'd ever seen. It only made me smile wider as I waved and made my way to the line to get my dinner.

It was petty, but it made me feel a little better.

After dinner, I needed to get out into the fresh air. Twilight had just fallen.

It was my favourite time of night.

Vex and I were simply soaring through the sky as it began to darken as we flew over the forest. Suddenly, I felt him stiffen beneath me.

What's the matter?

`There is something wrong. Down below, something doesn't feel right.`

I want you to teleport into that clearing and tell me what you see.

I leaned over the side of his body as he banked and spotted the small clearing in the trees.

I'll continue to circle overhead.

We'd been practising this, making sure I landed standing, not sitting, as I had the first few times. I shut my eyes briefly and made the jump. Stumbling slightly, I looked around the dark forest, squinting as I tried to see what Vex was sensing.

Move under the cover of the trees on your left.

I summoned flames to my palm, helping me see as night fell. I felt a prickle on the back of my neck.

I can feel something's off, too.

I think someone has done something terrible. Keep your eyes peeled. I'll continue to circle so I can see if anyone comes.

It made me feel better that he was keeping an eye out as I searched. My eyes landed on a mound of freshly dug dirt under a tree. I could smell the damp earth as I slowly approached, the mound at least three feet wide and eight feet long. I swallowed my unease.

Oh, gods. Do you think someone is buried in there?

Use your Voltrite powers to probe the earth. You should be able to sense their bioelectricity.

I set my flames into a ball and hovered it over the earth. I swallowed and wiped my sweaty palms on my pants. I stretched my shaky hands and slowly extended my electricity down into the dirt. I closed my eyes as I focused. There was *something* down there, but whatever it was, it was no longer alive.

I hastily pulled out my whisp and rang Lia. She answered on the third ring.

'*Hey Ria, what's up?*'

"Lia, I think I found a body," I whispered, stepping slowly away from the mound.

'*What the hell makes you think that?*' She was equally quiet, a door shutting in the background as she moved away from people.

"Vex sensed something off in the forest, so I landed and went to have a look. And there is a large mound of freshly dug earth the size of a grave."

'*And you know there's someone in there?*'

"I used my electricity to delve down there, and it's about six feet deep, and something large inside."

'*Shit. Where are you?*'

"I don't know, I'll ask Vex to send out our location to Cyndrithra. Perhaps bring Korin?"

'*On it, see you soon.*'

I didn't want to wait down here by myself, so I moved back to the small clearing, glad to see that Vex was still circling above me. It didn't take the others long to find me, perhaps ten minutes or so.

They set floating globes of fire above them as they landed, faces grim as they followed me into the trees. I heard Lia suck in a breath as we approached. Korin cursed, kneeling beside the pile of dirt, resting a hand on it.

"I can feel something in there. I'm going to see if I can bring it up. Step back, girls." He stood and hovered his arms over the earth as Lia and I stepped back. The ground began to shake, tiny piles of dirt tumbled away as it seemed to open before us. Korin cursed, shaking his head in horror. Lia and I stepped forward and looked down into the pit.

There was the body of Jason Simpson, the Ruleum cadet I fought only the other day.

Chapter
Twenty-Five

K orin sent Lia and I back to the academy and told us to keep this to ourselves.

Someone had murdered Jason and buried him deep in the forest. The question was: who?

Vex didn't want me to walk the halls alone, or if I did, to have at least five weapons on me at all times. I didn't mind, to be honest, because if my magic were to be blocked or depleted, I'd still be able to defend myself.

I was training extra hard to wield electricity at will and to keep my shield ready.

I began to get nosebleeds again.

Korin made up a tincture to help with the cramps, but he said only time could heal me fully.

It didn't take long for the news about the murder to get out.

The school didn't feel the same anymore.

A week later, P1 and Eli returned to the academy. Their reappearance caused quite a stir, as with them came Levi. It seemed that the professors were also a little on edge. It wasn't until that day, when the princes arrived, that another corpse was found, this time a body had washed up downriver.

It was Kortney, the bitch who filmed my fight.

It was probably horrible of me to think, but I wasn't too upset about that one.

I was sitting at my table with my wingmate's when the room hushed, and my skin tingled. I knew exactly who'd just walked into the room. It didn't take long for the girls to start calling out for the princes to come and sit at their tables. I hunched down into my seat, hoping Brodie wouldn't come my way. He hadn't spoken to me since I'd told him to fuck off.

With any luck, they had to sit over at the professor's table, or far away from me would work, too.

Two murders in such a short amount of time were unfathomable.

Cadets moved about in groups, jumping at sounds and magic flaring often. Professors were snappy, seen more often in halls, not to mention the guards.

Lia would check in with me every night before bed, our new curfew was now at dark.

"How are you coping with everything?" We walked together from the cafeteria before we would part ways at the stairs.

"Alright…" I said as a group of first-years hurried past. "I'm feeling a little caged in with all the new restrictions."

We nodded a greeting to a guard standing watch on the corner of the hall.

"Understandable," Lia agreed, playing with her ponytail. "Training is okay?" The principals passed, only Shields acknowledged us, which was no surprise.

"Yeah, it's fine. I'm making good progress. Korin seems happy, so that's good enough for me."

Mitch and Levi walked in from the courtyard, heads bent together, talking. They both looked up and smiled, slowing as if they were going to stop and chat, but Lia grabbed my arm and towed me onwards.

"If you need anything, let me know, alright?" She turned to me, still holding my arm.

"Thank you, you too." We hugged before parting ways. My feet were dragging as I wasn't ready to go back to my room just yet, especially when Ava would simply ignore me the whole time.

⸎

I'd managed to keep my distance from P1, but I was happy to see Eli, of course.

Every guard I passed in the halls, the ones stationed in the back of our classes, I could see the worry around their mouths, the bags under their eyes.

I lined up in the cafeteria, flipping a tray in my hand, when Ryler turned around and leaned against the counter.

"Hey, Ria. How are things?"

I looked up and smiled. At least he seemed to be normal. He had a plain black shirt with the sleeves rolled up, and matching black jeans.

"Good, well, as can be expected with what's happening. You?"

"Yeah, about the same, considering. So, teleporting, huh, that's epic." He smiled widely, his wheat-gold eyes sparkling as he ran a hand through his dark hair.

"Yeah, it was a bit of a shock when I figured it out."

"I bet. Your fight was amazing, by the way." He chuckled. "I see that they've sent some helpers. Do you think the professors are worried it might happen again?" He looked over his shoulder a moment before locking his gaze on me. "But having the apex squad here should scare them off."

"Apex squad?" I frowned in confusion as we continued to shuffle along the line.

"Yeah, the princes, O'Connell and Brown. They were the best in their year, so, naturally, they're the apex squad. I hope to be a part of the apex squad next year."

"They don't really seem to like each other. Did something happen?" I pried, hoping to get *anything*.

"Not my place to tell, sorry, Ria." Ryler went to leave, but I reached out and placed my hand on his arm, halting him. His eyes lifted from my hand to my eyes, softening.

"Please, Ryler? No one will tell me. Was it really that bad?"

"Ria." Another voice interrupted us, and Mitch made his way over. I dropped my hand from Ryler's arm as he winked at me and left the line.

"How are you? It's good to see you looking better." I smiled at his genuine concern.

"I'm much better, thanks," I smiled, looking him over with appreciation.

Had he filled out?

"Didn't realise you and Ryler Daniels were friends." His face darkened slightly, clenching his jaw.

"He's one of the only ones who doesn't fawn over me, hit on me, or give me moon eyes if I talk to him." I sighed.

Mitch nodded as he watched Ryler walk away, chewing on his bottom lip. He faced me again, looking a little tired. "How are you coping with these murders?" He shoved his hands into his pockets, eyes darting around the room constantly.

"It's horrific, but I'm coping as well as anyone else, I guess." We shuffled along the line, and Brodie's words came back to me. I felt annoyance at his bossiness, so I chose to ignore his orders. Prince or not, he wasn't my keeper, and I could talk to whoever I wanted. "How about you?" I looked up at Mitch, his eyes swinging down to meet my gaze. Our eyes locked for a moment before someone cleared their throat behind us. I hastily looked away and kept moving.

"It's concerning, that's for sure. Especially with what happened not long ago, as well." He murmured, keeping the conversation between us. He sighed, rubbing a hand over his face. "I can feel a dagger being lodged between my shoulder blades if I stand here much longer. I'll see you around." He touched my arm briefly before walking away.

--❧✦❧--

It'd been four days since the arrival of the Apex Squad, and I'd managed to avoid Brodie, much to my surprise. But I thought he might have been avoiding me, too.

We'd been given new rules: people weren't allowed outside alone, and not past nine at night, and were to travel with someone else at all times. The two bodies had been riders, and of course, we were suspicious of the infantry. They didn't want to share rooms with us anymore. I would love to have someone else in my room - much better than the sour-faced bitch Ava, who ignored me. The Principals shut down any talk of letting us switch roommates, claiming that we needed to drop our differences and learn to work together.

Fat chance of that.

Now, when I went out to fly Vex, I had to have someone else with me. Meaning that I couldn't practice my Voltrite powers anywhere. I could feel it crackling under my skin, the light bulbs began to blow again, and I tried my hardest not to touch anyone. Also, it didn't help that my hair was a frazzled mess with the electricity floating around me.

--❧✦❧--

We were allowed to run in the morning or evening, but the new rules were that we had to take our roommates with us. I didn't care that Ava hated me. I made her get her ass out of bed in the morning.

We didn't speak, and she always had to be in the lead. I didn't care, I just needed to get out and move.

"Hey, Ava," I called, already grinning, as I knew she'd ignore me. For the past two weeks, she'd never answered me.

"*What?*" She snapped, and I almost fell over in my surprise.

"What do you think about these murders?" I panted, keeping back far enough that I couldn't hear her breathing.

She was silent for a while, and I gave up any hope of her reply.

"Someone either with a grudge or obsessed." She grumbled, and I wasn't sure if I'd heard her correctly, but her words struck something in me.

It made sense, and we needed to figure out how the people were connected.

A loud roar sounded behind us. I stopped and grabbed two blades from my thigh sheath as I saw something that I'd only heard about.

A stormsteed sped around the corner and stopped beside me. I glanced at Ava, who'd simply kept running.

I shouldn't have been surprised that she'd left me for dead.

I turned back to the rider, the man pulled his helmet off, and Mitch greeted me with a cheeky grin

"What are you doing out here by yourself, Ria?" He lifted his leg over the side and sat sideways on his stormsteed. It was a gorgeous-looking machine, all black and red curves.

"I was with Ava, but she kept running. Guess I know where I sit on her list." I put my hands on the back of my head as I tried to calm my breathing. I'd pushed myself too hard that morning, it seemed. His eyes raked over me, his brown eyes dark and unreadable.

"Can I give you a lift back?" He smirked, and I huffed a laugh, shaking my head. "It was worth a try. Even if it's only a few hundred meters away." He looked down at his hands before placing his helmet on the seat and came towards me. He was just as tall as the twins, but more Eli's build than Brodie's.

"You're an incredible woman, Ria. I would very much like to get to know you." His voice was quiet, but I could feel the warmth of him as he waited for an answer. I blushed at his compliment, his heated gaze. He was a good-looking man, and I didn't know what the problem between him and the twins was.

I couldn't help but smile shyly back.

Sure, I'd been with men before back home, but it had been a long time since anyone had shown any interest in me.

"I think I would like that too," I replied boldly. I know that Brodie told me to stay away from him, but he'd given me no reason to.

"I'm glad you haven't let their dislike for me taint you as well." He pulled out his whisperglass, and we switched, inputting our numbers before handing them back. His fingers grazed mine, and I contained my shiver. It had been so long since I had been with someone.

I desperately wanted to know why they all didn't like each other. It couldn't be such a simple thing as infantry and riders not liking each other, surely? I planned to ask Lia once we were away from the princes.

I stepped back and looked towards the academy and sighed.

"I should head back and get ready for class."

He nodded and shot me a crooked smile before putting his helmet back on. He threw a leg over his stormsteed and started the dangerous-looking machine.

"Just a heads up, Voralyth tests you in ways you wouldn't imagine. And I look forward to getting to know you." He kicked the bike into gear and rode off as I shook my head.

Was I playing with fire with Mitch?

I woke one Saturday morning, and I felt my fingertips sparking, crackling against my blankets. It was still dark out, but I knew a storm was on its way.

Damn it.

I slid out of bed and rummaged through the drawer in my bedside table, but all I found were empty bottles.

Shit, I'm all out. I need to see Professor Korin.

You're not allowed to leave without anyone.

I know that!

Don't get cranky at me, just because you're feeling a little…prickly.

Hah hah. So funny. And you're not helping. I can't message Lia, she's spending time with Eli, and I don't want to interrupt.

Then I'll send for P1.

Ugh, please don't! I'll find someone else.

Too late.

By the stars, my dragon really was an asshole sometimes.

I heard that.

It didn't take long for Brodie to bash on my door. My roommate grumbled and threw the blankets over her head.

"Bye, Ava, have a good day!" I called loudly, her only reply was her middle finger.

I poked my tongue out at her as I answered the door and slammed it loudly behind me.

I couldn't stop my traitorous eyes from going straight to the handsome prince. And, damn it, he'd not long ago showered and smelled freaking amazing.

"Shall we then?" He gestured for me to lead down the hall. I gritted my teeth and walked away without speaking. I was still pissed at what he'd said the other day. I rolled my neck as another shockwave ran through me.

"Your scars are showing." He said softly, keeping step beside me. I pulled the collar of my jacket up around my neck, but knew it would do nothing to hide the ones that showed on my jaw and left cheek.

"Would you like me to get you a scarf or something?"

Did he sound apologetic? I turned to look at him again as his eyes trailed over my face.

"Look. I'm sorry for being a dick the other day," he grumbled. I stopped and crossed my arms, waiting for him to go on. He rolled his eyes and ran a hand through his still-damp, wavy hair. "I freaked out, okay? I know you were just following orders from Korin." He ran his tongue over his teeth, seeming to want to say more. I raised my eyebrows. "I don't want you to be like everyone else. It's refreshing that you aren't afraid to call me out on my bullshit. So, thank you for being honest."

I was not *expecting that.*

I opened my mouth to reply, but I had nothing. My mind was blank. I shut it again and simply nodded. He offered me a small smile, and I huffed a laugh back.

"Come on, McTavish, let's get to Korin before someone sees you and faints from being in your presence."

"Oh, that's rude. And I think she was ill..." he grumbled, hurrying down the hall.

"Nuh uh, she fainted from standing next to you in the line cause you're the prince." I put the back of my hand on my forehead and pretend to swoon. "Oh, Prince, catch me." He cursed under his breath as I collapsed to the ground. He stormed away. I picked myself up off the floor and ran after him, cackling like a witch.

A distant rumble of thunder sounded, making me shiver. Damn it, this storm was a big one. I shuddered and gritted my teeth, my fingertips sparking.

"Come on, let's hurry." He went to reach for me, but I yanked my arm away.

"Don't. I'll hurt you." I backed away, shaking my head.

"You won't hurt me, Storm." He reached again and took my hand in his, lacing our fingers together. There was only a small zap, but nothing compared to what I expected. With a wink, he plunged us invisible.

I will never get used to this.

Or the feeling of my hand linked with his.

We hurried down the last few halls until we reached the professor's door. He called for us to enter, and we wasted no time in slipping through the door.

"Ah, Nymeria, I was wondering if I would be seeing you today. I've been keeping an eye on the weather and had planned on dropping some bottles off to you this morning. And good morning, Brodie, good to see you again."

The kindly professor handed me a bottle to take straight away, and five others to stash in my bag.

"Thank you, Korin. You're a lifesaver." I could almost feel the scars dimming, the constant buzz under my skin dropping to a more pleasant hum.

"Now, I know you're meant to head off Brodie for the night, why don't you take Nymeria?" Korin turned to P1, and my stomach flipped. "Both of you head to the castle and come back tomorrow evening? The storm is meant to stick around here until Sunday night, and the principals have planned for the cadets to...mingle." He grimaced like he had to be the one to supervise them all. "I'll tell the principal's that it's strictly for training purposes, and that the king requests your help. If you leave now, you'll miss flying in the storm." With a cheeky grin, he pushed both of us out the door and into the dark hall.

"Well, looks like for both of our sanity, or not, we're heading to Sylvanfire." Brodie heaved a heavy sigh and began to walk back to my room.

Just the two of us.

Would we survive the weekend, or tear each other's throats out?

CHAPTER
TWENTY-SIX

I'd never packed so fast in my life.

I practically ran into Brodie when I left my room, slamming my door shut again with extra gusto. He raised his brows in question, a smile tugging at his lips.

"Dare I ask?"

"She's a bitch."

"Fair enough. Let's get out of here before someone sees us." He reached out and took my hand again, turning us invisible. I told myself I hated it, how he just grabbed my hand, but I couldn't stop the shiver that passed through me. And it definitely wasn't from the oncoming storm.

We expertly avoided the guards walking the halls, keeping a sharp gaze on anyone who passed. But Levi was lingering before the entrance of the courtyard, causing us to slow to a stop.

Brodie went to turn around when Mitch appeared, making his way right for us. Brodie backed us up until our backs hit the wall, keeping as quiet as possible.

"Hey, Levi," Mitch called as he handed him a coffee. "Heard a storm is rolling in, and they want the cadets to mingle in the gym." Mitch shuddered like he thought it was a terrible idea. "Something about forcing them to work together." He sighed, rubbing the back of his neck.

"Sounds like a nightmare." Levi groaned, smothering his yawn with a hand.

"It's not something I'm looking forward to." Mitch sipped his coffee. But his uniform looked a little wrinkled, like he'd been up all night. "As soon as our cover arrives, we need to leave." Mitch turned to stare down the hall, past where Brodie and I stood against the wall, keeping our breathing quiet.

The double doors swung open behind them, and the two spun on their heels, reaching for their swords.

"Whoa, easy." A guard put her hands up, eyeing the two with wide eyes.

Another newbie. We'd been getting new guards every few days, it seemed.

"Oh, sorry. You're Mia, right?" Mitch stepped forward and offered her a hand. She reached out hesitantly and shook it, looking around in awe.

"Yeah. This place is *insane*." She breathed, but quickly pulled herself together. "It's my first day. Where do you need me?" She stood up straight, pulling her shoulders back.

"You've arrived at the perfect time. Levi can take you down to the gym to meet the others." Mitch's lips twitched, fighting a smile. Levi, on the other hand, drooped a little.

"Thanks, asshole." He mouthed before introducing himself to Mia, and walked away down the hall with her.

But the door was still ajar, and Brodie used that as our chance to get away. He must have used his magic to make a noise a few feet away, forcing Mitch to walk over and check it out.

Without any other obstacles, we were finally outside and rushing onto the field.

I swore that Vex was grinning at me as I approached him. I promptly ignored him and mounted, my shoulders hunched as the rumble of thunder came closer.

Come on, let's get out of here.
`Impatient, are we?`

I don't want to stay here and get caught in the storm.
`Yeah. Sure.`

I pulled my jacket closer and snapped my goggles on. The sunrise wasn't far off, and the morning chill was still heavy in the air. The flight was peaceful, and, for the first time in a while, I enjoyed being in the air and simply flying. No tricks, no formation or practice. The stunning sunrise bloomed over the horizon in beams of yellow, orange, and gold.

We landed out back of the castle, the morning mist still clinging to the damp grass.
`Make sure you don't get into any trouble.`

You keep implying that I actively seek it out.
`You're a magnet for trouble. Perhaps stay indoors?`

Are you still here?
He grumbled down the bond, making me laugh.
"Meet me in the dining room. Also, the room you stayed in hasn't been touched." Brodie didn't give me a chance to say anything more as he walked away, leaving me in the entrance of the workers' door.

"Alright then." I gritted my teeth, hoping that I remembered how to get to the room I used to sleep in before Voralyth started.

I made my way up the stairs, trying to keep out of people's way, glad to finally make it to my old room. I dumped my bag on the bed just as a crack of thunder rattled me, a flash of lightning only seconds away. Rain pelted down in sheets, and I was glad that we got there before it hit.

Not wanting to get into trouble, I did as I was told and headed for the dining room.

To my surprise, no one was there. The doors into the kitchen were propped open, and it was utterly silent.

"Storm?" Brodie called from the kitchen, and I made my way inside. The smell of bacon was thick in the air. "Want bacon and eggs?"

"Oh, absolutely. Thanks." I was shocked. A prince who knew how to cook? I was intrigued as I sat on the stool by the island, watching him. He seemed to know his way around the kitchen with no trouble. He made a coffee in his fancy machine and handed it to me without a word.

"Thanks," I murmured, taking a sip and sighing in pleasure. I tried not to admire the way he moved, the muscles in his arms, the confident way he flipped the bacon.

Why is this such a turn-on?

I forced myself to move. I grabbed my coffee and went to stand by the large windows that overlooked the trees. For a kitchen, it had lovely views.

The weather was raging outside, and for the first time in a long time, I felt content in the middle of a storm. It was a big place, the chance of running into someone I knew was slim.

"Breakfast." He called out before my thoughts could spiral much further. I turned to see him placing my plate on the table and sat down opposite me.

The maids and cooks must eat in here themselves, rather than out in the dining room.

It was cosy and warm. Almost homely.

"Who knew you could cook, eh?" I smiled, taking my seat as I looked at what he'd prepared. He'd even made an omelette, folded onto some sourdough with a side of bacon. It smelled amazing.

"I used to spend some time in here with Moranna when I wasn't stealing cookies."

I laughed, shaking my head as I struggled to picture Brodie cooking as a child. I took a bite, and I couldn't help but groan.

Holy shit. This is the most delicious omelette I've ever tasted.

He stared at me mid-bite, eyes wide as his cheeks began to pink. I cleared my throat and finished my mouthful.

"That's bloody good, prince. Nice work." I forced myself to look away and devoured the rest. We ate in comfortable silence, my stomach pleasantly full as I drained my coffee.

"I'm coming here for breakfast more often." I stretched my arms out behind my head.

"Don't get used to it," he muttered, but I could see that he was chuffed with my compliments.

"Where are Moranna and the others?"

"Father gave them the weekend off. Usually, when it's terrible weather, he lets them head home."

We heard boots in the dining room, coming into the kitchen. Brodie jumped to his feet, but in came a saturated-looking Lia and Eli, grinning from ear to ear.

"Oh, you're both here!" Lia smiled and brushed back her wet hair, removing her sodden jacket. "We were hoping to miss the weather. I'm glad you're both already in." Her eyes flicked to Brodie, then back to me, lingering on our plates. "Shame we missed Brodie's famous breakfast. It smells amazing."

"It was the best omelette I've ever had," I confessed, rubbing my stomach.

"Don't tell him that. His head won't fit through the door." Eli joked, shrugging out of his own sodden jacket.

"So, when did you guys get in?" She'd been fighting a smile since they arrived.

"Just before the storm hit. I had to go to Professor Korin for more of my antidote, and he told us to get away for the weekend. I wasn't going to say no, especially when the principals wanted everyone to mingle the whole time while stuck indoors." I wrinkled my nose and Lia shuddered, making me laugh. "Yeah, that was my reaction, too."

"I know Father wants a word, so we'll catch up with you two later." Eli winked our way and left Lia and me standing in the kitchen, the former still dripping wet.

"Why don't you go and get warm, and we can catch up later? I'll just read in my room." I offered her a smile, and she sagged with relief.

We headed off, parted at our doors, and for the first time in months, I felt like I could finally relax.

Only an hour later, we were summoned into the royal wing, but it wasn't what I expected.

It was homely, warm, and plush.

The princes were lounging on the couch, and Brodie had his cap on backwards again as the twins played a round of cards.

My stomach knotted. I hadn't played since the night I was taken.

"You girls want to play?" Eli called out as the door shut behind us. Lia agreed and skipped over, but I saw how the prince's eyes were tired, their movements jerky.

They were pretending to relax, but something had happened in the time that we'd been gone.

"Grab a drink from the fridge, if you want." Brodie didn't look up as he dealt the round of cards, but I knew he was speaking to me. No one else had one, so I grabbed four cans of bubbly.

Knowing I needed to do something to lighten the mood, I decided to poke the grumpy bear.

I placed the drinks down and pinched Brodie's cap, shoving it on my head as I sat down beside him. He turned to me as if in slow motion, and I froze.

He leapt before tackling me on the couch and began tickling me.

Oh, gods.

I couldn't stop the shriek of laughter as I tried to get away from him, but he was relentless as he pinned me down. I wriggled and kicked, but he was too strong. We fell off the couch and landed on the floor with a thump. He straddled me, continuing his torture as I squirmed and laughed so hard I thought I would wet myself. I could hear Lia and Eli cackling as they lifted their feet off the floor. I tried to push his arms away, but he pinned my wrists to the ground above my head. I was powerless against him. His grin completely disarmed me. Both dimples popped as he laughed loudly. I'd never heard him laugh before, and the smile on his face shocked me so much I stopped struggling. His legs braced my hips as he leaned over me, breathing heavily.

Oh, by the stars, he's beautiful.

We just stayed there and stared, my breath heaving in my chest as I felt the zap of electricity fling between us. His fingers tightened around my wrists ever so slightly, his legs squeezed my hips as his beautiful eyes darkened.

"I think Ria should come with us tonight." Lia's voice was quiet above me. Brodie's head whipped her way, brows drawn.

"Absolutely the *fuck* not," he growled, his body tense in a whole different way. His legs pressed tighter against my hips, his fingers digging into my wrists, not enough to hurt, but I knew he was pissed.

"I've got a gut feeling about this, Brodie."

I looked at Lia from where I was still pinned to the floor. Even upside down, her face was set as she glared at the prince above me.

"The last time we ignored her gut feeling, it didn't go so well," Eli whispered, Lia reaching over and entwining her fingers with his.

"Fuck sake," Brodie barked, suddenly looking back down at me as if he forgot I was there. "Sorry," he grumbled, letting go of my wrists and sitting up.

"I don't mind. The view's pretty good from down here," I said casually with a shrug as I dragged my arms back to my side. His gaze locked on mine, making my breath hitch.

"What did you say?" Brodie looked at me with confusion, his brows bunched, making cute wrinkles between them.

"I said, I don't mind. The view's pretty good from down here."

"I thought that's what you said," he grumbled, a blush colouring his cheeks.

"Anyway, you're cute when you're mad. Especially when it's not aimed at me." Did I really sound that breathless?

He raised his brows at me, looking right into my eyes, as if he was trying to read my mind.

Shut up, shut up, shut up.

"I'll show you fucking cute," he mumbled, finally getting off me.

I knew we shared a moment. I knew we both felt it, how good our bodies fit together. His cheeks were still pink as he held out a hand and helped me up. He quickly moved away to the bottom of the stairs, arms loose by his sides, but his hands balled into fists.

"Get her fitted up then. We leave in an hour." He stormed away, slamming his door upstairs loudly.

"Well, that was interesting." Eli grinned.

Lia swatted his arm, but I could see a smile tugging at her lips, too.

We split off to gear-up, Lia handed me her spare set of leathers. I had no idea what we were doing, but this didn't seem like a trip to the cinema. Once dressed, we gathered in the main lounge room. Eli buckled a weapons belt on each of Lia's thighs and hips. Brodie glowered as he thumped down the stairs like a dark god.

"Storm," he barked, and I stood up straighter at the authority in his tone. "Tonight is dangerous, and we can't get caught." He came right up to me, so close that I could smell his aftershave. If I took a deep breath, my chest would probably have brushed his. I craned my neck to meet his hard gaze. "What we are doing is illegal, and you don't have to come." He murmured.

I looked between his green eyes, deciding that I could trust him, trust them.

"If I can help, I want to come." I breathed.

His gaze darkened, but he nodded his head once and dropped to his knees. My heart nearly exploded until I realised he was helping buckle on my weapon belt. His hands were on my thighs, causing my pulse to skyrocket.

I scolded myself for reacting so easily.

"We're breaking into a secret government facility where they have been known to...experiment on people," he murmured as he looked up at me through his beautiful, long lashes. His hands gripped the back of my thighs.

I didn't even think he knew he was doing it. I nodded in confirmation.

"How did you find out about it?" I breathed, caught in his gaze.

"I'd been sent to do some recon elsewhere, and overheard a conversation that pricked my attention. I followed them to a secret base, but I couldn't get in. That's why we're going in, to see what we can find out."

Eli sneezed, and Brodie blinked, looking down at where his hands were. He let go and stood, running a hand through his hair.

"I'm thinking that Brodie can make us invisible, and you can teleport and let us in. It will be so much easier than trying to break through their security doors." Lia offered me a grim smile, and I nodded. She pulled out a folder of photos and blueprints of the building we would be breaking into. I studied it until I was sure that I knew where I had to jump.

And what do you think of this plan?

`The plan where you're actively seeking out trouble?`

Yeah, that one.

`You could save lives if you're successful tonight. Stay close to P1.`

We did our final checks before we made our way out into the field. Brodie made sure no one saw us, the dragons included.

The power it must have taken to cover all of us was incredible.

Thankfully, the rain had stopped, but the thunder still rumbled around us, lightning flashing through the sky like bolts of blue fire. But I knew more rain was on the way.

"Alright, are we ready?" Eli made sure we had enough weapons, the open mental link between the four of us was locked in, and our leathers were reinforced in all the right places. I was handed a helmet and reflective goggles that took up half my face. Brodie approached and tucked in a loose strand of hair.

"We can't afford anyone recognising you, Storm. Make sure you keep this on at all times." His dark gaze bored into mine.

"Alright." I breathed, nodding my head slightly.

"Good." He turned and silently signalled Drathruin, who landed rather quietly for such a big dragon. She was the largest Sinvidia dragon I'd seen, and the bigger the dragon, the bigger the power. Vex even allowed her to land first, as she needed to lead the way. I was surprised as much as the others.

Don't get used to it, little storm.

Chapter Twenty-Seven

The rain pelted down like needles. And I was glad to have full-face coverage as the storm continued to rage around us. Vex blended into the night, like a shadow wraith through the clouds.

I lost track of how long we flew for, but Eli passed the time by running over our plan again.

So, Brodie makes us invisible, and Ria teleports into the compound to kill the cameras and opens the gate. We make our way into the building, Ria opening all the doors for us until we reach the security room. That's where we will gas the soldiers, and Lia will monitor the halls. Me, Brodie, and Ria will make our way to the interrogation cells, and I'll slip off to the back office and see what information I can gather. Brodie and Ria will see if they can manage to free anyone kept in the cells.

Sounded easy enough when explained like that, but what of all the people in the building? I had to make the cameras on us turn to static when we passed, and not zap one of us by accident.

What do we do once we get people out? How on Ardentis do we move them through the facility? Lia made a valid point, and one I'd been thinking about.

We'll figure that out when we get to it. But hopefully Brodie can make everyone disappear. Oh, and Ria. Have you been practising extending your electrical shield past yourself?

Yeah, I can extend it to Vex now.

Do you think you could cover us, too? Use our mental link to send it down? I'm hoping it will work against the heat signatures on the cameras.

That was actually a really clever idea.

That's a great idea, brother.

I know. I'm not just a pretty face.

I laughed as I tried to concentrate, closing my eyes and focusing on sending my shield down our link. It was almost like a silver thread that branched out in three different directions. I could just see it bloom over the others like a fine bubble of sorts. I was a little breathless.

It was taking more energy than I wanted to admit.

Absorb it from the storm around us, rather than depleting yourself.

I've done it, guys. I think you're fully covered.

I heard the others congratulating me, but I could only focus on one voice.

Well done, Storm. Brilliant work.

I blushed stupidly. Honestly, was I so desperate for his compliments?

We landed just around the corner from the facility, taking our last deep breath before we dove right in.

Alright, Storm, remind me where everything is on your suit.

Brodie approached, even though I couldn't see his face, I knew it was him. By the way he walked, the way he carried himself, and his shoulders were a little larger than his brother's. But it was also the magnetism that drew me in. I couldn't seem to look away.

I have sleep gas guns on each wrist and one on my chest. A knife in my boot, two daggers on each thigh, as well as a long dagger in my suit on my left

forearm, and a grappling hook on my right hip. He was nodding, and I thought I'd covered everything. He grabbed my hands in his and lifted them to my helmet, one on each side. My pulse thundered in my head, pounding out a loud rhythm.

Don't forget, on your left just here. He gently tapped his finger on mine above my left ear. ***Is your night vision, and here*** – he tapped my finger on the right side. – ***this is your gas mask***. He pushed in the small button, and the mask slipped into place. ***Are you sure you want to do this? And if at any time you change your mind, we'll get you out, no questions asked.***

I nodded my head in understanding.

I need to hear you say it, Storm.

Yes. I'll be sure to let you know.

Breathe, woman. Don't let him turn into a damn mess just because he's touching you.

Good. Let's go then. Don't forget to stay within an arm's length at all times.

I nodded, and we started walking. I was to go first and over the fence, seeing as I wasn't certain I could keep the others' shields in place when teleporting. They'd wait just out of the camera's view until I was over the fence.

I took a deep, steadying breath as the fence came into view.

Breathe. Focus. Jump.

I opened my eyes, and I was on the other side, and quickly made sure their shields were in place.

Okay, you guys are good to come over.

I got to work on the gate, sending in a tiny bit of extra electricity to override the lock. The faint click sounded, and I opened it just enough for the others to sneak in.

Right. First obstacle down. So many more to go.

Fingers intertwined with mine, and I knew who they belonged to without having to look. Not like I'd properly see him anyway. We were all just see-through, fuzzy-looking humanoid shapes.

The first door inside the building was the same. I teleported in and opened the door. It was a slow process, but we were getting in unnoticed. It was time for Lia to branch out and take control of the security room. The guards by the door were hit with her sleep gas, which made them disoriented and walk away, hopefully to their room for a nice nap. She snuck in and locked the door.

The next step was Eli getting into the computer room, to hopefully download information on the illegal stuff they were doing. Then Brodie and I would head to the cells to see if we could free anyone.

Brodie couldn't keep his invisibility around Lia and Eli so far away, that was why Lia was in the room with all the screens, keeping an eye on the cameras.

So far, so good. But my heart was hammering so loud in my chest it was almost distracting.

We hurried as fast as we dared. We hadn't passed anyone yet, but we could hear voices further down the hall. We pushed up against the wall and inched our way down. Now my hands were sweating inside my gloves.

"I've heard rumours, not only from here but also down in Drakeforge."

"Then we need to look into it. I want to know everything, and I want it done *now*."

"Yes, ma'am."

Footsteps faded, luckily away from us. But the person they were talking to seemed to still be there. We inched closer, my heart in my throat as I saw their shadow approaching.

"Please, tell me everything you know." The female voice sounded charming, soft. But I knew she was probably deadly as they came.

"I told you." The man's voice sounded almost pained as they gasped for air. "I don't know anything else. I don't even know what a Voltrite is."

My heart plummeted so fast I felt dizzy. Brodie's fingers tightened around mine until he was almost crushing my fingers.

"Such a shame, Mr Thorne. Looks like our methods aren't working. I'll be back tomorrow to see if you've changed your mind." She sighed as if she was disappointed in him.

"I've told you all I know," he croaked. My legs threatened to give way under me.

I know that voice.

Oh my gods, Brodie. I know who he is.

What do you mean? Who is that?

It's...it's Rex from Viscount Mordane's.

"Same time tomorrow, then, Mr Thorne. And don't worry about making any noise. There isn't anyone else down here. Just you and me." Her heels were loud on the concrete floor. She was coming right our way. I sucked in a breath and flattened myself against the wall so hard I almost hit my head.

She strode past, her long legs eating up the ground as she disappeared around the corner. As soon as she was out of sight, I moved. But Brodie pulled me back, hissing down the link.

***We need to be careful, Storm. Make sure the
cameras are down before we go in there***. His voice
was like steel.

Alright. I'll sort the cameras.

***No one else is coming your way, guys. You should
be able to get him out and back towards Eli.***

Thanks, Lia.

We hurried down the rest of the hall. I felt like
I wanted to throw up. It sounded like they'd been
torturing Rex for information.

I spotted him slumped on the poor excuse of a bed,
more like a plank with a tatty sheet. It was freezing
down there, even with all my layers, it was cold. I
wanted to run to Rex, but Brodie kept me beside him,
slowly approaching his cell. I wanted to weep at how
defeated he looked. His hair was matted and dirty. The
purple bags under his eyes and his gaunt cheeks were
enough to bring me to my knees.

"Rex," I whispered, grabbing onto the bars so tightly
my fingers ached.

"Silver Fox," he sighed and rested his head against the
wall, closing his eyes. I choked back my gut-wrenching
sobs.

"Rex, I'm really here. I'm going to get you out, okay?"

"Of course you are," He smiled, keeping his eyes shut.

I grabbed the lock and shocked it more than I probably should have, but I was beyond caring. I swung the door open, and his eyes flew wide. He sat up and looked at the door.

"Is that really you?"

I slipped into his cell, Brodie right behind me. "I'm here, Rex. Take my hand." I reached for his filthy hand and gripped it tight. A tear slipped down his dirty cheek. "I'm going to get you out, alright. You won't see my friends or me, but we're here. We are going to make you invisible, too."

"I thought you were gone. Never to be seen again." He gripped my fingers with surprising strength. I pulled him up, and he vanished, my shield slipping over him through our joined hands. A headache began to pound in the back of my head. I gritted my teeth and ignored it as I pulled him out of the cell. Brodie kept my other hand firmly in his as he towed us back down the hall. The lady from earlier was right, I didn't detect anyone else down here.

Lia guided us down each hall until we reached Eli, who was hiding behind the door.

But that was where our good luck ran out.

Guys, I think they're onto us! We need to get out! *Shit, shit, shit.*

We started running to the security room to get Lia. The lights flickered with my agitation, my nerves scattered.

"What's going on?" Rex whispered, struggling to keep up.

"We need to get out." I breathed, my fear a living thing inside me.

We won't be able to get out altogether. We'll have to split up. Eli was almost sprinting down the halls.

No fucking way. Brodie yelled, slowing for my sake, because I still held Rex's hand, who looked like he wanted to collapse any minute.

We won't make it to Lia in time! Eli sounded panicked, and I didn't blame him.

You guys go ahead, I'll teleport Rex out and come back.

I heard Brodie growl his opinion on the matter. A big fat NO.

That's a good idea, Ria.

No, it isn't!

We don't have time to argue about this!

I will NOT leave her behind!

As if I didn't already have a headache, I would've had one now for sure.

I stopped and tried to shake Brodie's hand away, but he locked on with a death grip. Eli continued sprinting ahead.

Rex was wheezing like a pair of bellows, his hand shaking in mine.

Rex can't keep up like this. He's about to faint.

You haven't been able to teleport two people, Storm, let alone someone as big as him.

No better time to try.

No. What if you can't?

Have a little faith, prince. I tried to joke, but my tone gave me away. I was scared, not just for me, but for all of us.

Let go, and I'll see you soon. I can plunge the building into darkness if that'll help. I offer, hoping it was enough to convince him.

Yes please! Lia called, worry colouring her voice.

Don't do this, Storm.

I'll see you soon. I stepped back, and he dropped my hand. I didn't know why that hurt me to let him go. *Go, Brodie.*

You first.

They need you to keep them invisible. I'll kill the power and keep my shields up. Go.

I closed my eyes and touched the wall of the building, using the storm thundering outside to flow through me and into the building. All lights popped in a shatter of glass, and everything went black. I shakily reached up and switched on my night vision. I heard Rex curse behind me.

I felt a trickle of blood run down my nose and into my mouth.

No time to think about that, we needed to get out. Brodie cursed and sprinted down the hall towards Lia and Eli.

"Hold on to me, Rex. I'm getting us out of here." His fingers tightened around mine as I shut my eyes again and drew on Vex's power to give me that extra strength I desperately needed.

CHAPTER
TWENTY-EIGHT

G uys, they're closing in behind us.

I'm almost there, keep running towards me.

I've left dirt soldiers guarding our backs.

The barely controlled panic in my friend's voices was enough to settle my fear.

`You can't make it in one jump, little storm. Be careful.`

I closed my eyes and jumped as far as I could, Rex barely containing his cry of surprise. I jumped again, and I'd made it outside the gates. I staggered a step, blinking away the stars dotting my vision.

"Stay here, Rex. They won't hurt you. They're ours."

"What?" he breathed, shaking before he landed on his ass, his legs had given out.

"I'll be back as soon as I can." I focused on the link to the others, closed my eyes and took a deep breath, then jumped. Thankfully, they were close enough for me to make it in one leap. I nearly landed on someone, their startled gasp letting me know it was Eli. They were huddled in the corner by the rear entrance.

Sorry! Who can I take next?

Lia. They both chimed at the same time. I didn't hesitate as I grabbed her hand and jumped. I took a breath and landed again.

Eli, this time.

No, you go.

No arguments. Take him next, Storm. He pushed Eli towards me, and I jumped back again in a heartbeat. I stumbled, and Brodie caught me as my legs gave out from under me. My bloody nose was running freely now.

You're burning up, I can feel it through your suit. He hissed, and my vision swam.

I'm...fine... but his hand tightened on my arm as he held me upright.

```
You're going to burn up if you jump
again!
```
 Vex roared into my head, making me wince.

I have no choice. I'm not leaving him.

Brodie picked me up into his arms and ran. I could hear boots thundering our way, and there was no chance I could shield us anymore. We hit a dead end, there was nowhere else to go.

Get yourself out, Storm.

I'm...not...leaving...you. I brought everything I had in my burning body, and from the storm around me until my skin prickled.

Storm, don't do it.

Just...because you're a prince...doesn't mean you...can tell me...what to...do...

I made one last jump, and blistering pain swallowed me whole before my feet touched the ground.

—◦✦◦—

My breath hissed between my teeth as I gasped awake.

Burning, blistering heat filled my body like I was bathing in acid. I had to bite my lip to stop myself from screaming out loud so hard I tasted blood.

"Finally. Nymeria, can you hear me?" a voice rumbled above me. A whimper slipped past as another wave of heat passed through me. But I tried to nod. 'You hit burnout, and you're incredibly lucky you had a water wielder with you. Otherwise, you'd be dead."

You're lucky I don't kill you myself for that stupid fucking stunt.

"Close your eyes and hold your breath." Brodie's stern voice ordered from my left, and I obeyed. Delicious, cold water poured over my head and down my back. I sighed as the next shudder of heat lessened.

"Cut her singlet off, Brodie."

I felt the cold press of metal start at my neck and slide down my back, and my singlet fell away. I pulled it off and wrapped my arms around my legs, resting my cheek on my knees. Another bucket of cold water washed over me, and my lungs no longer felt as if they were on fire.

"What the bloody hell were you thinking?" Brodie hissed, his anger choking his words, they were barely more than a growl.

For once, I agree with the boy.

I winced, both voices too loud in my pounding head.

"Leave her be. I expected better from you two." The Doc aimed a narrowed glare at the brothers, who shuffled on their feet. I no longer felt the link open between the four of us.

"I'm glad you're going to be okay, Ria. Thank you for coming back for us. We're all in your debt." Eli rested a gentle hand on the top of my head before walking out.

"Right, take this whole tube every two hours for the next forty-eight hours. I'm afraid you're going to look a little pink for a few days." The doctor sighed, worry bracketing his mouth. I whispered a thank you as he walked out, the surrounding water finally cooling off. My teeth began to chatter as the last of the heat left my body.

"Who did that to you?" Brodie's voice was so quiet I thought I'd imagined it. I peeked over my shoulder to see his dark gaze on my back.

"When I was in the arena." I started closing my eyes. "When I didn't put on a good enough performance, the guards took turns whipping me." I heard his sharp inhale. I opened my eyes to see his hands balled into fists before he reached for a sponge to finish wiping down my back. I closed my eyes again as the soothing motion lulled me into a comfortable silence.

"If I ever go that way, I'm going to make sure I burn it all to the damn ground." He growled, his tone opposite to his gentle touch as he swept my hair over my shoulder. "Come on, let's get you out." Brodie's voice was now soft and gentle, and I couldn't stop the tears that spilled over my still burning cheeks. He reached into the bath and hauled me out, not caring that I was naked and getting him all wet. He placed me down on the bed and wrapped a towel around my shoulders, tucking me in.

"I'll fetch someone to help dry and dress you."

"No, please stay. I'm too embarrassed for someone else to see me like this," I rasped, my throat still feeling a little raw, and to be honest with myself, I didn't want him to leave. My tears still fell in a silent stream, and I couldn't seem to stop them.

"Alright," he murmured and started drying my hair with another towel. He pulled me to my feet, and being such a gentleman, he didn't even look as he helped dry the rest of me. And I was surprised I didn't even feel a little embarrassed. Once dressed, I plopped back onto the bed, feeling utterly exhausted.

"Hop into bed, you're going to need to rest a bit." I didn't think I'd ever seen this side of him before. He tucked me into my sheets and ran his hand over my head as if I were something precious. He cleared his throat, took a step back, a muscle ticking in his jaw. "I'll be back in two hours for your remedy." He turned to walk away, but I reached out and grabbed his hand. He paused and looked down at our entwined fingers.

"Thank you, Brodie. For everything." I whispered, giving his hand a small squeeze. He returned the gesture, clenching his jaw again before walking away. I think I fell asleep before he was out the door.

⸻❖⸻

Every two hours, he woke me up, held the back of my head with one hand, while the other held the glass vial to my lips. The liquid was bitter on my tongue, but each time I had it, my head felt a little clearer, and my skin didn't feel as sunburnt.

I woke on my own, stretched, and I actually felt...good. Well, much better than I did before. I looked over and saw Brodie asleep in the armchair beside my small table, a timer counting down until the next remedy was due. He looked exhausted. Bags under his eyes as he slept. The timer was about to go off again, so I reset it before it buzzed and woke him, and downed the third last vial on the table.

I threw a blanket over him and relieved myself in the bathroom before sitting on the bed again.

`Glad to see you're up and about.`

Me too. Sorry about earlier, well, no, I'm not actually. I wasn't going to leave my friends behind, and I'd do it again.

`That's what I'm worried about.`

Vex growled, but he sounded resigned. `That grumpy prince is very upset with you, too.`

I know. I sighed. *When isn't he?*

`We need to get back to the academy, there has been another murder.`

No, surely not?

`Once P1 is awake, we'll leave.`

I let the prince sleep for the next few hours, but he woke, looking confused until he saw me sitting on the bed.

"Wh...what...what time is it?" he stretched and yawned, looking a little sore as he rolled his neck and winced.

"It's about five thirty. Don't worry, I've been taking my remedy every two hours."

"You should have woken me." He frowned, rubbing his eyes.

"You needed some rest, too." I tried to look serious as his gaze reached mine, but he just huffed a laugh. He stiffened, his eyes glazed over slightly as if he were having a silent conversation.

"We need to get back to the academy. Something's happened." He stood, ran a hand through his beautiful onyx hair, and came back to me. "Your friend is on the mend, some antibiotics and food in him, and he'll be fine. He's staying here to give what information he can."

Rex.

I'd completely forgotten we'd found him. I felt shame slam through me, hard enough to force me to fall back on the bed.

"I need to see him," I breathed, finding strength in my legs again. "I can't leave without seeing him, please," I begged, pleading with my eyes as I stood in front of Brodie. He sucked on his teeth briefly before giving me a tight nod.

"You need to be quick. I'll take you to him." He turned on his heel and walked out. I was close behind as we took hallway after hallway. I noticed he wasn't in a fancy room like mine, but it was a hundred times better than a cell. The room was light and airy, the curtains blowing in the faint breeze from the open windows. He was standing, looking out at the surrounding mountains. He turned when he heard the door shut, a wide grin split his gaunt face as he saw me.

"Ria!" he called, running to me and wrapping me in the tightest hug, spinning me around. I laughed at his joy and how happy I was to see him again. He put me down and grabbed both of my arms and simply stared. "You've grown." He grumbled, and Brodie barked a laugh. No doubt my face was as red as a tomato, and not because I was still pink. "I've missed you, my little pain in the ass." He lightly punched me in the arm, but I was so damn happy to see him.

Rex's okay. He's here.

I'd never thought I'd see him again.

"I've missed you, too." I breathed, unable to wipe the smile off my face. "I need to leave, but I'll be in contact, okay? And I'll be back to visit. I'm just attending Voralyth Academy, a few hours' flight from here."

His eyes widened, face going a little pale.

"You're a rider?" His fingers tightened on mine. I felt horrible that I had to leave him so soon.

"I should have gone back two days ago. I'm sorry, Rex." I feel tears begin to well behind my eyes, making my throat tight.

"You don't need to apologise to me. You saved my life, and I'll owe you that debt forever." He gave me a watery smile. "Just let me know when you're back. It seems we have some things to catch up on." He had to clear his throat. I nodded, hastily wiping away a stray tear.

"I promise, Rex. Rest up, I'll talk to you soon." I wrapped him in another hug before forcing myself away. "I'm really glad I found you," I whispered, but the sad look he aimed my way made my heart clench.

"Be careful, little fox. They're after you, and will do anything they can to get you."

I felt sick. It seemed like the Viscount was trying to hunt me down, or was it the government?

I swallowed and offered him a small smile. "They'd have to catch me first." I winked, and he shook his head. I waved and left, knowing that if I didn't, I wouldn't leave at all.

Brodie ducked into his room to grab our packs, which Eli fetched for us earlier, and made our way down to the flight field.

I wiped my tears before snapping on my goggles, Vex silent for once as I mounted and settled in for the two-hour flight to Voralyth.

We had a murderer to catch.

Chapter Twenty-Nine

We arrived to chaos.

Brodie was swamped as soon as he was inside, but not before he barked at me to return to my room immediately. My whisp pulsed in my pocket. Lia was calling me.

"Hey, Lia. What's going on?"

'Did you just get in?'

"Yeah, just now."

'Good, meet me in the social rooms.' She hung up, and I quickly made my way there. I opened the doors, and she pulled me inside, locking it behind us.

"Lia, what's going on?"

"There's been another murder this morning."

"Vex said, but didn't say who." I hated the tightening in my chest.

"It's Mick, I mean Wingmaster Skirvington." Tears pooled in her lovely hazel eyes. My breathing hitched.

Oh, no.

"What? When?" I backed up until my back hit the wall. All I could see was his smiling face and kind eyes.

"I'm sorry." Lia stood beside me and threw an arm around my shoulder, hugging me as I caught my breath. Lia's whisp pulsed, she sighed before she answered. "Yeah, I've got her with me, yes, she knows, yes, she'll be okay. Alright, see you." She put her whisp away and gave me a sad smile. "Just the prince checking up on you." I could only nod, too numb to feel much else. "Come on, I'll walk you to your room."

I didn't remember the walk back or climbing into bed, but my alarm woke me the next morning, and I struggled to get out of bed.

Mick's gone. Who will be our new Wingmaster?

Murdered by some sicko that they haven't caught yet. I rolled over and heard a crinkle of paper. Frowning, I shoved my hand under my pillow and pulled out a folded piece of paper.

HoW wElL dO yOu KnOw YoUr RoOmMaTe?

WhY aRe OnLy RiDeRs DyInG?

What the actual fuck?
`Someone's trying to divide the jaws and boots.` Vex grumbled, `keep your damn eyes peeled.`

And they're doing a good job of it. This is going to cause anarchy.

My hand shook as I re-read it again and again. I didn't care what time it was, I grabbed my whisp and raced into my bathroom and rang the first person who came to mind.

'Storm? Is everything alright?'

"Not really. I've just found a note hidden under my pillow...it's about the murders." I whispered, feeling a little ill. He cursed a string of filthy words.

'I'm on my way.' He hung up, and I hastily dressed. Brodie bashed on my door only moments later. He must have a room here in Sinvidia to get here so quickly. Ava, the asshole, grumbled and shoved her head under her blanket as I opened the door.

"Come with me." Brodie reached in and pulled me out by the hand, plunging us invisible in an instant as we raced down the hall. He didn't even knock as he opened Professor Korin's door, and I found Lia and Eli already there, with a scraggly-looking Korin yawning into his cup of steaming coffee.

"You got a note too, I'm guessing?" Korin handed us a mug that I accepted with thanks and a warm smile.

"Sure did. Do you think it's someone trying to wedge more of a divide between us?" I leaned back and sipped my coffee, the smooth taste warming the cold feeling growing in my stomach.

"Yes. But also, how well *do* you know your roommates?"

"Mine's fine. She'll speak to me when in our room, and when we have to work together. But I wouldn't call her a friend." Lia shrugged, like that should be the norm.

"Mine refuses to even look at me, let alone speak to me. I know nothing about her."

"Hmm. The principals think it helps build bonds."

"I think they're trying to push shit uphill. They need to accept the fact that boots want nothing to do with us." Eli downed the rest of his coffee, placing his mug on Korin's desk.

"Roarboard is going off." Brodie sat forward and showed us his whisp. Someone plastered the same note we found all over the aetherweb socials, and comments were pouring in.

"Shit. This is going to blow up." Korin sighed loudly, rubbing a hand over his face.

I sat back and tilted my head to the side, thinking.

"What are we going to do about these murders?" I had to clear my throat. Mick being killed was a huge loss. It still didn't feel real.

"I don't know, but we need to do something. It can't continue." Korin perched on the edge of his desk, deep in thought. "There has to be a pattern, we just need to figure out what it is."

Eli's whisp rang, breaking the silence.

"Father," he answered and nodded, but his face dropped. "Things are happening here that they need our help with." He was cut off, and he paled a little. "What do you mean, replacements?" He scowled, and I saw Brodie frown out of the corner of my eye, crossing his arms. I bet Eli was broadcasting their conversation through their mental link. "Yes, sir. We'll be sure to leave when they arrive." He hung up and sighed. "We've been summoned back to the castle. Apparently, we're needed there more than here right now. And he's sending out four riders and two more soldiers to fill in. Two for each house, total."

Korin's whisp rang next, and he gave us an exasperated look before answering.

"Good morning, Euan. Yes, I've heard. I have your sons with me as we speak." He began to pace, nodding as Eli had. "There was a note placed in every room. I'll send you the picture." He paused a moment before shrugging. "I don't know. There have been three murders, Euan. Things are getting serious. They're your sons, don't forget." His face darkened, but he turned away from us, walking over to his bay window. "Okay, sure thing. Talk soon." He sighed as he put the whisp away and levelled a look at the prince's. "Looks like you two are headed off and will return once your father no longer needs your help."

We stood and made our way out as Korin sat behind his desk with his head in his hands.

"What now?" Lia asked, gripping Eli's hand tightly.

"You watch your goddamned backs, and tell us if you find anything." Eli's face was dark, mirroring Brodie's. "This is bullshit." We began our way through the halls to the cafeteria, and only a handful of people were here, and they had all their heads bent together, talking furiously.

"Shit is about to hit the fan, and you two need to stick to each other," Brodie mumbled, sticking close as we came to a stop.

"It's a bit hard when we're in different houses, Brodie." Lia shook her head, giving me a sympathetic look.

"Then stay close to your wing."

"I would if mine liked me. They tolerate me at best. I've only got Theon." I mumbled, feeling a lump form in my throat, tears stinging my eyes.

Don't cry, damnit!

Eli and Lia turned away as Brodie gave me his full attention.

"Then you need to keep up with your training. Make them too afraid to try anything." He gripped both of my arms as he moved closer. I refused to meet his gaze as I tried to swallow my tears. "Look at me, Storm." His voice was low and soft. I blinked, trying to clear my eyes before I met his hard stare, the green a little darker today. "You're one of the strongest people I know. Don't trust anyone other than Lia and Korin." He raised his brows, waiting for me to acknowledge it. I nodded slightly, closing my eyes briefly. "You've got us, and your dragon, who would burn the world for you. Keep moving forward, one step at a time."

Noise blasted into the cafeteria as cadets barged through the doors, whispering and clumping into groups.

Jaws vs Boots.

It's begun already.

I saw Mitch storm through the doors, Levi on his heels. They aimed right for us, and the twins groaned. Brodie let go and stepped back slightly.

"I'm guessing you know what's going on?" Levi asked Brodie, at least those two got along all right.

"Yeah, we've seen the note. Eli and I have been summoned back to Sylvanfire, but another four riders and two soldiers are on their way. We'll leave when they get in."

"You're leaving? After what has just happened?" Mitch asked incredulously.

"We've got no choice, O'Connell," Eli growled, curling his top lip. I rolled my eyes. These guys were meant to be men, not teenagers.

"Did you get one, too, Ria?" Mitch turned to me, looking concerned as he took a step closer. Brodie not so subtly moved to my side.

Protective ass.

"Yeah, and Lia too." I was glad that the urge to cry had left as I cleared my throat. "I'm afraid things are about to get messy."

"My thoughts exactly. We're going to have a meeting with the principals any minute now. But please make sure you're careful." He pleaded, taking my hands in his. I heard Brodie scoff beside me, but Mitch completely ignored him.

"I will. I've been training, and anyone who tries to attack me would be stupid, because Vex would avenge me." I attempted a smile, but everyone's face was set in a hard glare.

I'd do more than avenge you. I'd burn that whole academy to the ground.

Got it.

Three professors walked in, six figures trailing behind them with grim expressions.

They must be the reinforcements.

"Looks like it's time for us to leave," Brodie grumbled, and Lia's face fell. Eli and Lia walked off to grab Eli's bags before he left. I waved goodbye as I suddenly felt awkward standing between Brodie, Mitch, and Levi, as the silence stretched on.

"Walk me out, Storm." Brodie's voice was gruff, but I nodded, waving to Mitch and Levi. For the first few meters, we said nothing. Cadets ran past, sticking to groups from their houses.

"Make sure you call me if you notice anything, and I'll be out as soon as I can."

"What about your father?"

"I'll deal with him later. There are more important things going on here."

We were out in the courtyard, the wind howling already, the clouds closing in. It was meant to rain for the next week. Winter wasn't far away.

"And whatever you do, stay away from O'Connell. Levi's a good guy, but I don't trust Mitchell. He and his father are up to no good." He turned to me, raising his hand, then dropping it again. "I don't mean it because I'm jealous, but because I know what he's like. He will do anything to get what he wants, and especially if it's something his father wants." Dread dropped into my stomach like a stone.

His father worked for the government. In that facility, we broke into on the weekend.

"Alright. I'll keep my distance."

He opened his mouth, but shut it quickly, frowning at me.

"You agreed with me too easily." He murmured, looking suspicious.

"Do you want me to argue with you, prince?" I raised my brows and crossed my arms, but he shook his head, dropping his hand.

"Perhaps another day, Storm. I need to get going." He turned and walked to the flight field, but looked over his shoulder. "And try to stay out of trouble." I flipped him the finger and poked my tongue out before turning around to get back inside before the rain started.

CHAPTER THIRTY

Shouting, cursing, and magical tantrums filled the hall as cadets showed their feelings towards this morning's note in our rooms. The Boot cadets yelled that it was the riders. The Jaw cadets yelled that it was the soldiers. I actually felt a tiny bit sorry for the professors and principals. I was sitting next to Theon, who looked like he'd had no sleep since yesterday. He was sitting ramrod straight, glaring at the principals. They took our whisp's off us as we entered, and to me, that didn't bode well.

"Why did the princes leave?" He whispered, his hands clenched tightly in his lap.

"The king summoned them. They'll be back once they're finished."

Theon nodded, taking a deep breath. The principals called for quiet, setting off a loud bang to get our attention.

"Enough! You will remain with your assigned roommate and continue classes as normal. Someone is trying to create a divide between us, and we will not stand for it. We have eight extra guards here to help keep an eye on things. All ex-cadets who used to be in your houses. If you see anything unusual, you go to them. If you hear of anything suspicious, you go to them." Principal Shields boomed. She glared at us all as the six new 'guards' took a stand on the stage. Mitch and Levi were already up there, looking stern and a little formidable.

"Oh, great. I've heard of some of those guys, and they're power-hungry assholes." Theon grumbled, shaking his head. "And the woman with the blonde hair, she's the worst of them all."

I glanced up to the stage and properly looked at our new 'guards.'

There was the woman with fierce yellow eyes that matched her straw coloured hair. She has a serious resting bitch face as she glared down at all of us.

Galadron, for sure.

Her dragon, Vixra, is just as savage. Keep your distance.

The other Galadron soldier was Mitch. I should have guessed, but I never thought to ask. Levi was a Furora, and their rider was a man with shaved brown hair, skin so dark it reminded me of burnt coffee, and hazel eyes that looked more brown.

The rider and soldier for Sinvidia were both female, and they greeted each other like old friends. Their smiles were warm, and they embraced each other in a firm hug. The Ruleum soldier had braided black hair, harsh light blue eyes and at least three facial piercings that I could see. Tattoos peeked out of her leathers, her makeup was flawless. She had a stormsteed helmet tucked under her arm and looked formidable as hell. The rider was more on the slim side, but his long blond hair was down around his shoulders in messy waves. His dark blue eyes winked at a few girls who giggled and blushed. He looked more like a surfer than a rider.

"We've come up with a plan to make you all start to get along." Grumbles filled the room, and nerves filled my belly. "We have devised a plan for you to be sent out into the forest with your roommate, and you will need to work together if you want to survive." Gasps were sounded all around, and my nerves grew. "You'll be given a map and that's it. You will need to work together to find your supplies if you want food, water, weapons, and shelter. The Jaw cadets will be cut off from their dragons and magic, to level out the playing field. You'll have to face whatever beasts dwell in those dark shadows, because they'll happily have you for their dinner."

The hall was completely silent. I think everyone was too shocked to speak. I could practically feel Vex's anger down the bond.

"We thought we'd try something different from our usual first-year initiations."

This was the first time doing something like this? And they thought now was a good time to try it?

Utter madness.

"We'll begin randomly selecting eight pairs next week, with no notice, nothing. You will simply wake in the forest. You won't get your whisperglass back until you complete your mission. If someone tries to get in contact with you, they will receive an automated response that you are in studies and won't be contactable for a few weeks. If it's urgent, they can contact us directly." Principal Shields looked exhausted as she looked over us.

"We need you to take this very seriously. We will not tolerate any more disgraceful behaviour, and every single one of you will be closely watched. This affects your end-of-year scores as well. Dismissed." Principal Peterson crossed his arms, glared at us, before stalking off the small stage. The hall exploded in yelling, cursing, and complete chaos as the principals left, the professors ushering us out.

"Are they *insane?*" Theon hissed, keeping close as we were jostled about. "Cutting us off from our dragons and magic? Diabolical."

"Ava likes to pretend I don't exist, so this is going to be a blast." I grumbled, already dreading the day I'll be 'randomly' selected.

We were given the week to study the beasts that lived in the surrounding forest, the edible plants and berries, and how to light a fire. Vex continued to grumble and complain, and apparently, he wasn't the only one. I spent my time trying to keep busy and not dwell on the fact that Mick was gone, and I couldn't speak to Rex, either. Brodie promised me that they would set him up at the palace to get back to health. But I still didn't feel right just leaving him there.

They've given us print-outs of fun facts about the animals that roamed in the woods surrounding Voralyth.

The Gulgron*: Don't let the "frog" label fool you. A Gulgron is the size of a carriage, with a throat that can swallow you whole and a croak loud enough to rupture eardrums. Its bulging eyes are rimmed with festering* *green-and-black boils that ooze when it breathes. If you hear it before you see it, run faster.*

The Nimurra*: It looks like an ordinary bird until it opens its beak. The Nimurra's call induces intense hallucinations, turning allies into monsters and the sky into fire. While you're disoriented, it strikes. First, it goes for the eyes. Then the rest. Death by a thousand pecks.*

The Zephyros: *At a glance, it looks like a wild horse. Then you see the fangs, serrated, finger-length, and made for tearing flesh. The Zephyros is fast, aggressive, and carnivorous. If one starts galloping toward you, don't stop to stare. It's not coming for a pat, it's coming for a meal.*

Last but not least, ***the Noctheris****: The nightmare of Ardentis. A Noctheris is a twisted blend of bat and human. Humanoid limbs, and leathery wings webbed between its arms and legs. Its head can rotate a full 180 degrees, and it's the size of a five-year-old child. It's shriek? Ear-bleeding. It's tail? Barbed, venomous, and paralytic. Its claws? Sharp enough to gut you in a single swipe. You'll hear it in the dark, and if you do...it's already too close.*

Can't wait.

I was hunched over a table in the library when I heard two guys arguing behind me.

"I'm telling you, she's the Silver Fox."

My heart plummeted, and my hands began to sweat. I held my breath as I listened.

"Don't be stupid. You're letting the thought of getting gold cloud your judgment." The other one hissed, trying to keep their conversation quiet.

"She has to be. She's short, has silver hair, and can fight like a hellcat. She fits everything I've heard." The other dude sounded too excited for my liking. "Regali said he'll even pay good money for solid information on her whereabouts."

Regali.

My blood froze as I recognised the name.

The rogue dragon rider.

"Listen to what you're saying! You're seriously considering handing over a fellow Sinvidia rider for gold?"

"But she's not, she's a Tenebrae. Not one of us."

My stomach flipped over itself. I knew they would never accept me. I slowly blew out my breath, hands curled into fists.

"She chose *us*. One of the most powerful riders in the whole of Everdra chose Sinvidia. That's got to mean something, surely?" He was pleading with his friend, and I'd nearly heard enough.

"Just think about it, will you? All that gold." I could practically hear the glee in his voice.

Nope. I'm done.

I pushed my chair out with a loud screech and walked towards them. I reached their table and slammed my hands down, they almost jumped out of their freaking skin.

"Maybe next time, you can talk a little quieter. This is a library, and I'm sure you don't want people overhearing your conversation." I glared, and they stared back with wide eyes.

"I'm talking him out of it, I swear, Nymeria." The one on the left stammered, but the other one was now looking me over.

"Just remember, if I heard it, then so did Vexirion. And he's the type to burn now and ask questions later." I narrowed my eyes at the other one, who was still staring.

Asshole.

`His dragon will hear from me, and I'll make sure to pull him apart limb by limb before I feed him to a Zephyros if I hear a whisper of them contacting the rogue rider.` Vex thundered, quick to anger.

I walked away, not caring that I should be with someone at all times. I was so caught up in my own head that I didn't see him until I ran headfirst into his chest.

"Sorry!" I blurted, stumbling back. He reached out to steady me, holding onto my arm.

"Hey, Ria. Are you alright? You look a little pale." Ryler furrowed his brows with concern as I gathered my thoughts, but I couldn't stop the rush of emotions that came to the surface and poured out of me. My face crumpled, and a sob burst through my tight throat. "Oh, Ria. Come here." Ryler wrapped his arms around me, and I melted. It had been so long since anyone had simply held me, comforted me. He ran a soothing hand up and down my back as I tried to reel myself back in. I felt like such a damn mess these days.

"Not even my own house respects me." I sniffled, trying to take a calming breath.

"Then you should have picked us. We would have loved to have you in Galadron." He chuckled, rubbing my back. We stood there for a few moments, and I began to feel a little awkward. "I'm sorry. They're idiots. You deserve better."

"Thank you, Ryler, for letting me fall apart on you." I huffed, feeling embarrassed that I let it happen.

"Hey, we can't be strong all the time." I could hear the smile in his voice. I stepped back, but he kept a hand on my arm, the other hand tucked a bit of hair behind my ear, and his knuckles grazed my throat in an intimate gesture. He left his hand on my neck, his thumb grazing my throat. His eyes darkened, his pupils growing as my pulse skittered.

"Your brand must be huge if just a claw is this big." He murmured, tilting his head to the side as his gaze travelled over my throat. "I'd love to see the whole thing one day. I'm fascinated by different brands." His voice was soft, but I suddenly felt uncomfortable. I was saved from blurting out the first thing that popped into my head by Levi and Mitch strutting around the corner.

Thank the stars.

Both of their eyes narrowed on Ryler's back and the intimate hold he had on me. They stopped on either side of us, crossing their arms and widening their stance.

"Ria, just who I was looking for. Would you mind coming with us?" Levi turned his gaze to me, and I hoped he could see my relief.

"Sure, no problem." I stepped back, forcing Ryler to drop his arms.

"Daniel's," Mitch drawled, looking him over in obvious distaste.

"O'Connell. Brown." Ryler matched Mitch's tone. But his eyes softened when they landed on me. "I'll catch up with you soon, Ria." He winked, a smile tugging at his lips. I gave him a one in return and nodded my head. No one said anything until he was around the corner.

"What the hell was going on there, Ria?" Mitch asked a little too harshly, his voice stern. He cleared his throat and tried again. "It looked like you were uncomfortable."

"I don't know how it got to that. He asked if I was okay, and I kind of broke down. He comforted me, then it got weird." My cheeks blazed with embarrassment. I looked down at my shoes and kicked an imaginary rock.

"I don't want to sound like McTavish, but it's probably best you stay away from him. He was weird, even as a first year." Mitch sounded worried, and Levi had those little creases between his brows. I met their eyes and nodded. I couldn't explain it, but that whole interaction made me feel a little nervous.

"Did you actually need me for anything?" I turned to Levi, who shook his head.

"Nah, just saw that panicked expression on your face and thought that was the easiest way to get rid of him. But you shouldn't be out here on your own. We'll walk you back to your common room." He smiled kindly, and I nodded, falling into step beside them. I felt like they were my guards, one on either side, as we wound our way through the halls.

"Don't worry too much about your upcoming mission with your roommate. I'm sure you'll smash it." Mitch offered me a smile I couldn't return.

"You don't know her. She hates me. I'm going to fail the mission for sure." I grumbled, annoyed about the whole thing. They shared a worried look, but shook their heads.

"Then it's a good chance to break the ice and get to know each other." Levi tried to lighten the situation, but it made me not want to do it even more.

"I remember my mission, and it made us become friends in the end." Mitch's smile dimmed as he blinked, jaw ticking. Levi cleared his throat.

"You don't know her. She refuses even to look at me, Levi." I moaned, huffing out a long breath. We reached my common room door, and I thanked them, dragging my feet all the way to my room, where I hoped Ava wasn't there to ignore me.

CHAPTER
THIRTY-ONE

I awoke to bird song, a light breeze that cut right through my blankets.

Wait.

My eyes flew open, and I gasped, dread settling in my gut like a brick.

I looked like it was my turn to spend three days with my roommate. She was dozing away to my left, still completely oblivious to what was going on.

The bastards took us while we were sleeping. No wonder they said we wouldn't know it happened. They drugged us in our sleep and dumped us in a part of the forest we didn't know. I stood and tried to get my bearings. It was still dark out, the sun maybe an hour away from rising. My mind tried to rack through the beasts that dwelled in the forest.

Gulgron's, Nimurra's, Zephyros' and Noctheris'.

Awesome. This is going to be super fun.

Panic set in as I could no longer feel Vex's bond.

Breathe. I can get through three days without him.

I hope.

I heard a twig snap behind me and wasted no time in shaking my roomie awake. She grunted, telling me to go away.

"You need to get the fuck up now, before we become something's meal, damnit," I growled, shaking her again, and her eyes snapped open.

"Fucking hell." She barked, jumping to her feet. She looked around and came to the same conclusion.

"I don't have a map, so maybe you do. I wasn't going to search you for it." I grumbled and tried to peer into the trees surrounding us, but it was no use. I couldn't see anything.

"Alright, alright. Just calm down, will you?" She growled, searching her pockets only to come up empty.

Seriously?

I looked around, and something white caught my eye. I raced over to see a small note nailed to a tree. I yanked it off and unfolded it.

**FIVE STEPS, FIVE TRUTHS, FIVE CHANCES TO FAIL.
IN SHADOW AND TEETH, YOUR FATES SET SAIL.
SEEK FIRST THE INK THAT KNOWS THE LAND,
THEN DRINK WHERE NONE WOULD DARE TO
STAND.
FEAST IN THE PLACE, THE HOLLOW ONES DREAD,
ARM WHERE THE SKIES WHISPER LIES,
AND THE SHRIEK SEEKS SIGHT.
FIND STEEL WHERE SHADOWS CIRCLE IN FLIGHT.
AND SLEEP WHERE THE SKY DOES NOT REACH.**

"What the fuck does that even mean?" Ava barked, trying to snatch the note out of my hands. I took a step back.

"Just calm down, will you?" I echoed the words she said moments ago. She sneered at me as she crossed her arms and glared. "It's obviously a riddle for us to find our supplies. It looks like we need to find the map first."

"No shit. But where the hell do we even start? That riddle is nonsense."

The sun finally began to peek over the horizon, and the temperature dropped. Our breath puffed out in front of us as we rubbed our hands over our arms. I searched the grounds for any clues, and I spotted a tiny, dark drop of something on a leaf. I picked it up and smeared it with my thumb.

"It's ink. Seek first the ink that knows the land. Look around for any more ink spots. It might lead us to a map." We both began scouring the ground for any more clues. Ava spotted another one two meters away in the trees.

"Here!" she called, and I hurried over.

"Do you think they go in a straight line?" I mused, looking around for more.

"How should I know?" She scoffed and wandered off. *Screw you, bitch.*

It took us another ten minutes to find another one. This one was about four meters from the first, and not in a straight line.

"There has to be a pattern we're not seeing," I mumbled, trying to figure out what it could be. By doing this, it was an easy way to lose each other. I thought back to where we found the first three, and realised it had to go in a zig-zag pattern. I rushed in the opposite direction about six meters and found another.

"It is a pattern, but it zig-zags and gets further away by two meters each time," I called. Ava nodded as she came my way.

"Hope you're right, rider." She grumbled and walked away towards where, hopefully, she'd find another.

"You know, I don't even know your last name, as you've decided to refuse to speak to me, remember?" I said just loud enough for her to hear. She mimicked me, pulling a stupid face as if she were pretending to be me.

"What's your problem, anyway?" I asked bluntly.

"Found another." She admitted with a frown. She took a deep breath and blew it out before meeting my gaze.

"I didn't want to like you, so I didn't give you the chance to even think about being friends."

I stared at her in shock. My mouth might have popped open slightly.

"Why? That's just ridiculous. You don't even know me."

"Because I don't *want* to know you. I know what the death rate is like here, and riders are one of the first to die in their first six months, as they're still bonding with their dragons. So, no, I don't want to know you."

I was speechless. How the hell do I respond to that?

"And you already arrived with everyone knowing your name, tied up with the princes and the all-popular Vidalia Fairchild. So no thank you."

"Wow. If that's how you want it, then fine, by all means, continue like I don't exist." I stalked past her, eventually finding another ink drop. It was slow going, and it had been a few hours, but we finally managed to find a dead Nimurra, its feathers soaked in ink-like blood. We approached hesitantly and saw that it was at the base of a tree with a rough map burned into its bark.

I looked back at the riddle, the next clue only said: Then drink where none would dare to stand.

"That's got to mean down by the creek, where the Gulgron's live?" I looked up at Ava, who was glaring into the distance like she'd rather be anywhere else.

"Spose so." She shrugged.

I rolled my eyes and shook my head as I looked at the map.

"The closest mass of water is about four kilometres, give or take, away from here."

"How the hell did you work that out?" She scoffed, folding her arms across her chest.

"I was counting from where we woke up, and looked at the map here, and that was eight kilometres, and the distance looked about half that on the map."

"Right. Whatever you reckon."

Oh my goodness. This woman is going to do my head in.

"Well, I'm going to head that way. You can either come or stay here. I don't care." I looked at the map one last time before turning in the rough direction I thought would take me to the next clue.

I heard a loud sigh, and her soft footfalls behind me as we trudged in silence through the dark trees. A distant cry of a bird sent shivers over my skin, making me feel a little on edge. At least we didn't have the Lekkah, which were native to Faritia. Those large cat-like beasts sounded terrifying.

A few hours passed, the sun now directly overhead, and hotter than I imagined, especially when winter was only around the corner. I was sweating in my leathers, slightly put out that someone had stripped and dressed me when I was knocked out.

I could hear a distant croak, nothing loud enough to do any damage, but still loud enough to give me goosebumps.

What else did the riddle say? Then drink from where none would dare to stand?

I snuck along, keeping low as I started to smell the beastly amphibians. Something caught my eye, and I saw two canteens hanging in a tree, swaying over the water's edge. I turned back to see Ava frown, holding her nose as she finally caught up with me. I silently pointed towards the canteens, and she nodded, pointing to herself first, then back to the tree. I shrugged and gestured for her to go ahead. If she wanted to go climb the tree, she could knock herself out.

Ava crept through the marsh, stepping slowly, keeping low to the ground and remained hidden amongst the reeds. I slowly made my way to another tree, hoping to get a good look at the Gulgron-infested marsh for the safest place to fill those canteens, as I could guarantee they were going to be empty.

Ava scaled the tree, the branches swaying as she climbed. The limb where the canteens were hanging wasn't that big, about the size of my thigh. I was halfway up my own tree when I reached the right height to overlook the marsh. Deep rumbles echo around, as if they were communicating with each other.

By the gods, they're huge.

Ava's branch shook, and some of the Gulgron's bulbous, festering eyes started wandering around. I tried to catch her eye, to tell her to slow down and be quiet, but she was ignoring me as usual. A few of them started to wade through the water towards the tree where Ava was.

Shit, shit, shit.

I shimmied down the tree, around the back of the frogs, to try to catch her eye. Not for the first time, I wished I had my magic. I had no plan and no idea what I was going to do, but I had to do something. Not only if they croaked, which could knock her out of the tree, but their stupidly long tongue could probably reach her up there, too.

I need to cause a distraction.

Everything fell silent, and it seemed like the marsh held its breath.

It sounded like a thunderclap in a drum. I felt the vibration from behind the beast as its throat ballooned, ready to go again. It was horrendously loud. I would hate to have that aimed at me. I heard Ava scream, slipping on her branch, as she struggled to hold on, her legs dangling.

The frogs moved as one, croaking low, their throats rumbling. They were much faster than a beast of their size should be. A grotesque, black tongue shot out, hitting the trunk of the tree only centimetres from Ava.

Shit. I need to do something.

"Hey! Assholes!" I yelled and instantly regretted it as all the frogs in the marsh spotted me and saw that I was a much easier target. They croaked excitedly and began moving my way, eyes blinking and tongues lashing.

Fuuuucccckkkk.

I ran. The water splashing up around my shins as I crashed through the shallow water, the reeds whacking my legs with dull thwacks.

"Run, rider!" Ava bellowed. I hoped she bloody got those canteens and was filling them as I ran for my fucking life. I could hear the frogs thundering behind me, and some reeds to my right exploded as a tongue ripped them from the ground.

Oh, my gods. They've got too long a reach.

Another thunderclap sounded, and it was almost like the sound wave that took me down. I was knocked off my feet, flying through the air as my head pounded. I landed heavily in the shallow water and rolled instantly, getting back to my feet as another tongue lashed at me. It hit me on my left ankle, and I cried out in pain as it yanked and twisted at the same time. I went down, landing face down in the water as it slowly dragged me towards it.

Think, think, think, damnit.

I turned and watched the beast pull me in, its bulbous eyes glowing green as its throat swelled, ready for another knockout croak. I didn't think, I just acted as I slapped my hands down into the water and threw everything out of me in a rush, a scream tearing out of my throat.

It was almost like it happened in slow motion. Energy rippled out of me and into the water. The first Gulgron stiffened, its eyes swelling until they popped, and rolled over onto its back, eyes steaming. One by one, the Gulgron's eyes exploded before they flopped over onto their backs. The tongue around my ankle fell away, and I shakily got to my feet. Smoke filled the air, and a disgusting fried frog smell wafted on the gentle wind. I gagged, trying to get as far away from them as quickly as possible.

"I guess that's one way to do it." Ava drawled, two full canteens hanging over her shoulder by the straps.

"Let's get out of here." I coughed, Ava gagging as the wind shifted our way. She handed me one in silence, clenching her jaw.

"I suppose I should thank you for distracting them." She grumbled, holding her nose. We continued walking in silence. "Thanks." She muttered, and I couldn't help but smile, huffing a laugh through my nose.

"You're welcome." We walked until we could no longer smell the roasted frog and pulled out the riddle again.

"Feast in the place the hollow ones dread. I think I've read somewhere that they call Zephyros 'hollow ones' and they apparently don't like places that have been burned." I mused, trying to remember what I saw on the map.

"There was a burned-out camp I saw on the map not too far from here, perhaps about four kilometres," Ava suggested, still looking a little pale. I gestured for her to lead the way.

I lost track of how long it took, as my body didn't appreciate me using my Voltrite powers so suddenly, and through whatever block I was supposed to have on my magic.

I could feel it beneath my skin, but it slumbered.
My stomach cramped a little as we walked in silence.

365

Chapter
Thirty-Two

We smelt the ash before we could see it.

The burned-out camp was eerily quiet, some of the stone buildings still leaned on crumbled angles. We checked all the old buildings, making sure to turn over everything.

I found something that looked like a dragon scale buried under a stone. The shimmering green scale felt warm to the touch, about the size of a shield. Underneath was a cache of dried ration packs in a backpack. I hastily threw it over my shoulders and tucked the dragon scale under my arm.

"Rider?" Ava's voice sounded shaky as I made my way out of the crumpled building. "We're not alone." She breathed, and I stopped at the doorway. I heard a gentle chittering that sent chills over my skin. I should have remembered that places like this, that have seen blood and death, attract Noctheris. The sound echoed around us, starting in one tree and moving around. By their chitters, it sounded like they had us surrounded.

I spotted Ava leaning against the outside of the building I was in. I slowly made my way beside her.

"I've got the food."

"Good use it will do if we're fucking dead. I can spot at least six Noctheris." She hissed, and I followed her gaze. Yep, I could see their freaky humanoid figures, their bald heads turned at a sharp angle, their long, barbed tails swishing below the branch they were perched on.

"Any ideas on how to get out of here alive? Got any of that...whatever that was back at the marsh?"

"I can try, but I don't think I've got much left in me." I could feel the cramping begin low in my belly as my body fought whatever I had in my system. "I think I'll be lucky to be able to run. My body didn't like what I just did."

"So you're as useless as me then." She didn't say it to be mean, just a fact.

"Pretty much."

A scraping against bark echoed around the camp, light but deliberate. Then another, as each beast repeated the sound. A high, piercing, blood-curdling shriek lanced straight through my skull like a dagger made of sound. I dropped the dragon scale as my hands flew to my ears, Ava whimpering beside me.

The Noctheris hunched over the branches like nightmares wearing skin, their heads turning too far, necks cracking. Even from here, I could see their claws digging into the wood of the branch. They took flight and landed in one fluid motion, their claws dragged on the ash-coated stones, twitching in the half light as the sun decided now was a good time to set.

I fumbled for my dagger, only to remember we hadn't found them yet. They were next on the stupid riddle. The Noctheris crept closer. One opened its mouth, wide and black, showing rows of needle-like teeth. It shrieked again, and my knees buckled.

Blood trickled from my nose, my vision tilting as the sounds reverberated in my head. Ava was shouting something, but it was all noise now. It was as if my body had decided to stop working as I fell to my hands, chest heaving. Out of the corner of my eye, one of them lunged.

This is it. I've failed. I'm about to die.

I saw Ava swing a branch at the Noctheris that was almost on me. She shoved the branch straight into its open mouth. The creature reeled back with a guttural scream, wings flailing, knocking another beast into the base of a tree. Ava spun on her heel, grabbed me by my collar and dragged me backwards into the ruins half-collapsed building.

"On your feet, rider." She hissed, voice ragged. "Or I'll carry your corpse the rest of the way just to gloat that I'm better than you."

I gasped, blood on my lips as I shakily pushed up off the ground. The screaming in my head had lessened, my vision beginning to settle. I rose, weak, but defiant. I saw something shoved into Ava's ears, blocking out most of the Noctheris shrieks. She shoved the same thing into my ears, and I nodded my thanks. I could hear the creatures approaching us, surrounding us. But this time, I wouldn't fall to their call.

Ava reached into her ponytail, dug around for a few seconds and pulled out a lighter. The sneaky thing must have stashed it in there in preparation. Clever girl.

She flashed me a wicked grin and got to work creating a fire from a half charred bit of wood. I hurled rocks at the creatures as they tried to approach, hissing when my aim hit home.

"Here, they also aren't fans of burning alive." She handed me a stick with a rolled-up wad of material on the end. I looked down to see that she'd torn her shirt. I took the stick, sucked in a long breath before we charged out of the ruined building together.

The creatures shrieked, but this time, I was ready. I poked the flaming end into one beast's face, right in their horrific eyes. Another I hit in the chest, the smell of burning meat was enough to make me choke. One by one, we slowly took them down. Half of them took flight, screeching into the night as we finished the others off.

We were both panting, bleeding, and downright fucking had *enough* of this bullshit '*bonding mission.*'

"I think we should skip the next step and just find the shelter. I need to sit down and eat something." Ava panted, leaning on a tree and wrapping a strip of her shirt around the cut on her arm. I was doing the same for a gash on my leg.

"Agree." We were silent for a few beats. "I would have died if you hadn't pulled me out back there. Thank you." I met her steely gaze, hoping she could see my sincere thanks. She shrugged like it was nothing.

"Yeah, well, don't get used to it." She muttered, slinging the precious pack of food over her shoulder. "So, sleep where the sky does not reach. Should be easy to find." She drawled sarcastically.

"I'm sure it's just around the corner. A nice king-sized bed each, with a shower and a butler to wait on us hand

and foot." I matched her tone, and she surprised me by laughing properly.

"Yeah, and handsome men to give us foot massages and feed us grapes."

"And don't forget chocolate-dipped strawberries and wine."

"Ugh, I could really go for a nice glass of whiskey right now." We looked at each other and burst out laughing. We were hysterical, but it felt good.

"Gods, we're losing our fucking minds." Ava laughed, wiping her eyes and smudging soot on her cheek.

"Are we thinking that there is a shelter that's hidden from view, perhaps? That the sun and moon don't reach it?" I shrugged, hoping we didn't have to fight our way through beasts to get there.

"Yeah, that's what I was thinking too. But where the hell do we even begin to start looking for something like that? Oh, hang on." She scrubbed her face with her dirty hands, smudging the soot even more. "I think I saw a valley on the map. It seemed to be in the middle of this godforsaken forest."

"Yeah, I think you're right. I'm guessing if we head west, we should find it?"

"I don't have any better ideas." We both shrugged, looked towards the sky to gauge where west was, and started our slow trek towards hopefully a shelter.

We put out our flaming branches, as we didn't want to attract any unwanted attention. But we kept them for when we found our shelter. The silence between us wasn't awkward, and I liked to think that we'd made it over some sort of hurdle. We were far from friends, but at least we didn't hate each other anymore.

We found the valley, a creek flowing through it like a snake in the moonlight as we carefully made our way down the bank. Branches and sticks clawed at us, pulling at our hair as we eventually reached the bottom. And of course, we found it only by sheer luck. We'd reached the end of the valley, a towering wall of rocks behind us that seemed to hold no clues. I leaned against a wall of vines, hoping to rest a moment, when I fell through it with a cry. I landed heavily on my hip, pain flaring bright as I hit the slightly damp stones. But I'd found an entrance into a cave, behind the vines, and under the stones.

We set to work foraging for kindling and made a fire. We both groaned out loud when the warmth began leeching into our weary bones. We emptied the pack to see what food we'd had.

Dried meats, some sort of biscuit with grains and nuts, hard bread, some apples and oranges, and peanuts. We made sure to split it into three days' worth and ate our ration for today.

It settled into my stomach with a groan, the cold water washing it down and making me shiver. There were no signs of animals being in here, so hopefully we wouldn't be disturbed.

We stoked the fire, lay down on the hard stones and tried to get some sleep.

It was going to be a long night.

Morning came too early. The birds were extra loud to my sore ears. I rolled onto my back and stared at the roof of the cave, Ava's quiet snore loud in the small space. I stretched, my body aching everywhere as I took in my injuries. A deep gash on my thigh, but at least it had stopped bleeding. A few cuts and bruises on my arms and hands. But, I think I made it mostly unscathed.

I waited for Ava to wake before handing out some fruit to start the day, draining our canteens. At least we could refill them here in the creek outside, but I had a niggling feeling that we should return to the marsh.

"So, you're not as stuck up and pompous as I thought you would be," Ava smirked over her shoulder as she refilled her canteen. I barked a laugh, shaking my head.

"Yeah, I could say the same about you. Still a little bit of a bitch though."

"Oh, that's me being nice." She chuckled, and I finally felt that we might actually like each other at the end of this. If we got out alive.

"So, where were you hiding that lighter before you hid it in your hair?" I put my hands on my hips, watching her stand and stretch.

"Trust me, you don't want to know." She wrinkled her nose, and we both burst into laughter. "Same with the stuff to put in your ears."

We checked the cave, making sure to bring our pack and set off again for the marsh. Ava also agreed that she had a feeling about it.

We were beginning to recognise some of the landmarks in the forest, so it didn't take us long to reach the eerily quiet marsh. We kept low, keeping to the reeds and climbed a tree to get a better look, and what we saw was enough to raise the hairs on my arms, goosebumps prickling my skin.

A giant mech suit was on the outskirts of the marsh, hauling a dead Gulgron out of the water, and about six people crowded around, in something that looked like armour. I thought the suits were a myth.

We couldn't hear what they were saying, but they put the frog in a large net, securing it with ropes as the mech suit powered up, wings extended on either side and took off into the sky, the dead Gulgron swinging grotesquely underneath it.

I turned to Ava, who looked at me with confusion. We needed to get closer to try to hear what they were saying.

Down the tree we shimmied, creeping through the reeds until we perched in a tree behind the group.

"The Basilisk should reach the base in a few hours. Let's clean up and leave before we're seen. I don't feel much like killing anyone else today." The man who spoke looked very familiar, but I couldn't place him.

Kill anyone else?

"Pack up and head out. Vaelin will be able to tell what killed these frogs, and hopefully it's as easy as hunting down a rider." A woman spoke, she had blonde hair tied back into a braid, fierce light grey eyes and cheekbones that were so sharp for a woman. She looked a little scary. "Regali, make sure no one sees us."

"Yes, Lysara." The man replied, looking around the marsh with narrowed eyes. I made sure to stay hidden, and Ava was doing the same.

Regali.

No wonder he looked familiar.

He had to be related to the rogue rider Regali.

CHAPTER
THIRTY-THREE

The woman knelt by another dead Gulgron, poking it with a gloved hand.

"Something fried these creatures, and I want to find out who, or what." She stood, removing her gloves and handing them to someone else. "If you see anyone else, kill them on sight and dispose of the bodies."

My skin tingled at her threat. They obviously weren't meant to be here.

The six of them wandered off in the other direction, making sure to keep an eye around them.

What the hell? Who are they? Where did they come from?

We waited until they'd been gone for at least ten minutes before we made our way down the tree, sneaking off back towards our cave. We didn't speak, too worried that they might hear us.

"Who the bloody hell were they?" Ava breathed as we entered the safety of our cave.

"I've got no idea, but I don't think they wanted anyone to know they were here. And I've never seen anything like that suit before."

"Neither have I. Even in the military, they don't have things like that." She'd gone a little pale, twisting her hands together. "My mother is in the military, and well respected too. I'll mention this to her once we get out."

"Good thinking. How about we try to find these bloody weapons?"

"Yeah, I was thinking the same thing. Then hopefully we can just come back here and chill out. I'm sick of all these asshole animals trying to kill us."

We found the map tree again and studied the burned clue in the bark. I read the riddle again.

"Arm where the skies whisper lies, and the shriek seeks sight. Find steel where shadows circle in flight."

"That's got to mean Nimurra's, surely? Fucking hate those things." She grumbled. "Here, use these for your ears, but I'm afraid it won't work as well as it did for the Noctheris."

"Thanks." I took the small globs of Blu-Tac for my ears. Not my preferred choice of thing to stick in my ears, but if it would help save our lives, I'd take it.

"I've read that they like to nest in a forest glade or some shit." Ava sighed, stretching her arms and legs with a grimace.

"Yeah, that's what I was worried about. Somewhere that's foggy and dark?"

"Must be to match their dark souls." She grumbled. I laughed, agreeing with her. We set off to find the possibly most dangerous part of this mission yet.

Hours we walked, swearing that we got lost an hour ago, but lo and behold, we found ourselves deep in a forest glade choked with fog and light-dappled vines. Tree limbs arched overhead like dark ribs.

It was too quiet. Not even a breath of wind.

"I don't like this place," I whispered, afraid to talk any louder.

We had to crouch low under branches and twisted vines until we heard the distant flap of wings. Not one or two. But dozens of Nimurra's. Their forms shimmered, more shadow than bird. Their cries were high and unnatural.

Not caws, not shrieks, but something worse. Something that slid into your ears and coiled behind your eyes.

"They're illusions," Ava whispered as they began circling high above.

"No, they're not." I breathed, scanning the treetops. "I think they're waiting for us to look away." A feather drifted down like ash, iridescent, dark green, with a sharp sheen like obsidian. Ava caught it, her breathing hitched.

"They're gone. I think...I think it's clear." Her voice sounded odd. I turned my attention to her instead.

"Ava, they're still here." I reached out to grab her shoulder, but I paused. Her eyes were wide with panic, and she began shaking her head.

"The forest, it's melting." She whispered and reached out to touch my face, her hands shaking. "Oh my gods, your face." She opened her mouth to scream, but I slapped my hand over it instead.

"Ava! Look at me," I growled. "The hallucination's not real. Focus." She blinked, once, twice. She sucked in a long breath and blew it out, slumping a little.

"Th...thanks." She rubbed her eyes, but I started to feel nauseous. The birds' calls were potent, even from down here. We began searching on our hands and knees, the damp soil soaking into our trousers. Under low-hanging branches, over raised tree roots, we crawled, getting more frustrated by the minute.

A large tree, just ahead, caught my eye. It was covered in scars, marks so deep in the trunk of the tree that something must be here.

"I think it's here." I breathed, quickly looking over my shoulder. I saw branches swaying above us, and a feather floated down not far from us. Ava scrabbled ahead, digging at the base of the tree. She eventually found a stone slab with a dagger and wings carved into it. She turned back to nod at me, and I hurried over. We lifted the stone with a grunt and discovered a cache of weapons. We quickly hauled them out, shoving them into our packs as the birds began circling again, their shriek getting closer. I made sure my ears were plugged, but didn't see the stray Nimurra that had broken away from its group and was making its way right for us until it was right in front of Ava. She screamed, throwing her hands over her face as the bird swooped for her eyes. I swung one of the short swords at the creature, nicking its clawed foot. It screeched and looped around, coming for round two. I threw a blade to Ava, who stayed hunched close to the ground. It was as if it had summoned the rest of its flock, as they dove as one. They swarmed us like a dark cloud, their cries harsh enough that my head ached, my eyes stung as my mind started to sway. The forest turned into a pretty flower-filled clearing. Vex and Brodie were there, lying in the sun. I felt relieved seeing that they were here, and I was finished with that stupid mission.

A scream broke through the silence, but it was quickly silenced.

"Brodie? What are you doing here?" I tried to walk towards him, but my limbs didn't want to obey. He opened his mouth to speak, but nothing came out. And his eyes didn't look right. I frowned and turned to Vex, his golden eyes more orange as they seemed to turn a little fuzzy on the edges.

This isn't right. Something's wrong. I felt a sharp pain in my face, and I gasped, throwing myself to the ground.

This. Isn't. Real. I chanted.

I cleared my head and opened my eyes to see a mass of Nimurra flocking around us, Ava screaming, face bloody where they were trying to get to her eyes.

Fuck. We needed to get out of here, *now.*

I swung my sword around my head, taking out three of the nasty beasts and made my way towards Ava. I grabbed her hand and pulled. She cried out, swatting me away, but I slapped her in the face. She gasped, but her eyes cleared.

"Move!" I barked, and she nodded. We got to our feet and ran, keeping our heads bowed as we fought through the dark fog and twisted vines. I didn't know how long we spent in that fucking glade, but it felt like days. We eventually got out and into the sun, our chests heaving and faces stinging.

I turned to Ava, who has cuts to her face, neck and hands. I was sure I looked the same.

"You saved me," she gasped, trying to catch her breath, wiping the blood from her cheeks.

"Don't make it a habit," I replied, wiping my own face with the bottom of my shirt. Ava coughed a laugh, collapsing onto the ground. "Come on, I need a wash and something to eat," I grumbled, brushing the dirt from me. I helped pull her to her feet, and we wearily made our way back to our creek and cave. It felt like the middle of the night when we arrived. The icy cold water made my teeth chatter, but at least I felt a little more clearer-headed. We were in no mood to take on any more creatures. So we lit our fire and settled in for the night.

I really, really hoped they got us out of there first thing in the morning.

I never thought I'd hear myself say this, but I've missed your voice in my head, little storm.

You're not getting soft on me, are you?

Just get up and walk to where you woke up that first morning. From there, you can teleport back to the academy.

I sat up, rubbed my eyes and looked around.

Hang on. We were still on the mission.

It seems like you've gotten rid of the block from your magic. Now, get the hell out of there.

"Ava!" I shook her awake, and she brandished a knife at me, blinking awake. "Bloody hell, girl." I gasped, rolling to the side only just in time.

"Why did you wake me?" She mumbled, huffing out loud and dropping the knife.

"I can teleport us back to the academy. We just need to walk to where we woke that first day." I summoned flames to my hands, it sparked at first before stunning black and silver flames danced at my fingertips.

"Oh, you got your magic back, and we can leave!" She jumped up off the floor, dusted herself off and gathered her things.

"If we leave now, we should make it back in time for breakfast," I said wistfully, dreaming of coffee.

"Oh, thank Kamari. I would kill for a croissant." Ava yawned, stretching her arms, her joints popping like tiny cannons in the quiet cave.

We wasted no time in heading out. The sun hadn't risen yet, but we were familiar enough with the forest now that we knew which way to go.

We arrived in the field we woke in, and guessed it was about seven in the morning. Just in time.

"This better work, rider." Ava didn't look impressed as she looked me up and down.

"Just shut up and hold on," I grumbled, grabbing her arm and holding tight. My skin was tingling, not having my magic for two full days made me feel on edge, my magic begging to be let out. I shut my eyes, pictured the middle of the cafeteria and jumped, making sure I kept Ava with me.

We went from the silence of the forest to the loud, echoing noise of the cafeteria full of students. A few shrieked, a lot shouted as they pointed at us.

"Oh, my gods! They're back!"

"They're filthy!"

"What the hell happened?"

"What did you have to do?"

Perhaps arriving in the middle of breakfast wasn't the best idea.

My stomach grumbled, and I shook off the cadets surrounding me, heading straight for a tray and loading it with sausages, eggs, bacon, toast, beans, and a triple-shot coffee. I hadn't replied to anyone yet, not until I'd eaten something. Ava followed, plonking down beside me.

The voices faded away as I focused on chewing my food, tasting it, savouring it.

"This is the best thing I've ever eaten," Ava grunted, as she shoved another bite of pastry into her mouth. She had to hold up her hand to shut up the others who came over asking question after question.

"Uh-huh," I grunted back, closing my eyes as I chewed on some bacon.

"Can someone tell me how you two ended up back here so early?" I heard the authority in the voice and paused mid-bite as Principal Shields came to stand opposite our table, glaring at us.

"You weren't meant to be picked up until this afternoon." Growled Principal Peterson beside her.

"My magic returned this morning, we followed the riddle and got everything on there."

"The riddle didn't exactly specify what time we needed to come back," Ava said around a full mouthful of croissant, spraying crumbs onto the table.

"Fine. I guess we'll allow it. Take yourselves to the infirmary, you're both a mess. And I expect to see you both in your first lessons." Peterson grumbled, walking away with a dirty look. I sagged into my seat, a hysterical laugh bubbled up through my chest, and I turned to look at Ava, who also seemed to be struggling to contain herself.

We lost that battle and fell about laughing until we were crying. People looked at us with confused faces, scraping their chairs away slightly. We finished our food and excused ourselves from the cafeteria, making our way down to the infirmary. We were in good health, just our few scrapes and bruises cleaned up, and we were sent away, just in time to make it to the first lesson.

Great. We didn't even get a day off.

CHAPTER
THIRTY-FOUR

I t was as if we didn't just spend two nights in the middle of that fucking dark forest, fighting for our lives. Oh no, we were thrust straight back into training, getting our asses kicked because we were tired and aching. The rest of the day dragged on with painful slowness, and by the time I sat down after dinner, I remembered that I hadn't checked my whisp that was waiting for me in my room.

Oops.

Three missed calls, and four pulses.

Lia said you're back. How was it?

Are you okay, Storm?

Why aren't you answering me?

For fucks sake, Storm, answer your whisp!

Uh oh. Someone seems cranky.

`Yes, he is. So you better call him back before he comes over here himself. You don't want to see him when he's angry.`

Alright, alright. Sheesh.

He answered on the first ring.

'Took you long enough.' He growled, and I couldn't help but smile. Same ol grumpy prince.

"Hi to you too."

'What the hell went on out there? Lia's giving me nothing.'

"That's because I haven't seen Lia yet, and we're the first ones back."

'How come no one else is back? Lia said you two looked like hell.'

"Because my magic returned this morning, I got us out of there. And yes, it was fucking *hell* in there. We nearly got eaten by Gulgron's, Noctheris', and Nimurra's. I would have died if it weren't for Ava. Hang on, something's happening." I took the whisp away from my ear as the common room broke out into wild chatter. Ava came over, looking a little pale and out of breath.

"They've just returned with the other cadets. Only three survived. The other three are dead, well, they can't find two of them."

I shakily put the whisp back to my ear as Ava wandered off to speak to her friends.

Dread settled into my stomach.

"Did you hear that?" I breathed.

'I did. What the bloody hell were they thinking, sending first years out into the goddamned forest weaponless, for three days? It's completely fucking insane!' He growled, *'I need to tell father.'* He hung up.

I sighed, poking my tongue out at the whisperglass.

"Bye to you too," I grumbled. I forced myself out of the comfy armchair by the fire and slowly made my way to my room, where I stood in the shower for way too long, then collapsed into bed.

The Principals decided to revert back to the old initiation to help us bond, seeing as they received so much backlash from the cadets about the forest missions. I just wished that we weren't the first group to get dropped out there, then we could have avoided it altogether. But Ava and I were at least speaking now, on friendly terms, but we were still far from friends.

While they talked it out with the other professors, classes resumed as normal.

Dragon Lore was probably my favourite class, as we learned about all the different dragons. Mostly the main four here, as they didn't get to see the other three rarer breeds very often, so Professor Jamieson tended to ask me questions about Vex.

Vex wasn't giving me anything, so I just had to go off what I had slowly begun to figure out. He especially didn't want me to tell them about the dragon stone in his chest. So I told them that the dragon and their rider are only allowed to know how they bonded, much to the professor's disappointment.

History was a bore. I'd never been a fan and struggled to pay attention. Ava helped when I needed it, as I could then help her in training with sparring.

It seemed to work out pretty well, and I was glad to have a girl I could talk to in Sinvidia. Theon was his usual self, but our studies were getting more difficult by the day, and any spare time we were studying.

I'd hoped that I would have made some more friends here by now, but they still kept their distance. Even at school on the island, I struggled to make friends.

So I trained, flew Vex and focused on my studies. I tried to avoid awkward conversations with Ryler, but he'd just smile and wave. Was I overreacting? The murders were still a constant thought niggling the back of my mind.

Levi and Mitch would often train with me in the evening when I didn't want to sit in the common room by myself. And my room was too depressing to just sit in. So I worked out with my weapons and the training equipment.

The new guard from Galadron - Michelle - was a complete bitch, sour face to match. She strutted around like she owned the place, sneering at me every time we passed in the halls.

I had no idea what I did to piss her off, but I was getting over it. Ava began sneering back, and I didn't think it would take long before a fight broke out in the corridors.

The other guards were at least friendlier. They would offer small smiles when we passed them in the halls, but they were there at every turn. I wouldn't be surprised if the murders stopped, only because we couldn't get a moment alone.

Our new Wingmaster was only appointed two days ago - Piper Lancom. She seemed nice, coming around and introducing herself to everyone in our house. But I wasn't going to get my hopes up about making a new friend.

"I've been thinking," Theon murmured as we sat in the common room, closing our history books. I looked over and waited for him to continue. It was just us down here now, everyone else had gone to bed.

"I might be clutching at straws here, and I don't know how Mick is tied in with it, but the first two were publicly horrible to you."

Goosebumps broke out over my skin as I thought about it. He was right, Mick was lovely and never said a bad word about anyone, but the other two didn't hide their dislike for me.

"Perhaps he was in the wrong place, at the wrong time?" Theon continued, scratching his chin. He met my gaze and shrugged. "I'm probably way off, but I don't know what else it could be."

The rest of the first-years were pulled into their bonding missions around the academy, and a bunch of rooms were off limits as they did whatever it was.

The ones who completed it simply rolled their eyes and continued not speaking to their roommate. Some of them hated each other more than before.

It was almost as if they didn't want us to get along, just pretended to try.

"Ria, what are you up to this weekend?" Mitch asked as he finished his round of leg presses. I didn't miss Levi's pretend cough from over at the weights station.

"No plans." I huffed, focusing on my skipping.

"They have a fair in Sylvanfire. I was just wondering if you'd be interested in going?" He kept his face straight, but I could see Levi grinning in the mirror.

Have those two been planning this? They look suspicious.

I *did* want to go. But I was also hoping someone else was going to ask me. But it was Friday night, and the fair was tomorrow.

`Don't wait for him to come to you. Otherwise, you'll be a pile of dust by the time he realises.`

I huffed a laugh. He wasn't wrong there.

"Yeah, sure. Why not?" I chose to ignore Brodie's earlier warning to stay away from him.

His answering smile lit up his whole face, and I couldn't help but smile myself.

"How about I pick you up, say, at seven? I know it's early, but it takes a few hours to get there."

"Sure, sounds like a plan." I set the skipping rope down, stretching my legs and arms before collecting my bag. "Well, I'm off. Night." I waved to the pair who were grinning, but Levi chased after me.

"Wait, you can't walk back alone." He shook his head, and I wrinkled my nose before nodding.

"Of course. Thanks, Levi." I smiled, and he fell into step beside me.

"Seems like you're fitting in alright." The halls were empty at this time of night, only a few of us were allowed out with an escort. Korin had worked his magic for me.

"Yeah, I guess so." I shrugged, not agreeing with him, but I didn't want to get into it. "How are you coping here rather than in the castle?"

Levi tried to hide his smile, but I could see how pleased he was.

"It's great. I'd love to be here full-time, actually. I'm going to ask at the end of all this." He had a spring to his step, and I couldn't help but smile as well.

"That's good. Hopefully, they have a spot open for you."

It wasn't long until I'd reached my door. I thanked him and said goodnight.

But I was surprised at how excited I was for tomorrow.

Mitch knocked on my door at seven sharp, and Ava grumbled as I whispered a goodbye.

He wore a pair of dark jeans, black boots, a navy blue shirt under his leather jacket, and damn, he looked good.

"Hey." I smiled, feeling excited for the first time in a long time.

"Hey, ready to go? You look lovely, by the way." He winked, and I rolled my eyes, but my stomach filled with something that felt awfully like butterflies.

Huh. Weird.

We quickly made our way through the quiet halls, most people still in bed. The academy had a large garage out the back, but mostly for the professors, but seeing as Mitch was here full-time as a guard, he was allowed his own transport. Over in the back was the beautiful black and red stormsteed that he rode the other day. It screamed dangerous, fast, and exhilarating.

Mitch handed me my own helmet, helping me buckle it on with a faint smile.

"You might want to hold on. But I promise not to go too crazy." He patted the seat behind him, and I laughed, climbing on.

"Don't go slow on my account. I like it fast."

"Well then, what are we waiting for?" He revved the engine, and it growled to life, the sound almost deafening in the garage. I wrapped my arms around his waist, and we took off like a shot. Dark trees and forest tore past as we sped down the winding dirt road, the dust kicking up behind us.

I couldn't stop the joyful laugh that burst free. I felt like I could finally take in a deep breath and not have to be someone they expected me to be. I couldn't wipe the grin from my face as we sped through the countryside, Sylvanfire approaching too soon. I could have ridden for hours.

We parked out the back, and Mitch placed our helmets on the handlebars.

"So, how was it?" He grinned, his brown eyes sparkling as he leaned back on the bike.

"I loved it, thank you. Didn't know how much I needed that." I felt a little shy, so I shoved my hands into my pockets.

"Come on then, let's see what sort of things they've got." He led the way. The fair was in full swing, even if it had just opened.

Rides. Games. Food. Drinks. A stall for everything you could think of. Mitch bought us both some games and ride tickets, and the roller coaster was the first one up.

I'd never been to a fair before. We didn't have them back home, not like this anyway. We only had markets with the occasional ring toss. The rollercoaster was super fun, but the haunted mansion wasn't so much. I didn't want to admit how I had clung to Mitch's arm when a vampire jumped out at us. Mitch laughed, but happily kept my hand on his arm until we'd finished.

I didn't think I'd ever laughed so much in my life.

I lost count of the rides we went on. But I couldn't wipe the smile from my face.

"What would you like to do next?" Mitch asked with a smile as we made our way through the fair. Everyone here was so happy, and I carried a silly stuffed teddy bear that Mitch had won for me. I didn't want to admit it, but I loved it. No one had spent time like this with me before, and I was sick of being alone.

"I'm actually starving."

"Oh, good. Me too." He led me towards a food truck, and the smells that were coming from it were divine. My mouth started to water just thinking about it. "What would you like? My shout."

"I've never had any of this before, so I have no idea. I'll have whatever you're having." I shrugged, and he stared at me with a shocked expression.

"You've never had fair food before?" He looked confused. I laughed and shook my head. "Dagwood dog? Soggy crinkle cut chips with tomato sauce?" I shook my head, and he looked at me with mock horror. "Then we must get you some!" He said in a ridiculous voice, lining up to order.

"Yes, sir." I saluted, unable to wipe the smile from my face. "Mitch?" I fidgeted, suddenly feeling a little nervous.

"Hmm?" He turned, eyes twinkling in the sun.

"Thank you. For all of this. I can't remember the last time I'd had this much fun." I felt my cheeks blaze, but his expression softened as he reached out a hand to grab mine. He squeezed my fingers gently.

"You're welcome, Nymeria. I'm glad you're having fun. I am too. I haven't smiled this much in a very long time, so thank you." We stood there holding hands, just smiling at each other.

"Next!" The man in the food van called, and I realised he was talking to us.

"That's us." I chuckled, and Mitch's eyes widened before he spun around, ordered chips and a Dagwood Dog each, and an energy drink to wash it down.

"Thank goodness you eat actual food. So many girls these days are so fussy." He mumbled as we went to take our seats at a nearby park bench. He handed me my lunch, and I breathed it in.

"Smells...interesting." I eyed the Dagwood dog but made sure to dip it in some sauce before taking a bite. Mitch watched with interest, popping a chip into his grinning mouth.

"So, what do you think?" He rested his chin on his fist, fighting back a laugh.

"It's...kinda gross, but kinda delicious at the same time." I didn't know what to think, but I made sure to finish it so I could make a proper decision. "Yeah, I stand by that. Yuck but yum." Mitch shook his head and laughed, his face lighting up.

"Yeah, that about sums it up perfectly." He winked and popped another chip in.

"How were you able to get us a pass out of the academy for this? It's been on pretty heavy lockdown lately." I took a mouthful of the energy drink I was never allowed at home, and no wonder, too, the sugar in it was enough to keep me buzzing for at least two days.

"I have some leeway with Peterson, I think he's scared of my father, so he lets me do what I want, mostly." Mitch chuckled, but mentioning his father chilled me.

I would get skinned alive if Brodie knew I was here with Mitch. I didn't know what else to say, but I could feel Mitch's eyes on me.

"So, what would you like to see now?"

I took a deep breath and looked around. The fairground was buzzing with young families, teenagers, and even some adults, like us enjoying themselves. The sun was shining, not a breath of wind either. A perfect day.

"Could we perhaps go see the ocean? It's been so long since I've felt the cool water on my feet, the sand between my toes."

His answering smile was actually beautiful.

"Absolutely! We'll head off as soon as we're finished, if you like?" He opened his mouth as if to say more when a hand clamped down on his shoulder. I looked up into the face of Mitch's father.

Vex growled into my head, feeling my unease and not helping the situation.

"Son, I didn't know you would be here today."

CHAPTER
THIRTY-FIVE

Captain O'Connell smiled at me like he'd just won a show bag.

Vex growled louder. I leaned back and placed my hands in my lap.

"Father? What are you doing here?" Mitch looked up over his shoulder, a crease between his brows.

"I could ask you the same thing, but I see you're here with Miss Everhart." He pinned his dark brown eyes on me, and I had to fight a full-body shiver as they locked on mine. It felt like he could see into my soul.

"You know Nymeria?" Mitch asked, looking a little confused as I tried to smile back, but I felt frozen, pinned under this man's heavy stare.

"It's lovely to see you again," he stuck out a hand, and I forced myself to reach out and shake it. His grip was so firm that the bones in my hand ground together, instantly making them ache.

Fucking asshole.

`I'll burn him to cinders if he stays any longer. I'm just around the corner.`

Did you follow me here?

`Yes. I'd be a fool not to.`

Nosy dragon.

"You too, sir," I said as politely as possible while he grinned evilly at me.

"I'm sorry to break up this little *adventure*. But I'm afraid I need you to come along, son, I have something important I need to run past you. government business, I'm afraid I can't discuss with commoners."

Fuck. You.

I wanted to shout the words, but I knew when to keep my mouth shut around men like him. Instant bad guy vibes.

"Then why are you here at the fair?" Mitch tipped his head to the side, brows drawing down further.

"That's none of your concern," the captain's eyes travelled over me again, and I made sure not to shrink down into my seat.

"But father, I gave Ria a lift here on my stormsteed. She doesn't have a way of getting back." Mitch started to protest, but his father cut him off with a hand in the air.

"She's a rider, no? Can't she take her dragon home?" He turned to me with raised brows, smirking.

Mitch opened his mouth, but I cut him off, too.

"It's okay, really, Mitch. Vex isn't far away. I'll be fine." I tried to ignore captain asshole, who still stood behind him, almost sneering at me. Mitch looked conflicted, so I reached out a hand and placed it on his, squeezing it slightly. "It's okay. I'll see you back at the academy." I nodded, but he still didn't look happy about it. And to just show off, I'm sure, Vex soared overhead, landing on the field designated for riders and their dragons.

"Ah, the dragon himself. Such a powerful beast, to bond to such a small girl." Captain O'Connell drawled, and I saw Mitch's shoulders rise, a muscle ticked in his jaw. I stood, bracing my hands on the table.

"Then it's a lucky thing a small girl like me can handle a beast like him. They're all the same, though, in the end. Men and dragons are very similar." I smiled, but it lacked any warmth. But I looked down at Mitch, who looked like he'd rather be anywhere else. "I'll see you later."

Don't burn me for that. I'm trying to-

`Yeah, yeah. I know. Shut up and get over here before I do something stupid.`

I sculled the rest of my drink, grabbed my food containers and dumped them in the bin on my way through the fair. I was seething. Wanting to hit something. Or light something on fire.

My steps were stiff, my hands were balled into fists at my sides. My jaw ached from clenching my teeth together so tightly as I approached Vex. His tail was swishing like an agitated cat as he growled at anyone who got too close. Safe to say, everyone was keeping well away.

We didn't speak on our way back, the academy looming in the distance as the sun disappeared into the trees.

A few pulses pinged on my way back, but there was no use checking them while flying. My luck, I would drop the damn whisp and never find it again. I checked it once I flopped down onto my bed.

I am so sorry about my father. I feel
so angry about the way he spoke
to you, but for some reason, he
has something against riders. Please

don't think I feel the same way. I
hope you got back okay?

> It's fine. It will take more than that
> to upset me. I had a wonderful day.
> Thank you so much.

I did too. Thanks for coming with
me. I'll make it up to you another
day :)

> I'll hold you to that ;)

—⦿✦⦿—

I yawned wide as Professor Yates and Shields droned on
in history class. Noah Richards, a Ruleum Boots cadet,
sat on my right scribbling notes into his book, and on
my other side sat Wally Ferguson, a Furora Boots cadet,
who was doodling in the back of his book. They'd rarely
spoken to me since the school year had started, so I knew
nothing about them.

"Who can tell me how long Voralyth has been an
academy?" Professor Yates called. He liked to pick on the
riders, calling them out and making us sound stupid if we
didn't know the answer. I was really starting to hate him.

"Everhart?" He smirked. He looked like a vulture today, dressed in droopy black clothes and beady eyes.

Goddamn it.

"I believe it was about four hundred years ago, Professor." I'd studied with Ava last night, and thank the gods he asked me something I remembered. His expression went from smug to sneering.

"That's a very broad answer, anyone could have guessed that. I expect you to research the exact date for the next class."

"Yes, sir." I automatically responded, internally giving him the finger.

"What an ass," Wally said under his breath. "He should just retire already." Wally didn't look my way, but continued to doodle away. I gazed over and my mouth almost dropped open. His art was spectacular.

"Wally, your drawings are amazing," I whispered, trying not to get the attention of Yates again.

"Thanks, I'd rather draw than listen to that old windbag drone on." He shrugged like it was no biggie.

"You could sell those." He'd drawn two dragons soaring through the sky over the trees, as if he were looking straight up from the ground. The detail was spot on. "Is that Vex?" I'd recognise that tail and horns anywhere, even if it was all shaded with pencil.

"Yeah, I saw you once when you were flying off with McTavish. He's a beautiful dragon, perfect to sketch." He quickly looked my way for the first time, a faint smile tugging at his lips. "I don't mean to sound creepy, but I like to draw people too." He slid a piece of paper over, and I realised with a start that he'd drawn me. It truly was stunning. He'd captured me perfectly. "You can keep it." He turned away and went back to his drawing.

"Thanks," I murmured, folding it and putting it in my bag. I didn't know how to feel about that.

"Can you guys not? I'm trying to pay attention." Noah grumbled, his notebook full.

"Sorry, Noah. But I don't know how you can pay attention. It's dreadfully boring." I murmured as I heaved a sigh. I'd barely taken any notes. Ava was going to kick my ass for that. I looked up just as Professor Shields took over, thank goodness.

"Voralyth has housed riders and soldiers for the past hundred years, hoping to end the divide between us. We are yet to crack that nut, but we're hoping one day we can move past it and work together. We've been fortunate to avoid large-scale conflicts requiring our cooperation since the invasion eighty years ago."

That got my attention.

Shields wandered across the room, eyes skating over each student.

"It showed us that we can work together when we put our differences behind us. And we were able to take back the land they had secured, and with minimal losses. But we can't get complacent. We must try harder. There have been attacks on the coastal villages, so the king has stationed small groups of riders and soldiers at outposts throughout Everdra. And so that will be your duty when you graduate. You might get the choice to pick where you would prefer, but I think they tend to move you to another location after a five-year stint in one place."

Will that be my fate then? To be a guard at some outpost or small town?

`No. The king will want you for his own personal guard. You're too powerful to waste in some backcountry town.`

"I want you to research the war, and catalogue where they landed, how they were able to take us by surprise, and for so long. How we could have avoided it, and what you would do in that situation. You're dismissed." The room burst into noise as we packed up our bags and filed out. It was the last lesson of the day, and I was keen to get out on Vex before it got too dark.

"Ria." Mitch was waiting by the door, casually leaning on the frame with a wide smile on his face. I hadn't seen him since the weekend. I smiled in return, slowing my pace as he fell into step beside me.

"How was history?" He looked down at me as we walked, the others pushing past us without a care in the world.

"Yates was in fine form, as usual." I shrugged, "But Shields wants us to research the war eighty years ago."

"Ah, they'll never let us forget that one. I wonder if they'll ever mention the..." He didn't get to finish the sentence when Levi popped up out of nowhere, out of breath.

"Mitch," he wheezed, placing a hand on the wall to steady himself. "We need to go, now. Oh, hey Ria." He waved halfheartedly, but I could see how pale he looked.

"What's going on?" Mitch instantly stood taller, looking around.

"No time to explain. Ria, you should head..."

"ALL STUDENTS TO RETURN TO THEIR COMMON ROOMS IMMEDIATELY UNTIL FURTHER NOTICE." Peterson's voice boomed through the speakers in the hall. Mitch stiffened, and Levi shook his head.

"Can I walk Ria to her room first?"

"Then hurry, we're needed in the principals office." Levi took off, and I turned a worried glance at Mitch.

"Let's go." He took hold of my hand, and we almost ran back through the halls. Most students were sharing worried looks as they hurried along.

"Do you think there's been another murder?" I breathed, nerves made me break out in a sweat.

"Yes." He was clenching his jaw, eyes darting constantly as he gripped my hand tightly. "I'll pulse you as soon as I know more." We reached the door to the Sinvidia common room. "I'll talk to you soon, okay?" He turned his full gaze to me, his brown eyes dark.

"Okay." I nodded, but as I turned to go, he tugged my hand, turning me back around. He dropped my hand, and his fingers slipped into my hair, angling my face up, and planted a kiss on my lips. Sparks shot through my veins, my fingertips prickling as the kiss seared through me. It had been so long since I'd been kissed. I didn't want it to end. But he pulled away, a little breathless as he looked through my eyes and into my soul. I was still trying to catch my breath when he gave me a shy smile, pink staining his cheeks. We were still just standing there, staring at each other.

"I..." His chest heaved, eyes darting over my face, and I huffed a laugh, knowing my cheeks must be blazing. My body felt a little too hot in my skin.

"Go," I whispered, giving his chest a little push. "I'll see you soon." His eyes sparkled, the brown lightning as he smiled at me, winking my way before darting down the hall.

Damn.

Mitchell O'Connell just kissed me. And I really enjoyed it.

CHAPTER THIRTY-SIX

There'd been another murder.

The rider was a third-year Furora cadet who had recently expressed his feelings towards letting Vex lead the riot of dragons when training. That Vex ought to stick to the back, seeing as we weren't proper Sinvidia, or any house here. I think I was starting to see a pattern here, and Theon was correct.

Every cadet who had either said something about me in a negative way, ended up dead.

So now I was worried about that, couldn't stop wondering if Rex was okay, and the loss of Mick still stung like a fresh wound. I doubted he said anything bad about me, but maybe he saw something he shouldn't have?

I thought Voralyth was going to be the best years of my life. But so far, I'd rather be anywhere else.

❖

Ava really doesn't hold back when sparring.

Her fists were flying at me, concentration etched onto her face as she danced around, trying to get me. She had really improved these past few weeks since our little adventure in the forest.

"Good footwork," I huffed, letting her take the offence.

"I know. I've got a good teacher. I saw you take down that Ruleum cadet." She smirked, trying to get past my defences. The double doors at the other end of the gym slammed open, getting our attention. The room quickly filled with soldiers dressed in black, guns on their hips.

This does not look good.

`Don't let them take you!` Vex yelled, *I'm getting Cyndrithra.*

"Cadet Nymeria Everhart." A blond woman called, and my stomach dropped so fast I felt nauseous.

That's the woman we saw in the forest, with the mech suit.

Lysara.

"That's me." I stepped forward, and Ava grabbed hold of my wrist. I could feel her shaking as she must have recognised the woman, too.

"You're a very popular woman. And we wanted to just ask you a few questions about you and your very special dragon." She smiled at me, but it was a cold, vicious thing. Her eyes were like steel, cutting right through me. "If you would come with us." She gestured behind her, where at least six soldiers waited.

Don't you dare.

I heard a roar in the distance, and Lysara's hand went to the earpiece in her right ear.

"I don't even know who you are." I planted my feet. Ava stayed right beside me.

"This is bad, very bad." She breathed, lips barely moving. I nodded very subtly.

"Of course. My name is Commander Toory of the Military. I have been asked to bring you in, just for some questions. It's been so long since we've had a Tenebrae dragon in these lands."

If they take you, I will burn them all. Vex roared again, and I felt the ground beneath me shudder as he landed outside.

"I see that your dragon is a little upset. Perhaps you could tell him we mean you no harm." She tried to smile again, but it looked stiff, like she wasn't used to doing it.

"How do I know that? You come storming in here with six fully armed soldiers at your back, demanding that I just come with you? To where? Why can't you ask me questions here?" I folded my arms across my chest and glared at her. A muscle in her jaw twitched as her eyes narrowed.

"I ask that the other cadet leave, so we can talk properly." I felt Ava stiffen beside me. I could sense her about to open her mouth to retort. I turned to her before she could get herself into trouble.

"Go, find Vidalia Fairchild," I whispered, hoping she could see the urgency in my eyes.

"I don't trust them. I'm not leaving until I know they mean you no harm." Ava didn't bother keeping her voice down as he turned hard eyes to the group before us.

"What's your name, cadet?" Lysara took a step, and I was tempted to stand in front of Ava.

"What does it matter to you? You're not here for me." She crossed her arms over her chest and widened her stance. I wanted to face palm at her attitude. Lysara didn't seem like the type of person to take it on the chin.

"You either tell me your name, or you get out of here before I arrest you for obstruction." Lysara snapped, and I saw the steel in her eyes, the way her hands twitched toward the weapons on her hips.

"Go, before you get in trouble too." I hissed, pleading with her. Ava turned sharp eyes on me, thought about it for a second, then nodded.

"I'm going to call my mum. Don't do anything I wouldn't." Ava glared at Lysara and the soldiers before bolting out of the room.

"Where's she going?" Lysara went to take a step towards Ava.

"You told her to leave, so she is. Now, what do you really want?" I got her attention back on me as Ava shot through the door and away.

"Tell your dragon to back off." She growled, taking a slow step toward me. "Otherwise, he won't like what I'll do to his precious rider." She advanced on me, her blonde ponytail swinging. She was wearing light leather armour, while the soldiers behind her were wearing thin metal.

I WILL NOT LET THEM TAKE YOU. He thundered down the bond. I winced as he roared. She lifted her hand to her earpiece again.

"I have guns on that stormblade that can take down a dragon, even one his size. So if you want him to live, you will tell him to *back off*."

Please, Vex. I won't risk them hurting you. I begged, my stomach felt like a pit of snakes as I thought about what they could do to him.

`If you go in there, you won't come out.`

Ava's gone to get Lia, and you've told Cyndrithra. I'm sure they can't hold me there forever.

`It's what they will do to you while you're in there that worries me.`

It looks like I don't have a choice.

`You always have a choice!`

"All settled then? Good, let's go." She strutted forward and went to grab my arm, but I pulled away sharply.

"How do you have the authority to come in here and take a cadet? On what charges?" I stood my ground, trying to bide time, anything so I didn't have to go with them.

"I'm from the Military, we don't listen to children and their dragons." Lysara snapped. She took another step, and I took one back.

"Surely you're legally able to tell me what it's regarding? You can't ask me some simple questions here?"

"You either come with us willingly, or we open fire on your beast." She snarled, wrapping her fingers around her gun.

I desperately ran through my brain, anything to stall them. The sweat ran down my back, pricking my scalp as panic began to worm its way in.

Did they know what I was?

"We will hurt him if he stops us from leaving. And you are a resident of Everdra, meaning that you fall under our jurisdiction, and if we require you to come in for questioning, then you will obey!" She yelled, the veins stood out in her neck as her face started to turn red.

"I'll come with you if you don't hurt him." I gave in. I wouldn't risk Vex.

No!

I won't lose you either!

She reached out again to grab me, but I backed away.

"I'm capable of walking myself," I growled, forcing one foot in front of the other as Vex seethed down the bond. I was ushered out the back door and along dark halls. We didn't meet a soul. I ignored my pulse hammering in my chest. How strange that no one was around. It was almost like it had been organised.

A stormblade was waiting on the roof, and a mad-as-hell dragon hovered nearby. No one was to be seen. I wouldn't put it past Principal Peterson or Professor Yates to be involved, they'd never seemed to like me.

I was shoved into the giant black machine, buckled in tight by one of her guards.

"You know he's going to follow and wait for me outside the building," I muttered, hating how fear coated my veins, making my palms sweat.

"Then I suggest he goes and finds something else to do. A bored dragon is a dangerous dragon."

"A dragon is only dangerous when you threaten their rider."

"We're not going to kill you, Miss Everhart." Her eyes finally met mine. They were as cold as ice.

"There are worse things than death, commander," I swore she could see right through me, and read my mind.

"Tell him to go to the palace, I'm sure he's dying to get reinforcements." A sting bit my neck, making me flinch as Lysara smiled evilly, and my vision turned black.

I'm getting really sick of waking up in different places.

The room was sterile white, the cold metal table biting into my bare arms as I raised my head. I was desperate to rub the grit from my eyes, but the handcuffs around my wrists wouldn't let them reach that far, seeing as they were chained to the table too. I felt a tug on my skin, and I saw a drip or something in the crook of my elbow, and sticky pads on my temples.

What the hell?

I couldn't feel Vex, and I knew that was their plan all along. Get me alone, cut off from everyone else.

I swallowed the nausea, the panic that threatened to undo me. The door opposite me opened, and in strode Lysara, looking like a cat who'd just had a saucer of milk.

She dragged the chair out slowly, the legs shrieking on the linoleum floor. She sat and linked her fingers together, angling her head slightly as she looked me over. She didn't speak, so neither did I. Time ticked by, the clock on the wall loud in the silent room.

Tick. Tick. Tick.

"So, Nymeria Everhart, if that's your real name." She leaned forward, arms braced on the table between us.

"Why wouldn't it be my real name?" I frowned, attempting to lean back and look casual.

"Because you're nowhere to be found. You simply don't exist. No records, no birth certificate, nothing."

I shrugged. But unease slithered through me. No records?

"Where did you come from, before you arrived here six months ago?"

"Nythevra." I was going to keep my answers short. I didn't want to give her anything. But I wouldn't be surprised if they had a lie-detecting machine on me.

"Who are your parents?"

"Carmody and Beau Everhart."

Small lies, some truths.

If I didn't exist as Nymeria Everhart, then I wasn't going to give them my parents' real names.

"Where in Nythevra?"

"Burmess"

I could tell she was listening to someone in her ear, as she smiled at me.

"I think we need to change our methods, Miss Everhart." She pushed her chair out and stalked towards me, pulling a device out of her pocket. It looked the same size as a whisp, but it was unmistakably a taser. "This here is one of our new inventions, and I've been dying to try it out. If you don't start telling the truth, then I'm going to use it on you." She threatened, a gleam in her eyes. I made sure to push my shield out around me. It was a struggle with whatever they injected me with, but I could just manage.

"What's your real name?" She barked, sitting on the table beside me.

"Nymeria Everhart." I met her glare, steel on steel. She clenched her jaw because she'd just been told that was the truth.

"Where are you from?"

"Nythevra."

She lashed out and hit me with the taser, but I was ready. It hits my shield, and a force of energy surged through me in a shockwave.

"What the?" She hissed, turning back to me. I fought a smile. "You can shield. Clever. But what about when I turn it up a level?" She flicked a switch, and the power intensified. I could hold it still, but if I did too much more, I wouldn't be able to.

"Hmm, level three then." She kept the damn thing on me, but decided to aim it at my chest instead. I could feel it trying to push its way through, but I gritted my teeth and kept my shield around me.

"Level four. No one has been able to get past this level before." She smirked at me, and I could see my shield was beginning to turn blue. "Level five." I could feel it now, my stomach was beginning to cramp, and I was breaking out in a sweat as heat bloomed on my chest where the taser was. "Level six." I felt a warm trickle of blood run down over my lips, and her face seemed to light up.

Sick, masochistic bitch.

I was struggling to breathe, my body ached as I fought to keep the taser's bite away from me. I bared my teeth at her as she pushed it harder into my chest until I could feel it burning me.

"F...fuck you." I spat at her as I lost consciousness.

Everything hurt. I couldn't open my eyes, they hurt too much. My teeth ached, my bones, everything.

So I lay on the table, trying to reel myself back in after what she did to me. I could hear voices far away, obviously on the other side of the two-way mirror. I had no idea how long I'd been there, but I would almost bet it had been longer than two hours. I heard the door slam and loud boots on the floor approached me. She yanked my head up by my hair, making me wince.

"Sit up." She barked, throwing me into my chair so I was slumped against the back of it. "We're going to try another method." She ripped the sticky pads off my head and applied new ones. I didn't have the energy to try to move. The blood had dried over my lips and chin, itching against the collar of my shirt.

One minute I was in the white interrogation room, the next, I was in a beautiful field of wildflowers. Vex was just to my right, and Brodie was walking towards me with a soft smile on his face.

"Brodie? What are you doing here?" I could feel the sun on my face as I sucked in a fragrant lungful of summer air. I loved this time of year. I was used to living in shorts and singlets back home.

"Your parents told me you were here." He stopped right in front of me, slipping a hand around my waist.

My pulse skyrocketed at his touch. But I frowned as I looked up at him.

"But my parents are dead, Brodie. You know that."

His face changed slightly, a crease between his brow.

"Of course, I know that. I mean, our friends told me I'd find you here. I've been looking for you."

What the hell was going on? Why was he acting like this?

CHAPTER
THIRTY-SEVEN

This was *not* normal.

I looked around, trying to figure out what was going on.

Calm, Nymeria. Just enjoy your day off with Brodie.

Vex's voice wasn't only different, he doesn't call me by my name, and sure as hell doesn't call Brodie by his name either.

"Nymeria? What's the matter? You look worried." Brodie's hands slid up to cup my cheek, and my thoughts scattered. I blinked as I took in his face. It *did* look like him, but he'd never said my name before.

This wasn't Brodie.

What's happening?

`Nothing's happening. You're overreacting.` Vex grumbled, and that seemed more like him. But something was *off*.

"Tell me what you're thinking? Why don't you tell me about your childhood? Where do you come from? It might take your mind of what's worrying you."

I swallowed and tried to step back. He let go, but looked hurt as I took another step away from him. I looked around the field again. I could hear birds chirping in the trees, and smell the floral scents of the flowers around us. I reached down and touched one. It felt so real. I picked the flower and examined it. Perfect. Nothing out of the ordinary. Brodie took the flower from me and placed it behind my ear, smiling at me.

"Sit with me?" He pulled me down to the ground and placed me in his lap. As much as I wanted this to be real, I knew it wasn't. "Tell me about your home?"

Something was tugging at my memories, but I couldn't grasp them. It slipped through my fingers as I tried to remember where I was, what I was doing before I woke in this field. A tree at the corner of my vision blurred, only for a second, but I knew that this was a trap. It was almost like a glitch in this vision they were forcing me to have. Everything slammed back into me, but I wasn't in the interrogation room anymore. They had somehow tricked me into thinking I was here with Brodie and Vex. So I played along and made the most of the pretend Brodie holding me.

"You already know everything, Brodie."

"Tell me again. I like the sound of your voice."

I almost scoffed, but that would give me away.

"I grew up in Burmess. It's a lovely coastal town on the eastern side of Nythevra. I grew up as an only child, and my parents died about four years ago. So I'd fended for myself until I had the dream from Vexirion." I was yanked out of this make-believe dream almost painfully as I woke back to the sterile, cold, white room.

"How did you know that wasn't real?" Lysara barked, fury written all over her face. I chuckled, smiling at her.

"If you're going to impersonate someone, then I suggest getting to know what they're actually like."

She stood and stalked towards me, and punched me so hard in the stomach that all the air was pushed out in one painful hit. I gasped for air as she punched me in the side of the face. My head cracked to the side and pain radiated through my cheek and jaw.

Fuck that hurts. I tasted blood as I licked my lips, my face throbbing.

"Tell me the truth! Who are you?" She got in my face, and I'd about had enough of her attitude.

"Why don't you go fuck yourself?" I smiled at her, no doubt with bloodstained teeth. She stood back and smiled at me, turning to the mirror behind her and nodding once.

She walked out, and someone else walked in instead.

Brodie.

What the fuck?

"Brodie?" I croaked, my lips cracked as I spoke.

"Why don't we stop this nonsense, and you just tell them the truth. Then she can stop hurting you." He stayed at the other side of the room, arms crossed, and his glare glacial. This was more like the Brodie I knew.

"Are you in on this?" I whispered, not wanting to believe what I was seeing. But they hadn't tricked me into somewhere else. I was still right here.

"Yes," was all he said, and I hated the tears that stung the back of my eyes, making my throat burn.

No. I won't believe it.

I shook my head, clenching my aching jaw.

"I don't believe you," I whispered, shaking my head, but he stalked over and leaned on the table.

"You'd better, because I don't want to hurt you." He tucked a strand of hair behind my ear, and I couldn't stop the sob that burst through. "Tell them, please." He begged, his voice breaking. I looked between his eyes, begging him to stop this. I shook my head again. He sighed, closing his eyes briefly. "I'm sorry." He breathed as he lashed out and hit me in the stomach, right where that bitch hit me earlier.

I gasped, hunched over to try and get some air into my aching lungs. He grabbed me by my hair and hauled me back. I made sure to meet his gaze, and I hoped he could see my anger, the pain. He injected something into my arm, and a burning cold filled my veins. It was *agonising*. I began to scream, the pain unbearable as it filled my body. I couldn't breathe.

"Tell them the truth! Who are you?" He bellowed, and I screamed even louder. I couldn't move, couldn't think, couldn't do anything other than burn alive inside my own body.

The pain stopped as quickly as it started, and I slumped forward, my chin resting on my chest, as I tried not to lose consciousness again.

"We don't have to do this. Tell them what they want, and they'll let you go." His voice was soft, and a gentle hand caressed my cheek. I could barely breathe or think, as my mind couldn't figure out what the hell was going on.

"Come on, sweetheart, tell me, is teleporting your only power?" He leaned back on his heels, wrapping his large hands over mine, still handcuffed to the table. I couldn't stop the tears that flowed down my cheeks, the sobs that were cracking my chest apart. I shook my head, scrunching my eyes together tightly.

"Tell me, you don't have to tell them." He breathed, so close to me now that if I were to open my eyes, I could see his beautiful sage eyes, his long dark lashes.

"No." I sobbed.

He moved so quickly that I didn't hear him until he injected me again, and this time, fire was burning inside of me. My throat tore as I screamed, my back arching off the chair as I thrashed, trying to get away from the fire.

Too much.

I couldn't handle it anymore.

I threw everything out of me in one last scream, and everything went black as the room exploded

"I'll fucking *kill* you!" A familiar voice bellowed in the small space. I sucked in a breath, and it burned my lungs like I'd swallowed glass. I must have made a noise, as someone stepped towards me, gentle hands brushed back my hair.

"I've got you, Storm. It's going to be okay."

No.

I flinched, opening my eyes and cringing away from the prince, shaking my head. I shrank away from the man who had just tortured me. His eyes widened, and he took a step back, but I saw pure fear spark in his eyes. He slowly turned to the door.

"What did you do to her?" His voice was low, lethal, and fear coated my veins. Eli stepped into the room, and I flinched away from him, too. He looked so much like his brother. Eli's eyes widened before he met his brother's gaze. Anger transformed his face like nothing I had ever seen before. At this moment, they both looked unrecognisable.

The two-way mirror was gone, completely shattered. The lights overhead were bare, the glass littering the table before me. The only light in here was supplied by the guards with torches. Before my panic could run away with me, Euan strutted in, looking thunderous.

"There will be hell to pay for this. You have not heard the last from me." He threatened, and at this moment, he had never looked more like a king. "Taking a rider without permission." He snapped, like the act was unthinkable. "Unchain her, immediately." He barked, Eli and Brodie at his back, their chests heaving, and weapons gripped tightly in their hands. I shut my eyes to try to calm my breathing.

Someone approached me, and I cringed away from them as they finally released my wrists from the cuffs. Euan knelt beside me, his face softening.

"Nymeria? Can you walk?" The kindness in his voice nearly broke me as I shook my head. I could barely keep my eyes open as it was. "Can Brodie carry you?" I shook my head, a tear slipping down my left cheek. I saw a muscle twitch in his jaw. "How about Elias?" I closed my eyes and gave one nod, another tear slipping out. I didn't open them. I didn't want to see the twins. I just wanted to get out of here.

Gentle hands cradled me and hauled me up against a solid chest, and we finally left this torture chamber.

I could hear a dragon roaring in the distance, the ground beneath us shuddering as he landed. Hot air blew against me, and I cracked open an eye. Vex's snout nudged me. I shakily reached out a hand and placed my palm on his warm scales. He growled low in his belly, blowing more steam over us. Eli didn't say a word, but carried me onto his back and held me the whole way back to the castle.

I was tucked into my bed, a doctor immediately checking on me after kicking everyone out. He hissed as he saw my chest, no doubt a burn there from the taser. He hooked me up to a drip, and my pulse skittered.

"It's going to be alright. I'm not going to hurt you." He tried to soothe me, but I felt like a completely shattered mess. "Sleep, Nymeria. You're safe now."

⁘

I was bed-bound for at least three days until I had my first visitor. I hadn't seen Brodie or Eli, and for that I was grateful. The doctor said I wasn't allowed visitors for a while, that my mental state wasn't ready.

Euan knocked on the door and slipped in with a sad expression on his handsome face.

"Nymeria, how are you feeling?" His voice was gentle, and he approached slowly. "May I sit?" He gestured to a chair by the window. I nodded, trying to give him a small smile in return, but my face didn't want to obey.

"I know you probably don't want to hear this, but we've been able to get the footage from when you were detained and interrogated."

My stomach plummeted, making me feel instantly nauseous. I broke out into a sweat, and the machine beeped as my pulse raced.

"I'm not going to show you. You're safe now. I just wanted to tell you that who you saw at the end wasn't really there." I could hear the pain in his voice as he sat forward, his hands clenched tightly together. "You saw Brodie, didn't you?"

I clenched my aching jaw, but nodded once, a tear slipping down. I'd tried my hardest not to think about what happened in there since lying in bed for the past three days.

"Brodie was here with me, getting ready to come and rescue you. They tricked you again, Ria. And you must know that he would *never* hurt you." He pleaded with me. "Since the first vision didn't work, they thought that would be the best way to break you. To have someone you care about hurt you in return, and I'm so sorry for what you went through." The king looked close to tears himself, his voice sounded thick as he cleared his throat. "I need you to know that."

I tried to absorb his words, to believe them. But every time I thought of Brodie now, I would break out in a nervous sweat, my pulse would thunder in my veins.

"I want to believe you, I really do. But I can't help my body's reaction. Even when you mention his name, fear shoots through me so much that all I want to do is hide, cry, and break down." My voice broke, my throat still sore from screaming.

"The doctor is hoping to be able to come up with something to help you, to banish this fear attached to him.

I have never seen him so scared before. And it breaks my heart to see you both suffering." He quickly wiped his eyes, taking a long breath before he was able to meet my eyes again. "Rest, Ria. I'll come back to visit you soon. I just needed you to know the truth, and that he would never hurt you." He gave me a tight smile as he let himself out of my room. I felt exhausted, mentally drained as I tried to process the news.

I should have known Brodie would never do that. But there was something inside of me that I couldn't banish. And I didn't know how long it was going to take me to move past this crippling fear of Brodie McTavish.

Chapter Thirty-Eight

On my bedside table sat a stunning single daffodil.

My breath caught in my throat. I hadn't seen one of those since I was home on the island. I didn't even think they grew here. With shaking hands, I reached out and brought it to my nose and inhaled.

These were my absolute favourite flowers.

Dad used to grumble about how stinky they were and that they made him sneeze. But it didn't stop him from picking them for me and leaving a bunch in my room.

I let myself cry for their loss. For the loss of Kai, wherever he was, and for all the people I'd lost on the way. All taken too soon, too cruelly. I put the flower back in the tiny vase and saw a folded note resting against the glass. I slowly unfolded it, the scrawled handwriting made me feel a little anxious.

Storm. I want you to know that I would never hurt you, not intentionally.
I need you to know that. I'll do all I can to help you overcome what they have done to you,
Even if it takes the rest of our lives. I'm sorry I wasn't there to stop it.
It won't happen again.
Your favourite Prince.
AKA: Cookie.

Despite my conflicted emotions, I laughed. I knew in my heart that he would never hurt me, but they did something to the chemicals in my brain, and even the thought of him made me anxious.

I hated Lysara Toory with every fibre in my body.

It took six dragons to stop Vex from destroying the building I was kept in, and he threatened to eat their cowardly guts every five minutes after our bond had finally come back, the drugs finally out of my system.

He checked in on me every three minutes. Or that's what it felt like. He was becoming a mother hen.

The doctor visited me twice a day, giving me things to drink while he measured my brainwaves when he asked me questions. I hated how I reacted when he showed me a picture of Brodie or mentioned his name. I knew in my heart, but my head didn't want to play.

Brodie left a flower every day on my bedside table. I didn't know how he got them there, but I appreciated the gesture. I didn't have my whisp, which was back at Voralyth in my room, so I couldn't even talk to Lia.

By the fifth day, I was feeling bored enough to get out of bed and go for a walk. I knew I shouldn't, because I didn't know how I would react seeing Brodie or Eli, but I needed to get out of my four walls.

I'd visited Euan and asked about Rex and if I could see him, but he was apparently away training with the guards at one of their outposts. I was glad to hear that he was fit and healthy again, but it felt like I'd imagined seeing him. The king had promised to get him set up with a false identity and a whisp, so I could get in contact. But there was still no luck in tracking down Kai.

I was finally given the full bill of health and could return to Voralyth.

I was halfway across the field when I heard my name being called. Fear shot through me as I recognised his voice, but I mentally told myself I was okay.

"Storm. Please, wait." I stopped, closing my eyes as I tried to steady my breathing. The doctor claimed that he would continue trying to figure out how to rewire my brain to let go of that fear. But in the meantime, I just had to wait and hope time would heal. I felt him come around and stand in front of me, but I hadn't opened my eyes yet.

"Storm." His voice sounded choked, and my lips wobbled as I desperately wanted to open my eyes and see him. But I was scared. "I wanted to see you before you left." He breathed. I swallowed my fears and opened my eyes. He was devastatingly beautiful, but I saw tears in his eyes. It was like a punch to the gut, the raw emotion on his face. I stumbled back a step as fear warred with the urge to hold him.

Tears slipped down my cheeks as my breathing became difficult. He lifted an arm, but I shook my head quickly, taking another small step back.

"I'm so sorry, Brodie," I whispered. The lump in my throat made it hard for me to speak, as my body screamed at me to run away.

"Don't you *ever* apologise for what they did to you." He growled softly, jaw ticking. "I won't let you push me away." He took another step towards me, but I took one back. Vex growled quietly, but didn't say anything.

"I can't help it," I managed, my bottom lip wobbling. "I need time."

"Nymeria, please know that I'd never hurt you." He begged, and my heart *broke*. He'd *finally* said my name. I couldn't stop the sob that cracked through my chest. I hung my head in my hands as I cried, unable to move. I felt him move closer, so slowly that he didn't startle me. "I'm going to hug you, okay? Just going to wrap my arms around you, and hold you." His voice sounded thick as I braced myself for his touch. It didn't hurt as much as I thought it would, but my breathing was erratic.

Two emotions were battling each other inside of me. They were both as strong as each other, as I struggled to stay on my feet. I had never been held like this by him before, and one part of me never wanted him to let go. He was warm, strong, safe. But the other feeling that was roaring at me was fear, pain, and suffering. He slowly stroked the back of my hair as I cried into his chest.

"I know things are going to take time, and I'm going to be here if you need me. And if you don't, I'll respect your decision." He rested his cheek on the top of my head. His whole body wrapped around me, and I didn't know how much more my nerves could take.

"Th-thank you, Brodie. But I need to go." I sobbed, and he let go, he stepped back and wiped his eyes. He nodded once and stalked away. Vex kept quiet for once as I hauled myself up his foreleg. I'd been asked to keep what happened to myself, in case anyone asked where the heck I'd been for the past week. Just had to tell them it was royal business.

I was keeping so many secrets that it was a wonder they couldn't see them floating around behind my eyes.

It was a silent trip back to Voralyth. I couldn't stop the tears, the pain inside of me as I struggled to pull myself back together.

Lia, of course, knew, and she wrapped me in the tightest hug when I landed, letting me cry on her shoulder for a bit.

"Mitch has been asking for you. Like, every day." She grimaced at me. I just nodded, unsure of my conflicted feelings towards him. I liked him, and that kiss the other day, it lit something inside of me that has been dormant for a long time now.

"He kissed me." I blurted, pulling her to a stop. Her eyes flew wide as she gripped my arm.

"He *what?* When?" She almost looked angry until she took a calming breath and blew it out. "Sorry, didn't mean to snap. But what? Is there anything else I should know?"

"He took me on a date to the fair the other weekend, and I had a lovely time, until his father showed up." I shrugged, feeling a little embarrassed. Lia's face paled as her fingers tightened on my arm.

"His father? What did he say?" She'd dropped her voice to a whisper.

"He was an asshole and made Mitch leave with him. Luckily, Vex had followed me there like some overprotective parent. But he dismissed me, called me a commoner and a small girl, so I left."

"Shit. Then you so happen to get taken in by the 'secret service' who Mitch's father works for." Lia scratched her chin, thinking. "For now, we'll just keep this between us. I'm sorry, Ria, but I don't think you should spend any more time with Mitch." She truly looked sorry, but I was quickly losing my patience when people kept telling me what I should and shouldn't do.

"Will anyone tell me what the hell happened between him and everyone?" I crossed my arms, raising my brows as I waited. "I'm not going anywhere until you tell me. I have a right to know, because Mitch is nothing but lovely to me. He's kind, treats me with respect, he's funny and makes me feel like a normal person. Nobody else here does." I'd dug my heels in, and I wasn't going to budge. Lia grimaced but gave in.

"Fine. I'll tell you. But let's head back inside." Lia grumbled, keeping a hand on my arm. We made our way through the back corridors so we weren't seen by anyone. Especially Mitch.

Lia poked her head around a door and pulled me in. It looked to be some sort of supply room. I turned and raised my brows at her, waiting. She sighed, took a deep breath and sat down on a crate.

"Brodie had a girlfriend for the last two years while he was here at Voralyth."

My heart sank, but sped up at the same time. I swallowed down the mixture of fear and longing at the mention of his name.

"Her name was Emily, and she had the most beautiful blue eyes." Lia smiled affectionately, silver lining hers. "She was perfect, clever, and brave. But, one day, she simply disappeared."

Lia looked away for a moment, clearing her throat. It felt like I had a lump stuck in mine.

"The last Brodie saw of her, she was having a heated argument with...Mitch."

My head snapped up, and I didn't know how to feel about that.

"Apparently, the last anyone saw was her getting into Captain O'Connell's stormchariot." Lia ran both hands through her hair, pulling bits out of her usually neat braid. "That's why Brodie freaks out about the whole Mitch situation, because he thinks that he's got something to do with her going missing."

"And no doubt he questioned Mitch about this?"

"Of course. Mitch said he didn't know what she was on about. She was ranting about being better, getting involved if he knew what was good for him. Don't let them walk over him." Lia scoffed, and I knew that she didn't believe him. And obviously neither did the twins.

"When did they graduate?" I croaked, not wanting to know more about Brodie's ex, but needed to know at the same time.

"They graduated four years ago." Lia looked down at her feet before meeting my eyes.

"They came to Voralyth when they were twenty?" I frowned. That seemed young.

"Sometimes when the dragon can sense great power, they bond when they think the rider is ready, and for them, it was when they were twenty. Sometimes, riders could be twenty-four before a dragon bonds them."

"Huh." I nodded, unable to think of anything else to say while everything ran through my mind at a million miles an hour.

"Are you sure you're alright?" I could feel Lia's eyes on me, but I knew if I met her gaze, I'd start to cry again.

"Yeah, I'll be fine. Let's go." I stood, needing to get some fresh air. "Did she know of their powers?" I blurted, turning back to face her as she opened the door.

"No, but I'm guessing she knew there was more to them than they let on. They were always away on weekends helping their father with things."

"And the king just sends them off on missions rather than finding someone else to do it?" I didn't forget Korin reminding his brother that they were also his sons.

"There isn't anyone else with those sorts of powers, and who works together so perfectly." Lia stood, closing the door behind us. "Come on. We'd better get you back. Are you ready?"

"Ready as I'll ever be." I sighed.

"Just a heads up, everyone heard Vex showing his...displeasure at the stormblade on the roof, and that he followed them away." She winced as we made our way down the hall. We hugged at the foot of the stairs, Lia telling me she was off to see Korin. I needed to go and freshen up first before facing anyone else.

I didn't want to go to dinner, but my stomach had other plans. I threw on my hoodie and tried to hide as best as I could as I made my way through the line, getting a large helping of carbonara. It had always been my favourite comfort food back home. I refused to let the thought of my parents shatter my calm façade. I needed all the help I could get right now.

I'd taken two steps when a shadow fell over me. I looked up into the worried face of Mitch. His brows were pinched, lips pursed as he looked me over.

"Ria, I've been worried sick. Where've you been?" He reached out as if to touch me, but thought better of it as I began walking to my table.

"I had to help the king with something. He needed some insight on Nythevra."

What a shit excuse.

"They don't have anyone else there they could have asked?" He fell into step beside me, a broody expression still on his face.

"I didn't ask, just following orders." I shrugged, standing at the end of my table, I saw my fellow cadets eye me with narrowed looks, whispering to each other.

"Then why do you have a bruise on your face, and why was Vex so angry the other day when a stormblade arrived? And followed it away?" He did look tired, with bags under his eyes. I hoped that wasn't worry over me.

"Just a misunderstanding. Everything is fine now." I couldn't meet his eyes. I hated lying to people who cared for me. He leaned down until his face was close to mine, his finger tipping my chin up to meet his stern gaze.

"You look unwell. Are you sick? I know something is going on, Ria. I saw Ava running through the hall like the devil was on her tail and heading straight to Lia."

This man is too observant, damn it.

`Don't tell him anything, little storm.`

I clenched my jaw before plastering a fake smile on my face.

"Everything is fine, Mitch, really. I just need some sleep, and everything will be back to normal." I sat heavily, stuck my fork in my pasta and twirled it slowly, unable to meet his gaze.

"Maybe next time you see them, ask them about my roommate, Jonas. He used to disappear with them on weekends, coming back exhausted and bruised, until one day he never returned. But rest up. I'll catch up with you soon." He stalked away. I tried to gather myself before I turned to Theon. I needed to ask someone about Jonas.

Is that what Mitch meant that they too had ghosts haunting them?

"All good?" He mumbled between a mouthful of roast.

"Yeah." I shrugged back, giving him a tight smile. He raised a brow, looked around before coming back to me.

"If you ever need back up, help with anything, just let me know, okay? I can be discreet and keep a secret." He bumped me with his shoulder and dug back into his food. I didn't know why it hit me as hard as it did, but the kindness made me want to cry.

"Thanks, Theon."

CHAPTER
THIRTY-NINE

Flight maneuvers were mostly safe, but sometimes, the dragons behaved like assholes.

We had a mixed class today to see how all the dragons would get along. So far, it was fucking chaos.

`Adolescent dragons are so temperamental. They get upset too easily.`

You used to be one a long time ago.

`Concentrate, before one of their temper tantrums takes us out.`

Can't you just growl at them to sort their shit out and behave?

What am I, their parent? No, they can learn to sort it out themselves.

I watched as a Ruleum dragon broke from the riot to dive into the river, dragging its claws along the water as a Galadron roared at another dragon for flying too close. I could feel Vex's annoyance down the bond, making me chuckle.

A lot of first-years bonded with a younger dragon, as their emotional intelligence was sometimes the same. For once, I was glad to have a grumpy old dragon.

Don't you dare call me old.

I laughed, but the smile was wiped off my face when I saw a scarred Galadron dragon roaring at a smaller Ruleum dragon, its rider hunching down on its back in fear. But the Galadron rider seemed to be encouraging the behaviour. The blue dragon attempted to dive away, but to my horror, the murky yellow coloured beast snapped out, and its jaws locked around the blue's throat.

Professor Jamieson yelled from the back of her large Furora, but the yellow only bit down harder.

We have to do something.

No. We're not getting involved.

Get your ass over there now! He's going to rip its throat out!

Fine!

Vex grunted in annoyance but made his way over towards the struggling dragon. He roared in their direction, and the yellow's eye swivelled our way, but didn't let go. I could hear the blue almost whimpering, and its rider was screaming for the other dragon to let go. I judged the distance and made a snap decision.

Don't you dare!

Watch me.

I jumped to my feet and ran along Vex's neck, reached his snout and leapt into the air. My arms and legs flailed as I soared through the air, landing just behind the Ruleum cadet.

"Help! Please!" She begged, but I was already moving. I ran up her dragon's neck and leapt onto the yellow's huge head, holding onto its small horns.

Get off there this instant! Vex roared again, so loud it hurt my ears. I planted my hand on the dragon's head and closed my eyes, ignoring the swearing from its rider, threatening to throw his dagger at me. But I blocked it out and focused on the bioelectricity within the dragon. I had only been practising this on Professor Korin, so it couldn't be too different, surely? I focused on the beast's jaws, working to take control and loosen its hold. I felt the dragons tilting, going in for a roll.

Shit.

Get off there now, Nymeria Everhart!
Almost there! Make sure you catch her.
Fucking adolescents.

I felt sweat beading my brow as my stomach began to cramp, but I'd nearly done it. I could hear the cadet swear and unsheathe his dagger.

Push, just a little more.

I could feel the dragon trying to resist me, but I won in the end. Its jaws opened just as we rolled. I could hear the Ruleum cadet scream as my eyes flew open, her dragon trying to stay airborne, but the blood was streaming out of its neck.

Catch them, Vex, please! I shouted. I was hanging on by my fingertips, my legs dangling in the air. But the nasty beast whipped its head away, and I went flying in the opposite direction to Vex. The yellow snapped out at me, just missing my legs. I heard other riders shouting and yelling, but I couldn't focus on them right now. He snapped again, and I shut my eyes and teleported back to Vex before his teeth closed around me. Vex was wrapping his huge claws around the blue dragon to slow her fall. He dropped them close enough to the ground before launching back into the air, straight towards the Galadron dragon and rider.

No one tries to bite my rider!

Uh oh.

He headbutted the yellow dragon right in the stomach, sending it toppling. He snapped out and grabbed it by the neck, almost crushing it as Vex was so much larger.

"Get your fucking dragon away from me!" I heard the cadet yell, attempting to get up and stab Vex with his dagger.

Oh, hell no.

I grabbed my blade and teleported again, landing just behind the rider as he was about to strike.

"No one touches my dragon, asshole. Let alone a bully like you." I grabbed hold of his collar and yanked him backwards. He grunted in surprise, slashed out at me as Vex bit down on the yellow dragon's throat. I ducked his swing, swiping my leg out and sent him falling over. Before he could get his footing, I grabbed both of his arms in a firm grip and flung him off over the side of his own dragon.

He screamed like a child as he fell.

I stood there and watched as he fell with a small grin on my face.

`Little storm.` Vex grumbled, sounding just a little amused.

Don't worry, I won't let him splat.

`Shame.`

I teleported down to the screaming cadet, tears in his eyes, as I grabbed hold of him and teleported us both back to the safety of the ground. There was quite a crowd gathered around to watch the show.

As soon as we landed, I shoved him away, causing him to fall on his ass.

"I wanted to let you fall. It's what you deserve after what you just did." I hissed, feeling my hands writhing in flames with my anger coursing through me.

"You fucking bitch, you'll die for that!" He managed to get to his feet before a fist smashed into his face. I stumbled back a step as a furious Mitch knocked him on his ass again.

"How dare you?!" Mitch boomed, pulling him to his feet again, only so he could punch him another time. "You cowardly, disgusting asshole."

"Alright, break it up!" Professor Jamieson ran over, blasting the two men apart with her magic. Professor Korin made his way towards us. Behind him, the shaking Ruleum cadet wrapped in a blanket, for some reason, she was sopping wet. Another roar echoed through the sky as Vex finally let go, flinging the dragon away from him.

"What the hell happened up there?" Jamieson yelled, crossing her arms over her chest as she glared at us.

"From what I saw, Professor, is that asshole's dragon was bullying the blue, and when she tried to get away, he lashed out and wouldn't let go. I could hear its rider encouraging it on. So I stepped in, trying to get it to let go." I ignored the grumbling from said asshole who was wiping the blood off his face, being helped to his feet by another in his house. Mitch came to stand by my side, his knuckles bloody.

"And then your dragon lashed out after he'd dropped cadet Davidson and her dragon in the lake. Why?"

"Because it tried to take her legs off!" Mitch yelled, and I turned to him, surprised that he saw that from down on the ground.

"Is that true, cadet Everhart?" Professor Korin came to my side, looking between us.

"Yes, professor. I teleported out of there just before he got me."

Vex landed behind us with an earth-shuddering boom. I could feel him hovering behind me, growling at the Galadron cadet, no doubt teeth bared.

"That's the second time he and his dragon have endangered someone's lives before." Mitch snarled, pointing at the scowling rider. "He shouldn't be allowed to stay here." I could hear a few cadets scoff around us, and I knew that they wouldn't kick him out for that.

"We'll be discussing it with Cadet Morrison. Back to your classes." Professor Jamieson called, ushering a smug-looking cadet Morrison with her. He flipped me the middle finger and a smile as he turned to leave. Mitch took a step after him, but I grabbed onto his arm.

"Leave it, Mitch. He's not worth the trouble."

"Yeah, he is. Another few fists in his stupid face might make *me* feel better." He turned to me, mouth pinched, eyes darting over me.

"I'm okay, really." I left my hand on his arm as I met his brown eyes. He reached up and covered my hand with his. He shook his head, huffing a small laugh. "What?" I asked, narrowing my eyes.

"You're a magnet for trouble, you know that?" A smile tugged at his lips.

"You're not the first to tell me that," I grumbled, rolling my eyes. "Come on, I need something to eat after that." The cadets began to scatter around us as the class was dismissed.

The cafeteria was extra loud when we entered, everyone watching something on their whisp with interest.

Not again.

I internally slapped a hand to my forehead, knowing that someone must have filmed that incident in the sky and shared it on RoarBoard. I expected my whisp to pulse any minute. But the thought was enough to send me to my knees with anxiety. My pulse began to race, my palms started to sweat as irrational fear surged through me.

I. Am. Safe.

He. Will. Not. Harm. Me.

It did little to calm my racing heart, but at least my legs didn't collapse out from under me as I came to a stop, breathing hard.

"Ria? Are you alright? You're terribly pale." Mitch towed me towards a chair and pushed me down as I blinked away my dizziness.

Gods, even a simple thought is enough to send me spiralling.

"I'm alright. Just a dizzy spell." I tried to smile, but I couldn't manage it. He frowned as he knelt in front of me, taking my hands in his.

"I know something is going on. And it's okay if you don't want to share it. But I just want you to know that you can trust me. I won't tell, and I want to be here for you."

Something caught my eye as they came towards us, their steps rigid.

Lia. She was frowning slightly. I returned my gaze to Mitch and forced myself to smile.

"Thank you, Mitch. You don't know how much I appreciate that." I squeezed his hands as Lia stopped at my side, clearing her throat. I didn't miss the hard edge in her eyes at our closeness.

"Please excuse us, Mitch. I need a word with Ria."

He looked between the two of us and got to his feet before levelling a hard stare at Lia.

"I hope all of you are treating her how she deserves. She's a person, not just someone with a fancy ability. Don't let her become the next Jonas." He stalked away, and I watched him retreat with a heavy feeling in my stomach. I turned to Lia, who ground her teeth, and looked like she was going to tell me off about it.

"I know, Lia. But I had a dizzy spell and needed to sit."

"I wasn't going to say anything. I just wanted to tell you that someone had filmed what just happened. It's all over the aetherweb." She pulled out a seat beside me, leaning back and watching the room.

"I guessed. I just had a slight panic attack at the thought of someone pulsing me about it." I ignored the thought's wanting to slither back in. I pushed them back.

"And also that the doctor has something he wants you to try." Her voice was softer as she looked at me, sadness in her eyes. "He won't call, not until you're ready."

I shouldn't feel relieved about it, but I did. I didn't want to have a meltdown in front of everyone. I just nodded, twisting my hands together as my fingertips sparked.

"What does the doctor suggest?"

"He says next week he wants you to return, and he can try something out. He's going to organise it with the principals." She reached out and touched my arm. I made sure to keep my electricity to myself. "I hate seeing you like this." She whispered, squeezing quickly before letting go. "Let's get something to eat."

The rest of the day passed in a blur. Everyone was gossiping about what happened earlier, and people made sure to keep out of my way.

It was like the first day again.

Chapter Forty

I hated pop quizzes.

But at least it was about dragons, not maths or anything boring like that. Professor Jamieson fired questions around the room in quick succession.

"Who can tell me what kind of tail and horns a Furora has?" She pointed to a Galadron cadet to my right.

"They have a club tail, with straight horns."

"Correct. What about a Ruleum dragon?"

"Curved horns to the side and a fin tail, for swimming."

"Correct, a Galadron?"

"Small horns and a feather tail."

Sniggers filled the room.

Everyone knew that Galadron cadets were sensitive about their dragon's tiny horns.

"Sinvidia?"

"Long horns that curve back, and a dagger tail."

"Good, good. What about the Tenebrae dragon?"

The room was quiet, and a few shrugged as they looked at the person sitting next to them. I sighed and put my hand up, seeing as nobody else seemed to know.

"Cadet Everhart."

"The Tenebrae dragons have horns similar to the Sinvidia dragon, with long curving horns, and a tail like an arrowhead."

"Well done, now, can anyone else tell us about the other two dragons? The Mallus and Pravius?" Professor Jamieson stalked the room, eyes roving over each student as she walked. "No? Looks like we need to do some work on the three rarer breeds. I know it's likely that you won't come across them if you remain in Everdra, but it's handy to know. The Mallus, commonly known as the brown dragon, or the celestial dragon. They have light and time perception, not as big as the Tenebrae or Pravius, but just as powerful. Their riders have brown eyes and can usually slow time or speed it up. Sometimes they have been able to go back in time, in rare cases." I hastily wrote this down in my book, interested to know more about them.

"The dragons also have horns that curve to the side, and curl around like a ram, their tails end in two spikes." As she talked, she projected an image onto the board behind her. The Mallus was a beautiful-looking dragon, their scales a shimmering chocolate, their eyes glittering like stars. She clapped, and the image changed to a stunning, proud purple dragon. Even the photo captured its expression that seemed to say - *I'm better than all of you.*

Pravius dragons are very proud and do not take well to being spoken to without respect and reverence.

Do you know many Pravius and Mallus dragons?

Yes. But they will never leave Durus.

Why? And why did you?

I wasn't stupid enough to ask, and I came here to find you, obviously.

"The Pravius dragon, or the purple storm dragon. They are a proud creature that can control electricity and weather. Their riders have purple eyes and usually can manipulate the electricity around them, and the weather in one way or another." I started. That was some of what I could do. "They have horns that curve forward and a scorpion tail. Whatever you do, don't approach a Pravius dragon. They are reported to be the hardest dragons to bond to, as they apparently want you to win them over before they allow you to bond. Not many survive."

The rest of the week flew by, and before I knew it, I was on my way back to the castle in Sylvanfire.

I was dreading it, the thought of seeing the twins had me feeling slightly ill. Lia was allowed to come with me, and she at least could tell them to keep their distance when we were out wandering around. I hated it.

I was a ball of nerves when I entered the doctor's office. He offered me a kind smile and gestured for me to sit. I told Lia I would be fine and to go find her prince. She didn't take long to convince.

"How are you coping, Nymeria?" He looked at me kindly from behind his desk, hands laced together.

"I have panic attacks when I think about...him." I swallowed, clenching my jaw.

"It's not something to be ashamed of, Nymeria. It's your body's response to keep you safe. But I think I might have something that can help lessen those feelings." He stood and wandered to a cupboard on his right, coming back with a little square machine and two small sticky pads attached with wires. I swallowed my unease, they looked very similar to what they attached to me back in the interrogation room. "I can see that this makes you uneasy, and I want to assure you that this won't hurt you. I promise. It's to measure your brain waves."

I tried to nod, but I couldn't stop the tingling in my fingers, the prickling on the back of my neck as my electricity tried to protect me.

He got me to lie down on the small bed and attached the sticky pads to my temples. I closed my eyes as he spoke about flying my dragon, the joy of true laughter, and got me to think of things that made me happy. He would then say the princes names, then quickly go back to something that made me happy.

We did this for about an hour, and I felt completely exhausted by the end of it. He was trying to get my brain to associate him with being something happy and safe. I was a trembling mess by the time I sat up.

"I've recorded this for you, and I want you to listen to it every night while you sleep." He smiled at me kindly, "I have a good feeling about this, Nymeria. And it might be worth looking at a photo of Brodie and Elias every day, repeating to yourself that you're safe, calm, and happy. It will be hard at first, but over time, it will get easier." Just their names sent a spark of fear through me, but I clamped it down, refusing to let it take me over.

"Good. Keep that up. I'll want you back here in another four weeks to check in. I'll have the recording ready for you by the time you leave tomorrow."

I made my way through the corridors, trying to remain quiet and hoping no one noticed me. I was supposed to pulse Lia, but I wasn't going to interrupt her time with her boyfriend.

We were only allowed a pass from the academy for the night.

I heard a gaggle of people coming my way, but it was too late for me to turn and hide.

The breath whooshed out of me as I spotted the woman who had to be the queen. She was dressed in a stunning blood red gown that whispered along the ground as she walked. Her chin was held high, and her blue eyes sharp and cold. Her black hair was slicked back into an intricate updo, her makeup flawless, and her blood red lips to match her dress. I felt like a startled animal as I moved to press myself up against the wall. She locked her eyes on me as she approached, standing too close than what I was comfortable with. She looked me up and down, and I managed to keep my shoulders back, my chin up, even though she was much taller than me.

"Who are you?" She commanded, narrowing her eyes at me.

"Cadet Everhart, your highness."

She almost scrunched her nose at me, but she stopped herself at the last minute.

"What are you doing here in my castle?"

"I came here to see the doctor, your highness. I'll be leaving first thing tomorrow." I kept my voice even, but my pulse was all over the place. Why did she have this effect on me?

I heard loud boots coming our way, but she didn't step back, didn't take her eye off me.

"Mother?"

Oh no.

No, no, no.

I clenched my jaw, my hands balled into fists as he approached. She finally turned to her son as he stopped at her side, but I didn't dare look his way.

"My dear boy." She crooned, but it sounded forced.

"Cadet Everhart?" He asked, but I focused on keeping my breathing normal, ignoring the tears pricking my eyes as I stared at the window on the other side of the hall.

"You know this...girl?" She asked, venom dripping from the tone of her voice.

"Yes. And she's been unwell. If you'd excuse us, I'll make sure she gets back to her room safely." He bowed to his mother before he stepped to my side. I was starting to shake now, my chest tight, vision swimming.

"It's alright. I won't let anything happen to you." I jumped as his arm threaded through mine.

I managed a weak bow to the queen as he led me away. My ears were ringing as I forced my feet to move. As soon a we were around the corner, he let go, and I slumped into the wall, hands on my knees.

"I'm not going to hurt you, Storm." He breathed, but I had to shut my eyes and think happy thoughts. I managed a small nod, but didn't open my eyes. "I hope she wasn't too horrible to you." His voice was so soft, laced with emotion as he backed away. I shook my head, and he sighed. "I'll get Lia."

"No. It's...okay." I whispered, eyes still firmly shut.

"I'm not letting you walk back to your room alone." He grumbled, but there was no bite to it.

"Then maybe walk in front, and I'll follow." I managed, my voice quiet as I struggled with myself. I opened my eyes and regretted it. His stare almost undid me. I gasped for breath and nodded my head for him to start walking. He mashed his lips together before walking ahead in jerky movements.

I counted to eight seconds before I followed.

My chest eased a little, and my vision stopped spinning. In front, I could see him, keep an eye on him and make sure he didn't do anything.

He's not going to, idiot.

I hated myself right now.

It was a slow trip back to my room, but we finally got there. He stopped a few feet from my door, but turned to face me. I sucked in a breath and opened my door, meaning to shut it on him, but he held the door open, and I flinched.

"Sorry." He murmured, stepping back, but I kept the door open. "Are you okay after what happened the other day?"

I yearned to reach for him, to wipe that sadness from his eyes, but just the thought of it shot fear through me so thoroughly that I wanted to fall into a heap on the floor.

So I managed a small nod, pressing my lips together.

"Good. I'll leave you be, then." He spun on his heel and stalked back down the hall. I let out a long breath and closed my door, falling onto my bed as I tried to pull myself back together.

⸺❖⸺

We were just returning from training when there was an ear-piercing scream. A cadet ran out of the change rooms, tears streaking down her cheeks. She was sobbing about something, but there was no way we could miss the word *body*.

Shit. Not another one.

I felt sick. The cadets exploded into chatter as Professor Potteira ran into the change rooms. A loud siren sounded over the speakers only moments later, and Principal Shields voice echoed around the room.

"ALL CADETS ARE TO RETURN TO THEIR ROOMS IMMEDIATELY."

The students around me almost bolted out of there, not caring about our things still in the change rooms as they ran to their rooms. Wingwarden Sean McDonald and Mitch burst through the doors, making sure that we didn't do anything stupid. We were herded back to our rooms like sheep, but I didn't miss the concerned looks from Mitch. We were the last to get to our common room, Mitch agreeing that he would escort us back so that Sean could go ahead. I was the last to enter as Mitch had placed his hand on my arm.

"Did you see anything?" He breathed, leaning in close. I shook my head, meeting his brown eyes.

"No, it was all normal when we got changed. It wasn't until Daphne came out screaming that we knew." Poor Daphne. It was her dragon that got mauled by the Galadron beast that day. She had found me later on and almost dropped to the ground to kiss my shoes. It was humiliating, but ever since then, she gives me a wave and a smile. She was a tiny thing, with the biggest glasses and long curly blonde hair that seemed bigger than her.

"Are you alright? I haven't seen you around much lately. I was starting to think that the others had gotten to you." He leaned back a little, an expression on his face that I couldn't read.

"I've been crazy busy. We have a history test coming up, so I've been studying with Ava. Our flight maneuvers have become almost impossible, and I'm still yet to master my flame-throwing. But no, I haven't been avoiding you." I smiled, and his answering grin lit up his face.

"So, what would you say if I asked you to come out on a date with me?" He took a step toward me until he stood toe to toe.

"How can I say no to that face?" I had to crane my neck to look at him, fighting a smile. His hands moved to cup my face, his thumb stroking my cheek.

"I like you, Nymeria Everhart. I can't seem to get you out of my head."

Chapter
Forty-One

The cadet who was found dead in the change room was the Galadron asshole Morrison.

The school was now on full lockdown. The only people who could come and go had to get permission from the Principals and the king. Safe to say that things were beginning to get a little scary. Luckily, my appointment with the doctor was allowed, but it had been brought forward by two weeks. I'd found that looking at photos and listening to the recording we did seemed to be slowly working. I didn't get anxiety looking at the pictures anymore.

I didn't know when my date with Mitch was, but he promised it would be soon. I found myself looking forward to it. It would be a good distraction, and I enjoyed spending time with Mitch. I didn't blame him for my being taken by the secret service, and I refused to believe that he had anything to do with Brodie's ex. There had to be more to it.

I busied myself with writing to Rex, asking how he was going, if he liked his new life. His replies always made me smile. He was making the most of the good food the good training, and he was quickly moving up the ranks. They were asking him to train the recruits. But he hadn't had any luck finding Kai. He's made more connections now and was asking them to pass along the information, trying to hear even a whisper of him.

He *had* to be alive. I wouldn't accept anything else.

I would know it in my bones if he were no longer.

Lia and I were chilling in the social room, the mood rather sombre from last week's murder. The count was now up to five, and they were no closer to figuring it out.

Theon and I had started to write down all the victims and what they did or said to me. Honestly, it wasn't much, one or two interactions, but always public ones.

Then we tried to figure out who was there, who would have seen it.

We weren't getting anywhere, as there were too many people to remember them all. Was it a professor? Another student? A guard?

The answer had to be there, but it felt impossible to grasp anything at the moment.

Ryler sat with his friends across the room and gave me a friendly wave. Mitch and Levi were playing a game of pool, teasing each other if they missed a shot.

It seemed so normal, but one of us here was a murderer.

Mitch and Levi were on duty, keeping an eye on things, but were allowed to relax a little. I found it odd that they had two boots in here, rather than jaws. But I was sure they had their reasoning.

Lia's whisp pulsed, so she excused herself to talk to Eli, and her other friends didn't bother speaking to me, so I didn't bother with them.

"Are you free tomorrow?" Mitch sat down in Lia's empty seat, ignoring the admiring looks from the other girls around us.

"I am." I smiled, turning to face him, ignoring their grumbling.

"Then make sure you're ready for me to come pick you up around ten." He winked before making his way back to the pool table, his short sleeves showing off his muscly arms as he shot a ball across the table. The girls around me sighed as they watched him, whispering about whether they should go and talk to them, or if Levi and Mitch had a girlfriend back in Sylvanfire. They obviously didn't mind that they weren't jaws.

I stretched and yawned, getting bored with just sitting there. *Might as well head to bed.* I stood to leave, and Theon popped up beside me. The man could move mightily stealthily for a big guy.

"I'm heading back, wanna pair up?" He shoved his hands in his pockets, hunching to make himself seem smaller.

"Yeah, sure. Thanks."

We walked in silence for the first few minutes, the only sounds were our boots on the stone floor.

"Don't freak out, but I heard the principals mention your name the other day, something about asking you a few questions about the murder victims."

"I'm not surprised, to be honest. It was only a matter of time." I grumbled, shuffling my feet.

"I'm not sure if giving them what we've been working on would be a good thing."

"I was just thinking the same. But something needs to be done."

"Just make sure you don't walk around alone. Let me know, and I'll make sure to come with you." He stopped me with a hand on my arm, his dark green eyes soft. He tucked his dark hair behind an ear. "And I don't know what happened the other week, but it can't have been good."

I felt a knot forming in my throat just thinking about it. I took a deep breath, ignoring my racing heart.

"I'm not allowed to say, but it's something that will take me a while to get over. I...I wish I could talk about it, but I can't. I'm sorry." I clenched my jaw, pushing back the tears threatening to spill. Theon nodded once, then again as he understood.

"Well, if you ever need to vent, I'm here. Apparently, I'm a good listener. Oh, and thanks for helping Daphne out the other day." It was his turn to clear his throat as we began walking again. And I swore I saw his neck turn red.

Oh.

I hid my grin.

"I'm not a fan of bullies. I'm just glad she's okay." We walked a bit further, the silence stretching between us. "So, you and Daphne, huh?" I didn't fail to see his shoulders rise slightly. I grinned as his cheeks pinked.

"We're not...dating. Just getting to know each other." He mumbled, and I smothered my laugh. It was sweet how shy he was about it.

"She seems like a lovely girl."

"She is."

We walked in comfortable silence the rest of the way, saying our goodbyes at our doors. I was glad something was going right for him.

Mitch knocked at my door, precisely at ten am. He was dressed in jeans, a fitting shirt and a leather jacket. He looked good. I smiled as he linked his arm with mine, making our way outside and through the trees.

"I hope you don't mind, but I thought a picnic in the fresh air might be nice for something different." His hand slipped from my arm and down to my hand, our fingers twining together. Warmth bloomed through me, the casual contact somehow feeling like something more.

"It sounds lovely."

We walked through the trees, and a field of flowers greeted us. I stopped dead, the scene hitting me like a hammer to the head. I gasped with shock.

I'd been there before. But last time I saw it, the prince and Vex were here.

The illusion that Lysara put in my head.

My breathing became laboured, and my hands began to sweat.

"Ria? Are you alright?" Mitch's voice came from faraway, concern lacing his tone. "Ria?" His hands were on my face, tilting my head up so I was now looking at him. "Ria, speak to me." He breathed, eyes wide. I clenched my jaw once, twice as I blinked, focusing on him. I managed a small nod as my pulse calmed.

"I...I just had a wave of déjà vu. Sorry. It took me by surprise, is all." I whispered. I cleared my throat and tried again. "Sorry, I'm fine." I took another deep breath and forced a smile to my lips. He didn't look convinced.

"We can go somewhere else, or I can walk you back to your room."

"No." I reached up and placed my hands on his wrists. "No, I want to stay. It's beautiful."

He searched my eyes for a moment longer before letting me go.

"Any time you want to leave, just say the word." He slipped his hand to mine again, leading me through the flowers to the middle of the field, where a picnic blanket was spread out, a large wicker basket on the edge.

I would use this to help move on, to rewrite that memory with this one instead. My chest eased as I sat down beside Mitch, focusing on him instead.

It was very romantic. He had everything I could want. Biscuits, cheese, dips, fruit, little scones with jam and cream, and some chocolate. He poured me a sparkling glass of apple cider, giving me a cheeky wink as he handed it over. The tart bubbles popped on my tongue, the refreshing taste a good distraction.

"This is beautiful, Mitch." I leaned back on my hands and took a deep breath, breathing in the floral scents of the flowers around us. I scanned the field, the trees before landing back on Mitch, who was watching me with his beautiful brown eyes.

"I'm glad you like it." His voice was soft, a smile tugging at his lips, but they fell slightly as his eyes darkened. "But I know something happened the other day that Vex was furious, and you've looked haunted since."

I swallowed and looked away, hugging my knees to me for a moment. I couldn't say anything, but I needed him to know at the same time. He deserved to know what monstrous things his father did.

But right now wasn't the right time.

"When I feel that I can talk about it, I will." I turned to him slowly, his whole attention wholly focused on me.

"The stormblade belonged to the government." Mitch's voice was barely audible, his eyes darting between mine, as if he were trying to puzzle it together. "You're the first rider bonded to a Tenebrae in Everdra...ever." He was trying so hard to piece it together. I couldn't let him.

"Drop it, Mitch. Please." I attempted a smile, taking both of his hands in mine. "Talk about something else."

His face paled as his thoughts ran wild. My pulse picked up.

"Tell me about your favourite things." I smiled, scooting a little close until our knees touched.

"I'm not going to let this go, but we'll talk about it later." He promised, and I knew that he would. He was too clever to not put two and two together.

But we talked about what made him happy, his favourite places to go to, and where he'd been on his stormsteed.

The minutes quickly turned into hours, and it was the loveliest picnic I'd ever had.

"I don't want to make you feel pressured or uncomfortable, but I wanted to ask if I could kiss you?"

My cheeks burned, but not with embarrassment. Butterflies took flight in my stomach, but I wanted to very much. I nodded, my heart rate erratic for a different reason.

He leaned in slowly, giving me time to move away if I wished. His hand reached up and cupped my cheek, his thumb caressing me. I closed my eyes as his lips hovered over mine, not quite touching. His other hand moved to the back of my neck, his fingers into my hair. I resisted the sigh that wanted to escape at being held like this. It had been so long since I'd felt wanted.

His fingers tightened as he leaned in, but a loud ringing broke the silence, making us jump.

He cursed under his breath as the whisp rang, and rang. I went to lean away, but he held me there, embraced in our little bubble. The whisp stopped, and he sighed, moving in again, but before his lips could touch mine, it started again.

"Ugh. I'm sorry, Ria." He groaned as he let me go, sitting up and digging around in his pocket to pull out his whisperglass. "Yes?" He barked, sounding annoyed. I used the moment to calm myself, my heart racing. "Really? You need me to come in? Why?" He scrubbed a hand over his face, closing his eyes. "You have to speak to the principals to get clearance first." He shook his head slightly before slumping, looking resigned. "Oh, right then. I'll leave in ten." He hung up and threw his whisp onto the blanket, keeping his eyes shut a moment before turning to me. "Ria, I'm so sorry."

"But you have to go?" I finished, feeling a little deflated. "It's okay, you go. I'll pack up." I forced a smile, preparing to start gathering the things to put away.

Mitch reached out, his long fingers wrapping around my wrist, stopping me.

"No, I'll pack it away. We can walk back together. I'm so sorry, Ria."

"It's fine, Mitch, really." I don't know why my throat felt tight, my chest constricted.

Why was I getting emotional about this?

"No, it's not. Look at me." He said softly, and for some reason, I couldn't meet his gaze. "Ria," he breathed, his hands tilting my head up to meet his soft gaze. I chewed on my bottom lip as he stared into my eyes for a moment before he moved. His lips crashed into mine, and I melted into his hold on me. Desire sparked to life as his fingers slid into my hair, his lips hot on mine. I moved up onto my knees, needing to get closer as he did the same. Our bodies pressed together as his lips moved along my jaw, leaving tingling sparks in his wake. My hands moved around his neck, my fingers burying in his hair. His lips moved under my ear, making me gasp. I had never been kissed like this before. He claimed my mouth again, his tongue exploring as I moaned, my body about to blaze and burn when his whisp rang again. He pulled away, breathless, hair a mess as he sat back and stared at me. I was almost gasping for breath, my lips swollen as I tried to remember what we were supposed to be doing.

"Damn whisp," he grumbled, searching for it as I flopped onto the rug, a smile spreading on my face. "I'm on my way, far out." He answered, putting a hand up to smooth his hair. "What? You're here waiting?" his face paled, then he began throwing things into the basket. "Fine, I'll meet you out front soon." He hung up and shoved it into his pocket. I sat up and helped, folding the rug over my arm. "I really have to go, sorry, Ria."

"Hey," I reached out and touched his arm, stalling him. "It's okay, really." This time, my smile was real as he moved towards me, a grin tugging his lips.

"I wish we could stay here a little longer, and see if I can make you gasp like that again." My toes curled in my shoes as he leaned in and kissed me quickly again, stealing my breath. "Come on." He winked, taking my hand and pulling me along.

We had reached the entrance when a dark figure stepped out in front of us, and I stopped so quickly it almost gave me whiplash. Mitch was pulled to a halt, and he turned back with drawn brows. My stomach dropped, my hands turned clammy, and my breathing became choppy.

No, no, no.

I tried to back away, but Mitch held firm.

Get away from her right now! Vex boomed, his anger a living thing through our bond.

"Miss Everhart, how lovely it is to see you again," Lysara Toory crooned, giving me a horrific grin that promised pain. I shook my head and pulled away again, but Mitch only held on tighter.

"Ria? What's the matter?" His brows scrunched together as he refused to let go.

"Oh, Miss Everhart didn't tell you we've met before?" She sounded so innocent as she continued to stare at me, as I struggled to stop my swiftly oncoming panic attack. Mitch looked between us, clearly confused. "I had Nymeria here in for a visit only a few weeks ago. Such fun we had." She almost laughed, like it was funny.

"Fuck...you." I spat, the words thick as I had to force them through my tight throat. "Fuck off back to the hell you crawled out of." I was shaking now, my fingers heating as my body wanted to fight back, lash out at this threat. I shook off Mitch's hand, balling them into fists before I zapped him, dropping the blanket.

"What the hell are you talking about?" Mitch spun to Lysara, was almost yelling, standing in front of me now. "What did you do to her?"

The boy clearly doesn't know what they truly do.

Not helping!

"I just asked her a few questions, played some games." Her fierce gaze never left mine. My chest was heaving, caught between fury and fear. "I hope to have you in again soon." She leaned toward me, and I so wanted to smack that smirk right off her face.

"Over my fucking dead body." I stormed past, unable to look at her anymore as my hands crackled. I could hear Mitch yelling at her, but I didn't want to stick around her any more than I had to. Loud boots echoed on the stone floor as someone ran after me. Fear lashed through me, but I forced myself to calm as he called after me.

"Ria! Please, wait."

"I don't want to talk about it. I can't." A sob choked me as he put a gentle hand on my arm, halting me. I buried my face in my hands as I struggled to breathe, to keep control as my electricity sizzled inside of me, the light bulbs flickering around us.

`Deep breath in, then out. The nasty vermin snuck in through the roof like the rat she is. Don't let them see how she affects you.`

Easier said than done, Vex!

`Keep moving before you blow. I can feel the electricity building in you.`

I took a deep breath and pushed past Mitch, unable to look at him.

"Ria, please, speak to me." He jogged beside me, pleading in his voice. "What did she do?"

"I can't, Mitch. Please, don't make me. I can't." I begged, almost jogging now. "Why don't you ask her? She seemed happy enough to tell you. I need to be alone." I ran, leaving him behind me as I sprinted through the halls.

CHAPTER
FORTY-TWO

I ran headfirst into Ryler, successfully knocking the little air out of my tight lungs.

"Ria, are you okay?" He looked at me worriedly, holding onto my arms as I struggled to catch my breath. I could only manage to shake my head. My skin wanted to crackle and burn, and I needed to get out of here. "Can I help you? Has someone hurt you?" His eyes darkened, his fingers tightening on my arms.

"N-no, I'm just having a panic attack. I-I need fresh air." I gasped, pleading with him. "I need to go." I pulled away and hurtled down the back corridor that led to the courtyard, barging through the door and out into the trees.

A bit further, too many people close by. I'm on my way.

I could feel Vex getting closer the further I ran, my lungs burning. I stumbled to a stop, fell to my knees, and buried my face in my hands as I fell apart. My skin crackled. A blinding white and blue haze covered me in sparking waves. A shadow passed overhead, and I knew it was Vex. I shuddered through wave after wave of electricity as it passed through me and into the cold soil beneath me.

The doctor hadn't given me anything to cope with *her*.

The waves finally passed as I lay on the ground, curled into myself. I didn't remember falling over or Vex approaching me. He nudged me with his snout, his hot breath blowing over me as I blinked open my eyes.

I think you should call him.

I flinched, afraid to move from my fetal position to glare at him.

You can't be serious?

I am. I think seeing her has overridden any lingering fear that you have for him.

I pushed myself into a sitting position, shakily reaching for my whisp. I stared at the screen for a moment, trying to find the courage to open my contacts and find him.

I slowly scrolled down the short list, his name on the screen making me flinch.

My finger hovered over the screen, Vex nudging me with his snout again, making me press the call button. I narrowed my eyes and gave him my best glare, but he just snorted in return. I slowly lifted the whisp to my ear just as he answered.

'Storm?' He sounded surprised, his voice incredulous.

"I..." I paused, having no idea what to say.

'Is everything alright?' His voice became louder, stern as he spoke.

"She was here." I breathed, hating how my voice shook. But I didn't know if it was from hearing his voice or leftover from seeing her.

'What?' He barked, cursing away from the whisp before coming back. "What do you mean she was there? What happened? Why?" It sounded like he was moving, his steps loud.

"She was here to pick up Mitch." I couldn't speak any louder, and I was still crouched on the ground, Vex's snout touching my leg in a comforting manner.

'Where are you?' It now sounded like he was running.

"In...in the forest. I needed to be alone. I needed to let it out." My voice faded as my throat burned, and I hated how he wrung so many emotions from me.

'I'm sending Lia to find you. Stay away from the academy. She'll pack you a bag, and you'll come here.'

My fingers tingled with nerves, but fear didn't drown me at the thought of returning to the castle.

"But we're not allowed to leave." I stammered, trying to come up with an excuse.

'They will when the king tells them.' He growled. Vex nudged me again, and I reached out a hand to rest on his snout. *'Thank you for calling me. I know it's probably really hard for you.'* He sounded quiet, reserved, and I wish I could see his expression. I was surprised to find myself wanting to see him and not run away from him.

"Vex didn't give me a choice." I huffed, and he snorted a laugh.

'Well, I'm glad to hear from you. I'll see you soon, fly swift.'

"Thanks." I hung up, dropping the whisp on the ground and shaking out my hands, taking a deep breath.

I did it. I spoke to him and didn't feel like I wanted to fall apart.

I must remember to thank the doctor, or perhaps Vex was right. I was more afraid of her than him.

`Of course I'm right. Pick yourself up, brush yourself off, and prepare to fly.`

It didn't take long for Lia to find me, Vex telling Cyndrithra where I was. She was slightly pale and out of breath. She told me that Ava asked her twenty questions while she packed me a bag, making sure that I was okay. It warmed me slightly that she cared enough to ask.

"How the hell do you know she was there for Mitch?" She crossed her arms and gave me a stern look.

Damn it.

"I was with Mitch at the time when we ran into her in the hall. She pretty much told Mitch that she had tortured me a few weeks ago." I spoke to my feet, refusing to meet her disappointed gaze.

"She didn't?" She breathed with incredulity. "What did Mitch say?" She sounded shocked.

"He kept asking what happened, what she did, then ran after me because I had to get out of there. He was furious."

"He doesn't know what they really do there?" She asked softly, and I shrugged.

"I think he figured it out. I think that's why he was so mad. She promised to see me again soon." I cleared the lump in my throat, threatening to choke me as fear reared its head again.

"We won't let her." She touched my arm, giving me a sad smile. "You'd better get going before Brodie flies out here seeking you. I'm glad you felt that you could call. It would mean a lot to him."

"I didn't have a choice, a certain grumpy dragon thought seeing her took over my fear of him."

The grumpy dragon snorted in my direction, making me roll my eyes. I took the bag from Lia with thanks, shrugging on my flight jacket.

"Fly safe, hopefully I'll see you soon." She wrapped me in a tight hug, holding me for a moment before leaving.

The flight didn't seem to take long. I was so lost in my thoughts that we touched down just as the sun began to set, but it seemed like we just left the academy. The temperature dropped swiftly as I shivered, glad to be heading inside.

Two figures were waiting for me as I slid down Vex's leg, he didn't growl, so I figured I knew them.

`I'll be close by if you need me.`

Thank you.

Brodie and the doctor were waiting for me by the entrance, the former hanging back a little. My pulse sped up, but it wasn't enough to make me want to have a panic attack.

"Nymeria, it's good to see you. I can see that you've made progress." The doctor smiled widely, shaking my hand as I reached him.

"I think I've just had a shock therapy that might've helped." I tried to laugh, but it fell flat. Brodie took a step forward, eyes intent on me. I took a deep breath and met his gaze, giving him a small smile. He took another step when I heard someone quickly approaching. Rex stalked around the corner and wrapped me in a bone-crushing hug.

"We'll catch up with you later," The doctor and Brodie walked away, but my heart felt a little lighter. My shoulders were not so heavy, especially at seeing Rex.

"Hey, kiddo." He stepped back and lightly punched me on the arm.

"Hey, mountain man," I smirked, feeling a wave of gratitude pass through me. "You look better."

"I feel a thousand times better. I've got some news, not about Kai, but about your parents." His voice dropped, taking my stomach with it.

I nodded, and gritted my teeth as he led the way inside, and up, up, up the winding staircase. Once the door was closed, we leaned on the railing, overlooking the trees and the land stretched out before us.

"Before I was ripped away from the viscount's, I overheard many conversations between Regali, the leader of the riot, and the horrible man of the house."

My heart wanted to stop, to freeze time as I dreaded what I was about to hear. But I needed to know.

"It wasn't originally the viscount's idea to come and take you. He heard about you from someone in the government." I could feel Rex's eyes on me, but I couldn't face him. It took everything in me not to stumble back, only my fingers gripping the rail kept me upright.

"Agents came to the palace often, because he's secretly working for them, and using the rogue riders to do their dirty work. No one would know it was the government planning all of this." He sighed long, as if the story tired him, or perhaps it was just everything about it that saddened him. "A woman with long blonde hair visited, walking with another agent, when the viscount heard their conversation."

I would almost bet anything I owned that it was Lysara. I tried to ignore how my body froze, my stomach roiling.

"She said that there were rumours of an Arcborne they hadn't caught yet, but only young, perhaps not into their power yet." He angled his body toward me, and I finally met his gaze. It was filled with unbearable sadness.

"Your father..." he croaked, and I had no idea what he was about to say, but I felt sick. "Your father used to work for the viscount, but he saw your mother being dragged down into the dungeons, kicking and screaming. But he'd heard what the viscount claimed, that she was half Arcborne."

My entire world stopped.

Was my mother like me? And she never told me?

Rex didn't give me a chance to fall into myself as he ploughed on.

"Your father fell in love with her, broke her out, and escaped to the archipelago. The viscount was furious and hunted for them endlessly. They married in secret. But their names weren't Albert and Heather Everhart."

I shook my head, not wanting to hear anymore.

"Your parents' real names were Robert and Maya Ashbourne."

I stumbled back a step. No wonder Lysara couldn't find my birth certificate. Nymeria Everhart didn't exist, but I could guarantee that Nymeria Ashbourne did.

"How do you know all this?" I breathed, stumbling back another step until my back hit the stone wall behind me. His eyes lowered for a moment as he seemed to think about what he'd say next. It felt like I couldn't breathe.

Everything I thought I knew was a lie.

"I knew your father, we used to be friends." He met my eyes again. "When you were brought in, I didn't recognise your name or looks, your parents had darker hair, so I didn't know you were their daughter. Not until just before I was taken." He turned away and looked into the sky for a moment. "He tried to get me to go with him, but I couldn't. I never saw him again, but I swear that I will find your brother." He sucked in a long breath before blowing it out. "When two agents arrived to take me away, I heard them talking to the viscount about another Arcborne, but somehow, when they got there, the island was sacked, and not a person remained. The viscount pleaded ignorance, of course, and that it looked to be the work of the rogue rider. He claimed he didn't control them, and they apparently did what they wanted, and probably sold all the people as slaves." He shook his head angrily, "they claimed that they'd found the viscounts escaped prisoner, and that she had a full-blooded Arcborne child."

It took everything in me to remain on my feet.

"The viscount was furious that they didn't tell him sooner, raged and threw things, then, when they asked to take me away for 'questioning', he yelled at them to get out of his face, and to hunt you down. But the government would never let him have you, they want you all for themselves."

My legs couldn't hold me anymore as I slid to the ground and hung my head in my hands.

"They'd already had me for a short while, until I was broken out only weeks ago." I croaked, and Rex growled as he knelt beside me. "They wanted to know what else I could do, I think they knew what I was." I looked up into his tear-filled eyes. "I'm scared, Rex. Everything I thought I knew is a lie, and I don't know what to do."

Rex wrapped his arms around me, holding me tight as I broke down, my chest constricting.

It hurt so fucking much.

The sobs burned my throat as I gasped for air, as I wrapped my arms around my legs, burying my face in my knees. Time didn't matter up here, and I didn't care how long I sat there and fell apart.

"I will do anything in my power to keep you safe, but I need to find your brother. I'm leaving tomorrow to begin my search. But you needed to know, little fox." He stroked my hair as I attempted to control myself.

"Thank you, Rex, for everything." I hiccupped, wiping my tears on my sleeve.

"Stay safe, kiddo. I'll speak to you soon." He knew I needed time alone. I didn't even hear him leave, but I wasn't alone for long. I knew it was Brodie without having to open my eyes. He didn't speak as he sat down opposite me, just keeping me company.

I waited until my tears had dried up. I would no longer cry for my parents. I wanted revenge. I looked up at the prince of Everdra as he gazed up at the twinkling stars above us.

My body didn't panic, my heart rate remained the same, my chest didn't tighten, my palms didn't sweat. It was as if he felt my gaze, he lowered his face and met my eyes. I reached out my hand, and he extended his automatically, our fingers twining together.

"Thank you." I breathed, my throat still too tight to say much.

"You want to talk about it?" He was just as quiet, but his fingers held tight. I shook my head, unable to look away. And I didn't want to, not yet. "He told me I'd find you up here." A moment passed, but I didn't know what to say. "You've come such a long way, Storm."

I huffed a small laugh, shaking my head.

"Feels like all I've done lately is go backwards." I croaked, finally breaking our gaze as I looked up at the stars.

"This here is more than I imagined. The fact that you can stand looking and touching me means you've come a long way."

I gazed at him, just to prove to myself that I could, and he gave me the smallest smile. I felt my lips tugging at the corners, even though I felt like a mess.

"Come on, let's get you inside. Your fingers are bloody freezing." He gave me a smug look, and I rolled my eyes.

"So bossy," I grumbled, but I couldn't stop the smile as I let him pull me to my feet.

CHAPTER
FORTY-THREE

Ever since Rex had told me about my parents, my mind refused to quieten.

My mother was half Arcborne. Did that mean when she got struck by lightning whilst pregnant, it made me full Arcborne? Was one of her parents one, but not her? I had so many questions, but I had no idea who could answer them.

I felt incredibly alone.

I woke early, feeling restless. I got up, dressed and decided that I'd go for a run to clear my head. I made sure to stick close to the trees, staying away from buildings.

The morning fog was still heavy on the ground as I ran, my chest finally starting to feel clearer. I pushed myself, needing to think about anything else. I had been ignoring Mitch's pulses. I knew it wasn't his fault, but each time I thought about opening his messages, I felt ill.

He knew what they did there now. He was too smart not to put it together. He now knew that Lysara had tortured me, broken me. It made my shoulders feel tight just thinking about it. I ended up turning my whisp off.

I was coming up to a thick patch of trees, a small creek nearby. I would stop there a moment and catch my breath. Vex had grumbled as I left, not to get into any trouble, as he had flown further away to get some breakfast. I promised him I would be on my best behaviour.

I cupped my hands in the stream, the water icy cold as it bit at my fingers. It made me shiver as I drank, the cold a shock to my stomach. I only stayed a few minutes to calm my breathing before I headed off, the birds in the trees waking up, calling to each other with wild abandon.

I'd just cleared the trees when it fell silent.

Not one bird chirped, they didn't even take flight. A creeping sensation crawled over the back of my neck as I stopped and looked around. I couldn't see anyone behind me, no one amongst the trees. But the feeling wouldn't go away.

Get out of there, little storm

Don't need to tell me twice.

I began to run back to the castle, but I only made it a few feet when something dropped out of the sky in front of me, shaking the earth as it landed with a boom. The birds screeched and took flight all around me as I stared at the mech suit now standing in front of me.

It looked smaller than the one I saw in the forest around Voralyth, but no less deadly. It took a step towards me, reaching out with its long, metal arms.

`Get the hell away from it! I'm too far away to get there quickly!`

Panic threatened to overwhelm me, making my head spin.

`Teleport, Storm!`

I took a deep breath to do just that when the mech suit sprayed me with putrid smoke, making me cough.

God's, not again.

My magic shut down inside of me, disappearing like the morning mist as I tried to grab it. The bond with Vex slipped away, and true panic took over. The machine advanced on me, eerily silent as it began to run.

Fuck.

I turned and sprinted, my head feeling cloudy thanks to the smoke. My feet didn't want to do as I wanted, they felt heavy and floppy. I fell to my knees, rolling away as it reached down to grab me. I kept rolling, but it made me so dizzy that the trees were warping together.

Get a fucking grip on yourself!

The suit finally reached me as I was getting to my feet, its cold, metal arms wrapping around my waist and hauling me up. I kicked and thrashed with everything I had. I hated how tears choked me, falling heavy as I sobbed, feeling completely useless. I reached for one of my daggers and shoved it into its face. It spat and hissed, its arms dropping me. My legs collapsed, and I fell in a heap. It kicked me so hard I rolled a few feet, the breath knocked out of me. I lay there gasping, struggling when one of its large feet landed on my chest, pinning me to the ground. I grabbed its ankle, trying with all my might to move it, but it was too heavy, too strong for my feeble attempts.

I heard a roar in the distance, the flapping of wings of something approaching.

But it wasn't Vex.

A dark shadow passed overhead, and something crashed to the ground, shuddering the earth beneath us so much the machine had to take a step back to steady itself, but not enough for me to escape. I turned my head to the side and saw a furious green dragon bellowing, baring its teeth as its rider ran straight towards us. Drathruin approached, her tail swishing like a cat as she came at us from my left and Brodie on my right.

He's come for me. Again.

Brodie moved like lightning, swift and brutal as his sword embedded itself in the mech suit. It shuddered, its body jerking, the foot pressing down heavier on me, making me cry out in pain.

I couldn't breathe.

I'd never seen Brodie look so furious. He looked like a dark, avenging god as he gave the mech suit everything he had. He doused it in burning green flames so hot that it made me sweat. A small panel on the side of the suit opened, a dark metal tube protruding, and it looked like a gun.

No.

I tried to reach for my dagger, but it was still pinning me to the ground, its damned foot half the size of me. Brodie came at it again, and the suit stumbled a step, enough for me to push it off and roll away. I finally managed to get to my feet when it swiped out with an arm, knocking me breathless in the stomach. I went flying, landing heavily against the trunk of the tree. Stars flashed in my vision. Brodie cursed as I heard a loud thump. Heavy steps stomped my way as it ran back towards me, arms outstretched.

"Nymeria!" Brodie bellowed, grimacing as he got to his feet, but fell. I could see blood on his face as he struggled toward me. The mech suit wrapped its cold, metal fingers around my arms in a painful grip, yanking me to my feet. It still had my dagger protruding from its face, and Brodie's sword in its back.

"Nymeria!" Brodie yelled again, crawling towards me, and the sight of him like that broke something inside of me.

"NO...MORE!" I screamed and delved deep inside of myself. Through the smoke and haze, I saw it. A tiny flicker. I grabbed onto it with all the strength I had left and threw it out of me with a scream that tore my throat. It covered the mech suit in a blue haze, cracking and popping as it invaded the machine. Its fingers tightened on my arms, the pain almost too much as it began to spasm and jerk. I kept feeding my electricity into it, my throat raw as I continued to scream. Its fingers jerked open, and I fell to the ground in a heap, no strength left. The machine stumbled back a step before a green tail smashed down on its head. It fell to the ground, shaking the earth around us as its head rolled away from its body. Tangled wires and cords poked out, showing that no one was inside. It was remotely controlled. Brodie reached for me, panting and bloody.

"Please tell me you're alright." He breathed, his hands on my face as I lay there. I couldn't get up. I had nothing left.

"I'm…okay…" I gasped, hating how weak I felt. I could feel warmth on my face, blood running into my mouth. He wrapped his arms around me and brought me into his lap, holding me tight against his chest. His heart beat like a drum under my ear, steadying me. We sat there until his breathing steadied, and my head started to clear. He hauled me into his arms, staggering to his feet as he limped to Drath. The dragon had the machine pinned under her claws as she lowered herself so Brodie could climb on. He stopped a moment, thinking.

"Sorry, Storm. But I'm going to have to haul you over my shoulder for a bit." I swear I could hear humour in his voice.

"I'm not a sack of potatoes." I groaned, and he huffed a laugh before hoisting me over his shoulder. I grunted with the impact. He slowly made it onto Drath and settled into the saddle. He moved me until I was sitting in front of him, his strong arms wrapped around my waist.

He seemed to be breathing just as heavily as me.

We flew back to the castle, both quiet, trying to get our heads around what the hell just happened. Brodie plunged us invisible, claiming he didn't want anyone to see what

Drath carried, but I knew it was a strain on him to keep it going.

She dropped the mech behind one of the garages, covering it with a tarp before quietly sneaking around the castle to get us as close to the workers' entrance as possible.

Brodie grunted as we hit the ground, still cradling me in his arms.

"I can probably walk now," I whispered, not wanting anyone to hear us. He didn't deign a response as he continued limping through the door. "Goddamn stubborn asshole," I grumbled, and even though I could only see his outline, I knew he was smiling.

It was a slow trek through the halls, but we eventually made it to his room in the royal wing. As soon as the door shut, we became visible, and he set me gently down on the bed, making my throat tight.

"Your ribs," he breathed, slightly out of breath for once. "Can I see?"

I nodded and flopped down on his bed. I huffed a laugh, but my fingers shook too much for me to lift my shirt.

"You...do...it..." I grumbled, not having the energy.

His gentle fingers slowly peeled my shirt up, leaving it around my chin. His expression darkened the further it went. I could see too many emotions swirling in his beautiful eyes. His cold fingers gently probed my ribs, but

I couldn't take my eyes off him. He looked up, his lips parting slightly. He cleared his throat and pulled my shirt back down.

"Nothing seems to be broken." A muscle ticked in his jaw once, twice. I just nodded, taking a deep breath, but it burned in my lungs. "You need to rest." He scooted me up the bed and tucked me in, the blankets up under my chin. He turned to walk away, but I managed to grab his hand, halting him.

"Stay with me, please." I croaked, throat raw as he looked at our hands.

"Alright," he whispered and came around to the other side of the bed, kicked off his shoes, and climbed in. We lay there staring at each other for a moment, butterflies finally making an appearance. I slid my hand towards him, and his hand shot out, twining our fingers together. The warmth of his hand on mine, the comfortable blankets lulled me to sleep, and I didn't fight it.

Chapter Forty-Four

I rolled over and face planted into something warm and smelling like cedar and pine. I blinked awake, hearing a startled grunt coming from the other side. A strong back, wide shoulders and a mess of wavy black hair greeted me. Brodie. He rolled over and looked at me with raised brows, surprised to see me, then he remembered.

His expression darkened, and I swallowed my nerves. Since he was no longer in shock and worried about my welfare, he was now going to lecture me, no doubt. I could feel it. He climbed out of bed, turned to face me and slowly crossed his arms across his wide chest, taking a deep breath.

Here we go.

I scrambled out of bed, not wanting to take his attitude lying down.

"What the *fuck*, Storm?" He growled, his chest rising and falling with barely contained anger. His soft bed eyes disappeared *really* quickly.

"What? Am I not allowed to go for a run? Or is it because I didn't ask for your permission, your high-and-mighty?" I whipped, anger flaring in my belly as I glared at him. He glared right back.

"Of course you're allowed to go for a run. Just not by yourself. For fuck's sake, have you forgotten what happened last month?" he growled, taking a step towards me. I crossed my arms, fighting the sudden urge to hit him.

"Of course I haven't forgotten, you asshole! It lives rent-free in my head, causing me to have panic attacks, and to wake up every fucking hour, drenched in sweat and panicked!" I took a step forward, lowering my arms by my side, poking him in the chest with my pointer finger. "You aren't my keeper, so why the hell are you so pissed off about it?" I demanded, my anger a living, breathing thing inside me. Him of all people, should understand the hell I've been through.

"Because I..." He took a deep breath, settling himself as he glanced at the ceiling. "Because I fucking care about you, okay? I care so much it hurts." He gritted his teeth and looked me right in the eye. His honesty rattled me. I didn't think he felt like that, or anything other than severe annoyance, most of the time. "I have a damn near panic attack almost every time you go back to that fucking academy. You're a magnet for trouble, Storm. And I can't stand the thought of you spending time with that asshole O'Connell, he can't be trusted." My eyes darted between his, seeing only the truth. "I'm sure Gehenn himself knows I'm the worst choice for you, and that I'm the last man you'd ever want to be with. But I just can't get you out of my head." He breathed, looking the most vulnerable I had ever seen him.

"One: you don't tell me how I feel. I've wanted you since I first saw you. Two: you've stayed in my head like a fucking limpet, nothing I do can shake you free. And I don't want it to. I've been thinking you're simple for not picking up my hints." I raised my brows, my nails digging into my palms.

"Oh, I've been getting them alright. I've just been trying to ignore them because this would be a terrible idea." He breathed, taking a small step towards me.

"Oh, no doubt a very bad idea," I mumbled as his hand moved to cup my cheek before sliding down to my throat, applying just the right amount of pressure as he used his thumb to tilt my chin up. My anger slipped away, turning into something else.

"The worst." He whispered as his thumb caressed my throat, making me bite my bottom lip. His eyes dilated, his fingers tightening slightly. Pleasure rocked through me as his gaze turned hungry. "You know what? Fuck it." He yanked me by my neck, and he kissed the hell out of me. Heat exploded everywhere, my need a living thing inside me as I hit him in the chest with both hands, grabbing fistfuls of his shirt to pull him closer to me. He growled into my mouth as I opened for him, letting his tongue sweep in and claim me in the best possible way. He backed me against the wall, his body flush with mine as I lifted my legs and wrapped them around his hips. He moaned before breaking the kiss, trailing his lips along my jaw. I used the moment to try to catch my breath, but it was no use. I was a raging bonfire. He nipped that spot just under my ear, making my back arch into him.

"Oh, Brodie." I moaned, unable to keep quiet. I felt his lips tilt into a smile against my neck.

"You know, that might be my new favourite sound." He mumbled as he continued to kiss my neck.

"Oh yeah, what was your first favourite sound?" I gasped, wanting his lips on me everywhere.

"Your laugh."

Oh gods.

He ground against me, and I had no idea where I ended, and he began. A pounding on the door broke the hazy spell cast over us, making me gasp. Brodie slapped a hand over my mouth with wide eyes.

"What?" He barked, going rigid beneath me as he glared at the door.

"Don't get pissy with me, asshole. I'm not the one who just dumped a ruined mech suit in dad's garage." Eli growled through the door, "Dad wants you in his office, now."

"Fine. I'll be there in a minute." He sighed, tucking his face back into my neck, making me melt again.

"Not in a minute, now. He's fucking pissed."

"Fine! Fuck, you're so annoying." He groused as he turned his beautiful eyes back to me. "You're going to have to let me go, little storm." He smirked. I could get lost in his eyes all day. I unwound my legs slowly, not wanting him to let me go.

"I'm going to turn you invisible so you can follow me, then I'll pretend to get you from your room, alright?" He whispered, planting a light kiss on my neck, making me squirm.

"Alright."

He winked at me, fixed his hair, straightened his pants and yanked open the door, glowering at his brother. I snuck out around him before he shut it.

"We'll need to make a quick stop." He drawled, walking away from Eli.

"We don't have time-"

"If dad wants the full story, then yeah, we do." He stormed away down the halls no one speaking until they reached my door. He knocked and swung it open enough for me to slip in and run.

"Storm, you're coming with us," He yelled into the room, letting his magic slip from me as I walked out of the bedroom.

"Alright, alright. No need to shout." I grumbled, plastering a frown on my face as I took in the twin brothers blocking the doorway. I grabbed my jacket that I'd left there this morning and shut the door behind me, and followed them down the hall. No one spoke as we made our way into their father's office, the king looking a little put out as he met his son's eyes.

"Oh, Ria, good to see you. I didn't realise you were involved."

Eli shut the door and settled into a chair against the wall, as Brodie and I took the two facing his desk.

"Yes, your majesty. It's kind of all my fault." I still sounded a little croaky, my throat aching, not from the devastating kiss that had shocked me to my core. The king's brows knit together as he stared at me.

"You can call me Euan, when it's just us."

"Yes, sir. I mean, Euan." I mumbled, feeling awkward at the casualness he allowed me.

"So, care to tell me what happened?" His father leaned back in his chair, eyebrows raised as he waited. I had to clear my throat again, turning the attention my way.

"I went for a run, and just as I turned back, a mech suit dropped out of the sky and tried to kidnap me."

Eli gasped, and his father's eyes widened in surprise.

"Vex was too far away to get to me quickly enough. Just as I was about to teleport, it sprayed me with nullifying gas." I swallowed my nerves. Brodie cleared his throat, folding his arms across his chest, leaning back in his seat.

"That's when Drath changed course." Brodie took over, and for that I was thankful. "I was heading back from scouting when she got the message from Vex. We swooped in when the suit had its foot on her chest, pinning her down." He growled, leaning forward as he gripped the arms of the chair.

"Fucking hell," Eli whispered from behind me, earning him a raised brow from his father.

"Language, Elias." He reprimanded.

"It wasn't easy to take down." Bruises had begun blooming on the prince's face.

"What of the person controlling it?" Euan asked, sitting back in his chair again.

"There was no one inside. It was remotely controlled." Brodie dared a glance my way, but I refused to look.

"By the Gods, are you alright, Ria?" Euan asked, the concern in his gaze made me more emotional than I expected.

"I'm f–"

"Don't you dare say fine," Brodie growled, staring at me again. I gave him a healthy dose of side eye.

"I am fine. It's just a bruise."

"A bruise from your collarbone to your navel. It nearly crushed your fucking chest!" He yelled, hands balling into fists. It was time for Eli to raise his eyebrows. We were glaring at each other when Euan cleared his throat.

"Son, take Nymeria to see the doc. She can stay here a while longer while we investigate this suit before returning to Voralyth. Toory isn't allowed on academy grounds anymore unless she has permission from me."

"Yes, sir." Brodie stood, waiting for me to come with him. I heaved a sigh and got to my feet, saying goodbye to Euan and Eli. We were silent for the first few moments, Brodie looking broody and grumpy as usual.

"I should have brought you to the Doc as soon as we got back. I was just so upset. And then I pushed you up against the fucking wall." He rubbed his face with a tattooed hand. "Fuck sake, I'm so sorry, Storm. I knew it was a bad idea."

I reached out and grabbed his hand, yanking him to a stop.

"Now, just you wait a minute," I growled, gaining his attention. "I don't regret what we did. I know you wanted it. Hell, I've wanted to do that for a long time. So don't you dare say you regret that kiss." I was pointing my finger in his face, my emotions all over the place as laid into him, his eyes wide. "And I'm not letting you off that easy. We're going to finish what we started." I turned and began walking again, letting him follow if he wanted. I heard him curse quietly as he came after me, grumbling the whole time.

The Doc cleared me, telling me to take it easy as my bruised ribs might ache with too much strain. Brodie leaned against the wall, brooding the whole time before walking me back to my room. I peeked at him from the corner of my eye, not sure what to do from here.

Mitch kissed me only the other day, and now I've kissed Brodie.

I'd never had this issue before.

I had lots of words bubbling around inside of me, but I didn't know which one to start with. I turned to face him as we reached my door. I could see his eyes were clouded. He opened his mouth, shut it, opened it again, then shut it. A laugh burst from me. I slapped a hand to my mouth as his eyes narrowed.

"Look. I-" I started, but he froze, eyes turning distant. He turned as Eli raced around the corner, breathless.

"We need to leave. Slaves being transported tonight, and if we don't get there and stop it, they'll be lost." Eli's chest was heaving, his eyes wide with horror.

"I'll change and be right back down." Brodie's expression changed in a heartbeat, but I grabbed onto his wrist.

"I'm coming."

"No," they both said in unison, a matching frown on their faces.

"I can help! I can teleport, remember?" I argued, standing up straight to make me seem taller.

"You were just drugged and attacked. You're too injured." Brodie growled, "No."

"Eli? Please? You know I can help." I pleaded, and his face softened.

"No, don't go preying on his weakness," Brodie growled. Eli turned to his brother, opening his mouth to argue, but Brodie ploughed on. "Where we are going is dangerous, and many lives are at stake. I won't risk you, not when I just nearly just lost you." He stepped closer, eyes locked on me as his hand moved to cup my cheek. I tried to remember how to breathe. "Ria, please." He breathed, and damn it, he was not playing fair, saying my nickname for the first time.

Eli's whisp rang, he answered, and we heard his intake of breath before thanking them and hung up.

"Brodie, Ria might need to come with us after all." I turned my gaze to Eli, whose eyes were wide, face paling. "That was Rex, and he said he's found Kai."

CHAPTER
FORTY-FIVE

"He's found him?" I choked back the sob, turning back to the prince who still held onto me. "I have to come, please, Brodie. It's my brother. What would you do?" His eyes softened before he rested his forehead on mine.

"Gear up, and you're to stay at my side. Understand?" He breathed, and I nodded. "We meet out front in half an hour." The twins stormed away, and I darted into my room, quickly finding my things. It didn't take me long to strap on my weapons, tying my hair back in two braids, tucking the ends in. My heart was in my throat at the thought of seeing Kai. After four years, not a day went by that I didn't think of him, and where he was, what he was doing.

Was he a slave? Is he working for the slavers?

`You need to keep focus on the mission ahead, don't let emotions cloud your mind.`

I'll try my best. But this is my brother we're talking about.

`And potentially hundreds of other people, too. I don't like this.`

I half ran down the corridors, adrenaline spiking through my body, leaving my fingers tingling.

Brodie and Eli were dressed to the max with the weapons. It was a wonder they could walk under all that steel. Eli was on his whisp, talking to someone, speaking in hushed tones. Brodie met my gaze and instantly changed course to come my way.

"My father said that if we leave now, we'll arrive just before they start to move them. He's been watching this one for a while now, and when Rex offered to help, father sent him right there." His gaze was heavy on mine as he reached for me. "I can't bear the thought of anything happening to you," he breathed, his fingers twining with mine. I squeezed back.

"I'll be fine. You always seem to be there to save the day." I smirked, giving him a wink. But he didn't smile back. "I'll rest on the way there, I promise."

"Here, the doc gave me something to help you heal a little quicker, and it also masks any pain for a while. Just be warned, it can sometimes do more harm than good."

I looked down at the little vial he handed me, a cloudy liquid swirled inside. I uncorked it and downed it in one, the sickly sweet taste making me scrunch my nose up.

"Ready? The others will meet us there." Eli wandered over, looking stern as he stood beside his brother. They had never looked more alike than they did in that moment.

We mounted our dragons, and took flight. The stars had begun to twinkle into existence, the clear night unusually warm for this time of year. It was still a few weeks away until it was winter.

I felt the mental connection open in my mind, Eli blasting into my head in a volume that I'd never get used to. I wish I could turn it down a little bit.

It gave me too much time to think on the flight to Crudelitas. The place was known for its brutality and backward ways. I just hoped we could get in there, free the people, find Kai and get out of there. Rex obviously knew what needed to happen.

We flew for almost twelve hours. I'd fallen asleep in the saddle, only waking when Eli's voice boomed into my head, startling me awake. We made a quick stop to relieve ourselves, eat something, and then continued on our way.

It was twilight when I saw the glittering lights of Crudelitas ahead. The city was much larger than I expected.

Alright, we're going to land over by the trees, at the base of the mountains. Rex is there waiting, and will guide us to where we need to go. He said the slaves are due to be moved at dawn onto two separate containers. Regali is there, keeping an eye on things.

My stomach knotted at the thought of seeing that man again. How I would love to put a blade through his head, or even better, to get Vex to burn him alive.

`I thought I was the scary one here?`

You wouldn't do it for me?

`I didn't say that. I would love to flay the skin from his bones and throw him piece by piece to the sharks. But you're not usually the bloodthirsty type.`

I am when it comes to the people I love.

`Good to know.`

I was barely able to get off Vex by the time we landed. Brodie came over and help me, so I didn't fall on my ass. He gave me a sympathetic smile, tucked a strand of hair behind my ear, and slipped his hand into mine. It felt so natural now, like it had become a habit.

Rex is approaching from our left, with Lia, George, Piper, and Levi.

Five figures approached, wearing all black and blending into the night. Lia gave me a surprised smile when she saw me tucked in beside Brodie.

Good to see you, Ria, although you both look a little beat up. Korin mentioned, looking us over.

You can blame a mech suit for that. Brodie grumbled, his fingers tightening on mine slightly.

A mech suit, you say? By the gods. Korin shook his head, his brows bunched. *I hope you both are alright.*

We'll be fine.

Conversation over.

We need to head over to a warehouse on the southern docks, that's where they're keeping everyone. They have seven guards surrounding the building, and one at each door. So ten altogether. I'm not sure how many there are inside, but I'd wager perhaps half a dozen. I could feel Rex's gaze landing on me, nodding slightly. It was still strange to see him out of the viscount's palace.

Good to know, thanks Rex. Right. Let's head out. You all know the rules.

We moved out, the dragons agreed to stay here, or worse case, fly in and snatch us up from the streets if things went to shit. Plus, they needed to stay hidden from the rogue rider's dragons.

Brodie leaned down, his lips at my ear.

"You're to stick to me like glue, remember?" He breathed, squeezing my hand.

"I remember," I whispered back, nerves fighting with the adrenaline in my system. I didn't have time to be nervous. Not when Kai was here.

We slithered into the city like shadows, not wanting to use up Brodie's magic too early. Not when he might need it to cover a lot more people soon. The streets were busy, people bustling about everywhere, calling from their wagons and stalls set up in the street. We made sure to wear clothing with hoods and to keep them up at all times. It would do no good for the princes to be recognised.

I felt a prickling at the back of my neck, like we were being followed. I turned, making sure that there wasn't anyone there.

"What is it?" Brodie whispered, leaning back down again.

"Probably nothing, it just felt like someone was following us."

"Keep your senses open, it could be someone who's seen our weapons and wants to steal them. Some of them can be pretty desperate." He pulled me in closer, our arms brushing as he kept us in the middle of the group. Eli was doing the same with Lia, who was unrecognisable in her giant coat.

It didn't take us long to find our way to the docks, the briny sea air unmistakable. I sucked in a long breath, suddenly missing the ocean. I used to take a swim in its blue depths at least once a day. I hadn't seen it in over four years.

We kept to the shadows, counting the guards that patrolled the docks.

That container there called the Charge, and the one next to it, called Infliction, belong to the rogue riders.

I made sure I committed them to memory.

Would it be too obvious if I got you to melt them?

`Maybe a little, but I would happily do it and find out.`

Back-up plan, perhaps?

Levi and Piper snuck away and scouted the warehouse, pretending to be drunks out for a walk before making their way back to us. They confirmed what Rex had told us. Each guard had a gun and a sword on their hip.

Where is Regali now? Will he be watching the people being moved onto the containers himself? Brodie folded his arms over his chest, looking at ease, but his eyes were constantly darting around.

I'm not sure, I didn't get to stick around long to find out. He's a stab now, ask questions later, kinda guy.

I kept my mouth shut. I didn't want to see that asshole, because I would end up killing him and jeopardising the mission.

"Are you alright, Storm?" Brodie's voice broke the anger buzzing through my body. I needed to stop thinking about the rider and concentrate on Kai.

"I'll be fine."

"I heard a rumour that some silver-haired fox broke his nose. Is that true?" He chucked in my ear, making my toes curl in my boots. I loved the sound of his laugh.

"The asshole deserved it."

"No doubt, you savage little thing." He ran his nose along my cheek, making me suck in a breath at his closeness. Was he trying to distract me on purpose?

"I know what you're doing," I murmured, making sure to keep quiet.

"I don't know what you're talking about." He breathed, tickling my ear, making my heart rate jump. My neck prickled, and I had that feeling again that we were being watched. I rolled my shoulders, ignoring it.

Is there a way we can keep Regali distracted enough that he won't notice us sneaking in? I asked, hoping to stay well away from any rider. I had to ignore my feelings and be the bigger person, so I made sure to look straight at Rex. Even in the darkness, I could see pain in his eyes when he looked at me.

Eli and Lia are going to set off a series of smoke bombs by the docks, hoping to cause a distraction. And that's when we'll move into the warehouse, where the smoke will disguise us, and the slaves escaping out the side door and down the alley. Levi and George will be waiting to show them through the streets and into the fields, where wagons are waiting.

Seemed easy enough. But I knew even the most thought-out plan could go wrong.

Alright, we need to move out now, Eli, Lia, you head off.

Rex seemed to have fallen into the team leader role rather naturally. But I guess he'd been here scouting longer than we had. I didn't mind in the least. I wasn't born to lead.

Eli and Lia disappeared into the dark, blending in with the shadows. My heart beat at an unnatural rhythm, my nerves getting the better of me.

"Easy, Storm. Everything is going to be okay." I didn't realise Brodie had his thumb on the inside of my wrist, where he could feel my pulse. "I won't let anything happen to you. And if this all goes to shit, I want you to teleport out of here."

I began to shake my head and opened my mouth to retort, but he cut me off.

"I mean it. I'm not letting you in there until you promise me you'll get yourself out." He'd lowered himself until he was level with me, his eyes dark and dangerous. He let go of my hand, only to cup my face. "Promise me, please, Ria."

Damn him.

"Fine," I grumbled, unable to say no to this man. He leaned in and gave me a whisper of a kiss, enough to set me alight before he leaned away again. A loud explosion sounded from down the docks. People screamed and began to run, panic setting in.

Time to move.

We kept low and headed to a side door, waiting for the guards to go and check out what happened. As soon as they took off, we moved. Brodie cloaked us, and what I saw inside made my stomach roil.

Too many people were shoved into cages.

Children, women, men, elderly. Anyone and everyone was there. They looked down, beaten, tired, and dirty. I had no idea where they had come from, but they had skin coloured from all over Ardentis. The smoke made its way into the warehouse, making a few of them cough. But that was our chance. The room looked clear of guards, the last one hesitating by the door as another explosion went off.

We moved silently. Brodie let his power drop so they could see us. The people were startled by our sudden appearance, but quickly quietened as they realised what we were doing.

I didn't have time to be scared, I was too busy ushering them to the side door and down the alleyway, then back again. There had to be almost three hundred people there. More.

We were down to the last cage, the last explosion only sounded minutes ago. The warehouse was thick with smoke. I'd pulled my shirt up over my mouth and nose, so I didn't start coughing when something sounded behind me.

"I wouldn't do that if I were you."

I stopped dead in my tracks.

I know that voice.

I turned slowly, swinging the door open wide and ushering the people to run. They froze, too scared to move with the tall, dark figure approaching us.

Nymeria, run! Rex yelled, but he was too far away. I almost felt Brodie's attention snap toward me as the figure approached.

"Go, get out of here!" I hissed at the people behind me, they startled, then bolted. Brodie began to run.

"I'm afraid I can't let you leave." He was close enough that I could see his outline. He was huge. His face was no longer kind, but pulled into a hard mask that matched his eyes as he unsheathed a sword from his back.

Kai was still slowly moving toward me, swinging his sword lazily. I was frozen. I couldn't find my voice or remember how to move.

It's really him.

Fucking move, Storm! Brodie bellowed as he was halfway towards me. Kai didn't even look at him.

"Why aren't you moving, girl? Cat got your tongue?" He took a step toward me when I was tackled from the side, Brodie knocked me to the ground. I landed heavily, but Brodie managed to take the brunt of the fall.

He leapt off me as Kai swung his sword down, ready to cut him in half.

NO!

I shook off my shock, jumped to my feet and watched in horror as Brodie and Kai fought, their swords clashing. I yanked my hood off and pulled my shirt down from my face, ready to start yelling when another guard rushed in, heading straight for us. I didn't have time to think as I unsheathed my own sword and prepared to take on the guard coming my way.

I barely held my own against his attack, as the man was holding nothing back.

We're almost there! Eli yelled down the link, but he might be too late. It seemed that Kai and Brodie were evenly matched. I decided I was not going to play nice anymore. We needed to get out of here.

I channelled my electricity down through my arms and into my sword, using it like a conduit as I spun and pointed it at him. A bolt of blue snapped out and hit him right in the chest. He froze, a gasp escaping his lips as he flew through the air and landed heavily on the ground. I turned to see Brodie kneeling on the floor, and Kai standing above him, sword raised.

"NO!" I screamed and began to run, but someone beat me to it.

A shock of blond hair moved into view, and shoved Brodie away just as the sword came crashing down. It happened as if in slow motion. Kai blinked in surprise at my shout, and at the man who was now under his sword.

The blade was embedded to the hilt right into the chest of Mitchell O'Connell.

CHAPTER
FORTY-SIX

"No, no, no!" I shouted, crashing to the ground as Mitch struggled to breathe. I turned to Kai, tears in my eyes as I screamed at him. "What have you done?" I ignored his wide eyes, his gasp of horror as I cradled Mitch's head in my lap, smoothing his hair back. "Mitch, what have you done?" I sobbed, my heart tearing in two as he coughed, the next one, blood sprayed my chest.

"I tracked your whisp. I needed to know you were...okay." He coughed again, his face turning horribly pale. "I'm...so...sorry...Ria." His body shook as I fought past my own tears.

"Shhh. It's okay, I'm the one who's sorry, Mitch."

"I just...want you to be...happy...Ria. I..." He shuddered, his breathing became laboured.

"Oh, Mitch. Please, stay with me." I sobbed, holding onto him so tightly. "Please, I can't lose you, too. Please." I grabbed his hand and held on so tight, but he had no strength left, his lips began to turn blue. "No, no, no." I sobbed, leaning down to plant one last kiss on his lips.

"Th...thank you, Ri..." His body turned limp as the light left his eyes. The warehouse was silent except for my cries. I was filled with such grief that I wanted to burn this whole fucking city to the ground. I gently placed Mitch's head down, ran my fingers over his eyes, and closed them for the last time. I heard Brodie coming towards me, but all I could focus on was the man standing motionless beside me.

"Ria? Is that really you?" Kai gasped, dropping his bloody sword.

I turned to him, and my body began to hum. Blue lights flickered at my fingertips, small cracks and hisses tingled all over me as I began to glow.

"Storm, look at me." Brodie approached, but didn't get too close. I was burning, and all I could focus on was the man who murdered Mitch.

"Little punk, I'm so sorry. I didn't know it was you. Please," He begged, his brown eyes pleading with me as he showed me his palms in surrender.

"Little punk is dead. She died a long time ago." I growled and took one step towards him. Eli and Lia burst into the warehouse, puffing as they took in the scene.

"I'm so sorry. But you need to leave before you're caught. I'll help you get away." He turned to Brodie, seeing as all I could think about was exploding.

"Storm, it's your brother, Kai." Brodie stepped in front of me, and I took a step to the side, but he followed. "Look at me!" He yelled, and I flinched, forced to meet his gaze from the authority in his voice. "You will never forgive yourself if you hurt him. You've been looking for him for the past four years."

The words wormed their way into my brain, past the blue haze that was begging to be let free, to raze and burn.

"We need to go," Eli called, kneeling beside Mitch. Lia was quietly sobbing into her hands beside him.

"He's right. The guards will be back any second." Kai sounded panicked, taking a step toward us. But I couldn't seem to turn this electricity off.

"I can't shut it off." I breathed, fear leaking into me. "It wants out." I hissed between my teeth as my body started to shake. "I won't be able to hold onto it for much longer."

"Then aim it at his containers. Melt them into the ground." Kai's voice triggered something in me, and I was running.

"Storm!" Brodie yelled behind me, but I could run fast when I wanted to.

"Get Mitch's body out," I cried, choking on my tears as I burst outside into chaos.

I saw Regali himself yelling at his men to sort the mess out when he turned to me, his eyes widening. He took a step towards me, looking confused and shocked. I shook my head, gave him a savage smile as I aimed the energy building inside of me right at the two containers on the docks.

They exploded in an almighty *boom*.

The shockwave sent everyone on the docks flying backwards as the containers disintegrated before our very eyes in a blast of silvery blue. I instantly felt better as the electricity left my body. I stamped down on the flow before I burned out. Silence followed, the only sound was the water lapping at the side of the docks, ash floating in the air like grey rain. Regali picked himself up and ran straight for me. I stood and let him get close enough to make him think he had me before I flipped him the middle finger and teleported out of there.

I arrived in the warehouse, and Brodie and Kai were arguing, the others were nowhere to be seen.

"What the fuck did you-"

I didn't let Brodie finish speaking as I grabbed his hand and Kai's and teleported us out and back into the field.

"-just do?" Brodie finished yelling, but stumbled a step as he realised we were no longer in the warehouse.

"Kai, you're with me." I grabbed his hand and pulled him with me toward Vex, who I swore was grinning at me.

That's my girl.

It was rather spectacular, wasn't it?

Kai wobbled on his feet for a moment, the abrupt change of scenery no doubt making him a little unsteady. I shoved his back, forcing him to climb Vex's leg and into the saddle. He was muttering the whole time about hallucinating. I refused to think of Mitch. I'd wait until everyone was out of danger before I could afford to break down.

Everyone ready to head out? Brodie will camouflage us so the rogue dragons won't see us.

Quiet agreements echoed around me. But I was not. My heart still felt like it'd been left back in the warehouse.

"You're a dragon rider?" Kai asked in disbelief as Vex hunched down, preparing to launch into the sky.

"Hold on." That was all I said as we took off into the night, the others right behind us. The wagons were well on their way out and heading to Pyrelith before taking refuge in Sylvanfire, Cindralis, and Nythevra.

"Nymeria," Kai began, but I shook my head. Not ready to speak about anything just yet.

"Later, Kai." I croaked. "We'll talk back at the castle."

"Castle? What the hell is going on?"

"Trust me, you're going to need a stiff drink when I tell you everything," because I knew *I* was going to need one when I had to acknowledge everything that had just happened.

We stopped for brief breaks. Piper and Levi joined us hours later after they were sure the wagons were fine to continue on their own. Korin had given them the names of people who would help them.

Kai nodded off halfway there, his chest leaning on my back as he snored in my ear, head on my shoulder. Even after all this time, the idiot still snored like a chainsaw.

I still couldn't believe we found him.

He seemed hardened by the years that had passed, but who wasn't?

The castle came into view, and I sighed in relief. We landed with a jolt, and Kai almost fell off in his surprise.

We were dirty, tired, hungry, and in need of some TLC. We shuffled our way inside, Moranna fussing over us, forcing us to sit down at the table and eat. It was the last thing I wanted to do, but she was having none of our objections. To my surprise, Brodie sat next to me, his unusually dark eyes lingered on me a moment before he reached out for my hand.

"I'm sorry." He breathed, not breaking my tired stare as he twisted his fingers with mine.

"Thank you. Me too." I had to look away. I didn't want to break down in front of everyone.

Kai was seated at the end of the table, looking a little shellshocked. But Rex pulled out a seat beside him and began chatting quietly. I swallowed as I looked around the table at the people who had begun to mean something to me. The mood was sombre, many eyes flicked toward me and away again, no doubt unsure of what happened between Mitch and me, but I could feel Lia's gaze the heaviest.

We were finishing up when the double doors flew open, and the Queen of all people waltzed in with all her finery, a gaggle of people behind her, peering in.

"Oh, I'm glad you're all here." She pretended to sniffle, wiping at the non-existent tears in her eyes. "But I'm afraid I have some terrible news."

Brodie's hand tightened on mine before shoving it under the table, away from the queen's hard gaze. She sniffled some more before delicately clearing her throat, her voice emotionless.

"The king is dead."

Acknowledgements

The first thing I want to say, is that this book is my *favourite*. I loved every second of writing it, even editing it I didn't want it to end. I think this book / series was the one I had to make sure I got right before introducing to you all. Nymeria & Brodie's next adventures are begging to be written. But that wont be the last of this world. I've got two books with Corlette at Duskmire Academy, and two books in Emberhollow with Calix, then followed up with one big finale with all three female main characters.

But until then, I'd like to thank those who made all of this happen!

Thank you Glen, my rock, and the one who keeps our wild little family together. Thank you for encouraging me to get out of my comfort zone, (riding crazy mtb tracks and stupidly high waterslides) and believing in me. My son who's nine years old wanted me to thank him for one line he helped me with, so thank you Harry, and of course I have to thank Ella, my seven year old for loving dragons as much as me.

I love you all to the moon and back.

Thank you Blake Polden, my fellow author, and book bestie. You've helped me so much with this book, and to be honest, all the others. I'm constantly annoying you with weird questions and glad that I have a fellow weirdo who gets the excitement of a new pen. Pen Heads forever.

Thank you to my amazing Beta Readers!! Emily Nalu, Sam Sauer, Amy White, and Kerry Costello. Your words mean so much to me, and help me find the holes I've missed, patching this book together chapter by chapter.

Thank you to my amazing editor Mae from Taking Root Editorial. Your wise words and help made me confident that I'm putting my best work out for the world. You're a joy to work with!

Thank you Rachael from Cartography Bird for the absolutely stunning map and cover. I'm in awe each time I look at them! I can't wait to see what you do for the other covers of The Ardentis Chronicles.

Thank you to my friends and family for always supporting me, you guys mean the world to me.

And finally, to you, the reader.

Thank you for picking up this book and stepping into this world with me. I hope you love reading it as much as I loved writing it. If it spoke to you, made you feel something, or gave you a moment of escape, I'd be so grateful if you left a review. Your support means the world to me xx

ABOUT THE AUTHOR

Alice Cornelius lives in the stunning island state of Tasmania, Australia, with her two kids and husband of fourteen years. When she's not writing, you'll find her mountain biking through the bush, camping under the stars, swimming upriver, or chasing waterfalls – always in search of her next great adventure.

Flicker is book one of The Ardentis Chronicles, with six more to come! With many more stories brewing, this is just the beginning – so keep an eye on her socials for updates, sneak peeks, and general bookish chaos.

If you enjoyed this book, leaving a review would mean the absolute world.

Stay weird, stay wild, and thanks for reading. xx

Ever catch secrets hiding between the lines?
If this book swept you away and you're craving a
front-row seat to the wild ride that is writing the next
one, I'm summoning a small circle of brave, sharp-eyed
beta readers. Think: early drafts, raw scenes, plot twists
before they're fully tamed – and your name etched in the
acknowledgments as part of the inner circle.
You'll need a love for fantasy, a soft spot for romance, and
the ability to be honest without stabbing me in the heart
(too hard).
If you're up for the adventure, magic, mess, mayhem
and all – send a raven (or, y'know, an email) to:
alicecornelius@outlook.com

AUTHOR'S NOTE

IGNITE is a stand-alone, DARK Irish Mafia Romance with a primal game of survival. It does contain content and situations that may be triggering to some readers.

This book is explicit, intended for readers 18+.

Please enter Decadence at your own risk. For a full list of triggers please see my website:

www.lunamasonauthor.com

Please keep in mind, the first third of this book, may give the illusion that it is *lighter* dark mafia romance, as it gives rom-com vibes, the main characters are hilarious. Do not let that fool you. **You will be slapped in the face with a brick of dark romance by the halfway point. Enjoy x**

To keep up with Luna's chaos, find her on social media:

Instagram: @authorlunamason

Her FB Reader Group- Luna Masons Mafia Queens

Sign-up to her newsletter here: https://bit.ly/3SShFuW

And if you want signed books, store exclusives and all the *naughty art,* you can purchase directly from my store:
www.lunamasonbookstore.com

*Yes, you can have a primal kink and still have zero interest
in actually running.
So, grab something to drink, relax, and let Conan Quinn
chase you down, claim you, and savagely ruin you.
And the best part? You get to* **keep cozy and stay spicy**.
Just keep flicking those pages…